THE ASSASSINATION OF GABRIEL CHAMPION

A Novel

ANGELA CAROLE BROWN

HAIKU HOUSE

H A I K U   H O U S E

Published by Haiku House
U.S. Copyright Registration No. TXu 845-933
ISBN-13: 978-0615771243

Book Jacket Design by Angela Carole Brown
Cover Photograph by A.A. Riley
Author Photograph by Jim Henken
Portions of "Leda and the Swan" by W.B. Yeats appear courtesy of © Grainne Yeats.

Visit the author at: **www.angelacarolebrown.com**

Printed in the United States of America

ACKNOWLEDGMENTS

Writing this book has been quite the journey, and I am forever indebted to my treasured tribe, those who were vitally along for the trip.

To David Bills and Clifford J. Tasner of the Writers Workshop, who were ruthless with me in all the best ways. To Jon Adolfi and Chris Haller, my quite instrumental editors. To my first agent Helen Breitwieser, who was more supportive of the book than it deserved at the time. To René Norman, who, at the start of this journey, opened up the world of art I thought I knew. To Roxanne Salazar-Bronson, her zealous feedback, and her psychologist's insight. To Annette Monteleone and her keen designer's eye, my trusted location scout and dark alley accomplice. To authors Kergan Edwards-Stout and John Edward White for their counsel and community. To Irma Breakfield for her marketing and street-team assistance, and her pep rally spirit. To Pam Brown and Cormac Ferguson, who expanded my world by regaling me with tales of their own worlds, therefore operating as valued consultants, which gave crucial fuel to the passages that take place in Tanzania, Ghana, and England. To Paris, the City of Light, with whom I continue my torrid love affair, to this day. To the late master of cinema, Anthony Minghella, who, in 2000, allowed a total stranger to accost him and hand him her manuscript, long before it was ready, and his willingness to actually read it, and to give her his sage critical eye and gracious enthusiasm. To the nearly twenty years it took to nurse this book into its rightful being. Without the arc of time, maturity, and patience, both as a writer and as a human being, it would still be an infant.

Lastly, to the memory of my beloved stepfather, Fred Hicks, who so fell in love with one of the book's characters that he would engage in vigorous arguments with me over how I should resolve said character's life. I can think of no greater example of pure love and authentic moral support.

I have lived with these characters longer than most marriages. They are inside of me, in my very blood, and I am ecstatic at the thought of finally letting them walk out into the world and introduce themselves. My eternally-encouraging support system made that possible, and for them I am grateful.

THE ASSASSINATION OF GABRIEL CHAMPION

PROLOGUE

Winter 1971. Los Angeles

In a linty pocket of the city that hosted no art, nothing beautiful or ironic or mythic or devastating, but with lights he'd always found arresting and eager, Arthur Hughes Dufresne lived. He did so in a tenement dump on Carondelet Street near MacArthur Park. His girlfriend at the time called it Arthur's Park, laughing in a perpetually boozy gurgle, "Les go down to yo' park, baby. Das my baby's park!"

Their life together, Arthur and his fair Ophelia, was a smashed, tanked, under-the-table, pickled, stewed existence. They slid across Wilshire Boulevard every afternoon, shuffling their feet in a Short Dog stupor toward Arthur's Park to meet up with the group. This consisted of the one-legged Mexican vet from Boyle Heights who was fond of telling jokes, his head-to-toe tattooed old lady who looked too hardcore to be into men but who always donned a flawless cosmetic about her exotic eyes, the toothless, ruthless White broad who was ready to die from liver failure and had a loud, emphysemic laugh, and the Limey who sang and played an eroded guitar for spare change. Arthur and Ophelia were the only Blacks in the circle. Actually, the Limey was Black too, but you couldn't tell that to Ophelia.

"Ain't no niggahs I know talk like dat."

One night Ophelia didn't come home. Days passed, which wouldn't have been the first. It usually meant she needed Arthur to bail her out of the drunk-tank. He woke up on his fourth morning alone, stumbled over to the icebox, and started in on a bottle of muscatel.

He sat by the windowsill in a filthy pair of socks and boxers. His ocher skin shined with sweat, though it was colder out than most L.A. winters. Dirty, tree-branch dreadlocks wrapped themselves around his neck like an octopus on a kill. He nursed an erection with a skin-cracked hand that probably did more damage than good. It was already a painful erection because his penis was currently battling a venereal something, and the idea of blood rushing through that sickly stalk to instigate the pus that was already seeping out of the tip was a bad one. But he couldn't help it.

He drank virulently, hoping to lose his hard-on, hoping to pass out, hoping to forget Ophelia. The more he drank, the more pissed he became. Pissed and pissed off. He watched the whores down below in the park with their big asses and bad skin. He couldn't avoid calling up the memory of each; the foul breath, the old hair grease that smelled vaguely of pork, the sour whisky that was reeked from open pores, the necrotic musk of having seen no soap and water in an eternity, the sour-sweet stench of disease. It was a love/gag reminiscence that got him stroking himself. If he could just beat himself off, then maybe he could be done with this obsession.

His crusty hand grabbed the monster that refused to be taken down and yanked it. He wanted to yank it right off. *Where the fuck is Ophelia!*

He knew he'd have to go down at some point and bail her out, but was in no condition to walk straight. The world spun in a nauseating swirl, until at one point he leaned over to vomit out of the window. Second story. And he even nailed someone below.

"What the—you motha-fucka!" came a voice from the sidewalk.

"Who you callin' mu-fucka, mu-fucka? I'll come down'ere kick yo' ass, niggah!"

Arthur's slurs didn't exactly bounce against as much as get sucked up by the brick walls of the surrounding tenements.

He held his cock full-throttle, curd dangling from his mouth, and didn't skip a single stroke during the entire purging exchange, even aiming his member at the unfortunate citizen, who disappeared around the corner disgusted.

"Mu-fuckas sayin' sump'n to me," he mumbled to himself, moving back away from the window. "I got'cho mu-fucka right HERE. Sheeit! Betta take yo' ass on roun'at corner. Aaaggggghhhhh!"

He squeezed out a tiny spew, but couldn't tell if it was semen or pus. He no longer felt exquisite release, only the burdening that would precede it and the absence of burdening that followed. Frankly, any sensation was better than the one it replaced.

Without bothering to clean up after his ejaculation, he bundled up and left the apartment with his bottle in hand and dragged his feet over to the park to drink with his group, squinting up at the glassed skyscrapers of downtown Los Angeles in the distance that glared an unmerciful sunlight.

They all sat and listened to the gathering of transient tunesmiths, who assembled every day in the park unless it rained, and who lived so profoundly on the edge of their lives that they played their raggedy graveyard of guitars and drums and noisemakers not with the laidback, front porch, blues-making languor that might be expected of vagrant culture, but with a mordant cry that almost had embedded in its dense cadence the words *"I am here."* Couple that with a sub-text of time running out and you had a drug equally as beguiling to Arthur as his bottle.

He connected with this mad music, a portal that could easily take him somewhere beyond the L.A. that did not love him. It took him there today, wherever *there* was, and threatened to make him human.

Time got away from him, and before he knew it nightfall had come and he'd forgotten to go get Ophelia. *Fuck it. It won't kill her to spend one more night there.*

Eventually everyone dispersed and slinked into the chilly night, and Arthur stumbled back home, higher than a kite, pissed off, lonely. When he opened the door to the apartment, Ophelia stood before him in a soiled, stretch-nylon dress and scuffed vinyl heels. A pair that had virtually twisted her feet into a bunion sculpture from being so cheaply made, they were the pair she always wore, a last desperate effort at femininity. She hastily rummaged through various drawers and closets, sloppily stuffing clothes in a duffel bag while nervously smoking cigarette after cigarette. At one point, as she tried to coordinate a balled-up jacket in one hand, the draw-string of the duffel in the other, and a cigarette barely holding onto her pursed lips, she dropped the butt on the unmade bed and frantically commenced to stamping it out. Arthur ran over to help her, but was so consumed with what he was seeing before him that he began shouting even as he stamped out sparks.

"Where in fuck you been!"

"Not now, man! I gotta git to da bus station."

"What da fuck you talkin' 'bout bus station? Hey, bitch, I'm talkin' to you!"

The yelling was ritual, but was usually reserved for who wasted the county checks on shit, or who was gonna clean up that puke. It was always a given that they'd be together forever, no matter what the arguments were. Even when they both fucked everything that moved and knew it of the other, it was always Arthur and Ophelia. He collected disability checks, food stamps, county assistance, and whatever else the government was offering. She hustled. He pimped her. They grifted together. And now she was getting on a bus? What had happened in four days time that she was suddenly out of there? And who had bailed her out of the tank? He demanded answers to all of the above, lacing the demands with assorted *bitche*s, *cunts*, and *fuckin' whores.*

"Look, I need to git outta dis hole 'fore it suffocates me. I done fount me somebody who can git me da bes' shit anywhere, and I am hoppin' on'at motha-fuckin' gravy train. You can believ'dat one!"

"You ain't goin' nowhere, cunt!"

"Fuck you, niggah!"

She grabbed her duffel and a carton of cigarettes lying on the table, as Arthur stumbled in confusion and rage. How could she be doing this? Just casually puncturing this hole in his heart without a moment's notice? His every waking thought was of his life, however putrid it might've been, with Ophelia. He never assumed it would be any other way. When Children's Services had taken her kid away only months before, it was Arthur who took a bath, put on clean clothes, and went to court to speak on her behalf. When she was sick with TB, and the numerous times she'd suffered alcohol poisoning or the clap, and the time she got the crap beaten out of her by some john, it was Arthur by her side. Arthur was the one who told her she was beautiful when she had long ago stopped being beautiful, and would give her his last sticky nickel if she asked for it.

He stood lingering in these glimpses of icky nostalgia for so long that he almost let her get out of the door. He looked up and caught her making her way out, when he picked up the coffee table and hurled it at her. She dropped the duffel, ducking the table and being thrown off her balance in the process. Just as quickly, she got up and threw a table lamp his way, gashing him in the forehead and knocking him clear to the floor.

In one second flat, the door was slammed behind her and Arthur was left dazed and bleeding. A good minute passed before he got to his feet again. When he finally managed it, he trudged hastily down the stoop steps onto Carondelet and into the bitter pitch of night. He spotted her in the distance, hastening across Wilshire toward the park he'd just left. He hastened too.

The swap meet hovels, porn houses, 99-cent stores, and accompanying neon, loitering in the distant Alvarado Boulevard foreground, dizzied him and rendered him nauseated, but MacArthur Park's looming lake glistened in the night, and this lured him into something more romantic. Reflections of the city's lights danced off the lake's surface, shifting and waving. Eager. Arresting. Always. The street was busy with cars, even though it was close to two in the morning, but deep within, except for a few snoring winos, the park was empty and still, and only the water moved, like two lovers beneath sheets.

He loved his city. It did not love him back.

Ophelia stumbled clumsily in her tattered heels, trying to maneuver the duffel, her purse, and a grimy polyester fur coat that practically swallowed her up. Random blouses, skirts, panties, and nylons fell out of the duffel, as she tripped and toppled her way across the park's grass toward the lake, grabbing each item up and stuffing it back in.

Arthur still followed, a profuse trail of blood running from his forehead into his mouth. Though everything was obscured by the shadowy, crescent-mooned night, he could see her silhouetted figure sneak into the wooden alcove that sheltered the rental pedal boats. Wasn't she supposed to be getting on a goddamned bus?

The effects of his alcohol had not been gentle with him this night. The beaning to the head didn't help. It pounded, and his hands shook. He'd already vomited once, jerked off twice, and had prayed to die. And now he was to be slapped in the face with this betrayal that was too effortless?

The angrier he grew, the more his head became a parade drum. His heart pounded too. So unbearably, in fact, that he came near to collapsing, and his breath pumped visibly into the brisk air.

He sneaked up from behind her in the partially enclosed boathouse of this urban wilderness, noticing that her coat had been shed and was lying clumped on the ground. He yanked her around to face him, startling her. In one swift move, he grabbed her elbow and bashed her face simultaneously, flinging her hard to the ground and interrupting a clumsy attempt at a heroin injection. Her rubber-roped arm came down first, to break the fall, as the other hand shot out in front of her to block any more blows from Arthur. With the hypodermic still lodged in her arm, dangling and pulling at the corroding flesh, a trickle of blood and pus oozed down toward her hand.

Before he could even think his next thought, Arthur straddled her, doing his drunken best to temper her flailing arms, with needles, vials, and caution being thrown to the dirty Los Angeles winds.

Ophelia screamed her greatest efforts at attracting attention. Probably hoping some wino would amble over to see what the matter was. Or maybe some neighboring apartment dweller would hear her cries and call the police.

"Fuck you, motha-fucka!" she screamed, veiny eyes pushing their way through her skull.

"You goddamn whore! I oughta fuckin' kill you!" Arthur wailed. His pain snuggled its fat ass right inside the crevices of his already taxed heart.

He had known profound betrayal in his life. What was one more? He sobbed, as he felt all of his hate for her swell.

She found her moment, as Arthur's weeping quite overtook him, and struggled to her feet, wrestling with her besotted suitor. But Arthur's focus was back, and he grabbed her and thrust her up against the back wall of the boathouse, with only the shining lake and the rested pedal boats in her sight.

He was all but ready to murder her when his cock was suddenly ten feet long and as wide as the Third Street tunnel.

Whyyy!!! he screamed to himself. Why did a hard-on have to plague him now? Distract him from this crucial dilemma of silencing the screaming hysteric? And what of that anyway? Had he actually hoped to accomplish some stupid thing by running after her? What ridiculous folly had he pictured?

"Sorry, baby, I don't know what got into me, wantin' to leave you like that. You forgimme, sugar? Les make up and go fuck."

That would never be. And at that moment he fell to such beastly weeping that his chest and lungs heaved.

Ophelia's struggling was relentless. But with the effects of his fortified wine, his rage, and his hard-on, Arthur was even more so.

He had her up against the wall, frantically knocking his erection against her, repeatedly, like a dog, hoping to beat himself off so that he could stay focused and get back to the matter at hand. But before he knew his next conscious thought, he had her dress hiked up, cock breaking out of his pants, a fucking missile. And within one thrust, it was inside of her.

He did his best to cover her mouth of its screams, and simply endured the wild flailing of her arms. Hair yanked. Ribs punched. Face scratched, gouged, torn. Skin thinly slivered by sharp fingernails.

He had her firmly pinned against the planked wall and skewered atop his violent erection. He thrust, and thrust, banging the life out of her uterus. *What of it! She should never be a mother, anyway!* He drove, and drove, grabbing hold of some part of her and the wall to get his leverage. His hands clasped tightly, clumsily smearing across her mouth, which bit at him like a dog. He tried to find a foothold, gripping her neck, as he proceeded to pummel the woman out of her.

Like a turned-off teapot her screams gradually withered to a warbled whistle. The hollowness that was already in her eyes from having been a drugged skeleton for a hundred years was now of such emptiness that she might as well have been dead. Her spirit had already begun its descent out of the violated body.

Minutes later her screams were finished, but his rape was not. The rabid dog continued. The more he pounded, the larger his cock grew, until it was larger than even him. It increased, and expanded, and burst forth, and sprang up into the sky, taller than the Hotel Edwardian, which loomed above them, and wider than the expanse of the black lake before them.

The limply hanging woman pierced on the other end grew smaller and smaller, until she disappeared against its breadth. And like the fly, was suddenly squashed.

Poof. And gone.

With his penis not even emptied, he collapsed beneath her. His breathing, stabbing the air in violent billows, was all he could hear in the sudden silence, and which was just about to undo him. He waited for the tornado to suddenly whip and whir over his head again, and knew he would be too beaten to fight her any longer. He'd let her go this time, he decided. Watch her run from his life forever. Endure the last few "fuck you"s for the road. And bear it. As he'd borne all else.

And suddenly the stillness, against which his breathing magnified to loud clangs, stunned him, and silence bled over his heaving frame. It was a silence that lasted and would not die. It stretched, and mutated, and dripped in droplets to derange his head. No sound, no movement. The woman did not run, or scream, or swing, or spit, or fight, or declare, or pronounce. She did no drama. She and drama were done.

He looked up in a jerk and found his trembling hands cramped around her variegated throat, which bulged and striated between his fingers. Upon her face was pasted a frozen, gaping mouth, opened wide like some nightmarish Munch or other, howling the end of her life. He jerked away in a flash, and her perished form fell in a dull thud to the pavement.

"NO!!! NO!!! NO!!! NO!!! NOOOOOOOO!!!" barked the rabid dog.

He dove back in, shaking her violently, trying to jolt life back. He grabbed her face, pleading with it, begging it to answer, but it would not. His own face bulged in an aneurysmal boil, as he straddled her limp body.

He seized. He puked blood. He pled. Staggered. Damned God. Cursed her dead self. The dead self with which he now had to reconcile.

Eventually he collapsed to the ground, unmoving, save for his convulsive sobbing. Hours passed in this deed. Two clumps of flesh, like drops of dung, lay on the blacktop pavement. He wondered if she would ever stir. He waited for her to stir. He prayed to a God he no longer believed in that she *please stir!* But the stillness lingered and would not remorse with him. It was a tawdry stillness. A slutting, teasing whore. Just like the one beside him, who was now no more.

A tiptoeing dawn finally startled him out of his catatonia. Blood and puke caked itself around the circumference of his blue lips. Dried tears crusted his swollen eyelids. Disoriented, he nevertheless realized he had to work fast. In a frantic haste, his eyes darted this way and that. He hooked his arms under hers, taking care not to be seen, and dragged her to the edge of the lake, where clusters of small boats floated. It was a difficult drag.

As he caught his pounding breath, he stared deeply into the black waters until they hypnotized him. His hands, outside of his own conscious will, nudged at her body until it rolled into the water, and he cradled her head in his dirty grip, clumsily immersing it and holding it there, as his hands endured the sharp stabs of frigid water, and Ophelia's torso and limbs were slowly engulfed, and she was eventually swallowed up by the blackness.

These were shallow waters and man-made. Bodies of the drunk and derelict were routinely found when the lake would be seasonally drained. And this next time around they would uncover Arthur's fair Ophelia, who, like Hamlet's own, was now sunk by *"her garments, heavy with their drink"* into a watery grave.

He watched her as her eyes stared back up at him, beneath the bed of waters, her reflection dancing in the turquoise of early light, a willowy specter. Even after she disappeared, fading slowly like a movie blackout, that stare haunted him. And would haunt him forever.

It will haunt him forever.

Daniel Cross knew this because twenty-five years after that night, in the year 1996, but a short sprint toward the new millennium, he and Arthur Hughes Dufresne were practically brothers.

They'd met fifteen years ago, after Arthur's prison stint, and after Arthur had already become a writer and a changed man. How many times that changed man had opened his heart to Daniel and confided every detail of the horrific event in a driven ritual was beyond calculation. As Daniel thought of it even now, a quivery bead of sweat hung from his temple but refused to fall.

Daniel knew that he was the only person to whom Arthur had ever spilled this nightmare, which made him feel oddly privileged. He also knew that were it ever to be shared with another, that other would never be a woman.

Ever since the day he first learned of it, Daniel had been trying his damnedest to reconcile that tale. When he wasn't hearing it from Arthur, he was replaying it in his own head furiously. Doing what Arthur was doing, he supposed. Trying to deconstruct it. Get inside of it. And perhaps the only reason the fixation even existed was because enough voices in his head told him that he shouldn't be Arthur's friend. That he should stay away. But he would never abandon Arthur.

Daniel hadn't even been in this town long, from London originally, when they pumped his stomach at L.A.'s County General in '81 and dumped him in the waiting room from Hell. It was Arthur who came to his rescue, picking Daniel up in his own '59 Beetle and taking him back to Art's place on Fifth Street. Arthur would die for him; Daniel knew this as surely as he knew anything.

It is single-handedly what has made him even more determined to remain Arthur's friend, and to figure out this enigma.

Every time he has ever tried to put that night into thoughts, however, and uncover what could possibly take any man there, a most disturbing thing has begun to happen. It has started to become Daniel's tale. Perhaps even shamelessly embellished with his own touch of the theatric. Did Arthur ever even say, for example, what the weather was like on that evening of twenty-five years ago? Or has the sense that the night was biting cold simply been birthed from Daniel's great love for the sensuous? And what about all those eager lights of an artless L.A.? Was this Arthur's conjuring, or Daniel's? He couldn't honestly say any longer. But the details have grown more queasily intimate every time he has recalled it. And he has truly begun to fear that maybe he is getting inside of it.

This, then, is Daniel's tale. His and one other's.

Yet it must be warned that this apologue of Arthur's will never fall far from it.

ONE

Summer 1996. Los Angeles

Who cared about Dick and Jane?

Her head was beginning to implode from being stared at by the dreaded black hole, into which she would easily fall given half the chance, and she couldn't get a word written.

Once out of the hospital, she began spending endless hours upon endless days bleeding into endless weeks listening to Pharoah Sanders and Alice (not John) Coltrane, because her head felt like their music sounded. Like Hell, and fire, and blood, and chaos, and orgasms. She raged as they raged, and paced the floors of her artfully decorated Santa Monica Mountains living room, blasting music, eating very little, and periodically soaking in a tub to soothe her beaten body, which had been stitched and sewn back together like Frankenstein's creature. And she still couldn't get a word written. Her face had been bloodied and blistered. The collarbone had been fractured. As had the left eye-socket, requiring a bandage to make sure she didn't lose the eye. There'd been bruises to the ribs and legs, but the primary damage had been to the face. That's if you didn't count the actual violation of rape. The pain had been blinding. No more, so much, as she'd finally been able to stop using the nausea patch that had been placed behind her ear, and was taking fewer and fewer painkillers now. At least physically, things were getting better. But her head still swam with forensic what-ifs, and the doctors wanting to run more tests, and her publicist refusing a statement to the press, which had a modest enough interest in the bestselling authoress, and finally screaming for everyone to stop. Just stop.

Please stop.

She knew she'd be hearing from the publishing front any day to start going over a proposal and preliminary outline for her next book, to which she was contractually obligated. But how could they possibly expect her to enter the world again and pump out another book? Instead, for weeks after being released from Cedars-Sinai, she drowned out the ringing phone with furious music and didn't engage at all.

And yet with all of that swilling about in the oversized load that was her head, none of the thick detritus contained the act itself. There was no memory of it. Not the slightest recollection of a detail. No smidgen of the scenario ringing. Neither the glint of a violent image, nor the stir of a brutal sensation.

One minute she was seeing a performance piece at a gallery on Melrose; and the next, the ceiling of an emergency room. If some private dick ever went looking for a predator, they'd never think to look within the bowels of the art gallery circuit. And, of course, that's where Nona Childe could always be found, loitering the alleys of the art world sub-cultures amidst the local painters and sculptors, or the coffeehouse spoken-word kids who'd listened to way too much Jim Morrison but were at least alive and vital and creating. It was what she loved best about her life, and it was virtually impossible for her to buy that one of those visits could've ever parlayed itself into some random mugging. Apparently, though, it was so. And there was no private dick, besides. Cases like these numbered in the thousands in L.A. Not even her literary weight helped to get her special treatment for her case. The police's unofficial position was, *"Just be happy you're alive. Some aren't so lucky."*

Rape. The heaviness of that word — growling first consonant, the most jarring vowel of the five, percussive last consonant, and even the silent vowel that hovers near, like the rapist himself — clanged in her ears.

And while she seemed to have blacked out this moment in question that she was trying desperately to recall, like an itch at the center of the brain that you can't quite reach with your finger, no matter how violently you shove it into your ear, she was constantly reminded that her legs ached deeply and had for weeks now. She was certain her entire womanness had been pummeled right out of her.

"A love supreme. A love supreme. A love supreme. A love supreme."

Today Nona Childe glided across the wood floor of her living room, naked in this 102-degree weather, wearing nothing but her mummified face, chanting Coltrane (John, this time), hurting to his wailing saxophone, crying upon the sound, knowing that he'd felt pain as she was feeling pain, and begging to be lifted out of this weight, as Coltrane was lifted. Coltrane had wings.

She stood in the center of her split-level, hillside, Mid-Century Modern that flooded light into her living space via one completely glassed wall that showed a distant Pacific below in its vista, and stared at the two expensively framed Basquiat originals on her east wall, her two most prized possessions, bought on the streets of the East Village during college, when she was barely twenty and the artist was barely The Artist. Basquiat hadn't overdosed yet, hadn't even become Warhol's prodigy yet. Today, with a book that had once held court on the *New York Times* bestseller list, Nona Childe could afford a Basquiat at its present worth. Back in the day, she had bought the pieces for the price of a wink and a smile. It was the era of her buying lots of paintings and sketches on the streets from artists living in boxes. She craved the very idea of being some poor soul's savior in the name of art. She still had every one, all of which, except for the Basquiats, occupied wall space in her bedroom or her office, some even packed away in storage. But only the Basquiats found their way to the living room, because only Basquiat eventually made himself into a near legend. She wasn't even aware of the caste system she'd created among her children.

Though one was a minimalist invocation of Basquiat's SAMO tag, while the other was a wild confluence of words and pictures, crudely drawn and bloated with color, she liked to call them her twins. And the twins were her soul mates, meant to be in her life, meant to carry her through disappointed loves and financial challenges, straight to the rooftop of true reward.

She imbued them with magic, gave them the reverence of God. She would bow before the twins long before she ever would a figure of Jesus Christ. Her Christ was the abstract allusion of dreadlocks and blackness, playfulness and pathos, beauty and ugliness.

Whenever she would bring them into any home, dating all the way back to studio apartments with barred windows, the space was officially anointed, protected from all ills. She practically credited the twins with her freakish ascent as a published author. She loved her Basquiats as much for being statements of arrival as for being statements of art.

The twins were also the romantic litmus test. If a potential suitor didn't notice them on her wall, if he didn't have a clue who Jean-Michel Basquiat was, then he wasn't worthy of getting in her bed, much less her heart. It also didn't hurt if said suitor followed the meridian directly to type, and could, even vaguely, resemble the tragic life of a young, wretched beauty like Jean-Michel.

At present, she stared at the twins and struggled to put a narrative on the idea that their good luck and anointment had failed her the night of the alley.

She suddenly needed to escape, either because the walls got too close or because that damned tenor player was just too heartbreaking for her to take any longer. Before Coltrane even arrived at a proper cadence, she slipped into an old pair of patchwork jeans and her rock boots, grabbed her purse, always some giant bag of a contraption flung over a shoulder, and flew the coop.

She looked like a face-lift patient, which in L.A. would be the assumption from strangers passing, but went out into the world anyway, driving to Miracle Mile, passing Brown's Bakery, which sold the best pumpernickel in the world, and taking in an exhibit at LACMA of the new contemporary collection. She could roam these halls unbothered, as the art on the walls would be anyone's only notice, and not the bandaged woman, whose face could easily rival a de Kooning, but after a bit she gave up, got back in her car, and hair-pinned her way to Erewhon Natural Foods on Beverly Boulevard.

She was too itchy to soak up art today. Instead, she parked a block away, walked to unburden her restless legs, and pursued an urgent need to reconnect with a longtime crush. Perhaps she could succeed in shooing rapists and acts of rape out of her head, and shove something lovely in there instead. The object of this crush already lived in her journal. Very first entry: *December 10, 1995. He is a brooding Heathcliff.* That was six months ago.

The first time she'd seen him was while feeling tomatoes. His was a face so beautiful that it was almost womanly. She had looked up and seen his gray eyes staring, which were so softly translucent that they countered all the fury his beautiful face had held. And it seemed to hold a surprising amount for an L.A. guy who shopped at health food stores. It was the eyes that caught her attention. Next was the pitch-black hair, streaked with hints of gray, falling in great waved locks to the middle of his neck. Forty, maybe? Maybe older? She'd never been good with that kind of thing. His lips had been full and lovely, like a Black man's, and because he was so beautiful any race would've been glad to claim him. With his mongrel looks, olive hue, and searing, colorless eyes, she knew that many probably did.

A brooding Heathcliff.

She had loved being able to attach a bit of poetry to a man who, for all she knew, might've actually been a grease monkey who scratched his crotch in public and was fond of saying *"pull my finger"* on a first date. The luxury of fantasy was that she could tailor him any way she saw fit, and she saw fit to make him a museum man, someone who haunted those corridors alone, weeping at *Pygmalion and Galatea* on his day off.

After six months of eyeing and spying, she discovered that he was easily as alluring in the spring and early summer as he had been surrounded by all the holiday tinsel and lights of their first encounter.

In all that time, they'd never spoken a word. It had always been a case of the two of them catching each other's eyes, and the polite smile and nod of the head to acknowledge that, *"yes, I've seen you here before."* Who decided that they shouldn't have spoken? But then it became this game that was too far into itself for anyone to suddenly change the rules. Instead, they just kept on with the Smile & Nod Dance, that peculiar mating ritual that only humans seem to do so superbly. Advance, retreat. Dip and bend. The clumsier the better. The cute, little, imperfect foibles that are adorable in the beginning. But only in the beginning.

She'd never seen him with a woman, and he'd never done the kind of shopping that was for two. All the strange herbs he'd been examining the first time she saw him had given a clue. Thick roots of Yerba Buena, the bark of Slippery Elm, giant, dried Jakarta bees, gnarly, burly stems of this and that, bought in bulk. This had been a man on some sort of medical mission. If there'd been a wife at home, he would have also had cute little aesthetically packaged canisters of Republic of Tea in his cart.

She'd always seen him in dark colors and coats, even in the warmer months; lapelled vests, corduroys, worn, buckled boots, leather. Not a jeans and tennis shoes kind of guy. Not a Los Angeles product, she'd finally theorized.

On a couple of occasions he'd had a book under his arm, but she'd never been able to catch the title. Had it been one of those genre paperbacks of international espionage or cyber intrigue, she would have known she had a pop lug on her hands. Not necessarily an unintelligent pop lug, but lug nonetheless. Had it been a Windows manual, no. Simply, no. Not interested in computer geeks. Nona Childe loved artists. If it had been something literary, she would have given it up to him right then and there. And if it had been her book under his arm, she'd have fallen over from a dizzy spell, stood back up, and married the man on the spot.

Marry me, beautiful health food store brooder. Be perfect, and marry me. Deliver me from this shaking between my legs and my eyes.

TWO

"*Champion* is a champion," the New York Review of Books had read. He'd already known her face from the book sleeve photo, but it was easily the third or fourth time seeing her at Erewhon before he was certain it was she. If this was the author of *The Assassination of Gabriel Champion*, then he had to paint her. That book had upended his life, and the creator of that book had a pixie's face with a luminous smile.

Today, reeking of paints, solvents, glues, and turpentine, Daniel Cross gave yet another stab at painting Nona. He'd already been trying for a couple of months. He didn't even know her; what right had he to call her by her first name? Ms. Childe. MRS. Childe, perhaps? Didn't matter. Husbands never got in his way. He closed his eyes and pictured this woman with whom he was growing rapidly obsessed. Her book sleeve photo didn't do her justice. In the flesh, she bore a serene Modigliani face with a fawn's neck; vibrant, dark eyes set deeply in; short, cropped hair of tiny ringlets; a crooked mouth with an overbite that was damned erotic; and burnished caramel skin. She was the classic hippie girl or flower child. She had the *ohm* sign tattooed on the small of her back, which she often allowed to peek out from beneath a pair of patched jeans and a shortish blouse, a second tattoo of some sort of tribal origin that wrapped around and crawled up her left arm, and a diamond in her nose. His guess on her age was early thirties.

For weeks of trying, he paced his flat, puffed fag after fag, sipped or swigged, depending on his mood, a bottle of Old Forester, and threatened to pound the walls. But he'd done that little bit of tantrum before and never to good ends.

He paced the broiling room with brush in hand and couldn't decide whether to open the windows to let in some air, or draw the monstrous shades to block out the sun. He'd been renting the dilapidated warehouse downtown on Santee Street for the past five years, and in that time he'd really done a job on it.

The place had been in good enough shape when he'd first moved in, but the freight lift entrance, cement floors, exposed brick walls, and floor-to-ceiling French windows were now entirely scribbled over with the fury of his active head. If there was an idea he couldn't lose, right there on the spot, paint brush in hand, he would jot it on the nearest wall. Or a quote. Or a telephone number. Or dried cum that he'd never bothered to wash off after an especially horny and frustrated evening of artist's block and masturbation, which numbered many.

Not one square inch of flat was untouched by his antsy vandalism. A Henry Miller insanity dripped in black acrylic in one corner. Blood-red spray paint splayed a Jim Carroll anecdote in another. A midnight blue oil stick scribble from Alan Watts's head covered one of his giant windows. A Manchester punk scene sentiment that had been a proper bloodletting in his youth spilled across his floor in smudgy, messy charcoal, which grew more smeared and abstract the more he walked across it. Sayings and wisdoms and doodles and song lyrics were scribbled everywhere.

He stared at this tapestry of mad, and let the dizzying circus of his graffitied flat derange him. He took a good, long, 80-proof guzzle this time, just to help the derangement along, and which just about landed him on his knees. Every slice to the innards reminded him of his trip to County General.

He had genuinely tried to kill himself, but hadn't succeeded. Just ripped up his guts good. Ever since then he practically lived on Maalox. That, and a complicated network of branches, herbs, bugs, and weeds that a Chinese herbalist had prescribed for him after the wreck done to his stomach.

He was too much a fan of Old Forester, though. It was a cheap high, and he'd be damned to give it up. He figured if it didn't kill him, it would have to make him a monster. At least he felt like that after a taste — like he could scream the roof off the building or jerk off an atomic bomb. That was when his best work was in him. But did he really want to take a stab at this canvas in a completely slobbered stumble or raging roar? Who was this Nona Childe, damn it? And why did he need to paint her? Was she going to torment him the way the others had?

The portraits of all the women he'd ever loved or lusted after leaned against a remote wall, stacks upon stacks of canvases, like a gaggle of bored whores waiting for a gig, and stared at him. The portrait of Dorothy Favor came to mind.

He had discovered her one night at the Orchid Club, and even though it'd now become his regular hangout, and she remained the house singer, he had yet to introduce himself to Dorothy to this day.

On that first night, she sang *In A Sentimental Mood* as though it were his very requiem. He remembered every inch of that evening, yet it was almost three years ago. The band had just finished playing the fastest version ever of *Giant Steps* he'd ever heard. He remembered chuckling when he saw the bass player's face. Horror might've been accurate, but this bloke was welcoming the challenge with a predatory leer, and it was burning. Neville was the bass player's name. Lived out of his car. He and that huge, wooden canoe he called a bass.

Scant applause had followed their 'Trane, because there was barely anyone in the club. Neville then leaned into the microphone and introduced her. And as the words "Dorothy Favor" formed on Neville's lips, she walked out from the back room and everything else in the world for Daniel stopped. Dorothy Favor wore ancient, thrift-store prom dresses and wilting flowers in her wigged hair. Her lips were full and her teeth perfect. But upon closer inspection, as the lens of Daniel's eye zoomed in past the perfectly applied rouge and mascara, he caught the faint murmur of age. Lines. Crow's-feet. Tiny, broken, spider-web blood vessels decorating her weather-worn complexion. Lips whose flesh accordioned every time they parted to sing, and the lipstick that bled between the crevices. The metal in her capped teeth. She was even more of an intrigue.

Here was a woman who'd kept all her beauty in a purse. It had to be a large purse, he'd imagined, for there was a whole lot of beauty that she commanded. He remembered thinking that she might not deliver the goods, that they'd be as false as her wig. He'd been wrong. She spat forth her Ellington like a feline, and he ran for his life. With only a memory stamped on his chest, he painted her that very night.

Women demonized and mesmerized Daniel Cross, and it would always be so. Today that woman was Nona Childe.

A stranger. A radiant face on a sepia-toned book sleeve photo. But Nona was no longer myth, as he'd now seen her in the flesh countless times. She would smile at him. He would try to smile back, but smiling was unnatural for him. He was more accustomed to being in constant brood mode, even when he wasn't brooding. Or maybe he was always brooding. Maybe it was all an act. After all, women tended to like dark, tormented men who wept at paintings or recalled some distant memory when listening to jazz.

He would weep at a painting or reminisce to Charlie Parker for this beauty. He would get on his hands and knees and beg her to let him into her creative process, and all the while he'd be astonished that the words *"His strokes are not strokes at all, but gashes in the flesh of this life"* could've even come from her imagining. And he'd be deliriously happy to be so astonished.

The first time Daniel read *Champion*, the opening passage made him drop the book on the floor as if he'd picked up a hot iron. He promptly shuddered, picked it up again, and continued to read, neither knowing his life, nor the happenings in it, until he was done with that tale. He read that four-hundred-page haunting in thirty-six hours, then sweated himself to sleep.

She had written about a tormented painter. Friends who had read the book came to him in ridiculous droves, saying, *"Have you read the Nona Childe book? She's that new author cleaning up on the bestseller list. You've got to read this book, Daniel. Her main character, Gabriel Champion, is YOU. It's eerie!"*

Though he despised being part of any faddish mob scene, he did run out immediately and purchase it. He wanted to know who had the nerve to think they could capture any painter's life in any astute way. He expected to have much fun deconstructing this coffee table scribbler. Writers of that pop brand were always about gross stereotypes, and if his friends were saying that this portrayal was uncanny then it meant that he was being reduced to one. And he'd be damned to be so reduced. He'd already been far beyond wishing some rich society matron would discover him, fall in love with his inner James Dean, give him money, introduce him to society with exhibits, let him bed her once in a while, and turn him into some sort of long-suffering pop phenom legend that no one understood but everyone clamored to.

Actually he could've easily given her the long-suffering part. But he'd been far past all the rest; all the crap he knew this bird would be writing about, and he could probably have predicted it word for word, because it's what they all wrote about.

All he'd ever wanted was to connect, spinal cord to spinal cord. He was smugly challenging this new authoress to capture that in a character. And with a one-two punch, he was felled before he'd even hit the ring. *The Assassination of Gabriel Champion* became Daniel Cross's doppelgänger.

In the past few years, he had started to become somewhat of a West Coast art scene phenomenon. The fact that he exhibited so rarely, any longer, only piqued the critics' fascination with him. They were so full of lofty art jargon about tension, and fluidity, and negative space, and discovering the new Klee or Feininger, and blah, blah, blah, fucking, dick-sucking blah. But none of them had even come close to saying about his work: *"His strokes are not strokes at all, but gashes in the flesh of this life."*

"Gashes" was what he wanted. And the first time he saw his author-demon-beauty feeling up tomatoes at Erewhon, he wanted her own heavenly gash to wrap around his hard-on.

For six months of accidental encounters in a grocery store he had debated introducing himself to Nona Childe and letting her into his world. But he wasn't sure she deserved such cruelty, so he decided to paint her instead. Every time he lifted the brush, however, flashes of *Champion* would hit him and he couldn't engage.

Then she stopped coming. He hadn't seen her in weeks. He wondered if she'd moved away, and realized the git he'd been in neglecting to tell her what her book had meant to him. He hoped she was just out of town on business. A book tour maybe? Or on holiday in the French Riviera with some writer boyfriend who's probably also a bestseller, and they'd eventually go off to have little bestseller babies and live happily ever after in their bestseller sprawl, and fuck all that. Today she was his, goddamn it. Or would be, if he could ever get her to the bloody canvas.

He dabbed. He sat. Got up again. Chain-smoked. Drank. Dabbed some more. But these strokes could never be called gashes. He paced his flat barefooted and felt the clotted wonder of spilled paint on the floor. His toes were often black with the volatile perfumes of ether and enamel. His hands were a fright, too, with his fingernails, on more than one occasion, falling away from the bed of his fungal fingers. They grew back more mutated each time than before.

And if his ulcers weren't the by-product of his encounter with shoe dye, then they were no doubt the result of his penchant for smoothing out the fibers of his paintbrushes with his mouth. He was certain the poisons in his gut would one day carcinogenize him. Although if the shoe dye hadn't managed to do him in (that nasty bit of business back in '81), then perhaps he was doomed to stay alive and blocked forever.

He needed to get out of his studio but quick. Before the damned walls started closing in.

THREE

She didn't actually want to run into him. What she wanted was to be where their flirtations had taken shape, sit quietly with a beverage, people-watch on the boulevard, and remember. But though it had been a little over six weeks since she'd last stepped into Erewhon, who should be sitting at one of the sidewalk tables with an iced coffee and a newspaper? Did the man live here?

Yes, she'd been panging for this encounter, but not today, not while looking like Rocky Marciano. She still needed a few weeks. A few months. A new life.

She pretended not to have seen him.

"Ms. Childe."

She turned his way and was instantly stricken that he was speaking to her when he never had before. And aroused that he knew her name. It had to be from the book. That had been her perfect fantasy, him knowing her work. But not now, not this way. She felt deranged and hypnotized by her conflicted head.

"I'm sorry," he said, standing. "I didn't mean to startle you. It is Nona Childe, the writer, whom I've been waving at over the past several months, isn't it?"

An English accent. In all of her romantic conjuring, mischievous and daring in the boldest of times, she had never considered that.

"Yes," she sputtered, then half laughed and felt ridiculous trying to look every way except his. Her face grew instantly hot with tears, but she couldn't tell if it was because of being caught looking like the Wreck of the Hesperus, or that he knew she was a writer.

"Christ, what's happened to you?" he asked. This was obviously a man who didn't even have cosmetic surgery in his consciousness, or the subject would've been more delicately broached. She liked that.

Her attack had been in the news, but maybe he wasn't a man who paid attention to local tabloids. She liked that too.

"Um—" she clipped, "—an accident."

"Bit of a nasty one, looks like. I hope the bloke was insured. Sorry you had to go through it. Is that why I haven't seen you for some time? I thought maybe you'd moved away, and I wanted to kick myself for not approaching you before—"

His voice. Finally. Six months of flirting with no words. Six months of wanting to hear it. Deep and warm. Alluring accent. More Rolling Stones than Royal Theatre, which was definitely sexier. It was too unbearably sensuous for this meeting. Why was he turning out to be everything she'd fantasized?

"—May I just say—I mean, you probably get this all the time, and the last thing I want to be is some annoying fan, but I found your book extraordinary—"

And then the fantasy was made complete.

"—It's moved me in ways that have been profoundly—I guess, well…revelatory…would be the word—"

Her head was reeling. And too much in pain for such an intoxication.

"—I just, if you're not in a terrible rush, I'd love to buy you a cold beverage. It just seems silly to keep waving at each other all this time and not to at least exchange names. Please. A quick one, then you can be off."

Yes! Yes! Yes! But it wouldn't actually come out of her mouth. Like dreams of running or talking, every limb, orifice, and muscle simply defies free will. This man was bold and seizing the day, which turned her on, but she didn't want to be turned on. Not today. Not while looking like Quasimodo. What would romance novels, mortifyingly in need of beautiful heroines, have to say about this one?

She'd come here, though, hadn't she?

He looked at her with a half smile. He had the most arresting face. Beautiful on a tired day. And he'd read her book.

"It would be just such an honor to sit and talk with the very writer that has changed my life. To put it as…unhistrionically…as I can, which I suppose is too late."

She chuckled with him. Nervous. A flummoxed laugh. His was perfect.

"One quick drink. Please."

He didn't have to beg, but he didn't realize that.

Nothing between them was uttered for several seconds. He was waiting for an answer, and she didn't know what she was waiting for. Some shift in the earth's polar plates, she supposed. Or simply for her knuckled head to calm down.

"Sure," she whispered. It didn't mean to come out like a frail kitten. She grew more self-loathing by the minute.

His eyebrows bounced. He smiled, pulled a chair out for her, and flagged down a waitress. She sat gingerly, as the collarbone was still a problem.

"What would you like?" he asked her, as the twenty-something approached.

"I'll have an iced tea, please."

"An iced tea," the pretty waitress repeated. "And you're okay with refills?"

"Good, thanks," he said.

As the waitress walked away, they now had only each other to face. He stared. Not so much at the swollen, purple and yellow flesh of her face and its grotesquery (more her self-pitying perspective than reality), but straight into her eyes, at least the unbandaged one. Her nerves bristled.

"I can't even begin to speak on the book," he began. "I mean...yet. Frankly, I don't know what I'd say to you. Although, I did ask you to sit, didn't I? I don't know, it just seemed ridiculous to keep passing each other and not to say hello."

She smiled in agreement, though smiling hurt. And she waited to hear his angle besides. She was considered a pretty woman. More freshly-scrubbed than centerfold. And she knew it. *But you, Mr. Gray Eyes, never took me on before, in your charming way, to woo me the way I'd wanted.* Today she looked like the victim of a head-on, with that head unbearably cluttered, *and you choose today to wink at me.*

Yet no matter how hard she tried, she couldn't even be angry enough at stupid fate to walk away, so stunning was this man who had read her book *(men just don't read fiction unless it's Tom Clancy)* and wanted to have a drink with her. In spite of smug opinions about romance novels, of which she had plenty, Nona Childe was a sucker for a romantic play.

"Daniel Cross," he offered, reaching his palm across the table for a handshake.

Daniel Cross. Daniel Cross. Daniel Cross. She could chant it the way she chanted *A Love Supreme.*

"It's nice to finally meet you," she managed, placing her hand in his. "I'm sorry it has to be under these circumstances."

"And those circumstances would be…?"

That he would address her hideousness for the second time turned her ears an irritating red. For, though Daniel Cross may have been a stranger toward whom she should properly keep a caution, what was more shallowly worrisome, by comparison, was the fear that he might find her repulsive. And without a response, her eyes began to glisten again. This time with shame.

He squeezed her hand and shushed her as she fought the urge to weep in front of this stranger, and assured her with his shushing that he wouldn't keep probing. She hated feeling fragile.

As the moment seemed to be on the verge of a tenderness between them, the waitress suddenly reappeared with an iced tea and broke the spell. They pulled away from each other, and Nona took a breath, wanting to give her tear ducts a good slap.

What was it about restaurant servers that they always seemed to show up at the most inappropriate moments of intimacy? Then stay too long, laying your glass on the table, offering you a napkin, taking up the emptied salt and pepper shakers, only to return with filled ones, and generally interrupting a moment that will never be gotten back?

They froze in their exposed display until the waitress walked away again.

"I'm sorry. I don't mean to be such a bore," Nona offered, pulling herself back up on her haunches. "But then I guess if you ask a woman to sit whose face looks like this, you've got to expect her to bring a little luggage with her, right?"

"Should I be wary?" he asked. "Of the luggage, that is."

"It's *your* party. I'm sorry. That was rude of me. It's—I'm sure it's just the heat."

"It's all right."

She sighed an exhausted note.

"So, what do you do, Daniel Cross?"

"I'm a painter. Not of houses, but of, of, of—although I have actually painted a house or two in my day—"

"You're an artist?" she asked, ignoring his stab at levity, and instantly spellbound. An accountant, a shoe salesman, even a doctor, and there'd be only so much interest from her. But an artist? Nona Childe had always been mad for these official peekers into the wondrously dank cavern of humanity. Not a malady was there more thrilling or contagious. This man didn't need to weep at Manet's *Blue Venice*; he created his own.

She resisted blurting *"I've two Basquiats on my wall."* It had been her calling card and her wooing tactic with every man she'd ever been interested in; a way of letting them know that she knew a thing or two. Her last boyfriend, a lawyer, had specialized in acquisitions for auction houses, so a line like that got him making breakfast for her at the end of the first date. Here she hesitated. Suddenly she realized how pretentious it made her seem. Or how desperate to be part of a couple. Today she was putting on the brakes. Best.

"You're an artist," she repeated.

"Well…I mean, ecchhh—"

It was as if he didn't want to claim it.

"—there's just something about that word, you know?" he offered. "To call yourself such is a bit…em…presumptuous, don't you think? Shouldn't others decide if what you do is actually art, or just some dirty laundry hung on a gallery wall?"

She laughed. It hurt to laugh. She didn't care.

"Tell me about life as an artist," she asked, choosing to ignore his disclaimer, and too smitten for sanity.

"Couldn't start with an easier one, could you?"

What was it about women? she suddenly thought, irritated. Everyone one of them, herself especially, fell in love with an idea long before an actual person, and could always be counted on to convince themselves that the idea was enough.

She was annoyed with herself that she was only partly present, the other part too busy steeping in a stew of self-hatred. She forced herself back to the conversation.

"What do you paint?"

"The world as I wish it to be."

"And what do you wish it to be?"

He stared at her for some seconds. "Aye, there's the rub." He reached into his breast pocket for a smoke.

She watched him contemplate her, as she contemplated him. It tried to be a flirtatious dance, but it was hard for her to shake disgust. Her pulse was rambunctious.

"So, are you one of those painters who frown on the idea of reproductions?" she asked, shoving critical voices aside.

"Ah, mass marketing, my favorite subject," he answered with a roll of the eyes, lighting a Viceroy. "I guess I've been on both sides o' that one at different times in my life."

"I suppose a lot of that must have to do with where you are financially."

"Why do you say that?"

"Well, I just mean—"

"Are you saying that money is the defining factor of our moral tenets?" he asked, leaning forward.

"I don't know if that's what I'm saying."

"Well, you'd be telling the truth if you were."

She liked his cynicism. She thought. Yes. No, she liked it. It was the cynics who would change this world. She wasn't one, herself, so it was a bit tart on the tongue, but enticing. And, of course, the true cynic always smoked unfiltered cigarettes, so she'd have to take the habit with the jewel.

"There's nothing like the real thing, that's for certain," he continued. "Texture. Depth. Energy. The fact that an artist's very hands made the canvas that's standing in front of you. A print, you see, the old bloke personally had nothing to do with. It's just a piece of paper that bears, at best, a dull simulation. In the real thing, there's still some part of that artist's spirit living in the woven fibers of the canvas. It's an intimate rendezvous."

She was suddenly struck by just how much she'd missed the boat in trying to capture an artist's spirit in her own book.

"You're right," she said, heartened and disheartened. "I mean—"

"But then I think," he interrupted, on a roll that clearly didn't include her, "why should some rich tosser be allowed to experience a 'real thing' and not, you know, Daniel Cross…nobody?"

"I'm not sure I follow."

"One of my favorite paintings is a Picasso that's housed in Paris," he proceeded to explain. "It's never traveled to the States. Not yet, anyway, as far as I know. It's called *The Muse*. And if it weren't for photography, and the ability to put that image in a book, I would never have known of it. Because when, at this stage in my pauper's life, am I gonna get the chance to go to Paris?"

"Sure, I get what you're saying—"

"And I mean, a book is where you should see it if you can't get to the real thing. Getting art to the poor masses is much more important to me than getting it to the elite few. But the real question is, should I be allowed to have that Picasso copy on my wall? Bought for ten cents in the poster bin of a novelty shop? Knowing that a thousand other people have that very same pop fake on their wall? Remember the days when everyone owned the same Venice Beach-bought Nagel in a cheap frame? Value does decrease with volume."

"But are we talking merely money?" she offered. "Or a kind—"

"You okay with refills here?" the waitress interrupted again.

"Yes," they both blurted.

The sun had begun to move their way, and the metal of the patio chairs was beginning to burn. Nona shifted in her seat to peel her skin away from it, as the waitress sauntered away, and a car honked to add to the chaos. *Damn it! Go away!* she begged of the entire Fairfax District.

"You were saying that value decreases with volume," she tried to get back. "But are we only talking money? Or a value that volume can't touch?"

"Of course, no, you're right on that one. But then I have to ask myself the question, would I want Dorothy Favor's portrait—she's a woman I once painted—on a thousand living room walls, or on a calendar for someone's desk, or a sweatshirt, or a coffee mug? Serving not only art but commerce, as well. Making her nothing more than swag? What does she mean then?"

Dorothy Favor. A woman he once loved?

"Then again," he continued, "what does she mean now, since no one knows her but me? She sits against a remote wall, stacked behind dozens of others. Does she transcend a spirit to its divinity? As art should do?"

"I guess not, if the spirit never gets the chance to see it."

"Exactly. And why not transcend a thousand spirits instead of just one rich fuck's? Sorry. Forgive my crudeness." Suddenly he laughed. "Never mind me and my rambling, anyway. I suffer from delusions of Warhol."

"No, not Warhol, right? He's the king of consumerism, the very concept you hate."

"Well…all right, I mean, I was just throwin' a name out there. But hey, I can't really say that I don't envy him that the world knows Warhol, no Christian name even needed to identify him, and not Cross. What does that tell you about my conflicted head?"

"It tells me that we're all paradoxes. It's what makes human beings so fascinating."

"Is'at what does it?" he asked, smiling.

She loved the way he habitually shot his fingers through the mop of hair that would periodically fall in his face, to throw it away from his eyes, especially if he was in the throes of some passionate discourse. He couldn't have made a single move, at this point, that would've displeased her.

Nona Childe had stopped resisting Daniel Cross. She wasn't altogether sure she should, but she'd made a decision. This man wanted her company no matter what she looked like or what she'd been through. And was a creature of such palpable passion that she could never imagine him being cruel. Was this her rationalization for the day?

"Have dinner with me, tonight," he suddenly said, as if he'd heard her very thoughts and was assuring her she'd be safe in his company. Polite and formal one minute, impulsively sexy and brusque the next. It wasn't an invitation. It was a directive.

She didn't know what to do with this enigma, and wasn't really in any condition to test the waters. Why now?

"My face isn't exactly presentable for a restaurant."

"Well, you're here, aren't you? No one's staring and pointing and storming the castle with torches."

"I, I, I—" She had to laugh at the image.

"Look, if it'll make you feel better, we've no need for a restaurant," he assured. "I'm not much of a cook, but I have a peculiar weakness for Persian cuisine. Ever had it?"

"Uh—"

"There's a dish called *kuhbideh* that I'm mad for at this particular haunt of mine. You'll love it. If you like Eastern food of any kind. Why don't I bring some to you with a nice Riesling."

Bring some to her? He wanted to come to her house? Her head spun in a panic, and she was angry that she was forced to consider this beautiful man in the same category as some predator.

"So, um, do you, do you, do you operate a separate studio in your, I mean f-f-for your work?"

He was clearly a merciful man, because he allowed them to go right back to idle chat without an answer his way, gratefully sidestepping the always entertained Mr. Goodbar scenario.

"I'm a true starvin' artist, darlin'. I paint, eat, sleep, and relieve myself all in the same lonely space."

"I'll bet your place is amazing," she said, envisioning canvas after canvas littering some crazy cottage. "Your studio must be something to see."

"Not really."

It was a cold *"not really."* Such a puzzle. Warm one minute. Strange the next.

She did tend to like them tortured.

FOUR

How could he tell this damaged beauty, who held some horrid secret she couldn't share, that his horrid secret was a warehouse full of canvases, all strewn about as if from a nuclear fallout, every one scrawled with messy attempts at capturing her? Her name scribbled on this and that, her book-sleeve photo copied hundreds of times over and plastered everywhere. His flat looked like it belonged to a serial killer.

He, on the other hand, wanted to know everything about her. Like, who the Hell did this to her, for one. He wanted to murder the vermin. He wanted to hold her close and caress her pain, and he wanted all her woes to vanish. An accident? Bullshit, this was no accident. A face to the windshield in a fender-bender, or even a clumsy slip down a flight of stairs, would never render this. This was human contact. Fists, or...Was it a stranger? A husband? For all he knew, she could be a perverse part in some ugly play of domestic violence that she couldn't seem to rise from under, or maybe didn't even wish to.

Of course, there was no way to entertain any of this without the ugliest play of domestic violence that Daniel's world had ever known invading his head once again.

Perhaps this wasn't the first time Nona looked like this, and that got him even angrier. Inviting him to her home might just expose more than she wished, and maybe that's why she wasn't about to. He couldn't blame her. *Stay away from every one of us blokes,* the better part of him wanted to warn. *Cuz I happen to know firsthand, darlin', that even the noblest of us have traveled first-class to Hell and back.*

Instead, he turned the conversation away from himself and asked more questions about her. Why had she become a writer? What music did she love? Did she believe in God? He seized the day like a man on a mission to conquer, just to keep inquiries about her injuries out of his head. He knew she wasn't about to disclose that to some stranger, nor should she. But it was driving him mad not to know.

"I'm not terribly religious," she offered to one of his many questions. Odd that she didn't acknowledge the Dharmic symbol on her back. "Which is not to say that I don't feel the existence of divinity. I very much do. It's just—I guess I could never reconcile the dogma of my church with the non-judgment of my art."

"Amen to that," he muttered.

"I believe art is divine, but beyond that, who knows? In fact, that very idea is sort of the basis of my novel."

Was she going to speak now on the very book that had sent him into near-biblical apoplexy? To discuss *Champion* with Nona Childe would be remarkable. But not yet. He started to interrupt, but she barreled through.

"I mean, myself, as a writer I, I, I—um…you know, as artists we try and assign beauty and poetry to every ordinary thing in the world. That's the artist's role. And it's an important one."

"Well, there are those who say that art isn't important at all. At least not as important as science or commerce or religion, those things that establish our culture."

"Bullshit."

"Of course, bullshit. But much of the world thinks that way."

"It's even more important."

"Of course it is."

"And the reason it's more important is because we live in a random and meaningless world."

"Wow. We've a good, old-fashioned existentialist in our midst, have we?"

"Call it whatever you want, it's just true. How else do you explain that so much bad happens to good people, or that so much fortune is bestowed on the truly undeserving? This isn't, at its core, a poetic world, where everything and everyone is part of a divine design."

Bless her heart for questioning everything. She was a vessel of exquisite melancholy.

"And yet it's crucial to our spirits that the world be poetic," she continued. "And so here's where our role comes in. It's the artist's duty to assign life its poetry. Because if we weren't able to make some sense out of our horrors, by imbuing them with irony, or lesson, or metaphor, or—you know, then this would just be a world of suicides."

"So, you believe that art saves lives."

"Don't you?" she challenged. "Or are you just in it for the Daniel Cross lunch pail?"

She laughed, or tried to, through all of that wreckage. A tiny light in a vast hole.

He sipped his drink, and watched her do the same. They endured the heat, and relished each other's company, though she seemed alternately content and wrestling. He tried to remember what she looked like before this injury, and every once in a while, with a pained smile, the woman behind those scars would emerge. He couldn't remember the last time he'd felt this connected to a woman. He mainly bedded them, and left his richest stimulation to the shaggy roundtable of his social, political, and artistic renegade friends. It certainly wasn't as if the two were identical twins. In this visit alone, he found out that she loved Coltrane, while he was partial to Bird. He preferred Fellini films, she loved the German Surrealists. Of course, they laughed to discover that both were suckers for just about any Monty Python bit. She believed God to be art, he believed him to be figment. But she was a thinker. Someone who loved life, truly, and challenged it every day.

"You're welcome to bring dinner to my house tonight," she suddenly said. "If the offer's still—"

"The offer is very much still," he returned.

They exchanged contact information, and he let her go until they would meet again later that evening.

He didn't know what changed her mind, but he vowed in that instant to never make Nona Childe feel as though she would ever have reason to fear him.

FIVE

He had her spinning. And, of course, the trouble with spinning is that there are usually moments of incredible intoxication followed by bouts of nausea. She was giggly and giddy, a bit of an annoying teenager, in fact, because she couldn't remember the last time she'd felt this way about someone and couldn't keep from placing his face right in her center view. But then she'd have to tell herself over and again, in a loop, to *be careful, be careful, be careful.*

And suddenly her head swam again with tests, and rehab, and therapy, and the importance of keeping levelheaded, and she was about to have her first date since all of this in less than thirty minutes.

She put Pharoah Sanders's *Thembi* on the disc player, because it was a primal scream and she could blast it loud enough to drown out the clutter in her head. She furiously set her low-to-the-ground carved wood dining table that required throw pillows all around it and the sitting of one's buttocks on the Persian-rugged floor, very opium-den chic. Nona's house was an ethnic mishmash and bore the charming eccentricities of the Bohemian. She dressed the table with her mother's silver, her colorful Colombian stoneware, and her favorite wine glasses, breaking one, *shit!* She marched to the yard and cut a bushel of apple blossoms, praying the gentle flowers would bring a peace to her table-setting, her home, and her, before her gentleman caller arrived.

She bathed, smoked a joint, lit some table candles, smiled at her Basquiats, which she hoped would impress Daniel, and promptly took off Pharoah Sanders. That might frighten him off. How about Nina Simone? No. Too strange. Not for Nona, of course, but Ms. Simone wasn't everyone's taste. Johnny Hartman? Now, there was one romantic balladeer. No. That might seem too blatant a flirtation. *Okay, okay, okay, take a deep breath, don't over think. Take a deep breath, don't over think. Take a deep breath…*

The doorbell rang just as she was in front of her bathroom mirror picking the remnants of a scab off the side of her eye. In haste, she re-taped the bandage against it and sprayed something freshly scented in her hair to take Daniel's focus away from her face. The choice of music at once forgotten when she had to go obsessing over this hanging wound, she greeted Daniel Cross at her door with a bristling anxiety and no romantic underscoring in the background. He was handsomer each time she saw him, and she was the Elephant Man.

"The food smells great," she squeezed out between threats of tears. *He's here. Enjoy him. Release the rest.*

He placed the packages of wonderful aromas on her kitchen counter and handed her a wrapped gift.

"D'you like Nina Simone?" he asked, as she unwrapped a CD of Nina's greatest hits. Life was funny.

They listened as *Black Is the Color of My True Love's Hair* commenced, and Nona, for one, was grateful that the silence was now filled with delicious sound.

"I'm surprised you live this far from Erewhon," Daniel said of her Pacific Palisades cottage. "You're such a regular there. I just assumed you were in the neighborhood."

"I did live there for years. I roomed with a girlfriend of mine all throughout my struggling writer days. Right near the tar pits. In fact, tar used to seep up from the sprinkler nozzles of everyone's lawns. Can't say I miss that part."

Daniel laughed.

"But once I moved here, I just kept haunting all the places I had once called home. I used to go to Erewhon back when it was on the north side of Beverly, further west."

"I remember it back then, as well."

"How long have you been in the States?"

"Em…lemme see, God, twenty-five years, I want to say. Could that be right? Well, since I was a teen. So, yeah, I guess somewhere around there."

"Wow. And I've only just found you."

She jumped at her own boldness, until she realized she'd only said it in her head.

"This house is amazing," he offered, as he floated about her living room.

"Thanks. I'm partial to anything Moroccan or Balinese or Tibetan, as you can tell. I love all the thick wood carvings and colorful textiles and handcrafted pots and things, especially against such a modern structure."

"Ah, bit of a world traveler, are we?"

"Uh, yeah, Pier 1 Imports and the Pasadena flea market. You don't even need a passport."

Daniel detected just the subtlest taint of self-deprecation in her aside. But as she charged full on, he didn't challenge it.

"This is actually the house I grew up in. My parents left it to my sister and me when they passed, and I moved back into it only just a few years ago."

"Really? You do realize how remarkable it is that you live in the house where you were raised? Myself, I've no link at all, anymore, to my boyhood."

"And where did your boyhood take place?"

"Section of London called Whitechapel."

"Jack the Ripper!"

"Yes, he has managed to supersede all other legends that Whitechapel could possibly boast."

"Sorry."

"Not at all. I lead the march in destroying whatever good repute it may have left. Not exactly the fondest of memories. And I haven't been back since. I've no more use for Dear Old Blighty. But I have to say again, I'm just blown away that you still live where you grew up and played as a child. That's got to be a testament to something...extraordinary."

She was curious about those un-fond childhood memories. Instead of asking, she waited to see if he would elaborate.

"So, you say you have a sister?" he asked suddenly.

"Yes, a younger sister, Thembi."

"Thembi?"

"She was named after a Pharoah Sanders album," Nona explained, laughing. "The avant-garde jazz saxophonist?"

"I know the album well, actually. Recorded, like, somewhere around 1971, '72, am I right? With Cecil McBee, Lonnie Liston Smith. Couple of other blokes I don't remember."

"Holy shit, nobody but a musician would know that album, or any of those players."

"Well, you aren't one. Unless there are other wonderful little secrets I've yet to discover about you."

"No, no, I'm not remotely a musician. Can't hold a pitch to save my life. Have no rhythm whatsoever. I'd like to tell you all Black folks have it, but…"

They laughed again.

"But my parents were both musicians."

"That's fantastic."

"My father was a trumpeter. Played in a lot of big bands. Mother was a piano player and singer. Sort of a Hazel Scott type. They were both so entrenched in jazz. And therefore…my sister's name—"

"Well, they didn't name her Sarah or Ella, so that tells me a little something about your parents' taste for the avant-garde. I like 'em already."

"Yeah, they'd like you too. Anyway, *Thembi* also just happens to be one of my favorite albums. I swear to God, I was playing it minutes before you arrived. I mean, talk about synchronicity."

"Yes, let's."

Everything that came out of his mouth seemed like a flirtation, though she couldn't be sure it wasn't just her imagination.

"Anyway," she continued, finding it best to ignore the flirtation, imagined as it might've been, "the house was left to both of us, but Thembi, who's quite a few years younger, wasn't interested in homesteading. She took an insurance policy instead and backpacked across the Sahara. And never came back. She'll probably end up living here with me again after she's done roaming the earth."

"And what about your roamings of the earth?" he asked.

"I haven't much."

"That's hard for me to believe, considering your book is fairly global right now. No book tours?"

"Well, yes, but—all domestic. Lots of Holiday Inns, and college auditoriums, and the periodic in-store reading or NPR interview."

"Again, hard for me to believe."

"I'm a first-time author. An unknown still, relatively speaking. At least in the beginning. And then the book grew legs of its own in the most unexpected way, so they just sent me back to the trenches to get started on the next book, since I am contracted. Consequently, there just hasn't been much travel for me, even on my own dime. I mean, I just never had the wanderlust that my sister's always had. I have, in fact..." she hesitated, ashamed at the assertion, "...never been out of this country."

"You? A writer? I don't believe it."

"When you really think about it, I have the perfect job. Writers get to cocoon and hunker down and isolate."

"Sounds a bit counter-intuitive, though, doesn't it? Writers write about the world."

"Well, we certainly think we do, don't we?"

"Sorry, am I being overbearing?"

"No, not at all, it's just...I don't know what to tell you. I guess I was just always the one who was dug deep in the earth."

"Well, that's all right. We need those too. You're the ones who ground the rest of us."

She handed Daniel a wine opener, and watched him open the bottle he'd brought. He poured them each a glass of crisp white, perfect for a hot summer night, and they walked out to her backyard. The lawn sat on a sloping hill that rolled down into a valley of sprinkled homes below, and beyond it was a brilliant vista of the Pacific. They strolled across the lawn to the edge of it, though it was tough to see the water now that the sun had set.

"Your parents must have done well for themselves."

"Are you kidding? They were musicians. They bought this plot of land back in the Stone Ages; way back when this whole Palisades, Santa Monica Mountains, Topanga scene was largely hippies and pot growers. That was way before everything got crazy expensive and all the hippies got run out and replaced with rock stars and record execs."

"Well, it's just lovely," said Daniel.

And as he said so, the ocean wind wafted the smell of him her way and the words *"lovely, indeed"* ran through her mind. It was a peculiar combination of tobacco, sandalwood, and good leather. He was probably an incense burner at home, and now the scents had settled into his clothing. It was a bouquet she would never be able to smell again and not think of this moment. They wandered back inside.

"Christ, are those real?"

Bingo! They stood before her Basquiats, and she instantly went into the anecdote she loved telling, of her East Village scores for a steal — mere minutes, it seemed, before Basquiat's paintings would change the art world. This evening was going perfectly.

After a bit, they set the food out on the low table. Cups of fresh basil and radishes and fragrant saffron rice accompanied unidentifiable stews and kabobs. She had to giggle to find that Daniel had a hard time crossing his stiff legs to sit on the throw pillows that surrounded her table.

The food was amazing to Nona, though she clearly got the feeling that she would find Burger King amazing at this moment. She laughed a lot this evening, for the first time in a long time, grateful that the burdens of her head were finally lifting. She could even forget for an instant that her face looked like a neo-expressionist splat.

They had talked so much at Erewhon earlier in the day that she'd been anxious they'd have nothing left for conversation this evening. As though she needed any help with anxiety. But she was wrong. They talked endlessly, debating the impact of the current war on art by the Religious Right. She thought it was an institution that should be gagged and bound, but Daniel's take on it was intriguing.

"Resistance to a movement is what creates the movement. It's what feeds it. You think Impressionism would be significant today if nobody had ever been angered by it? Or the Fauves? Or Dadaism? Somebody out there was outraged at each of those turns in artistic history, and that outrage is what compelled those artists to move forward and be in constant motion. As far as I can figure, the Religious Right exist in this grand design to agitate and fire off the next movement. So I welcome them. And as a person who creates, I am armed and ready. You see, and that's what's so incredible about your book, Nona. Your main character, Will Speck, he knew that, too, but he was incapable of arming himself with the proper weapons. So he armed himself with a gun instead." He suddenly laughed. "Listen to me. I'm telling you about your book."

"No, no, that's—I love that," she said. "You not only know my character, you know him by name. Like he's real—"

"He *is* real—"

She demurred. "You know what I mean—"

"Because he informs—"

Oh, if this is just a wooer's trick, Daniel the Perfect, then I am a sucker.

"What just gave me goose bumps, though," Nona chimed in, excitedly, "is that your analogy reminds me…I mean, eerily reminds me…of a fable by this German essayist—"

"Hans Gruber. *Das Fremde.*"

Her eyes grew wide.

"Okay, are you a mind reader? How on earth could you possibly have known I was going to say that name?"

"Because when I read your book, Nona, I swear to God I couldn't help but think of Gruber. He's in your writer's voice, your style. And all I kept thinking was, how does this woman even know who Gruber is? I mean, he was basically just a local Weimar Republic boy. Never became world-renowned. But I just knew he'd been an influence."

Daniel followed her into the kitchen, carrying dishes from the table, as she put on the tea kettle.

"Well, because I was a lit major. What's your excuse? I mean, like you said, he's pretty obscure."

"Gruber was a colleague of my grandfather's."

"Really?" she offered in a singsong bellow. "So, who is your grandfather that he would be hanging out with the likes of Hans Gruber?"

"An essayist, as well, but of even lesser renown than Gruber, if you can believe that. You wouldn't have heard of him."

"Try me. Remember me? The lit major?"

"Leviticus Rankin."

She merely stared, head cocked in furious curiosity and feeling too foolish to blurt any more "*oh-my-god*"s and "*really*"s, but could not contain the expression of quiet astonishment.

"Uh-oh, foot in mouth?" Daniel asked, at her odd agape-ness.

"Your grandfather is Leviticus Rankin?" Nona asked. "Whose work, especially the post-World War II writings, was the basis of my college thesis?"

"Come on, now," Daniel said, laughing. "You're pulling my leg."

"I assure you I am not. Oh my God, Daniel. How is the world this small? I mean I ate, drank, and shot up Rankin's writings my whole last year of school. He was considered somewhat of a brilliant nut."

"Well, that certainly was Grandfather."

"You do know that he's kind of a rock star."

"Right. In the small but mighty world of obscure East End essayists he's Keith Fucking Richards."

Nona blurted out a laugh. "This is just too much!"

"It does seem to be, doesn't it?"

"You realize I'm gonna need you to tell me everything about him."

"Well, if you did your thesis on him, then you could probably school me."

"No, I mean, what it was like to be in his life."

"Well, he died when I was a boy, so I don't really know a lot."

She didn't push, having already been given a hint of his difficult childhood. They simply offered each other a smile.

What stars were aligning to make this night so right? Leviticus Rankin's grandson and her!

Two pairs of eyes meeting in a moment's pause told her that she wasn't the only one recognizing the stars tonight. And she suddenly noticed a spider on the wall. The unswept dust bunnies in the corners. The kitchen clock ticking. The peculiar bouquet of Eastern spices and apple blossoms and tobacco. She could feel, hear, smell, and sense everything in this instant.

"So," Daniel nearly exploded, stabbing the moment, "is the publishing world as enervating as the art world?"

Yes, right, change of subject. Best.

"Well, considering that I have a book that's done very well, and it's my first published effort, there is not a person on this earth who would listen to me if I were to say so. Which isn't to say that it wasn't a struggle to get here, but then again anything worth having probably should be a struggle, right? Builds character, blah, blah, blah."

"So, what has built your character?"

"Hmmm. I guess…finally getting a manuscript out there that no one wanted for the longest time. The fact that there were others before *Champion* that never got a bite. Babies of mine that had floated around the workshop mill for years, and had been beaten and twisted into pretzels, and I kept getting *'write what you know, write what you know'* barked at me, which meant that clearly no one was buying what I was selling. And I really hated those words, because all I've ever known is a pretty comfortable life. And who wants a book about that? So, a year after my last unsuccessful trip around the publishers offices, I released into the wilds my crazy tale of Speck and Champion, these two symbols that had been born from my nightmares about myself. I waited for everyone out there to hand it back again with the same pronouncement. And when I finally got a '*yes*' after too many '*no*'s to count, I realized that my fears were going to be the only viable source for my writing. Except that I felt a little like the rapist, who exploits and violates—"

She used her own most recent monster as a metaphor, which she had the nerve to dangle in front of her own trauma, right here in the witness of her date, and dared it to give her away.

"My fears deserve to be left alone, don't they?" she finished.

"No, actually, they don't," Daniel offered, oddly strutting. "Go to the place you fear, that's what I always say. I mean, look at the book it gave you."

"I guess," she agreed, with a nod of the head that was still in the midst of deciding even as it was nodding. The idea would linger for the rest of the evening. And for a long time after, though she didn't know that part tonight.

"And just to show you how little confidence I had in myself at that point," she said, "I was practically apologizing, even as they were handing me a contract, for everything from writing such a bizarrely angular narrative to, to, to giving my characters such obvious names. Speck and Champion? Right? But then I thought, well, it is meant to be a sort of parable. The symbolism has to be somewhat archetypal, and in that way, I guess—overt."

"You don't need to defend it to me. I'm already a fan."

"I guess I am making excuses, aren't I?"

"You've arrived. Celebrate."

Why was she so hesitant to do so?

As she poured cups of tea, Daniel opened a Styrofoam of sugar cubes from the same bag that had contained all the other Persian goodies.

"Now, if we're going do this the way of proper Iranians," he said, "you've got to place this cube on your tongue first, then sip your tea. It really does make much more sense than the way we English blokes do it."

He extended a sugar cube from between his thumb and forefinger, but it wasn't intended for Nona's hand, she suddenly realized. His hand aimed straight for her mouth, one side of which was stitched and twisted still. She impulsively leaned in and opened her lips to a helpless hole. As the sugar cube gently slid inside, her tongue inadvertently grazed his finger, which sent a bolt up her thighs and down her belly to a centrally located wellspring of arousal. It must've hit him, too, because suddenly there was a lull in the chatter, a ceasing of movement, and a facing off of eyes. The awkward hole. Standard for every first date. Ordinarily filled with the first kiss. And which had just been teased by the first true touch. But she was hardly kissable.

It was in this instant that she became hyper-aware of her injuries again and noticed that Daniel now stared at her face unabashedly. Surely the wine.

The cube was disappearing on her tongue, and she quickly bowed her head to the steaming cup and took a sip of tea, lest his stare turn to a leer. His large hand came up gently to meet her face. It was so incredibly tender and so perversely awkward that she had to wonder for just an instant if he wasn't some kinky freak that got turned on by beaten women.

But the look in his eyes told her something different.

"What really happened to you?" he asked, pointedly. Her heart started to race, and it was suddenly hard to take a breath. She had avoided the question that afternoon, and he clearly knew there was something more sinister to the story. Again, it must've been the wine that made him so bold. But though he might've thought he wanted to know the answer, he did not. Her eyes began to glisten and her mouth pursed. Her tears had become tiresome. She could see why men grew exhausted of women.

His hands slid up both sides of her face to caress it, and his forehead leaned in to rest itself against hers. They were so close to each other, yet without the freedom to fall into wild lust. Gentle, chaste intimacy would have to do.

He finally pulled away and stared again with those searing gray eyes. Eyes saturated with melancholy and history. And maybe a little too much wine.

"I'm sorry. I don't mean to put you on the spot," he whispered. "Maybe some day you'll tell me. Maybe not. But...just something to think about…"

He did a kind of sniff thing which clinched his jaw, and launched.

"Whoever it was that hurt you, do not let him smother your spirit. It is large and looming. It is greater than him."

Maybe it was the accent, maybe her raging pheromones that blinded her like a fog, but every word belonged in a perfect sonnet. His proclamation deliberately made sure not to use contractions, of which Nona took notice, like the syntax geek she could be. Or like someone desperate to be in love. To be delivered.

SIX

The music at the Orchid Club was burning tonight, and he couldn't even lift his head from the spell he was under to watch the band work. Whisky didn't help, though it tried hard. No Dorothy Favor. She was the weekends. Tonight there was a trio — Billy somebody. A bloody genius, who was pissing Daniel off because he was uplifting the world in ways Daniel lately could not.

These blokes were fantastic, and probably poor, and likely turning down bar mitzvahs and weddings, and saying, *"Screw that, I'm gonna sit right here and make my music."* And it was brilliant precisely because there were no compromises.

As he ordered another shot, hoping to disappear into a stupor, the saddest discovery Daniel Cross ever made in his life happened right here in a downtown bar: He couldn't reap joy from the brilliance of other artists. It brought him no peace. It only caused him pain to experience it, because experiencing it was never enough. He needed to get inside of it, know how it worked, so that he could find the key for himself. He couldn't look at a Van Gogh and not hate the painter for capturing fury so uncannily and transcending spirit with the mere stroke of a brush. He couldn't read Tennyson and not reel from a broken heart because the poet caught beauty in a little poem the way one catches a moth in a jar. And he couldn't, right now, listen to this Billy Somebody's trio and not stew in his single malt.

Their music was too splintered with real life, too fraught with breath and blood, while a block and a half away on Santee Street, in the dungeon Daniel called home, lay canvas on top of canvas of Nona Childe's incomplete, unrealized image, while the woman herself dwelled in a beachy cottage of strategic sunlight and koi pond comfort, likely creating another masterwork that he would be unable to endure. His head ached from the uncut thought.

She's not cutting off her ear, damn it! Why do I need to?

He was far away now from sterile Pacific Palisades, and just had to grab a taste before heading home. And while he understood why Nona lived there, and had heard the whole story about her family being there before it had become *that*, he still wondered if the pristine frigidity wouldn't at some point begin to stain her. Take away her soul just a bit.

It wasn't as if he didn't understand the desire for comfort, but for Christ's sake, *that* community? That place was for nouveau-riche trash. Tanning salons, aromatherapy salons, Eastern spiritual salons, plastic surgery salons. Nona Childe did not belong there. Not the writer of that feisty opus that kicked his ass every time he thought about it. That place would drown her feistiness, and the only thing that would come back up for air would be a sopping, washed-out, self-help maven of warm, fuzzy, feel-good, coffee table crap.

Maybe she did need to cut off her ear. Or maybe he was just an asshole who was determined to project all of his shit onto her.

He got out of the Orchid quickly and stumbled home, down Eighth Street, passing the trains. It was a trek he'd made almost every night for five years and not once mugged, and he wondered if tonight would be the night. The dregs lived on Eighth Street, loitering in the storefront cubbyholes. Though, how could he call it loitering? It's where they lived. A stranger passing was the loiterer. And tonight that was he.

He'd been told by friends, who had warned him against strolling down Eighth, that he must've had an angel on his shoulder. But if there was one there, then what a cruel angel she was, for he floated into the Orchid Club night after night, got drunk, and floated home to paint or rail against himself for not being better than he was. An angel would not make him suffer in his miserable mediocrity or cause him to sink into the deep despair of obsession for a woman he barely knew and couldn't paint. This was no angel that sat on his shoulder, but a snarling imp who teased that his time was merely being bode until the day of his reckoning, when he would be smitten down by some shepherd of Skid Row who looked like Jesus and wanted his wallet.

Goddamn, he was drunk. And when he got drunk he got slightly Baroque. He wanted to get mugged. He wanted to be carried away to some chamber of horrors and have them beat it out of him. It? Whatever

IT was that he couldn't seem to get out whenever he stood in front of a canvas. Maybe it was the ghosts of all the brilliant madmen who painted with a bloody gust, and who jeered at him that he would never be as great as they were.

Oh, he might become rich and famous, though. The critics loved him. He was their little darling. *This* week.

All you need's a gimmick and a hook, and you too can get a big, fat grant and a Vanity Fair cover.

It had become a culture so desensitized, so lacking in the keen recognition of nuance, that what was required any longer to stir someone's soul was movement, noise, clangs and bangs, where news outlets were consigned to showing actual video footage of head-on collisions in order for the viewer to be impacted by the pronouncement of tragedy. And where art had to *stun* (*stir* just wasn't good enough anymore) by feats and stunts and concussion in order to be considered the legitimate New Art. Bob Flanagan hammering a nail into his penis before a live audience at a "happening" was considered art by those for whom the criteria was, singularly, that the deed be undared by anyone else.

Flanagan had been a performance artist battling cystic fibrosis and exploring themes of pain threshold, and there was certainly validity in the idea of a coping mechanism being raised to an art by the very involvement of an audience, a reaction, an impact, and a relationship. But the bottom line for Daniel was: How do you sell that?

He suddenly realized that in this drunken instant he was thinking more like an art dealer than an artist, and he surprised himself that he had, in one swift indictment, reduced his entire impetus to paint to his ability to make a living from it. Never mind the idea of art that was authentically experiential, completely stripped of the possibility of the repeat generation of dollars dealt from one collector's hands to another's. Commerce had always been the farthest down on Daniel's list of reasons to create, yet today it seemed to be the first, instinctive weapon he drew in this invisible battle with an invisible foe, for his (a mere painter's) rightful place.

The art world had been stricken with a bad case of the emperor's new clothes, and the rest of the world was guileless and gullible, including Daniel, who had started to believe the buzz about his own work. Maybe being *just* a painter was the gimmick assigned to Daniel by the critical circle.

And maybe in the end, he actually was starting to feel unworthy of the attention because, after all — all he did was paint.

There had been a moment in his life when everywhere anyone turned he was exhibiting. *This* gallery. *That* installation space. Celebrity-so-and-so's restaurant. The trendier the better. Determined, of course, by how many fruity variations of martinis they served, or if oxygen was on the menu. He would dutifully hang with the hippest, black-lipsticked, tongue-studded, goth-clubbing crowd. And he'd sip non-fat, sugar-free, double-double, decaf, latté soy grandés, while pontificating forth on the whys and wherefores of his latest piece. All the while glancing over someone's shoulder to catch a glimpse of one of his own creations, and knowing in his heart that it did not elevate or transcend. Then, in a second glance, he would catch a plump, round ass in his sights and make his move on some sensitive female, who would tell him that she was a poet and ask him if he'd come see her read some time at the Queen of Cups. And he'd go and pretend to dig her freeform, bebop wordplay, and take her home afterwards, and they'd shag each other mercilessly. And when he'd leave her place and catch a cab home, he'd once again find himself alone with his self-doubt and his poor-me snivels. And he'd drink himself to sleep. Eventually he stopped showing altogether. He withdrew and did nothing at all but paint.

Harper still kept him abreast of the L.A. scene, a scene lampooned by the entire East Coast, but which, in spite of an unfair press, had some serious legs: Which new phenomenon had an installation at Bergamot Station or the Temporary Contemporary; who was being written up in the Art Review; what shows were happening in The Brewery District; who was actually getting a shot at a LACMA exhibit. She did this just to get him jealous and fired up and competitive. He realized that as his agent this was her job, but he begged her to stop being a fly in his ear.

He exhibited only once in a rare while any longer, and one of those was coming up, which was why he was drinking more than usual these days and more ornery than ever.

"This one will be huge!" Harper had exclaimed a few weeks ago.

His first solo show in some years, and at the Hareton Gallery no less, was, according to Harper, one for the books.

"Daniel, Hareton is a very prestigious space, and the curator there is associated with the Whitechapel Gallery in London. This could be a real boon."

But these significances weighed little on him anymore. Harper had arranged the whole thing. A longtime patron of the arts and a burgeoning heavyweight in the L.A. critical circle, Harper Levy had been one of his dearest friends long before he had taken her on as agent. Now he was her pet project. The fact that Hareton was finally giving him its attention, after years of trying, was a credit to Harper's increasing weight in the industry.

"Why don't you consider pieces you already have?" she had asked, in what had launched an ongoing argument. "It'll take the pressure off."

"Because they've already been out there," he'd thrown back. "And if they weren't bought the first time out, too bad and too late. They can sit in this dungeon and pile up on top of each other, to be discovered after my death, if that's to be the will of fate. Or we can just have a rummage sale and offer them up at a quid a pop."

She hated his sarcasm. He hated his scattered focus. He had no voice. Or too many voices. But not one solid one that stated, *"Here I am, Daniel Cross, you can spot my stamp a mile away."* No one had to second-guess a Miró, with its sparse geometric droppings; or Rothko's bold blocks of minimalist color field; or the broken glass of Schnabel. But a Cross… *"Who?"*

And then the whole West Coast peculiarity. *"Why here? Why not New York?"* was a repeated question he was asked. He never answered those questions, not even to those closest to him, but Harper knew that he'd done New York early on, after he'd first gotten to this country. He was only a teen then, not even painting yet, only trying to stay alive. And he'd quickly discovered that it was a much harder place to starve and struggle. Los Angeles was, at least, without the bitter winters, in case he had to make his home from a cardboard box. So he hitchhiked west and never left, because after a lifetime of no anchors he'd just been desperate to dig heels in.

He'd been working night and day to get something ready, had thirty pieces done so far, and, with quintessential Daniel pathos, he saw his body of work as suffering a profound identity crisis: Pointillistic, expressionistic, surrealistic, abstract-figurative. Acrylics. Gouache on paper cut-outs. Oil pencils. Charcoals. Woodcuts. He painted on canvas, ceramic tile, sheet metal, any scrap of crap he could find. He had large installation pieces, and tiny jewelry box confections. It was true that Daniel Cross was exhausting to look at and exhausting to contemplate. Yet, though it was impossible for him to see it, this peculiar recipe of influences had actually formed a very distinct voice. A voice that demanded engagement and deciphering, with no quick and easy assessment. A voice that stayed with you.

A woman once told him that his paintings gave her a headache. He'd responded to her, *"then, Madame, my job is done."* He wasn't nearly as smug as he liked to come off. It was an exchange that burdened still.

Tonight, as he trudged his way up Santee, Nona Childe was all that was on his mind. Her likeness, in varying mutated forms, decorated his flat, but the woman herself was nowhere yet on those canvases. The real Nona, the one he would some day capture, or kill himself trying, was still lurking in the clumps of paint on his paint board.

SEVEN

At 2:45 a.m. he arrived at his studio, once again unharmed by the citizens of Eighth Street, and proceeded to try painting her one more time. A newly stretched canvas was bracketed onto his easel as he laid the paints before him. He meditated over his barrel of brushes the way a baseball player meditates on his selection of bats, and chose. Tonight he was burning from eight whisky shooters, but unlike most men Daniel was aroused more keenly with drink, so a hard-on was raging, as well. He blasted Joy Division from his boom box and turned off all the lights. He wanted to paint blind tonight, and he didn't trust his eyes to stay closed.

And though he was raging, drunk, and horny, there was no way he was going to give himself a go. Not now. Now was for Nona. He had her in his head clearly. Seeing her at dinner earlier tonight gave him a whole other angle to this beauty. To speak with her, hear the sound of her voice, the cadence in her speech, to learn the little quirks, the mannerisms, to witness her passion, her insecurities, to discover a bit of history. She was no longer an anonymous piercer of his soul. Behind that frightening mask of violence and stitches and gauze lurked an enigma who was reluctant to reveal her horrors to him. But he would uncover her. And though he would always be crippled with self-doubt, this was his true gift.

A wrath of hues flung themselves on the gessoed canvas as he grabbed his cock simply to soothe it and calm it down. Punk music screamed at him, with mad guitars and demonically flanged voices gunning him down like an Uzi. He could see nothing of his efforts in the pitch black of his flat, except her soul inside his head.

As stroke upon stroke built itself up around him, saturating the canvas, the darkness was liberation. At one point, he abandoned his brushes and let his fingers dig into the canvas instead. Praying for gashes.

Flashes of Nona's book threatened to invade his privacy and blind him even more than the darkness could. She had made the protagonist of her dark, art-world masterpiece a champion. She had even given him the name Champion, though he got a hint tonight that she regretted that choice. And she laughed at Daniel Cross's life and knew what even his friends, the ones who had originally told him about the book, did not. That he was not Champion. He was only a speck. He was Will Speck, her paradoxical antagonist, who lashes out and yearns to kill the world because he cannot paint it, who literally holds a gun to Champion's head and cries, *"Give me your gift or die!"*

Gabriel Champion is the divine transformer of souls. Will Speck only wishes to hitch a ride at first; an observer on the journey, until he can no longer suffice merely to sit in the bleachers, an innocent bystander. As Champion becomes increasingly celebrated, Speck becomes more and more invisible. Speck's gut is filled with an unwavering yearning to express. Or is his unwavering yearning actually for validation? This is merely one of the questions Nona's narrative poses. And whichever is the answer, like the thief or the rapist, Speck is compelled to claim potency and power by robbing Champion of his. The taunting seducer holds his victim at bay and tickles Champion's skin with the cold, phallic barrel of a gun. Speck demands that Champion open his head and share his Muse, as two cads might share a mistress. And Champion begins. He draws, and sketches, and paints against his will, and paces the floors, and wrinkles his brow, and dabs some more, and stumbles through his ritualized gyrations, and pisses his pants because he knows that on this day he will die. Speck intends to usurp the genius in Champion, as though it is a tangible thing that he can hold in his hand and take for his own.

These words swilled about in Daniel's head, his paraphrasing summation of her tale verily haunting him throughout the night, no matter how much he tried to rid himself of the apparition. It made Daniel brave his own ever-agonizing search for self-discovery. It forced him to realize just exactly how he, too, drew up his grand schemes daily, manipulating the people around him to be a part of his drama so that he might fuel some sort of genius. And finally it knocked the wind out of him, because he had already fought through a long and bitter life just to resolve that his not being a champion was all right.

He was suddenly yanked from his fever to contemplate a pragmatic question he'd been asked more times than he could count: Why hadn't he ever utilized a team of young painter apprentices, as many of the most well-known painters did, to create a kind of factory, to help facilitate his vision, and to make producing product easier? And, as if the questioners were in the room, Daniel posed the question back: Do you see, now, how abusive it would be to invite a crew to be a part of THIS?

In the midst of his sooty self-indulgence, he fell asleep. He couldn't tell for how long, but when he awoke — still dark out (darker still within) — he looked up at the shadowy canvas before him.

Out of the dusk he thought he saw her peeking out from the abyss. A tiny light. *Oh, Jesus Holy Fuck and Mary, Mother of God!* He stood stunned before her. Though it always happened, he would always be stunned. It was the way of pathetics.

He couldn't let himself turn the lights on yet, but even in the darkness she peered at him, a pair of sad eyes that had lost their fire. Her mouth was serene, and her downward gaze gave her a gentility that seemed, with this injury of hers, to be the dominant factor in her demeanor. In a spate of startling cubist wonder, he had fashioned her very soul. And that word. He didn't even believe in The Soul. It was a sentimental, religious bunkum of a word, for certain. But it would have to do, for lack of anything else to call this force, this presence that was clearly here. Clearly her.

He hadn't painted her injuries. Those scars didn't belong to her. Frankly, the ones inside her heart were much more visible. He had tried to temper them, but they wouldn't be tempered. She was radiant and melancholy and broken. But all the pieces and shards were there.

It was just a beginning. And he couldn't even smile. He was afraid if he moved even a breath, it would all suddenly go *poof!* and prove to have been merely a mirage.

The strokes were wild and calm at once, with the intimate meshing of warm siennas and sepias and dark crimsons and burnt oranges, working together the way a bass and a drum and a piano and a horn work together. A calm settled in him, but he wanted to be careful not to get too comfortable with this vision because he still had far to go.

He sank in his big chair and stared at her until it was daylight again. Here or there he'd approach to add a touch to the wet canvas. And he giddily drowned in her presence, doing everything in his power to block out further thoughts of Speck and Champion with more manic music. *Don't mess with this moment!* he begged of them.

The sun rose and sank some undetermined number of times before he was conscious of the world again, as he paced his filthy floor, naked except for his construction boots, paint brush in his left hand, bong in his right. He had stopped drinking some thirty-six hours before, and had long stopped being reprimanded by Ian Curtis's mad vocals. Dvôrák's Ninth Symphony now caressed his ears.

She continued to evolve, to open like a deep rose and give him some new inspiration that would take him back up to the canvas for one more stroke.

He nursed Nona Childe's most precious secrets, peeked in, then fell in, the deep hollow of her excellent self. He stood before her and told her he was hers if she wanted him.

"Daniel! Wake up!" he suddenly heard in his ear. "Christ, are you on another bender?"

He awoke in a stupor, not welcoming the nasally Canadian twang above him, in his ear, on his face. How did Christianne get in?

"What are you doin' here?" he barked. "I'm workin'."

Then he panicked. Had he dreamt it all? He stumbled to his feet, all naked, smelly, brute, six feet of him, and turned toward the canvas. There she was. Not a dream. Not a terrible tease. But here before him. He caught the breath that had skipped. He grabbed a pair of pants and forced his booted feet through the legs. Was it day or night? He couldn't tell for several seconds. Christ, it was roasting in here! He fastened his pants and swooped up his bottle of Old Forester, drenched in sweat, and commenced with a new binge.

"Jesus, Daniel, you didn't pick up the rents!"

The rents? What the Hell was she talking about? Then the fog began to clear.

"Has Slumlord Daddy come frothing again?" he managed through a hungover cloud.

"Screw you, Daniel! You're lucky I even fuck you, otherwise you would be outta here on your Limey ass. Daddy hates you. And the only thing keeping you in this place is me constantly coming to your pitiful defense."

"Well, it's a good thing you love to fuck, then, isn't it? Or is it just that you love sticking it to Daddy by slumming with the lowly artist types he despises the most?"

"You sure about that artist claim?"

"Fuck you."

"Bite me."

When Daniel had first moved in here, he'd agreed to a barter with Tensmith, collecting all the other rents and acting as a sort of landlord's assistant, in exchange for a cut rate on his own place. And Tensmith's daughter Christianne, bless her heart, was not only a good lay, but a good egg, who'd been the one to arrange all this for him in the first place. She alone was responsible for keeping him in his flat without any hassles from Herr Tensmith, and all he could seem to muster for her today was Asshole etiquette.

He stared at her standing before him, plump little sexiness in a tube skirt, tank top, and peroxided hair. But beyond Christianne, on his canvas, looming in the distance, was his other Her. More serene than all the Mona Lisas, more startling than all the Dora Maars and Marie-Thérèses.

Christianne suddenly snatched his bottle from him, spilling half the contents.

"Answer the question, Daniel! Are you on another binge? Because I can't keep bailing you out every time you neglect the one and only responsibility you have in this life!"

Christianne's shrill voice could outgun Joy Division any day. Nevertheless, Daniel was able to gather from her ranting that he'd been at this obsessive session for eight days. *Eight days?* How had eight days slipped past him? Yesterday had been his dinner with Nona, hadn't it? Later that night had been Billy Somebody and his trio, no? How on earth had eight fucking days gone by? His hangover was stupendous, his sense of time and space foggy, though several empty bourbon bottles adorned the floor, he was sporting an almost full beard, and he stank horrendously.

Christianne never got mad for long, but Daniel would at some point have to respond to her. He finally discovered, after piecing together her ranting, that she'd taken care of the rents herself after Tensmith had confronted her about it. She'd covered for Daniel once again. As always.

He truly did feel the bastard. She deserved someone who would love her, and that someone was not him. There simply was no connection. He honestly liked her a great deal; she was sweet, cute, sexy. He liked her so much, in fact, that when she had tried to leave him eighteen months earlier he had begged her to stay, on pitiful hands and knees. She'd actually grown tired of his aloofness and his unfaithfulness. Imagine that. But he couldn't help it. She was wholly uninspired, had no mystery about her, no gifts, couldn't carry on a conversation that caused even the slightest spark. How could anyone remain interested and faithful? Yet he'd become sullen to think she might be gone from his everyday existence. And all he'd had to do to make her stay, that one time, was to shed a single, well-dramatized tear.

"I'm sorry Chris, but you gotta leave," he tried to articulate on this blistering day, but was fuzzy and absent.

"Gee thanks, Christianne, for picking up the rents for me," she mocked, doing some whiny impersonation of him, "and sweeping up the stupid crap of my life that I just leave spilled all over this goddamned, filthy floor. Thanks a-fucking-lot!"

"I'm sorry, bloody Hell! Whaddaya want from me? Thank you! All right? Thank you for rescuing me from myself AGAIN! You're a saint, honey, honest. But I swear to God, you gotta leave. You know the rules. No one's allowed here while I'm workin'."

She couldn't possibly know that he was in the very throes of a kind of fever.

"You didn't exactly leave me a choice, Daniel. Everybody thought maybe you were dead or something. Harper's been calling me, because you don't answer your phone. We were all worried sick."

That high-pitched, nasally voice was enough to make him commit murder today. He begged her to leave. Her intrusion onto his intimacy with Nona was unforgivable. But she wouldn't. And when he reached the pinnacle of his frustration with Christianne, when he could not possibly have been more irritated, he did the only thing he could do.

Her tongue had always proven talented, and her tolerance level of his smelly body was almost enough to touch his heart. Their sex was seldom gentle. It was usually about two people so starving as to be rabid about it. They did not kiss softly; they devoured and bit and groaned. Their hands never explored; they slapped and prodded and clung to flesh for dear life. She pulled his hair. He flung her over on her stomach. It was a vicious dance that left them both exhausted but supplied. This time, however, he could only see the image of his great beauty on a canvas in the distance, unfinished, yet complete enough to frown on his beastly behavior. It killed him to see Nona's face as he pounded Christianne beneath him. It killed him that this was not Nona beneath him. Not her fingers clutching his waist. Not her legs clenching his torso. Not her mouth, which he longed to taste, touching his neck and face. He flashed on that marvelous moment at her house. *Eight fucking days ago, already?* His finger had probed her mouth to give her a sugar cube, and had accidentally brazed her tongue. The very thought revved him up enough to give Christianne a go. He felt deceitful and despicable for having this carnal moment before Nona's image. And it made him hate Christianne. Of course the more he hated her, the better they fucked.

When they finished, he couldn't look in her eyes. He loathed himself. For letting her violate his process. For being led by his cock. For even now catching her nipple in the corner of his eye, as she dressed, and wanting to grab it and suck it more. He sat on the edge of his mattress with his head in his hands.

"Now, will you please leave," he begged in a whisper. "And tell everyone that I am not dead, only working. And if they want me to produce for this upcoming show, then they'd better all leave me the fuck alone for a bit."

"All right, Daniel," she responded. He could tell she felt patronized by his fucking her. She was no match for him in a fight.

"And Chris," he added, as she turned back his way. "I'm sorry about the rents."

"Yeah, whatever."

As she turned to leave, she scrutinized Nona's face on his canvas. She would question him about Nona later. Happened every time. It was a line of questioning that always concluded with, *"Why have you never painted me?"*

Quietly she left.

This was his life.

EIGHT

While the pink and sparkly haze of romantic newness had certainly snagged her, Nona was distracted these days by inspiration. She spent days and nights staring at a computer, frantic for inspiration to show itself, brought to tears by its frustrating absence, cursing at the feeble words on her screen, pissed off that they were mediocre and would never cut it, and fearful of the ringing phone that she knew would commence soon enough from her editor if she didn't come up with at least the start of a rough draft for her new book. What she'd gone through to get *Champion* on the shelves — the soul-searching and journal-jotting, the risk-taking, the excruciating decisions about how to resolve the book, the too many cooks in the kitchen, the constant tug-of-war with her publishers, which would either make or break her career — was enough of a reminder to give anyone hives.

It wasn't that she couldn't write. If anything, she was writing insanely these days, spilling endless, run-on sentences onto endless pages. But what her head had to dump was not literary. It was some brand of unrefined rage that could never call itself good composition.

She had always kept a journal whenever she was writing a book. She'd found it useful in sorting out her wild head. But what she was writing today had nothing to do with the creative process. This was therapy. This was desperately trying to fill the black hole with a literary conceit, which had been her therapist's idea, though Nona wasn't sure to buy any of it. Mainly she was confused and frustrated.

Nona didn't tell her therapist about Daniel. She knew she would have *"are you sure you're ready for this?"* coming at her from all sides, and she didn't want to have to defend it. How on earth would she ever be able to say, without sounding like a sap in pink and sparkly denial, that some serendipitous force had brought Daniel Cross into her life, grandson of the man to whom she'd devoted her entire college thesis, and that she would be damned not to recognize that? She would surely have her face slapped and be told to wake up and get a clue.

Just leave me alone and let me enjoy this man! she screamed, in her imaginary argument, not only to her therapist and her editor but to the faceless predator that insisted on burdening.

Her second date with Daniel was a little over a week later. She'd invited him to meet her for a performance piece in the brewery district of downtown, which was as close to a west coast version of New York's meatpacking district as any nook of L.A.

"You and Kai will totally hit it off," she said over the phone. "She's been my best friend since high school. She's a true bohemian. Yoga teacher, meditation facilitator, and an amazing performance artist. I mean, just this complete experimentalist, who hosts these parlor performances around L.A. You will not be disappointed. She also used to be Irene, but don't ever let her know I told you that."

"She sounds great," Daniel returned. "Frankly, I could use a break from the madness."

He then rambled on about artist's block, and a difficult eight days, and being kind of insane. Insane she could relate to.

Earlier in the week she'd had the stitches and surrounding bandages removed, though the swelling and discoloration was still about her, her eye remained bulbous, and she'd graduated to a simple eye patch. Looking like some cartooned pirate marauder should definitely turn him on, she thought, with a roll of her one good eye.

She waited at the entrance on Traction Avenue with that anticipatory seizing that the belly loves to do at the most inconvenient moments. Captain Hook waiting in the balustrade. She wanted to catch Daniel's eyes and read what was in them at first sight of her eye-patched face before he would have the chance to offer up some false courtesy. The baggage served up with the seizing should've been more worrisome; nothing is the killer of a good thing like trauma, dense of content and daring to be reckoned with, strutting the ring with pomp. No one ever wants to take it on. Especially when it's someone else's. And doubly especially if you're only looking to get laid; she hadn't gotten a sense yet of whether this was Daniel's only angle.

When the house lights flashed with still no sign of him, she waded inside and took her seat, almost smiling at the grim satisfaction that the worst about Daniel Cross had been revealed, and ready to cry from chewing her own tail. She sat in the darkened performance space alone, as alone as one truly is in a crowd of others who merely cocoon you but do not have your back. Eye-patched. Afflicted. Jilted.

Loser. And then she realized that she wasn't sure if that was meant for her, or him.

Twenty minutes into curtain, Daniel tiptoed in with program in hand and the silent apologetic gestures to everyone he had to creep past in the narrow aisle. When she noticed him she wanted to fall on her knees with thanks, when, with anyone else, she'd have been affronted that they'd shown up so late. The seizing in her gut never ceased; only shifted. She hated feeling this desperate.

Lights were down, as she slid over in the pew to accommodate him, and only the dim glow on her face from the stage lights allowed him any glance of her. He leaned over to kiss her cheek, which pricked her nerves. They smiled at each other, turned their attentions toward the stage, and she barely breathed for the rest of the performance.

The various happenings, live art pieces, action poetry, and aleatoric song cycles presented were everything from sublime to subversive. Daniel whispered in her ear that he knew one of the musicians on stage performing tone rows on an upright bass; Neville was his name.

"This bloke's a burning bebop player. You gotta see his trio play some night at the Orchid Club."

They watched their friends together making music, making theatre, making art, and making life feel rich. But Nona could barely keep her attentions on the art at hand, due to being distracted by her conclusion that art was what she and Daniel were all about. Art was their whole existence. It was what had drawn each to the other. She concluded this somewhere between swagger and anxiety, and was in such a romantic fog that she missed a stage moment that elicited applause from the audience, and couldn't even recognize the irony.

As curtain call was being taken, and the house lights came up quicker than she was ready for, in the midst of applause Daniel turned her way.

"Thank you for this," he offered.

And that thing in his eyes that she'd been waiting for, that vaudevillian double take when noticing the shocking, just wasn't there. Although…

"May I say that you look positively swashbuckling."

She laughed outright. Such a laugh that she almost coughed it. And she breathed again, and giggled, and hated her girlish incontinence.

Everyone adjourned to a party at the Factory, a new hot spot that had just opened on Eighth Street. They walked into a multileveled warehouse with huge arched windows, cemented walls, crazy sculptures made from PVC pipe, and behemoth Persian rugs. The lights of downtown shined through the windows of this Warhol emulation in an eerie wash of color.

It was packed with artists whose works were about to make a dent on the West Coast scene. As Daniel, Kai, Neville, and Nona stood waiting for a table, Nona realized that she couldn't entertain notions of the black hole tonight. She'd begun the evening weighted down with fear and loathing. At this moment she was buoyant.

They finally sat at a table and drank Russian ales and ate borscht, having to scream at each other to be heard over the din, and a buzz in the room began to strike her as most profound. Daniel knew most of these artists, performance and otherwise, and many — who had never even met him — knew who he was. If they weren't coming up to him, they were glancing his way and whispering to each other. Nona hadn't actually considered the possibility that a bit of celebrity might exist for him, and suddenly she was even more intrigued.

Even Kai discovered that she'd seen some of Daniel's work before, but was only just now putting face to name.

"I saw a piece of yours at the Robert Berman Gallery a couple of years ago," she yelled across the table. "I think it was the only one you had at this particular exhibit. It absolutely blew me away. Nona, I think you were doing a book tour or something. I can't remember now why you weren't there with me. Oh my God, she and I are, like, the gallery divas!"

As for Nona, she was a bit spooked now. If Kai had heard of Daniel, why hadn't she? She'd always prided herself on keeping up with the goings-on in the L.A. art scene. And to discover now that he was quite possibly one of those forces? Beautiful face and brooding brow aside, this new mystery only added tenfold to his allure.

Kai was running her mouth on octane, but never without charm.

Daniel teased privately in Nona's ear: "This one here? A yoga instructor? Really?"

They chuckled together and kept the joke between them.

"It was an abstract," Kai continued, on the canvas she'd seen of Daniel's. "But if I remember correctly, it wasn't quite as graffitiesque as, say, the new-wave Soho kids. It was really much more minimalist—much more the West Coast thing. Except that I've always thought of West Coast minimalism as having a kind of serenity to it. This piece was anything but. It was a furious thing."

"Ah, I know the canvas you're talkin' about," Daniel finally inserted. "Yeah, actually that piece didn't sell. It went right back to my flat."

"Are you kidding me?" she blurted. "God, if I'd had the money I'd'a bought it. It was the best thing there that night."

"Thanks."

Daniel blushed, but Kai was such a force of nature that she didn't pick up on it. Instead, she begged him to tell the table where all that painting fury came from.

"Some kind of aching sore, I can only imagine," she seemed to answer for him. "I mean, oh my God, Nona, Neville—I mean, Nev, have you seen the piece? You guys, it was just that powerful. How would you describe it?"

Kai was a bullet train for sure, with Daniel alternately charmed and embarrassed.

"Well, thanks for asking. You don't know what it means to have someone actually interested in the process. But, em, you know, I...I...em..." He was genuinely struggling for words. "I'm happy to show it to you sometime," he motioned to both Nona and Neville, and clearly begging off from having to dissect his work as a crowd pleaser.

"No, no, but I mean—" Kai interrupted, insisting on a full rundown of the very brushstrokes. She took over where Daniel was politely unwilling. "—Um, it's this, sort of, well, first of all, it's massive. And it's this mixed-media abstract-figurative on this huge wood plank. And it's got these images of water rings from a drinking glass stamped in black over a hybrid image of a grand piano, I think, and a, sort of, human face in torment. And, and, and the imagery is literally made of scraps and pieces of rice paper, newsprint, splats of paint. And the colors are a sort of smeary mess of taupe, black, rust, amber. And I mean mess in only the best way."

The table couldn't help but laugh, though Nona could see the cringing politeness coming from Daniel, who had no interest in having his art piece reduced to a grocery list of the physical materials that made it up. Art was beyond the paper and the paint and the parchment and the scraps. It was the statement. The blood. The life revealed. She got it.

Kai did too, Nona knew, but Daniel couldn't possibly know this by the indelicate way the girl attacked everything. Kai gobbled life up and didn't regard its fragility, Nona pondered, especially the fragility of the art world. If anything, Kai laughed in fragility's face and dared it to *man up!* It was what Nona loved most about her girlhood friend, especially because she, herself, was so the opposite; Nona strode through museum halls with reverence, where Kai blew through, irresistibly gusting up the skirts of the literati.

As Kai spelled out Daniel's piece stroke by stroke, she shook her head in barely contained hallelujahs, reminding Nona fondly of the church ladies from their childhood who were just seconds away from jumping up and Jesus-shouting. Daniel tried hard not to look embarrassed at being raved about and exposed. He would periodically catch Neville's eye, or Nona's, here and there, and just smile through it.

In particular, however, when he looked Nona's way there was a slight lingering in the glance, something that almost stated, *"you and I have some engaging to do yet."* The contemplation made Nona's pulse flutter. This was definitely a sexual play, yet Daniel never abandoned his dutiful attention to Kai's praises to quite fully leer. And suddenly, as if he needed to regain control of the runaway horse, he chimed in.

"There's this piano player over at the Orchid Club on Wednesday nights. Right down the street from here, actually. In fact, it's where Neville and I first met. Anyway, this bloke's name is Billy…somebody. I don't know his last name. You wouldn't know him, would you, mate?"

Neville shook his head.

"Anyway, this piece Kai's going on and on about—and bless you, child—lodged in my head the first night I saw this piano player. His trio was playing *My One and Only Love*, which just happens to be my favorite old standard, and some drunken bugger, as I'm sure I've been on enough occasions, stumbles over to the Steinway. Now, this genius Billy—right?—

has been caressing this instrument in ways that are almost erotic. And Lord Stumbleton suddenly decides that it's okay to lay his sweating pint on it, while he leans in to slobber a request. All of a sudden this Billy bloke stops playing. I mean, right in the middle of this gorgeous passage. And he suddenly clears the Steinway of pint and asshole with one swoop'a the arm. And he starts ranting, to the shock of the other musicians, something like, *'I don't come to your house and take a shit on your dining room table, you little prick, so don't you lay your wet little drippy mug on this beautiful instrument. Have some respect, asshole. If not for us, then for IT!'* "

"Whoo-hoop!" the table shouted alternately. "Wow! Fuckin' yeah!"

"Amen," Daniel whispered quietly to his own anecdote. Nona was the only one who noticed it. He then looked directly at her, though he was still talking to the whole.

"And it only reminded me that being an artist is the loneliest job on earth. Every blood and gut of you spilled into the thing of your creating. In this Billy Somebody's case…aaghhh, some day I should really learn this bloke's name, yeah? Anyway, in his case it was this incredibly wistful song. As elevating as all the *Nessun Dorma*s in existence. And who cared?"

It was a rhetorical *who cared* that hung in the naked air, but really did beg an answer. They all stared at one another, having been quietly sobered by Daniel's story.

"I ran home that very night and started the canvas. And for the longest time I really struggled with that piece. You know, did it really say all that to me? Had I truly seized the hopelessness and the melancholy I was going after? And did it even matter if that's what I captured or not? It said something, right? So what, if some little old lady with her Gallery Guide rolled up in her hand and a cheese ball stuffed in her mouth says of it, *'oh, it reminds me of Paris and my romantic boat trip up the Seine.'* So be it."

"You know, I think I know that woman," joked Kai. "Oh wait, I AM that woman!"

Kai was incapable of going to the dark place that seemed to be Daniel's authentic familiar, and the table was grateful.

"Well, you obviously got past the hurdle," said Nona, "if it ended up on a wall at the Berman."

"I guess," Daniel responded. "Who ever knows, right?"

"In any case," Kai offered, more sobering than she'd been all night, "it was the best piece there that night. A true sin no one took it home."

"Well, Kai, how about this? For the remarkable honor of having made your acquaintance, and for giving us all such an incredible show tonight, why don't you be the one to take it home next time we meet up."

"I don't have that kind of money. But thanks for making me say that out loud."

"Who said anything about money?"

"No, no, don't do that, my friend. Don't fucking tease me like that."

"I never tease about a thing like that."

"You could pay your bills for six months with what you could get for that piece."

"Well, that's overstating it a bit, but it is just sitting in a corner collecting dust. It might as well be loved."

"Oh my God! Oh, believe me, it would be loved!"

"I've no doubt."

Kai squealed a perfectly sharp stab through the thick drapery of noise, and hugged Daniel until he almost fell off his chair. Nona sat and watched this most remarkable scene of generosity, and was reminded of the story she'd heard, for years, of Picasso once tipping a waiter in a restaurant by scribbling a pen and ink on a napkin for the young server. It made Nona smile. That story. And this one.

A quartet that had been setting up their instruments in a corner, unbeknownst to them, suddenly poured forth a wistful Miles composition, which quieted the din of the room to a dull hum.

When Kai pulled Neville up for a slow dance, Daniel felt obliged to ask Nona. She could tell he wasn't much on the tradition but thought he should at least extend the chivalry.

"Sure," she said.

"You'll forgive me if I pummel your feet?"

And before they knew it, they were in embrace. The kind that's okay, when boundaries and invitations haven't exactly been established yet. His right thigh nestled gently in between hers, a place of great pain lately, physically and otherwise. His hands cradled her waist to draw her to him. The warmth of him sent a prickle up her back and neck, which ultimately settled into a delicate simmer. Their cheeks rested against each other, as he buried his face in the crux of her collarbone. It unnerved her to have his face actually touching one of her scars, barely healed, but he seemed unrepulsed. And she realized in this instant that she was the only one repulsed and frightened by this injury. He would take it on, no matter how contentious the opponent. A faint hum from his breathing tickled her ear, and they floated on top of *Blue in Green*. Why couldn't Miles last forever tonight?

When the last note rang out and slowly faded, the four of them retreated to their table and ordered dessert. As for Daniel and Nona, they'd not quite gotten off this ride yet. He looked her way with his potent gray eyes, and when she looked back she would swear that he was opening himself up to her, beckoning for her to learn him as quickly as possible, as if there was some urgency in it. She could barely heed the conversation that had begun between Kai and Neville, or the murmured din of the rest of the place, for attempting furiously to hear what Daniel's eyes were trying to say. But the two of them couldn't very well keep the rest of the world locked out forever, so for the time being they dropped their eyeing pursuits.

The quartet continued to lushly underscore their evening, and eventually the table wound around to the subject of *Champion*, which Daniel and Kai both stressed to Neville he must read.

"This book's a manifesto, mate," Daniel jumped in. "It'll, it'll, it'll—if you've ever had, you know, any doubts about what it is you're here for—I mean, as an artist, and, and, or like, needed a connection that you felt you couldn't get—I mean, it's just—it's a slap in the face. I mean, not exactly a slap in the face, because it's, like, it's actually quite nurturing. But, I mean, not that warm and fuzzy crap—you know, it's, it's deadly—"

"It gets to the very heart of what it means to be compelled as an artist," Kai mercifully interjected, as Daniel was just about to trip over his own feet. "Every artist should have this book."

"But there's something else, besides, that's, that's, that's—"

Clearly unsatisfied with the collective appraisal thus far, Daniel took a beat and reordered his thoughts.

"Books are all about language and dialectic and argument. And here is a book that has managed to say everything in the domain of silence, in behavior and thought, a touch, an intention, a feeling. This book thrives by its very abatement of words."

He didn't stumble on that one.

He also gave the book far more credit for being a paradoxical wonder than it actually deserved, Nona thought, annoyed at the fact, so she was grateful when Neville mentioned Daniel's upcoming show and turned the conversation.

Eventually the evening wound down, as all evenings must, and she didn't know why it had to be so. It seemed almost willful in its insistence on not allowing her euphoria to extend until she was simply spent and empty; she could've gone at this for hours more. It had to insist, instead, that she drive home reeling.

They all said their goodnights, as Nona promised to come see Neville's trio at the Orchid Club, and Kai swore not to miss Daniel's opening.

Minutes later, Daniel and Nona found themselves curbside and alone. He stared at her as if a subject of the utmost importance was on his mind, and puzzled over how exactly to engage. He took both her hands in his, as he sought the words, and she loved the feel of his gnarled palms.

"I know I sounded like an idiot in there trying to tell Neville about *Champion*."

"On the contrary. You actually—"

"It's just that it's—oh, I'm sorry, you were about to say?—"

"No, no, no, go ahead."

She didn't want to have to confess that his spin had been more compelling than the book it was spinning.

"I really don't know how to convey to you just what your book has meant to me," Daniel continued. "And to be quite frank, I'm not sure you'd welcome hearing most of it."

"Why do you say that?"

"Well, that's just about—that's just my head. Suffice it to say that the honor to be in the company of the woman who has brought that book into my life is a great one."

"Wow," was all she could muster. The writer, the fashioner of words.

"My fondest hope, Nona, is that some day I'll be able to talk about it with you, without it taking me to the dark side."

He laughed, but she didn't laugh with him.

"Well, I certainly look forward to being as moved by your work. You weren't going to tell me about your exhibit, were you? We had to hear it from your friend?"

"I...I wasn't even thinking about it. It wasn't intentional."

His exclusion of this news only added to his mystique, because she would swear that Daniel had been wooing her this night.

They eyed each other keenly, and both snickered. It wasn't a laugh so much as a guarded harrumph, as though they were both ruthless opponents in a flirty game of hide-and-seek.

And suddenly there it was. The fantasy she'd been entertaining all evening long, of his hands caressing each side of her face and his mouth leaning in to kiss her. Except that in her fantasy his lips parted slightly as they rested on hers and were so softly sensual that she melted into him. In reality, for her mouth was still somewhat pulled from the scarring, he politely found a clean spot on her battlefield of a face and tenderly kissed her cheek instead. Oh well. It would have to do for now.

"Goodnight," he whispered.

"Yes, it has been," she returned.

As she got into her car and started the engine, she watched him in her rearview mirror. He casually walked down the street, turned right onto San Pedro, and disappeared.

She'd have to write about Daniel Cross some day. Gourd of melancholy. Blessed intrigue. There could be no more complex or solemn a creature in all of the world's literature, she thought, as hyperbole drenched everything tonight.

He was her Heathcliff.

NINE

Nona met Kai at the entrance of the Hareton Gallery on Canon, and after initial hellos to Neville, whose trio was performing, they instantly parted ways, Kai down one corridor, Nona down another. It was the ritual of art-show-hopping, and they both knew to meet back at the champagne table some time later. Nona hadn't seen Daniel yet this evening, in fact not since their evening at the Factory, but got the feeling that he was the sort to relish his anonymity, likely overseeing the whole event from some comfortable shadows and steering safely away from the world at large. As she made her way through the milling, she watched as art critics and patrons alike turned up to see what she imagined as the rarely surfaced recluse who painted with a fury. That was the word Kai had used.

Fury didn't even scratch the surface of what it turned out to be. Nona had been in anticipation of this moment since the day they'd met. *Show me what you're made of, health-food-store brooder.* And he surely did.

His portraitures were larger than life, but not in the way of the portraits of the Masters. Rembrandt and Raphael assigned divinity to mere mortals. There were no halos, literal or symbolic, adorning Daniel's subjects. He approached his from the opposite end. He took the noblest of God's creatures and turned them inside out, revealing to the world on a mere scrap of canvas all their basest instincts, everything wonderful and horrible revealed, tormented gods and goddesses. It was truth and sensual essence blasting through a veil of decorum and politeness. No quaint Still Life's here.

Leading up to this night, she had prayed he wouldn't be mediocre, because how do you tell someone what you think of their less-than-average efforts when they've lauded yours? But she wasn't prepared for this. In this presence, she was the one who felt mediocre. The work in this space was the proof of just how watery a portrayal her Gabriel Champion suddenly felt to her. What made her think she could capture the spirit of a painter? This before her was Gabriel Champion, not the conceit on her pages. When she'd first created Champion, she had contrived his genius by simply stating it. And all a reader had to do was to accept her words and imagine it. But how do you actually deliver the goods with mere words, when it is all about color and light and dimension and visual phantasm and blood? Here before her was the thing embodied.

As she walked the corridors of Hareton, each painting thrust itself upon her, one only more thrilling than the last and wildly different from each other. At one passing, she caught Kai in the corner of her eye.

"So what do you think?" asked Kai, approaching.

Nona shook her head, unable to gather thoughts. Then simply: "Wow."

That she seemed repeatedly to go back to that fine bit of eloquence worried her. She was supposed to be the artisan of words.

"I just wish I could find him to tell him how incredible his work is."

"Oh, he's here," said Kai. "I've already spoken to him. I met his agent too. Very cool lady." Kai then stared at Nona in that mischievous manner of hers, and sighed a breath of satisfaction. "Before you go off looking for him, though, I think you need to come with me."

Kai led the way down a narrow corridor past several other rooms, and Nona would swear that each painting they passed reached out to brush her like groping fingers.

As they turned a final corner, Kai didn't even have to point it out. There it hung on a wall alone, surrounded by a smattering of people.

She couldn't decide whether it was a good thing her not seeing Daniel before she saw this. It was called *Joyau*.

"That *is* you, isn't it?" Kai asked, already knowing.

"Oh my God," Nona whispered, stunned.

Though this austere piece before them was somewhat abstract-expressionistic, it was obviously her likeness. Yet it seemed arrogant to agree with Kai. No one had ever painted her before. To be honest, she felt a little unnerved. Daniel had proven to be such a remarkable exposer of souls, and here she was on a canvas before them, every breath and inch of her secret self weirdly laid bare.

She wasn't sure how she felt about Daniel letting himself in like that.

But hadn't she invited him? And wasn't it his duty as the artist to speak what he saw? This mirror of her darkness and light spooked her. And if there was one thing she had always loved above all else, it was being spooked by art. Nona Childe never needed a roller coaster ride to make her feel alive. Just give her a little artistic brilliance.

"Well, I don't know how you feel about it," said Kai, looking her squarely in the eye, "but I think this man's falling hard."

"Don't be a soap opera," Nona threw off, rolling her eyes, though she was fighting off her own teary telenovela. "We don't even really know each other that well."

"Didn't seem to stop him, did it? And speak of the Devil."

Nona looked up as Daniel approached. Finally. The Man. With a day's growth and looking like some kind of steampunk gigolo in an Edwardian-cut coat with ancient buckles, he didn't belong to this century.

He chuckled like someone caught in a naughty act when he saw what they were standing in front of.

Kai made her quickest exit. "More champagne. See ya' in a bit."

Once alone, they both stared at the canvas. An uneasy exaggeration of features. And yet they were features that could only be her. The short coils on her head, a set of eyebrows that were almost too close together. Explosive eyes. Implosive mouth. A curling in of her soul that was almost weirdly literal. The unnatural colors that spoke emotion rather than photo-real simulation. A brilliant wistfulness that was really much more brilliant on this canvas than in her actual face. But he didn't portray her scars. The sewn gash up her neck and adjoining her ear. The pulled mouth. The gross eyelid tumor under her patch that she would never let him see. This portrait was merciful and unmerciful at the same time.

"Well—" he eventually leaked. He tried for more, but seemed awkward and stumped.

She looked in his eyes and her own started to film. As much as she hated her penchant for easy tears, she didn't try to hide it this time. She wanted him to know what his work had done to her. She struggled for words, as he held both her hands and faced her like a gentleman comforting the grieving at a funeral. He had made this moment transcendent for her. How do you just casually thank someone for that?

"You ARE Gabriel Champion," was what she finally came up with.

"You know, I only ever had, at best, this distantly abstract concept in my mind of what Champion's work would be like when I was creating him. I mean, to make a fictitious character brilliant is merely to say so. Right? Or is it? Aaagghhh, I know I sound shallow. Obviously it takes more than just saying so. It takes building just the right blocks for the character that could render no other conclusion in the eyes of the reader. I just, I don't know...I just feel like I missed it. But you have—"

She stared again at the body of work before and around her, *Joyau* being but one in her immediate view.

"—You have brought Gabriel Champion to life."

She was so wrapped up in her own words that she hadn't bothered to notice how uncomfortable he seemed with them.

A moment later, after boring holes in her with those gray eyes, he leaned in to whisper in her ear.

"Come home with me tonight."

He was so blunt. Irritatingly sexy.

"I, I, I, um—"

What on earth was she trying to say? She wanted to go home with this man more than anything in the world.

"I'm not asking you to go to bed with me," he interrupted softly. "Not that I wouldn't...enjoy that, as well. But you said you might like to see where I lived some day. I figure I can't hide from you forever. And I guess what I'm saying is that I don't want to anymore." He smiled shyly. "We'll steal a bottle of champagne from this bore of a ball when it's over, and be out. Whaddaya say?"

The world must've been feeling unequivocally good to Daniel right now, if he was finally willing to open his home to her. He was a different man tonight. He seemed bright. And bright was not a word she would ever have used to describe the brooding Brit. Surely it had to be the fact that many of his pieces had already sold in the silent auction. He wanted to celebrate. And he wanted to do it with the weeping piratess.

She shook her head in agreement and then asked it. The question that was nipping at her ears.

"Why did you paint me?"

The second she asked it, she realized how fairly daring it was to assume, in front of him, that it actually was her in the portrait.

He peered at her as though the question were ridiculous. Or puzzling? Or…worse! *Shit!*

"I didn't have a choice," was what he finally offered, in a whisper.

He smiled again, though it was really more of an awkward spreading of the mouth. He walked away, disappearing into a crowd of accolades and buzz, leaving her to reel. She really should've known he would end up being this great. If she'd been about her keener judgment, she'd have sensed it in the eyes and the silence between his words.

I'll be paying more attention from now on.

A moment later she turned back to stare at *Joyau* again and imagined if she'd been painted by Rubens or Caravaggio. And because she had an inkling, this night, that Daniel Cross could be as important a figure some day, her mind raced with the magnitude of it. In three hundred years she might still live, perhaps haunting some wall in the Louvre, with historians discoursing wildly on the identity of the mysterious woman in the portrait. She could not resist entertaining the mischievous thought, and the chill of immortality raced through her.

After taking a deep breath and recuperating from the swoon, she went to find Kai, who promptly introduced her to Harper Levy, Daniel's dearest friend, and agent, and the one responsible for this show.

"You're the first woman to turn Daniel's head in a long time," Harper said, "and I'm not sure yet whether that's a good thing or not." She laughed and extended her hand for a firm shake. "It's an honor to meet you, Nona. I'm the one who first gave Daniel your book, so you can blame me. It's a remarkable work. I've been following your career, young lady."

"Such as it is," Nona responded. "I mean, it's the only one. I've hardly got a body of work."

"Don't underplay your accomplishments. The world will be hearing a lot more from you. I know it."

"My goodness. Well, thank you."

Nona was wonderfully overwhelmed by this tornado in an elegant Ann Taylor pantsuit and smart Joan & David shoes.

A small, frizzy-haired woman, in her early fifties was Nona's guess, and a feisty sort, Harper Levy possessed a straightforward manner and confident handshake. Nona discovered in five efficient minutes that Harper was the daughter of immigrants, had traveled the world, once living in Israel on a kibbutz, herding and cooking, once visiting the death camps in Poland, and was now the CEO of a company that funneled grant money into shelters. Agenting was not her career, but she'd made Daniel her personal artistic mission.

"He's my sole client," she responded when Nona asked how she'd come to represent artists. "I've just been active in the art community for so long, on the arts councils of MOCA, and the new Getty, and the Music Center, blah, blah, blah, that it seemed I might actually be able to be of service to my dearest friend, who is the most exciting artist to come along in years, but who is completely useless as a businessman."

They laughed.

"Anyway, I managed to get the art historian Michel Dugnac here. I'm trying to get him to take on the project of a catalogue of Daniel's work. We've already got a monograph on him in the works by June Steele—"

Nona glanced at Kai, who whispered, "The critic. Very distinguished."

"Thanks."

Nona learned quickly that it was going to take a lot to keep up with Harper Levy.

"—So I figure we can use that, tie it all together. And I'm hoping Dugnac might use his influence to get Daniel's work in the Musée Cantini in Marseille. To have Daniel exhibited in France would be a coup." She then laughed, as if she couldn't quite believe they'd come this far. "AND this particular show—fingers crossed—is meant to be a direct steppingstone to the Whitechapel Gallery in London."

"Daniel's hometown."

"Yes," she said, with a kind of reverence. "And one of the most prestigious galleries in the world."

"Well, he's certainly got the right woman working for him."

"Well, we'll see, won't we?" Harper answered, refusing to take credit for the immense résumé she'd just rattled off.

"You know," Nona began, "Daniel tries to play a good game of *'I'm not worthy,'* but I just—I should've known it wasn't so."

"I know, I know," Harper chuckled. "He does have a way with the unassuming, doesn't he? After talking with him for five minutes, you imagine the typical scenario of some guy who dabbles insignificantly in his basement and once in a while takes his stuff out to Venice Beach to sell on the boardwalk."

"Yes! You've nailed it. That's exactly what I was picturing. I mean, not the work itself—necessarily—and not to say that street artists aren't... you know, but I mean, to be honest, I just didn't know what to expect."

What Nona didn't express outwardly was just how spooked she was by Daniel's unexpected largeness. She now not only had a man of passion and gift, but of weight, as well, to contend with.

"Of course, if it were all left up to him," Harper added, "no one would ever see his work. But I believe in him and am determined not to let him leave this earth unheralded."

Nona and Kai toasted this vibrant woman's determination and thanked her for it, and all three toasted Daniel's success, as they watched him in the distance shaking hands with the Who's Who and knowing that it was only a matter of time.

As the evening wound down, goodbyes were said to Harper and Neville; and to Kai, who had just finished making arrangements for the delivery of the promised Cross original, and was on a cloud. Nona then found Daniel, who grabbed a sweaty bottle of Moët, and she followed him in her car as they exited the posh hub of Beverly Hills for the dubious hub of Downtown Los Angeles.

Thirty minutes later they arrived at Daniel's building and parked in an alley-accessed structure on Santee. The rickety elevator ascended, and the double freight door opened onto it. Daniel entered ahead of her, as Nona slowly moved about his studio, eyeing everything. Huge, arched windows, whose frames were badly chipped and bowing in places from water damage, surrounded them with a view of Los Angeles Proper at night. The windows stretched from floor to ceiling, Daniel's ceiling being a dusty chasm of tubes, wires, and ominous pipes.

One corner of the loft was piled high with industrial bins and milk crates filled with every scavenged thing one could imagine: Paints, felt strips, rolls of tarp, solvents, turpentine, glues, wigs, fragments of a Banana Republic mannequin, old 45s spilling over onto each other. A construction ladder leaned against a wall. Nona eyed books that were piled everywhere; in bookshelves, on tables and chairs, in boxes, stacked by Daniel's mattress with a half-filled bourbon glass sitting on a stack and a dead fly floating in it.

"Do you always use your books as a night stand?"

"Doesn't everyone? In my defense, I do at least read them first. Hang on. What is this?"

He noticed her tragic friend floating, and emptied the glass of its contents in a nearby sink.

"Sorry about this place."

She watched him walk to the center of his colossal palace of chaos and voltage to thumb through his mail. As he did so, the loft's energy awoke and swirled about him. How could he apologize for such a place?

Regarding the magnificent library contained within these walls, she started, "Let me guess. You were one of those annoyingly gifted students for whom studying was effortless and whom everybody hated. A book a day, right?"

He laughed.

"Where'd you study?"

"Never did university. I found there was no future for me in preparing for a future. I was already painting. Already out there. Thank God for books, or I'd be a lost man in a lost world."

"Did you just quote a Sting song?"

He laughed again.

As she floated about the room, the kaleidoscopic swirl of fragments and abstracts and scribbled messages on everything reeled her in with fascination.

Daniel poured two glasses of champagne, as she thumbed through some of his books and found — amidst *Magister Ludi* and *Thus Spake Zarathustra* and Miles's autobiography and Mao's Manifesto and Faulkner and Joyce — *The Assassination of Gabriel Champion*. She spotted some lesser works too, but preferred to group her own with the company of legend. She picked it up, rubbing her fingers across it, as if doubting its reality. Daniel quickly handed her a pen.

"Would you honor me?"

"Of course. But would you mind if I take it home with me, so that I can take my time and think about what I'd like to inscribe to you?"

"Just don't keep it. It's become my Bible."

Foreplay, schmoreplay.

She walked about, clutching her own novel to her breast, and felt validated.   As she roamed his loft, unable to restrain a smile, she approached nine different canvas studies on the same woman, all overlapping one another in a corner, a serene creature with hollowed eyes and a troubled mouth. She put *Champion* aside and rummaged through them. These weren't as abstract or as bold as the one she'd seen of herself earlier tonight. These were softer. In a way, a nod to da Vinci's *sfumato* technique. She couldn't take her eyes off of the compelling face.

"Is it true what they say about artists only ever having their own work on their walls?"

"Absolutely," Daniel said, handing her a fizzing glass. "We are our own biggest fans, you know."

"Yeah. Somehow, in your case, I doubt that. So tell me about these," she commanded, referring to the nine studies.

As Daniel joined her, they both stared for some time.

TEN

"Laura," was all he whispered.

"You must have loved her."

"Never knew her."

He took a swig, finishing the champagne down whole, and poured himself another. He brought the bottle down between them as they sat on the floor beneath Laura's many incarnations.

"She was a commission," Daniel began. "It was this older couple, stalwarts in the community, children all in the best prep schools, fraternity pledges, debutante balls, yacht club memberships, the whole blue-blood circus. And they wanted a portrait in memory of their dead mum, the matriarch, the children's grandmother. Now, I didn't like the idea of doing commissions. I'd done them before, and never to gratifying ends. See, because when the work has an agenda other than the artist's, that's when you can get into trouble. Now you're just a work-for-hire. Which is a completely valid job; it's just not for me. Da Vinci suffered that same dilemma, you know."

Nona grinned, he noticed, with her eyes to the ground. Some private joke to which he wasn't wise.

"But da Vinci was actually a bit mischievous about it," he continued. "He'd give the clients their commission, but with other added, hidden symbols and meanings, as if to laugh in their faces. Now, I'm not quite the brilliant rascal da Vinci was, AND this particular family was offering me obscene amounts of money. How do you turn that down when you're poor?"

"Well—"

"The answer is, you don't. So we shook hands, and the process began. An impossible one, I would come to later find, but then I've always been of the opinion that creation is a job for someone with at least a high school diploma or the equivalency. And at all times requires a crash helmet."

They laughed stupidly. Surely the champagne had something to do with such an easy penchant.

"In any case, I couldn't figure it out, you know? I mean, how could I possibly paint someone I never knew? It's not just a face you paint. It's a spirit. An energy. I mean, *Joyau* is a perfect example of that. It, it, it—"

He couldn't quite compose what he wanted to say. Then a second later he had it in his thoughts but wasn't sure he should offer it. Did he really want to invite her into his crazy head? She was such a nice lady, and had never done him wrong. But he found himself continuing anyway. Perhaps he figured that if he could show her the warts on this old toad, and still not frighten her off, then there might actually be something here.

"With your portrait, Nona, it wasn't until we looked in each other's eyes, touched, learned a few secrets. That's when it all opened up for me. Because that's simply what the process is. Before we actually met, I'd been struggling with it forever, it seems. I know. I sound like some disturbed fan."

He noticed that her glance shifted from him to floor upon that confession. He'd made her uncomfortable. But there was a strange smile, not even, about her face. Just a blip on the screen. She really was an enigma.

"In Laura's case," he continued, trying to redeem the story, "she was already dead. She wasn't anyone I ever could personally connect with. And there had never been a mutual path that either of us had ever crossed. I mean, she was from privilege, a world I knew nothing about. My only recourse was to study her from scratch, the way an actor studies a character on a page. So I started gathering, collecting, rallying around me all the trinkets that spelled her life. Anything her family could possibly dig up. Photographs. Letters. A handkerchief bearing the scent of lilacs and moth balls. Very telling, that one. Em...em...purses with old lipsticks glued inside. There was a pair of nylons, never worn, just packed neatly away in a rusted hope chest. This black, em, this brooch of black pearls and emeralds. Most of the emeralds missing. A very badly tarnished silver cup with her name inscribed. Kind of like a teething cup. And, em, an old floral-printed, moth-eaten, mothball-scented frock. Very frilly."

He looked Nona's way to make sure she wasn't wondering with

widened eyes if this batty painter was some creepy fanatic. But she seemed to smile at him, though he couldn't be sure it wasn't just politeness.

"Anyway, I placed everything on tables and chairs all around me and just sat for days, staring at the walls. At one point I held in my hand Laura's hairbrush, all embedded with tangled gray and black hairs. And slowly I lifted it to my nose to smell. I felt insane. I mean, it was only hair, right? What the Hell was I gonna get from hair? A hint of old Bergamot? I was just so frustrated, and trying my damnedest to get acquainted. She was a puzzle, you see, and I couldn't locate all the pieces. She was a wife. That much I knew. A mother. A lover. To me, a stranger. Just a virginal face on a tintype from 1923, or something like that. Hair neatly embracing a round face. Her smile was sort of a half smile, coy. What was I to do with that? I mean, this woman had lived another lifetime than me. I would've been this beauty's grandchild. Anyway, I took her dress in my arms at one point, and an image began to form. A boardwalk. A seaside stroll with a tall man. I bet she liked seashells. And purple urchins. Didn't like the wind mussing her hair, though. Always covered it with a chiffon scarf. Never talked much above a whisper."

Suddenly he laughed obnoxiously.

"Shit! Who was I kidding? She might've been a loud tart, for all I knew. D'you get where I'm going? I was inventing MY Laura. How would I ever get to know what she was really like? I was no closer. I wanted to scream the fucking roof off. So, what the Hell, I popped a few Black Beauties and just started."

Nona chuckled but never once contributed a single insertion to this mad tale. Surely she had wanted to keep this evening light, and here he was trying to take her into the caves. No wonder he'd had few proper dates in his life. And he just bulldozed right on through her laughter, because, of course, a madman obsessed...

"And to my amped and sweating dismay, my first strokes were simply rubbish. Imagine that. Color was wrong, light was wrong, approach and intent completely off the charts. I wanted to slash the fucking canvas to shreds, is what I wanted to do."

He'd begun to perspire. Part champagne. Part life. And he'd stopped looking Nona's way by this point.

"Instead I just sat. Week after week I sat with the sights and smells of

Dead Laura. Reading her letters, memorizing her penmanship, sleeping with her quilt draped over my legs." He suddenly laughed again. "Not a bit neurotic, am I?"

No laugh from Nona this time. Had he effectively done it, then? Was she thinking to herself, this very second, *'I'll just smile politely, for now, and sneak the fuck out when I've got an opening'*?

"You know, it's a silly story," he suddenly blurted. "Boring."

"Wait, what are you doing?" she asked, as if jerked awake from a dream. "You can't just give up mid-story. You don't reel someone in like that and then say, *'it's boring'*."

Was she serious? He didn't know whether to buy it, or to hand her the award for Best Patronization by an Actress in a Condescending Role. Was she really in this?

"Right. Well. Okay. So, I remember pacing my flat for countless unbathed days, and going through several fifths and an easy carton of Viceroys. I listened to Maria Callas day and night during that binge, because her weeping timbre was how I felt."

A moan from Nona's way, he took note. She liked Callas. Good.

"Then one day—one day I realized that I had done it. It was so out of the blue. I mean, there was no earthly rhyme or reason to it. No hint, at all, that it was even coming. It just did. After all the madness. And yes, mad was what I had become. I know, I know, as if I really needed to say that. But the moment was, like, I suddenly realized…that I was wearing her. As one puts on a cloak and lavishes in its feel. I wore her very life on my person. She hung from my limbs, nestled round my waist, perhaps a little snug in the arms, cuz I still wasn't really sure how to proceed, but so what! And every part of her was now in my grasp. I don't mind saying that I was a bit awed and trembling, but I also needed to shake that off, and the only way to do that was to just dive back in. So I did. Only this time, I went at it for twenty-three possessed days. No kidding. Not hours. Days!"

"You remember the actual number of days?"

"There is nothing more indelibly stamped on the brain in unforgivable detail like mania."

"Leviticus Rankin."

Daniel smiled. "The man certainly knew from whence he spoke. In any case, I was on a roll that couldn't be stopped and thanking the fucking

Heavens. Cuz prior to that I'd been just about ready to put a gun to my head."

He suddenly looked her way again and saw the glazing of her exposed eye. Was she despising this moment? Moved by it? Or feeling sorry for the mad lout?

"I'm sorry," he offered. "You really don't need to be burdened with this insanity."

"Please, god, stop already. Or rather DON'T stop...is...what I mean."

He stared at her for some minutes. She wasn't hating him. She wasn't afraid. She was on this train with him. And suddenly he was a schoolboy, as amped and sweating as in his Black Beauty days.

"It was her, Nona. It was Laura! I was strutting like a peacock. And that's just something I don't do. I mean, are you kidding? About my own work? But this was different. I was proud'a this one. I mean, IT was proud. And strong, you know? Like the woman herself. Yet at the same time sad and eloquent, like her love letters. And angry, like the cracked hand mirror that I can just so clearly envision her dashing against a wall in a divine moment of passion. And vulnerable, like the sad eyes I saw in every one of her photographs. And, and, and exquisitely sensual, like the woman I know she was. There was no longer any doubt in my mind. I remember, I kept circling it for fear I'd dreamt it. But it was real. And I breathed in the smell of her, which was beyond the paint, and the turpentine, and the stale bourbon, and the cigarette smoke. I stared at Laura until she bewitched me."

Then he stopped. Gave them both a chance to breathe. Thought about what he'd just said. It would seem that he'd been bewitched again in his life, wouldn't it? Because this woman sitting before him, with a ravaged face, and a brilliant gift, and the willingness to take his madness, and even love it a little, was managing to do something no other woman in his life had ever been able to do. She had compelled him to let down his guard, to open the door to a dungeon no one had ever traversed before, and invite her in, and allow her to gawk at the warted toad.

Only, she didn't gawk. She wept. And laughed. And maybe even loved him.

ELEVEN

Like reading Vincent's letters to Theo, she knew she was being allowed entrée into an artist's most intimate process, and she couldn't let this gem of a moment go. She got the feeling Daniel was purging some demon by unfolding this tale. He kept trying to stop, for her sake obviously, but she knew he needed to pour it out, and she couldn't resist getting inside.

What must this family have thought of his methods? They probably fumed when he started asking for personal things. She could just see them painting Daniel as some pervert who used this most elaborate foil by which to get off. *Isn't a photo enough? A diary! An undergarment! That sort of invasion passes the limits of propriety!* Then she flinched when she realized that passing the limits of propriety is exactly what a rapist does.

In an instant she shook it off. She would be damned to shove Daniel Cross in that category. Not this tender man who told as passionate a story as this one, and whose biggest flaw was probably that he fell in love too easily.

He was far away now. She tried to look into his eyes, tried to bring him back. After a moment, he looked at her squarely but didn't speak, which unnerved her. It seemed to be happening left and right this evening. After a solid minute of this weirdly awkward intimacy, she was the one to eventually break the silence.

"You fell in love with Laura, didn't you?" she declared.

There were several seconds of contemplation, during which he tried for an answer, but would stumble, stop, retreat, try again. Finally he gave a stab.

"I fall in love with them all."

She smiled at being so dead on. And she smiled at what it also meant. But Daniel sighed a deep one and laughed at himself.

"That is probably the most pathetic truth of my life."

"Is it?" she asked, hoping against everything that he didn't mean it.

That he didn't find falling in love pathetic.

He stared at the floor sullenly before lifting his head again. When he finally did, he had nothing else to offer except a hardened pair of eyes. She continued as cavalierly as possible.

"Well, after all that, Laura's family must've been in awe of the final result, yes?"

He smiled a sarcastic smile.

"Oh yes, they were in awe................of what a charlatan I was."

"What!" she sang. "You're kidding me!"

"No, indeed, I am not. I didn't get it at first, you know? But now I know all about agendas. See, they wanted something they could put on their mantle like a holy shrine, to decorate with flowers. They weren't especially interested in something they might actually have to ponder, get inside of! They wanted something they could readily identify. Like a police sketch! *'It doesn't even look like her,'* they said. *'It is the very essence of her!'* I said back. They asked me how I would know that. *'How would I know that? Are you people fucking daft? Human nature is my job!'*"

Nona noticed that there was absolutely no place, on this occasion, for his usual brand of self-condemnation. He knew he was an artist. He knew he wielded power with his brush. He'd just given himself away.

He laughed, but she couldn't laugh with him. He was sad. He was angry. Then suddenly he was delirious with champagne and laughter. Then angry again. It was a wild ride.

"The truth is, they'd've fared better taking her photo to the Venice boardwalk for a three-minute chalk portrait, and I told them as much. They called me a narcissistic dilettante, which, Hell, I probably am. And I called them visionless cretins, which they most certainly were. And they promptly stormed off with all of Laura's trinkets and whatnots. And without remuneration."

"I'm so sorry," was all she could offer, and which seemed so insufficient.

"Ecchhh, par for the course, yeah?" he answered, tossing it off as nothing.

"But you got the painting."

"No. Well, I mean yes, but I don't have it any longer. What you see here are all just the preliminary studies."

"Whatever happened to the finished portrait?"

"I burned it."

"What!?" she sang again.

"Don't, don't *what* me. Everything that I'd found most powerful and arresting about Laura had been trivialized by a loathsome pack of imbeciles, and I couldn't have that reminder looming in my head forever."

"Well, okay, I get that. I guess. But—then why aren't you haunted by these?"

"Because, they're not her. They're only ridiculous, ignorance-fueled attempts. Rungs in the ladder to the actual result."

"Ridiculous? Are you kidding me? Daniel, you are—look at these. I'm sorry, but you're wrong! I mean, I don't know the woman, but do I have to? In order to see that there is a powerful humanity in these studies? All of these are somebody. Okay, so maybe they're not the Laura that you had conjured in your head. Fine. Give them another name, if that'll make it make sense for you. Just stop refusing to see how wonderful these are. There is an entire collection of Monet's, all studies of the same cathedral, exploring the subject under varying light and color conditions. I know you know them. He put them all out there in the world. And they were only preliminary studies. Why can't these be that?"

He was annoyed by her proclamations and didn't respond.

"Are these next in line for the furnace?" she continued to challenge.

"Stay with me tonight," he commanded softly, his face suddenly upon her. This was the second time he had gone *there* when the world seemed to close in on him. She felt the rhythm of his warm breath on her eyelids, and sighed. She didn't have an answer.

"What's the problem?" he asked pointedly.

"Daniel. This?"

She indicated her face, the eye patch, the wounds and stitches, all with the circling of a disgusted finger. Disgusted with rape and men who rape. Disgusted with a face only Frankenstein's monster could love. And even a little disgusted with being pushed to spill what she was clearly not ready to share.

"This was rape. That's what happened to me."

Thiswasrapethiswasrapethiswasrapethiswasrapethiswasrapethiswasrapethiswasrape.

She wondered if to say it over and over would be to lessen its power.

TWELVE

"That's what happened to me," she declared, or he thought that's what she declared. He couldn't really be sure for having been completely cold-cocked.

Had he heard her right? Was she just now unleashing but the second rape-nightmare that had been confided to him in his life? One more for his brain to store away, and obsess over, and become plagued and tormented by? AGAIN? Was he now being told that he was the only one in the world wise to some twisted schematic?

"There's just a lot I'm going through right now," she continued. "I am barely sane these days. And taking this on with you…this, this, this wonderful, exciting possibility…I mean, I thought I could just tuck rape away, pretend it didn't happen, and enjoy your company, and I am enjoying it. I am just not ready to spend the night with you. I am not ready yet for that. And I know I run the risk of never hearing from you again…but…"

His heart pounded. Was she still talking? His ears had been boxed and were verily ringing. To have his worst theories confirmed, after having seen her that first day bandaged like some B-flick mummy, and wondering at all the wretched possibilities, was just too much.

Men always have a tough time with this one. They feel responsible and impotent for not being able to have been there at the needed moment of rescue, and gullible enough to believe that somehow their very presence in women's lives should be enough to ward away all evils. And when it's not enough, they feel less than men.

Daniel must've been glowering, because suddenly she looked anxiously his way and took his hands in hers. But he could only delicately slip his out of her clutches, for in this instant he feared his own temper and didn't want her to get caught in the crossfire.

Before he even knew his next thought, he'd hastily stormed to the far side of the flat and, without a fair warning, shoved his fist against a wall, which shook a nearby utility shelf and spilled some of its contents onto the floor. Then, just as quickly, he walked back toward her and wrapped his arms about her frame, holding her there for several minutes.

This horror had happened to her, not him, he thought with disgust, yet he was the one fuming about the room like some spoiled brat who hadn't gotten his way. He hated his own gender in this instant, as he pulled back and stared into her eyes. *How did this happen? When? Where? Who? Was it a stranger? Someone you knew?* All the questions he couldn't utter out loud screamed in his head and threatened a migraine.

She could see he had endless inquiries, but she simply shut her eyes and shook her head. Not now. She hadn't wanted to spill even the bit she did, but he'd pushed her.

Silence bled through the walls of the gauzy room like blood from some horribly wrapped head wound, as he held her tightly again. He was not a man who wept, but he wanted to cry so that she could see. He wanted to show her that all men weren't rapists and blackhearts. That some could be tender. Or maybe she would just think him soft. Women don't like soft in men. They always think they do, but no. So he re-strategized, bucked up, and calmly asked her if she'd like to take a walk.

"Sure," she whispered.

They descended his dilapidated lift, and stepped out into an eager Los Angeles night. After forty-five solid minutes of a talkless stroll down by the tracks, past the breweries, and through the sleeping garment district, she finally spoke.

"I've always loved downtown. It seems to be hated by...or feared, I guess...by the rest of L.A., but not me. It's unpretentious and unapologetic. I mean, look at this skyline. The City Hall standing out from all the clusters of high rise windows that are towering over it, but eerily lit as if it's some grand diva about to go on stage."

That made him smile. She was so easily swept.

"And the best of it," she continued, "is that it's filled with artists who know how to recognize the real deal when they see it. I mean, sometimes I hate living where I do, because, come on, look where I live. There's no hunger in my little beachfront town. I often fear that I'm disconnected from what matters."

"But it's your family's home," he offered, though he'd once entertained that same thought.

"I know. And it's what keeps me there. But this place. This is where I'd've chosen to live if I'd had no family home. I mean, it's got everything, the Music Center, Union Station, the Temporary Contemporary, Olvera Street—"

"The homeless."

"The homeless," she repeated somberly. "I think that's one of the main reasons I refuse to hate it. Because that's pretty much the same as saying I hate them."

"You're very compassionate."

"Yeah, what good does it do? It's not like I can save anybody."

"Maybe not. But it means that there's just one more person in the world the homeless don't have to worry about coming along and spitting on them. And that's a lot."

"It's really a sad state of things when that's a lot, isn't it?"

He watched her marvel at this black night, with its strange shadows made by all the monstrous, hovering rolls of textiles leaning against the insides of storefront panes, while the smattering of homeless men and women leaned against the outsides, huddling in their cubbyholes, making their homes for the night. Only the overlapped murmur of their mumbled, chant-like conversations pierced the silence and consoled like a meditation. There was something both melancholic and electrifying about this hub, and he found it thrilling that she recognized it, too, if perhaps giving artists a little too much credit.

"I don't know if I romanticize it quite the way you do," he responded, "so much as it's just about the only place I can afford to set up shop. I mean, I'd love to have a fancy space on Traction Avenue. Like that space where we saw Kai's show. But the real estate's ridiculous there. If I want the square footage I need, then Skid Row'll have to do."

"But that's exactly what I mean," she offered. "Traction Avenue's fine and all, but it's, like, you know, 'the hip place to be' these days. You aren't cutting a perfectly symmetrical hole in the knee of your jeans to affect some trendy grunge look. You got the hole there, torn and ragged, because you're on your hands and knees stretching canvases, and hauling buckets of paint, truly laboring over something that matters. What's alive about this part of downtown is that it doesn't sport fashionable affectation."

He quickly looked down at his trousers to inspect for any holes and feigned a panic. "So sorry. Meant to patch that rip ages ago."

She laughed outright on a dark downtown street, which pleased him. If he could play any part in lifting her burdens at all, he was gratified.

"Sorry. I know I can be Miss Metaphor."

"Are you kidding? It's charming."

He could see that she was still afflicted but was trying her damnedest to lift herself out of the bog and not draw attention. And while she went on and on about downtown, he could think of nothing else but this rape thing. He had a thousand questions. Still, he gave her what she wanted, which was an evening free of it. He held her hand and breathed in the night as rapaciously as she did. Small streams of smoke billowed out from the nearby factory stacks, and now only a distant freight whistle marred the tranquil silence. A floating thickness of clothing approached, asking for money, and Nona gave it freely. He too. For her.

They returned to his flat, and she stayed the night after all. They drank more champagne. And when they finished that, they drank bourbon. They talked. Or didn't. She told him only what she wanted about the attack, that it was mainly a black spot on her memory. And then they were off of it, because she didn't want to swim in it all night. They listened to music. Or they listened to the silence, which had already proven its friendship. They did not make love. She'd been clear about that. It was okay with him. And neither slept until long after the burnt-umber sunrise.

She called it magenta.

THIRTEEN

He awoke in a daze, hungover and cramped about the legs and spine, still wearing the same clothes from the night before, which seemed in his fuzziness to have been only minutes ago. His shirt was wrinkled and twisted about him. He looked around hazily, trying to put pieces together, and found himself alone. Searching around for the clichéd note on the pillow, he suddenly heard stirrings coming from his bathroom and was glad she was still here.

He stumbled out of bed and searched for a cigarette, licking his tongue across his upper teeth, which were appropriately furry after an alcohol-sodden sleep. The crud in his eyes only matched the tangled mess of his hair to rival the staleness in his mouth. But at least the finally located Viceroy tasted great.

He shambled over to the kitchen area to start a pot of coffee and spotted his Nikon on one of his worktables. It always had film in it; he was one of those blokes who took pictures of everything from the spectacular to the mundane.

As he sat waiting for the coffee to brew, he fumbled around with it and pondered the noises coming from the bathroom. They were female noises, the strains of delicate clangs on porcelain and against mirrors, and the rippling of the faucet, like tiny waterfalls. The sound of men in bathrooms always included lots of hacking, snorting, scratching, and farting.

The door was cracked ajar and he couldn't keep himself from creeping over to peek inside. What he saw piqued no voyeuristic arousal, however, but the ring of empathy. He watched her stare at herself in his mirror and loathe her face. The swollen discoloration of her cheek was unusually puffy, though most of her scabs were gone by now. Her injured eye was uncovered and was a frightening mutation of some twisted sculpture. The eyelid was sealed shut and bulged out tumorously, as she scrounged around for her patch.

It broke his heart. He could see what she apparently couldn't; that her own radiant face, the one hiding behind the mask of violence, was still there. And he knew she was looking for it desperately. He wanted to say, *it's right there, honey, just look deeper.* But he was already violating her privacy; she really shouldn't know that he was spying. For a moment longer he stared, recalling the night's events with a mixture of sadness and tenderness, then quietly tiptoed away.

Standing over the percolating pot, he fumbled with his camera more and thought how compelling it would be to seize such a moment. Before he knew it, she was shuffling along his cement floor, her own clothes wrinkled about her. As she approached, her face largely facing the floor, she looked up just as he snapped a shot. The flash of light shocked her. But what came next shocked him.

"What the Hell?!!!"

He stared, stunned.

"I'm sorry, Nona," he inserted as quickly as he could, unprepared for an explosion. "I thought you saw it in my hands. I just wanted to capture a—"

"Is this some kinda kinky shit you're into?"

"Christ! Nona, of course not!"

"What're you gonna do with that?"

"Nothing! I just, I don't—nothing! Jesus Christ, Nona, this is a bit hysterical, don't you think?—"

"Are you kidding me with this? I'm not some kind of hysteric!" she bit, hysterically.

"No, I know you're not. I'm sorry, I—"

"What the Hell were you thinking?"

"I wasn't. Obviously—"

"You wanna know what I wrestle with everyday? As if I should have to spell this out for you—"

"Nona—"

This was half-cocked.

"Do you understand that I am absolutely panicked because I can't find ME anymore? I don't know who did this to me, which means all I have to hate and to rail against is some abstract! And you want to capture that?"

"I won't even develop it, I'll throw it away. I swear, I never meant to cross a line, or, or—I just, I just, I use my camera to grab at spontaneous slices of life. Compelling ones, Nona! You're not a freak to me. But it was stupid of me. I'm sorry. I just thought, for sure, that you'd be all right with that. You and I have shared those kinds of wondrous moments before. But, no matter, it wasn't my place to presume. Please, forgive me."

She stared at the floor, arms crossed over her chest, clearly humiliated. As sorry as he felt, he couldn't help entertaining the exasperated thought that this over-reaction was so typical of women.

Finally she looked at him.

"You know your Laura over there?" she began, pointing at the canvas studies.

She wasn't about to give this up.

"Maybe I understand her family after all. Because when it comes to my own life, my PRIVATE life, I guess I don't want reality conveyed and my soul upturned either. I want something that uplifts me. Not exposes me. And, ultimately, that's what your talent is, isn't it?"

"I'm sorry. Please forgive me," he pled. But he'd also just been stung. If she'd been some bloke, and not the woman he hoped to someday bed, he'd have offered her a hearty *fuck you!*

He knew that she was more than just someone he wanted to shag, but he couldn't resist a moment to pout, even if it was to himself. In truth, he was afraid he'd blown something for good. She had just begun to trust him, had confided in him her nightmare, and this was how he'd chosen to repay her. He deserved her sting, if not necessarily her whole wounded play.

"Please, just let me offer this, Nona. Your scars don't define you. They only give you more power because they haven't taken you down, as they might've. You've told me this horror, and yet you still own yourself. It's only THAT…that I was trying to capture. You inspire me. In so many ways."

She stared at him in a manner that almost looked like forgiveness.

Then suddenly: "I have to go."

She scurried to gather her coat and purse, quickly putting on her shoes, spilling words in a careless haste.

"I'm leaving the country. I don't know when I'll be back."

"What do you mean you're leaving the country? I snap your photo and you respond by saying you're leaving the country? Look, I was wrong to do it, okay? But don't you think this is a little overly reactive?"

Don't dare call her an hysteric again, idiot.

"Oh, please. This was already planned. I just hadn't told you yet."

Her tone was cold.

"Is it work? A book tour or something?" he asked, confused.

"No. It's personal." She headed for the lift and started pounding the button near it. "I can't figure this…! How do you get this fucking thing to open?"

"Nona, talk to me," he demanded, clutching her arm. "This is crazy."

She stopped and turned. In spite of her scars, in spite of her meltdown, he found her quite beautiful this morning. Was it morning? Even in his panic, he was still fuzzy.

"Look, I'm not leaving because of you, Daniel. I swear this was already planned. Please believe me."

"All right," he answered, cautiously, waiting for the angle. "It's just—I mean, the timing."

"I'm sorry. I know what it looks like."

"Is it what it looks like?" he challenged.

"It's just something I'm doing." It was almost: *what the fuck is it to you?*

Her tone then changed, softened, and none too soon or Daniel was about to wonder who this tart was, and what she'd done with Nona.

"Look, when I realized that I wasn't stepping out of this hole, which is everything, the rape, this infuriating black spot in my memory about it, frankly even writer's block, which is a whole other typical and tiresome subject, I knew I just needed to get away for a bit."

"I understand." He didn't. He could be spoiled, and he could pout. But he tried not to.

"Ridiculously," she laughed, embarrassed, "I even thought that meeting some wonderful man might just take all of that away, and make everything instantly all right. But you can't be my magic pill, Daniel. As much as I thought you might."

"What about talking to someone?"

"I already have a therapist," she tossed off quickly, steering him away from something too personal. "And please, Daniel, it is not your job to fix my life."

He wanted to hold her, but she wouldn't be held.

"If I can just get somewhere where the shadows of my everyday existence aren't being reflected on the walls, then maybe I can stand a chance to clear the slate, get some perspective, something, so that what just happened right now doesn't happen again."

"I am so sorry."

"No, no, it isn't you. You see? That's what I mean. You didn't actually do anything wrong. I just—it's me. Something is already in me that would make it so easy for me to just bite like that. I just need to go away and, and, and rejuvenate. And come back not so raw and open-wounded. I need to have an adventure. That's all. Or not. Maybe just…quiet. I just, I just, I just need to go away."

"All right. It's all right," he tried to calm, but it was he who didn't know if it would be all right.

"But I'll be back. It's just for awhile," she assured.

He also didn't know whether to believe her. She waited patiently for him to work whatever lever would open the elevator lift, and he did, begrudgingly. She entered the lift and tried to smile at him, but it was limp.

Goddamn it, I can't have fucked this up because of a cloddish impulse.

"Can you at least tell me where you're going?" he asked. He still got the creeping feeling this was all extemporaneous; that she had no real plans and now had to come up with quick answers to appease him.

"To, to, to visit my sister," she stuttered. It sounded like a lie. "I'll call. Or write. I promise."

And then he watched her, behind the gated door of the lift, descend out of his sight.

FOURTEEN

He'd been looking forward to introducing Nona to Arthur. These two extraordinary artists, he'd thought, two fairly compelling forces in his life. But Arthur hadn't been able to make the Hareton Show. All he had said to Daniel was *"domestic problems,"* which, for Arthur, could've meant about a hundred ominous things.

Now that Daniel knew what he had just learned about Nona, how on earth would that ever work? And why was it so important anyway?

He knew the answer, of course. Arthur was family. More family than anyone with whom he'd ever actually shared a bloodline.

Daniel first met Arthur when Arthur was living on Western and Fifth, above an Equity-waiver theatre. It was 1981, the year after Arthur had been released from prison, and only a handful of years after Daniel had arrived in L.A. This hole-in-the-wall theatre was like something out of a Bukowski fable. And like Bukowski, Arthur wrote endless scribbles he called poetry, which was some of the most affecting work Daniel had ever read.

Daniel had been dating a lunatic actress at the time, who was doing a play at the hole-in-the-wall. There was never any audience, except for him, some random family members of the cast — and Arthur. Daniel was the boyfriend; he had to be at every performance. But he remembered it striking him as curious that this fair-skinned, scraggly Black man who seemed to be channeling Bob Marley with his thickly gnarled dreadlocks and shaman nature, and who didn't know a single soul in the cast, was also at every performance. Everyone whispered about the mysterious man who hung around. They all thought he was indigent and just looking for a place to stay warm.

One evening during intermission, Daniel decided to strike up a conversation with him. In one fell swoop Daniel found out that Arthur often sold blood and sperm, wrote poetry, and called himself Arturo when the inspiration hit him. Arthur used poetry the same way Daniel used painting. To pick up women. He also suffered by it and lived by it, as did Daniel, because though the pick-up ruse was real enough, something deeper had lured them to poetry and painting, respectively, in the first place. It was simply what they were. And it was what instantly connected them.

They did **est** together. They dumped **est** together. They would go see Marty & Elayne at the Dresden Room, or the Orchestre Surreal at the Purple Sleep Café, or Courtney at Jumbo's Clown Room, and debate all the suicidal poets — Plath, Sexton, Woolf — and play dominoes and poker, and drive down to T.J. to pay for women at Adelita's, and eat magic mushrooms and Black Beauties and Yellow Jackets at Burning Man, and booze it up, and smoke dirt weed, but Arthur did heroin alone. Daniel could never go there.

Before the Western and Fifth address, Arthur had slept on a cot at Transition House, downtown, where he'd been dumped as part of a release program after the time he'd served. He was such a paradox: a near-homeless drunk one minute, and holding down a job and running for local public office the next. He espoused the virtues of anarchy and atheism, or he thrust his Bible in your face, depending on the day of the week. He seemed to be always searching for Truth.

Ultimately, Daniel believed, Arthur found it in poetry, though he would probably tell you that he was still searching, or no longer cared. Poetry was Arthur's peculiar toy. One would never think it to look at him. Daniel had always associated poetry with some foppish, weepy manchild. And of course every woman wrote poetry. But men who hung out on Central Avenue, who drank out of a paper bag and adjusted their testicles at any given public moment, men who had drowned in the bleak waters of Hell, all these being Arthur, did not usually tend to write poetry.

Arthur had a Gil Scott-Heron voice, four-percent body fat, and had been growing the same dirt-colored dreadlocks his entire adult life. He was somewhere in his fifties, but like most Black men he seemed to defy aging. And though he had the mind of a man with an Oxford education, Arthur would never be caught dead in anything as institutionalized as university. The man was self-taught and book-saturated, and was one of the smartest men Daniel had ever known.

The thing was, Arthur could've gotten away with his crime so easily. Ophelia would've simply been counted among the many winos that stumbled to their muddy deaths daily and were fished out of the lake months later by the city. No one would've thought twice about autopsying this indigent woman to discover she'd been strangled and raped. But Arthur didn't choose that course. For days after that horrific MacArthur Park night, he roamed the streets in a stoned stupor, until he finally went to the police and told them everything.

After lengthy judicial red tape and a juryless trial, he was convicted of second-degree murder and remanded to Centinela State, where he served eight out of a twenty-year sentence. While inside, he suffered a massive coronary, surely due to his heroin withdrawals. And with only a thread of life left, locked up in a dingy prison hospital ward, he began to write. He'd done the odd bit of verse scribbling in his youth, but it had now taken on the more crucial role of lifesaver.

"Writin's what pulled me outta the swamp, man," he'd often said to Daniel. "I'd lost my soul. And that scared the shit outta me. Cuz a man with no soul should not be allowed to walk among human beings. I mean, yeah, I was fucked up on dope and shit, but it takes more'n dope to make you just wanna destroy life."

It was true. There was something eternally unsoothed about Arthur.

And every time that nightmare popped into Daniel's head — an agitating activity with a nervous system all its own — the chill of the unfathomable would race through him, and he always had to sit down to recover.

He sat now. Alone, in his flat. Burdened by a deadly nightshade. Abandoned by the only woman who had meant anything to him in years. Possibly for good, for all he knew. And, as often happened in the silence and the shade, plagued by Arthur and Ophelia yet again.

FIFTEEN

For twenty-four solid hours, Nona traveled by plane to escape the world she knew. She had only conjured the trip on the spot for shock value, an immature child's move. But once committed to the lie, she realized how awesome it was, how half-cocked she would look, how half-cocked she probably was, to have come up with something so brazen. And when she took a moment to consider it, she also realized it was probably her best idea yet. A trip away, for healing and perspective. A spiritual retreat. An about-time journey to a foreign land. Why it took game-playing with a man for her to divine this plan irritated her to no end.

Of course, only the rich could whim an adventure of this magnitude, and bestsellerdom had certainly made her that. An expedited passport later, her first, and she was on a plane to the other side of the planet.

She and Daniel had parted so unceremoniously that she couldn't get him out of her mind. Had she leapt irrationally at his taking her picture, which even she copped to at his loft? Or had she been wise to trust no one's actions, considering her baggage?

She flew across two continents with no answers to the nagging questions, and eventually grew tired, and determined that she really did need to put Daniel on the back burner for now and make this a true retreat. It wasn't as if she didn't desperately need the very thing she'd described to him during her moment of theatre.

She didn't see Thembi until she reached Tanzania. American Airlines had flown her from Los Angeles to New York, then to Zurich, and into Nairobi, where she stayed the night at the Nairobi Hilton. She didn't watch their cable television, or take advantage of their in-house spa, or even eat much of the room service she'd ordered. It was some dish of spongy bread and fried grasshoppers that scared her just a bit. Though, in truth, she couldn't have even managed a good old, comfortable, familiar American burger if it'd been placed in front of her.

She stared out of the window, looking down from her 20th floor room, in quiet awe of this other world, of her great smallness against it, her newness within it, and her puzzlement over how she ever drew the winning lottery ticket with her novel, when so many other writers, far more worthy, far more worldly, continued to struggle greatly. She fell asleep to that self-demeaning thought and a groaning stomach, and flew the following day, via East African Airlines, into the capital city of Dar es Salaam.

Thembi met Nona at the airport dressed in kanga cloth. They hugged ravenously, and Nona stared at details she'd never noticed in her sister before: The tattooed bindi nestled regally between Thembi's stunning eyebrows that symbolized a third eye Nona wished she could claim. The thick silver ring through the side of Thembi's strong nose. And only the wispy hint of her prior lustrous hair, cropped even closer to her head than Nona's short bob. Thembi even had some gray here and there, though she was only twenty-five. It made her look wise and centered. It had to be the place.

Thembi stared at Nona, too, but hers carried more pity than awe. And it wasn't because of Nona's eye-patched and bruised face.

"We need to seriously shed you of this belted, buttoned, western prison you've bound yourself in, and get you something that'll flow in the wind and caress you instead. What do you say?"

"It's good to see you, too, Peanut."

They had so much to catch up on, and Nona marveled at how wedged into this ancient place her baby sister seemed. She had the feeling Thembi could live here forever.

Though Thembi was indeed the younger sister, she seemed in every way the older. The itchy one, who, while in college, had run off to Russia to sing in a choral group as part of a student exchange program, Thembi was always working part-time jobs in high school, neglecting to devote the proper time to her studies, and saved enough money to hike through the Amazon one summer. Education plenty. This was a girl who had to roam.

Nona had been the homebody. The one who flinched at everything. Who always did what was right and responsible and safe. When offered the opportunity to travel with their mother to Europe one summer as a teen, the alternative being a summer job to help with her college tuition, Nona chose the job.

It hadn't always been that way. When they were children, Nona drew little Thembi into her bosom as though the girl were her own child, and kept her there like a note pinned to a blouse for school. She'd grip Thembi's tiny hand as they'd giddily ride the giant roller coaster at the Long Beach Pike, or the bobsleds in the snow at Santa's Village up in Arrowhead, or the pedal boats on the lake at MacArthur Park, or Mister Toad's Wild Ride. There was no excellent childhood excursion on which Nona embarked without her little peanut by her side, and today the little peanut would be the one to show Nona a thing or two about the world outside their little world.

Thembi had flown in from Lagos to meet Nona in Dar es Salaam, and they stayed with an older couple in their beachfront bungalow in Ocean Road. Friends of Thembi's who had taken her in when she'd first come to Africa, they themselves were Americans, who had forsaken the States twenty years prior. Right around the same time Daniel was escaping England, if Nona recalled the timeline of his story correctly. Everyone seemed to be escaping one world for another, for one reason or another. Except her. Until she realized that this very moment indeed counted.

Mr. and Mrs. Wenda, whose first names Nona would never find out, were ancient and grand. Mr. Wenda walked with a cane and constantly sang songs around the house. Mrs. Wenda, some years younger, was clearly the boss of the family, charmingly reprimanding Mr. Wenda whenever she'd catch him smoking a cigarette. They called each other Husband and Wife, never using their first names with each other.

They had mastered Swahili but never spoke it in the house. Mrs. Wenda held a certain disdain for Africans who held a certain disdain for her, being an American expatriate. She only spoke the language in town, and only if absolutely necessary.

"Kiswahili is a bastard language, anyway," she complained. "So how can they hate me for being an American? During Colonialism, when everyone was raping the land and selling off Africans to the slave traders, their pure Bantu language was ultimately diluted to include bits of German, Arabic, Portuguese, even English. This is the Swahili that is spoken today. Bantu I would love to learn, but it is largely a lost language now. I walk in the marketplace, and once in awhile someone will pass me and click his teeth, muttering under his breath, *mtumwa*, which means slave. That is what many of the indigenous people here call Black Americans. They laugh that we have embraced our European slave names. But I always bite back, 'get rid of the European in your own language and then talk to me!'"

Mrs. Wenda was full of feisty pepper and would laugh so hard at times that she would unhinge her false teeth.

"Please pardon my ignorance," Nona interjected, enchanted and fascinated, "but the name Wenda doesn't sound European to me. It actually sounds quite African."

"I simply refer to the general prejudice that exists toward Black Americans. You are not ignorant at all. Husband's family is from here originally. These very parts, in fact. He is African by birth. But there was so much civil unrest that his family migrated to the States just prior to Husband being born. That would have been around—1916, would that have been, Husband?"

"Something like, Wife."

Mr. Wenda was a soft-spoken man who said little. His family was of the ancient Kehe tribe, though it was explained that there were almost no pure Kehe left today.

"It is ironic," Mrs. Wenda continued, "that I am constantly pelted with these insults. My own husband is as black as ink and one of them for certain, and I forsook my European maiden name, Van Brunt, to take his African one. But, alas, I am easily spotted, being so fair-skinned."

Mrs. Wenda spoke slowly and deliberately, pronouncing every word as though it were a gem. Even when she got excited, her language was controlled. She and Mr. Wenda both spoke with a precision and care usually only found in people who have mastered English as a second language, though this was the original for both. They took pains not to speak as lazily as most Americans tended to do, and the result was that they actually sounded as though they had accents. Perhaps it was out of their cultural duality that they found attention to detail in language important.

"Please understand," Mrs. Wenda continued, "all Africans are not like this. Most are extremely affable and would take you into their homes at a moment's notice."

"Present company being the best of that example," Thembi piped in.

"Believe me, it is our pleasure. And most whom I know would do the same. It is simply the other examples that really get my dander up."

"Whatever you do, don't get her dander up," Mr. Wenda muttered.

Both Wendas had been professors in New York. Mr. Wenda retired his professorship in literature from Columbia in the fall of '72. And once Mrs. Wenda retired her own in political science from Sarah Lawrence a few years later, they returned to Mr. Wenda's homeland.

On this first night for Nona in their gracious home, Mrs. Wenda prepared a supper called *ugali*. A fragrant dish of white corn meal patted into a large cake and served on a huge aluminum platter in the center of the table, this ugali was garnished with beans and *mchecha*, and was accompanied by a meat and peanut stew. They sat on straw mats around the low table, and proceeded to dip their fingers in individual bowls of lemon water and scoop a palm full of the ugali into their cupped hands. With their thumbs they carved out a kind of tiny bowl from the meal, then dipped it into the pot of stew and feasted. Nona was reminded of the night Daniel had introduced her to Persian cuisine. This was easily as heavenly, yet she couldn't escape the gnawing reality that there was so much of the world that remained foreign to her, the writer. She felt the fraud.

During dinner, Nona and Mr. Wenda deconstructed every literary protagonist from Joseph K. to George F. Babbitt. Nona was ecstatic to have discovered in Mr. Wenda a companion of letters, and in both a fascinating chapter for her otherwise pedestrian existence.

SIXTEEN

The day that Arthur had told Daniel about Ophelia, Daniel remembered shuddering that he could know such a man and call him friend. Rapists and murderers were the stuff of pulp movies. They were hardly ever your neighbor, and they certainly weren't your dearest comrade.

Presently he sat at the Orchid Club on this night of no music, and overdosed on party mix and pretzels, while nursing warm beers and old nightmares.

Arthur's was a tale that had stunned on first telling, yet ultimately Daniel could give two shits what popular opinion might've held; the man he had come to know today was incapable of rape or murder. The man he knew had been extraordinarily lifted from that mire and delivered to redemption through poetry.

There were women who would shriek in disgust at this admission of Daniel's empathy. Surely Nona would be among them, having been on the other wretched end. But he simply knew a different Arthur. When given a second chance at life, Arthur had met a woman, fallen in love with her, and sired a child. Because of that bleak inferno from which he had come, and the life he had taken, Arthur had vowed to pay his penance by replacing the human soul that had been destroyed with one who would be nurtured.

Today Arthur's son, an extraordinary boy of ten years old, was the constant source of his conversation. Fatherhood was, in fact, the only constant in Arthur's life. That and poetry.

From the very beginning Arthur had vowed to teach his son to revere and regard womanhood, to esteem humanity, to recognize the beauties of the universe, to feed upon that, and to give it back to the world.

Daniel had never heard a human being speak like that in his life. There was an interminable sadness in Arthur, yet a remarkable love affair with life. People saw it in his eyes when they met him. When they shook his hands, there was an energy shooting from those hands that knocked people off their foundation. How could he be anything but the most astonishing poet?

He still did heroin of course.

Anyone else having gone to Hell and back would've been so scared awake by the trip that they'd have never touched another needle. Not Arthur. You couldn't reason with him about the futility of such things.

"I leave myself just clear-headed enough to write, make sure my son is raised right, and pay my rent. As it is, I'm plagued every day of my life by the demon that I was. And by Ophelia. If I let myself stay too straight—I gotta tell ya, Danny boy, I can't take seein' Ophelia's face lucid in my mind. She's gotta always remain a haze for me, or I'll be the one swallowin' shoe dye. And unlike you, my bungling friend, I will not fail at suicide."

"What about your son?" Daniel would ask, as he replayed endless conversations.

"What ABOUT my son?" Arthur threw at him defensively the first time Daniel ever challenged him on it. "My son'll never know the ME that existed before him. You understand that? That man is dead. And only mercifully kept at bay by a little numbin' out. Fuck, man, fuckin' Burroughs knew what he was talkin' about when he said a man could live forever on smack. I stop, I'm gonna fuckin' die, man. I mean, I'm sure I deserve to. I'm not gonna argue anybody that. But what I'm tryin' to do is be a father to my son. And I can't do that if I bite it from a fuckin' aneurysm or a fuckin' seizure, or, you know, like—fuck, remember my heart attack? What do you think brought that on?"

"I know, Art, but—"

"Naw, naw, naw, man, you know what? I wanna live. Okay? And I'm doin' it. May not be anybody's idea of body-as-temple, holistic, feng shui, vegetarian, high colonic, yadda yadda, and suck-my-dick-with-that-shit method, but I'm here. For my son. In the flesh. Fuck the rest. The trick is to never start, but I can't cry over that now, can I? Whatever took me to smack in the first place is what's fucked up. My son ain't never goin' to that place. I will personally see to that. I plan to give him this beautiful world on a motha-fuckin' platter, man. The wonders of this world are what'll keep Lorca from that pit."

That Arthur could still speak of a beautiful world after the life he'd led was a testament to something deeper and stronger than Daniel could ever hope to capture on a canvas.

And that was just it. He had always wanted to paint Arthur, but had frankly been afraid of the head he might open up. Today he felt compelled. Maybe it was because he had once again relived Arthur's tale in his mischievous imaginings, and with each reliving was given a slightly tougher hide. Or maybe it was because he now had a new horrid tale to ponder. And was still standing. How many more times in his life was this wretched theme planning to repeat itself?

He knew he had to paint a series that included both Nona and Arthur. This strange axis couldn't have been placed in his lap without a greater schematic in mind, intended for him to explore. And it couldn't possibly result in anything less than explosive. Crazy ideas began bouncing around his active head of a piece that would fuse the visual with the word and explore the polarity of darkness and light.

Of course, Daniel was anguished at the notion of even introducing the two of them, much less inviting them to collaborate.

"Boilermaker this time, mate," he ordered from bartender Otto.

"Sure thing, my friend."

Were Nona to ever learn of Arthur's past, Daniel was convinced, she would never be able to ratify the legitimacy of this human being, who was like a brother to him.

As he downed his shot and chased it with several gulps of his ale, he came fairly close to drowning out notions of just how sinister it would be to ally that brother with the new woman in his life. Knowing what he knew about each.

SEVENTEEN ·

She lay beneath the white mosquito net that draped her bed in the room she had all to herself, and wiped the sweat from her neck. Her head was heavy with its burdens. She was grateful that the Wendas had several rooms in their palatial bungalow, so that each girl could have her solitude while in these kind strangers' home, for she could already predict the need for periodic escapes. She stared at the world around her, an unfamiliar world filtered by the white muslin gauze, but still clear enough to tell her that she was alive and had a chance for renewal.

The ritual she came to establish in the following weeks in Ocean Road was that she would rise every morning to the smell of roasted coffee, from beans picked in the Southern Highlands. Before heading downstairs to join the others, she would meditate with some of the yoga asanas Kai had taught her. She'd then stroll the white sands of the Indian shores with Mr. Wenda, who needed to walk every day so that his old legs wouldn't atrophy. They discussed the works of Soyinka and Armah and Tutuola, and the aged lore compiled by African scholars. There was a world of literature that had never been taught in Nona's schooling. She was getting plenty schooled right here. Sometimes Thembi and Mrs. Wenda would accompany them, but they mainly grew tired of Nona's and Mr. Wenda's constant literary gab.

She and Thembi went into town almost every afternoon, and, being fair-skinned Black girls, they once or twice caught the insult from some passerby that Mrs. Wenda had described. When it happened Nona was actually tickled. She couldn't believe it was happening to her. She wanted to encounter everything.

They roamed bookstores, collecting the works of some of Africa's most prominent writers. They shopped for Makondé carvings and mud cloth, bargaining with sellers on the street. Downtown Dar was not unlike the dizzying streets of Times Square, and held in it the bewitching magic of its nightlife and music scene.

Every afternoon when they arrived back home to Ocean Road, Nona brimmed over with the awed chatter of her discoveries in this unfamiliar place. She sensed that Mr. and Mrs. Wenda found her innocent wonder precious, but she didn't mind one bit being the yearling here.

She tried to start work on her newest manuscript, and wrote incessantly, though her loyalties were irritatingly split between book-writing and journal-scribbling. There was so much about this place that she had to put on paper, and she couldn't seem to maintain a singular focus. Too much resplendency. Not enough harness.

On any given day she could find some new fascination that either enchanted or saddened her. The rhythm and pace of the city hypnotized, sliding and gliding by her, like a mournful horn blowing an intense dirge. She watched Moslem women, draped in their black bui-buis, roaming the marketplaces like ghosts. Their steely eyes peeking from beyond ominous garb haunted her. They moved in slow motion, or her head made it so. She watched one-armed men and women with hunchbacks, hollowed eyes, strange mutations and deformities, like some perverse Dali masterpiece. They stood on every street corner and lurked in every alleyway, the result of rampant protein famine. Milk and eggs had to be flown in from other countries, and meat was often gotten by the desperate means of poaching. She found herself breaking into tears constantly, as the eerie singing of the giant mosquito in her ear became a perpetual reminder of the disease that lived in this land. It was an unrelenting hum.

She and Thembi spent more time together in the weeks that followed Nona's arrival than they probably ever did in their entire girlhood. They were seven years apart, so they'd never really been peers until now. Thembi made and sold garments and jewelry in the many flea markets and bazaars the city boasted, braided hair, and helped promote her new fiancé's vocal group. She had designed her life precisely to fit the transient nature of the roamer. Nothing ever anchored Thembi anywhere. And while, in their youth, Nona used to warn her that it would be her undoing, it had actually turned out to be her greatest asset. Thembi was more centered, alive, and seizing the day than Nona had ever seen. Reaping all of the spiritual rewards of the true renunciant. And big sister Nona, bestselling author, and holding down the very comfortable foundation of their family home, was just about coming undone.

If Nona was smart, she'd learn a few life lessons here.

They never discussed the rape; Nona didn't want this trip to be about wallowing. But she still found herself crying at every turn, which was the same thing, wasn't it? And that became aggravating. She'd break down in the middle of market places and restaurants and bookstores. And Thembi never asked why. She just let.

What exactly Nona was purging she couldn't quite pinpoint. Fear? Mistrust? Anger? The rapist, himself? Did he actually live in her? Or had she simply become skittish through his deed? Her greatest dread was that her crying bouts might've been to garner a self-pitying attention. It was irritating to be unable to identify a specific tool, toward a specific culprit, toward eventual liberation. She simply couldn't give herself the luxury of weeping and be okay with not having to know why.

"Yes, you can," Thembi said one day. "There's no need to shrink it, Nona. That's your therapist's job, anyway. Just let it come. Welcome it. Instigate it, even. Cry until all the tears you have to give are simply finished, ducts emptied, hide toughened. Wait a minute! Why didn't I think of this before? I've got a brilliant idea. Let me give you a gift."

And so, after four weeks in Tanzania, Nona agreed to follow Thembi back to Lagos, where they were to meet up with Thembi's fiancé, and where Thembi would give Nona this gift she would not name.

Saying goodbye to Mr. and Mrs. Wenda made Nona's heart ache. Having lost her own parents early on, she knew that she and Thembi, both, had allowed themselves to snuggle inside the Wendas' bosom, and call themselves daughter.

"I'm convinced my parents sent you to us from their great beyond," Nona whispered to them, as they said goodbye in the airport terminal.

"Well, now, that is a design," Mrs. Wenda responded, "which only the most giving artist could possibly divine."

"And thank God for it," added Mr. Wenda.

Nona and Thembi climbed the step rail to their westbound Cessna, with the Wendas' collective proverb ringing in Nona's ears for the full crossing of the great Sahara.

She would never forget this extraordinary couple. Mrs. Wenda's wonderfully aromatic dishes. Analyzing great books with Mr. Wenda. The way each would finish the other's sentences and loved telling each other's anecdotes as fondly as if it were his or her own. Or weekends on their farm in nearby Bagamoyo, seventy kilometers outside the city, where the girls helped to shuck rice and pick casabas and milk goats.

Of all the memories that she would never be able to shake, however, the most compelling by far was the mournful, distant baying of the Wendas' female ass for days after a lion had strolled onto the farm in the middle of the night and devoured the male. It was a cry to which she felt profoundly connected. A cry she would hear in her head forever.

EIGHTEEN

The project of a catalogue by Michel Dugnac was officially in full swing. Dugnac had been completely knocked out by the Hareton show and wanted to claim Daniel as his own personal discovery. He'd have been just as happy had Harper simply disappeared, but Daniel would never let that happen. Dugnac was foretelling Daniel's overnight success, even though Daniel had been on this dogged road for twenty-five long years, and was even including that silly bit of slick Hollywood rhetoric in all the promotional materials. *Whatever. It's all hype. Call me anything you damned well please.* The monograph currently being penned by June Steele would also be included, and with everyone's contributions the sudden barrage of lawyers and contracts was dizzying.

Dugnac wanted to do a catalogue of the Hareton exhibit, which made no sense to Daniel since many of the paintings had already been sold to private patrons and would be taken out of the gallery within the month. Harper chimed in that her star client was presently working on a multi-media concept that would excite them all; her own rhetoric could easily rival Dugnac's for silly.

The fact that Nona Childe was an author of note was a boon, although Daniel had to admit, if only to Harper, to having taken liberties by including Nona's name without her consent. And the two of them seemed to pique everyone's interest in the mysterious poet who was about to make a splash on the scene. Daniel felt like the wheeling, dealing whore, but Harper didn't seem to think there was any moral dilemma in such self-aggrandizement.

After a business dinner that made Daniel's skin crawl, he and Harper argued like a married couple.

"You need to go out there and say to these people, *'I am worth your valuable time.'* There's no room here for false modesty."

"But, for fuck's sake, Harper, it's all style over substance anymore."

"Daniel, you're not posing with a life-sized cutout of Warhol for a snapshot to go in the Daniel Cross brochure. You're not selling toothpaste, my dear. This is a legitimate catalogue. Hell, only dead artists ever get this anymore. You should be thanking your lucky stars these people are excited by you. Aren't you the biggest proponent of getting art to the masses?"

"Right, right, but—"

"Look, not everyone's going to be able to afford a Cross original, honey. Not after how this exhibit has gone. But anyone can afford a book. My God, you would be in people's homes across America. A catalogue like this could get you into MOMA. Or The National Gallery. Or Paris."

"I know, I know, I know, I know all of that. It's just —I can't let it run away from me, you know? They're gonna hate me for this, but I need to have my hand on everything, you understand? I've got to have final approval on the color plates. They always screw up the color separation and the definition. I've seen it a thousand times."

"Of course. I know. I've made that clear. And by the way, you could never be accused of style over substance, my substantial darling."

They bickered every day, as this project got legally and financially assembled. Harper wrote grant proposals to arts councils and corporate sponsors. She wined and dined foundations and philanthropists, which Daniel could not be a part of because it all, frankly, made him sick. But she told him to never mind her business and to get his nosy self back in his studio and paint.

It was difficult, because even as inspiring as Arthur was, the whole concept was incomplete without Nona, and Daniel had no idea if he'd ever even see her again. It'd been over a month now, and she still hadn't written or called as promised. He may've really botched that one.

Of course he reacted to that bit of perceived rejection in the typically male fashion. He spent more and more time with Christianne in order to take his head away from thoughts of Nona, and pretended to love Christianne's company. He did boyfriend to the hilt.

One night at a dinner party thrown by Christianne's parents, he and Tensmith got into it over art. A strutting jingoist who, as soon as he'd amassed his fortune, had made a few attempts to culturize himself, William Tensmith was now pompously leading the march of the Right Wing's guidelines on what art should be. And though Tensmith would claim his love for art, and was actually a serious collector of what Daniel called "uncomplicated" works, Daniel knew that the old man hated him as much for being an artist as for shagging Daddy's Little Girl.

At one juncture in the evening, everyone at the dinner table fell completely silent, perhaps concerned that these two would end up in fisticuffs. The only sounds that could be heard besides two strong-willed men were the clinking of forks on china.

"How can you compare what calls itself art today with the genuine craft of a Michelangelo or a Rembrandt?" Tensmith asked.

"Well, I—"

"And what about these so-called street graffiti painters that are all the rage on the Right Coast these days, with these rap names and code names? Q-40 and SB-1, and, and, and—you know, what the blue blazes is that about? It's all gimmickry anymore."

Though Daniel had certainly had his own curmudgeonly moments about what constituted art, and would probably have commiserated with the old man under any other circumstance, tonight he knew that it was Daniel Cross Boyfriend To My Daughter who was on trial tonight, and not Daniel Cross Artist. Tensmith would probably have patted Daniel on the back if he'd known how much Daniel, too, tended to resent the new wave of rock star youngsters that was permeating the scene these days as much for their lithe, muscular bodies, brooding prowess, and sexy aliases, as for their creative statements, and that Daniel much preferred to call those efforts *stunts* over *art*. But he couldn't be Tensmith's ally this evening, because Tensmith was shoving him in that group.

"Art is ever-changing, and yes, some of it is gimmickry," Daniel inserted calmly. "But we all know that there was a time when even Picasso was considered a fraud and Dali demonic. Until, of course, they were legitimized by the powers that be. But, I mean, it's not like I'm saying anything you don't already know."

Daniel bent his inflections just curvy enough to suggest his sarcasm.

"You think you've got me pegged, don't you?" Tensmith asked in a sort of mobster sotto voce. Well, at least the old man got the sarcasm.

"I wouldn't presume to, Mister Tensmith. Sir."

"And don't even get me started on Pablo and Sal," Tensmith offered, with such disdain that he might as well have been speaking of the mediocre job done on his property by Pablo the plumber and Sal the gardener.

"Since when is airing the dirty laundry of your twisted head considered art? Those two might as well have just put their therapy sessions on display like the fucking *Jerry Springer Show* and charged admission. At least it would've saved wasting good paint and canvases."

Tensmith was enjoying his moment because he had an audience. He leaned back every few seconds to savor what he'd just spouted, smacking his clever lips and rubbing his clever belly. He was proud of his rants and probably thinking to himself, *"Bet no one's ever come at you with THAT perspective, hey kid?"*

Nothing was going to give Tensmith greater pleasure than to bring Daniel Cross down a button hole lower in front of a dinner party full of guests, and to show Christianne what a buffoon her so-called artist was. But Christianne wasn't having any of it. She got no better pleasure in this world than from defying her father.

"Okay, Daddy, now you're just embarrassing yourself," she blurted between mouthfuls of stroganoff and gulps of wine. "I mean, your goddamned Winslow Homers are fucking prosaic."

"Well, forgive an old man for wanting his art to actually have some skill to it," he ranted to the both of them. "How can you call just throwing some paint around art? I mean, Jackson Pollock? Give me a break! There's a lot of bullshit out there that dares to call itself art, good people."

Suddenly Tensmith was speaking to the congregation.

"And these two here are just gullible enough to buy it all."

He got some laughs. But others of his guests just stared into their soup.

"My dog can accomplish as much with a dripping paint brush hanging out of his mouth," Tensmith continued, snickering at his own jokes and feeling waggish. "Was Pollock saying something profound when he flung that paintbrush around like an epileptic? Well, let's see, the last time I was a clumsy mess trying to paint my garage, voila! I look down and suddenly my old, clumpy drop cloths have got validity. They're art! Now, if I stare at it just deeply enough, it's sure to say something profound to me, right?"

The few who had laughed with him earlier, surely his business cronies, amen'd him and growled their own discontents at the art world, which only fed the beast.

"The guy was a fucking alcoholic! Of course that's the best he could do."

He chuckled disgustedly. Daniel couldn't help but smile.

"It's all just some bullshit attempt to redefine art," Tensmith finished.

After patiently allowing the hubristic monster the full reign of his pulpit, Daniel poured himself another glass of Bordeaux and decided it was time to play ball.

"Well, isn't that the point of the continuing evolution of art?" Daniel asked, sucking the food from his teeth. "To redefine itself?"

"Then they should call it something else if they want to redefine it. Like CRAP, maybe?"

Laughter.

"Begging your pardon, sir—"

"Please, call me Bill. After all, you're almost as old as I am, aren't you?"

Touché! Tensmith was proud of that one.

"Fair enough—Bill—if calling it something else is really the answer, then your age-old untouchable art should've been called something else four hundred years ago, and something else again three hundred years ago, and so on, and so on."

"Meaning?"

Uh oh. Breaking a sweat, are we Tensmith?

Once in awhile Daniel would glance over at Christianne, who'd grown bored with them both, but this was too rich. There was an appetite in Daniel to push Tensmith's buttons.

"I'm only saying that your beloved art—if I may call it YOUR art—is perhaps not as unshiftable as you'd like it to be."

"Can't wait to hear this one."

"Just that it's been changing its face throughout its entire history. There was a time when the subject matter of artists was exclusively that of mythological characters and religious mysticism. Art was meant to hail the nobles. It was law, in fact. But as ages passed, and the political climate shifted, it ultimately evolved to include the more engaging subjects of everyday people and places. It was the art of the proletariat. We know this work today as Impressionism. Very controversial in its day. Yet we call it art."

Take that, you pompous fuck! You aren't the only educated bloke in the room.

"Yes, but what you don't get—"

No, no, asshole, you've had the floor. Daniel bulldozed right on through any possible insertions from Tensmith.

"THEN there came a point in history, as a new generation began to understand the workings of the subconscious mind, when art began to present a more psychological symbolism in its subjects. A pathos, more than a likeness, for example, might be what was portrayed. Such as in German Expressionism. Or even your pals, Pablo and Sal. And still called art. But surely I'm not telling you anything new, your being such a scholar on the subject, and all."

The end. Thank you! Goodnight, Los Angeles!

Daniel sat back and watched the tremble in Tensmith's cheeks.

"Don't think that you have uttered one single fact with which I am not already familiar, or that you're dealing with one of your sidewalk caricaturist colleagues who wouldn't know a Manet from a Monet."

"Again, sir, I would never presume—"

"Maybe you actually can enlighten me on something, though, Daniel. Tell me," Tensmith practically commanded, and then abandoned the train of thought as he reclined and beckoned for his wife to bring over the humidor. He opened the intricately carved box to a neat formation of Stradivarius Churchills and motioned for Daniel to help himself. It was a gesture of honor that Daniel would be the first offered, before it went around the table. It was Tensmith's way of regaining the lead and assuring Daniel that he'd not been gotten to.

Tensmith took one himself, moistened the cigar with a pompous ring of puffing lips, and picked his thought back up.

"So tell me. What does some ten-foot by ten-foot canvas of nothing but a big block of blue, with, say, a tiny little yellow drip in the corner... exactly...mean?"

Wrapping his own smiling lips around the nice Dominican blend, Daniel offered, "Well, minimalism certainly has its—"

"Oh, it's got a name, does it?"

Tensmith's smile was even bigger.

"Sorry to say it does, my friend."

A brave soul from the table chimed in.

"You know, I have to say, I've never gotten minimalism."

"Well," Daniel offered eagerly, "it's really about form being upheaved and artists starting to exam alternative ways to explore, as well as viscerally respond to, color, light, negative space—"

"No, no, no, no, no," Tensmith interrupted, "it's about SKILL being upheaved, and people who want to call themselves artists conveniently rationalizing their untalented bullshit and lack of craft."

Daniel was starting to keep a mental log of how many *bullshit*s had come out of the old man's mouth so far. He also laughed to himself because Tensmith may've actually had a point there. Daniel had certainly known his share of con artists in the art world, but he wasn't about to give Tensmith credit for anything.

Tensmith chuckled in that haughty way that begs accompaniment, and felt good about his regained lead.

"And besides," Tensmith continued, as he nodded to all the original Wyeths and Rockwells and Homers on his heavily-insured walls, "I really don't think I need to have art explained to me by a grown man who still plays with his paint sets and refuses to go out and make a real paycheck."

Ouch! We aren't even trying to mask it with politeness any longer, are we Tensmith? Did the crowd even respond? Daniel could barely take notice for the clang against his eardrums. *Okay, mate. You called it.*

"Well," Daniel began, "I guess the world will always have two camps, won't it? The ones who truly love art and its boundlessness, and the ones who simply use it as a weapon to exclude and divide."

"All right!" barked Christianne. "That's enough! I swear, the two of you are so fucking self-important! Frankly, who gives a fuck either way? Nobody. Thanks. Buh-bye!"

Assorted giggles and head-lowerings came from the rest of the ten odd guests. Ignoring the screeching bird, William Tensmith and Daniel Cross simply eyed each other like two tigers, backs arched, teeth dripping, hairs raised, hindquarters ready for leaping, and barely caring that anyone else was even in the room.

"The only reason you are even being tolerated here tonight," Tensmith leaned over and whispered through salivating lips, "is for my daughter's sake. If it weren't for her constantly pleading your sorry case to me, you wouldn't even be allowed through my front door."

Yeah, Billy boy! Now, would somebody please pass the salt?

Daniel had to give it to the old man. Even with the venom in his eyes, Tensmith never lost the smile. And Daniel had never had so much fun at a dinner party in all his life.

"Daddy!" screamed a mortified Christianne.

But Daddy was already mounting the garish staircase of his Newport Beach coven, steam puffing out of his red ears and cigar smoke trailing behind.

"Please excuse my husband, Daniel."

MRS. Tensmith. Smallish woman in a cardigan, sensible flats, and an unnatural red coloring to her hair, who'd remained practically silent, serving her guests and running back and forth to the kitchen, until this moment.

"He just got back from Oak Crest, and it always takes an emotional toll on him. He's irritable with everyone these days. It isn't you."

Oak Crest was a fat farm for rich fucks. Tensmith had been trying to lose the same gut for twenty years. This family was a French farce. Christianne's bulimic sister was busy disappearing into the bathroom every fifteen minutes and coming back out with a shiny finger and rancid breath, while Daddy probably had a chocolate cake hidden in his sock drawer right next to the .357 Magnum.

Why Daniel had even agreed to come to this circus was beyond him. Christianne was not what he wanted in his life. He'd even made up some elaborate excuse as to why he hadn't been able to invite her to the Hareton opening because he knew Nona would be there. Something like, *"this one is for industry only, honey, and I'm really, really, REALLY sorry."*

It was perhaps ironic that just when Christianne was attempting to install him into her insane family, he was looking for a coward's way out. A task made doubly hard by the fact that when two years before she had threatened to leave him, he had successfully begged her to stay.

And why had he gotten so much pleasure out of sticking it to Tensmith, anyway? The old man was a benign enough bag of wind.

Daniel was restless these days, agitated and impatient on a good day. Ready to pounce on anyone and anything, it seemed, and on this particular day Tensmith was as entertaining a target as any.

He was angry at Nona, and he knew it. She was the only thing on his mind these days, and he hated being enslaved by that. He had barely painted at all in the past month, and that only meant one thing. A woman was once again foiling his work. Would it ever end? Arthur and Harper had both been unbelievably supportive during his dry spell, but he had simply hit a wall. And the wall was Nona Childe. She was supposed to be a part of this creation. A part of his life. Without her here, it remained an incomplete vision with a gaping hole. Project. And life.

Nona, where the Hell are you?

NINETEEN

She and Thembi arrived in Lagos after a bit of red tape regarding their visas. First order of business, after checking into the Imperial Hotel, was to visit the University of Ibaden, where Thembi was considering enrolling.

William Mwelase, Thembi's fiancé, met them at the campus and introduced himself, instantly calling Nona Bride-sister. Upon sight of her husband-to-be, Thembi was the giddy kid Nona remembered from their childhood. It had, after all, been a whole month since Thembi had last seen him. And Nona suddenly realized that, though she had perhaps tried to shove her own pang aside, she missed Daniel terribly.

They traveled the following morning, by train, passing through William's hometown of Porto-Novo, into the energetic city of Accra, where they passed their time recuperating from the hard seats of the train, roaming the city, collecting artifacts, and eating odd and amazing food. Sometimes not so amazing, but Nona's courage to try new things was definitely improving.

After a day or so of sightseeing, Nona finally mustered the courage to ask Thembi about this "gift" that had been promised.

Thembi looked her squarely in the eyes over a couple of Dr. Peppers at a food stand.

"There's a guide that William has arranged who's going to take us to Cape Coast."

"Okay?" Nona said, oblivious to a significance.

"…To visit the slave castles."

Nona had heard about these. Ancient forts that had housed the ones who were being stolen away to America. Prisons that were now museums. She took a breath, which rattled unexpectedly, started to play with a piece of thread hanging from her skirt. And smiled.

"Okay," Nona whispered.

Thembi took Nona's hands in hers, still cold from the bottles of pop.

"I think it's an experience that'll do you good. It will be difficult, but that's the point."

What was the point? Nona wondered, annoyed, but was too wing-weary to ask it. Instead she just shook her head. Obedient, docile, without free will. A child. Only capable of handing the responsibility of her emotional health over to someone else. Wing-weary, for sure. They'd had such a pleasant and peaceful time with the Wendas. Was this part really necessary?

A couple of days later they arrived in Cape Coast and their guide rented a lorry to transport them the rest of the way. The anxiety became palpable.

She flashed on that evening at the Hareton Gallery, meeting Daniel's agent, Harper Levy. The two had hit it off like sisters, and had talked about everything. Harper had told Nona of her visit to the Terezin Concentration Camp outside of Prague, and how the experience had been simultaneously spirit-shattering and spirit-building.

"It will threaten at first to devastate you," she remembered Harper saying. "Only then to make you grow ten feet tall."

Nona wondered if the stature with which Harper carried herself was because of her boldness to stare that part of her history, her ancestral cord, in the face. Was this what Thembi had in mind? Sure, Thembi had rambled on about the catharsis of weeping. The girl never said anything about building fortresses.

You have to be ready for that kind of work!

After a long travel, they arrived. As they advanced on the turbulent wheels of the lorry, which jerked them violently about, and had wearily done so for a good hour, Nona saw a structure growing larger in the approaching distance and monstrously expanding, as they approached, to tower over them. Her heart began to pound. They all got out of the lorry and dusted themselves off.

They were greeted by a gentleman who offered to take them through. He had a steely coldness about his eyes. Nona could see why. She couldn't imagine having his job, guarding the ghosts of the wronged.

No one else seemed to be here. Only the men who worked the place. She wanted to ask why, but didn't want to talk. Maybe Thembi had arranged for a private tour, which sounded awfully Red Carpet for something of such ancient, terrifying, and sacred ritual. Or maybe she actually was surrounded by people — ridiculous tourists with cameras and silly hats — but couldn't see them, because in the chamber of fear there is only you, alone in your world, abandoned by humanity, taking on the great ghosts one by one, like some Spaghetti Western gunslinger.

Her head swam with nonsense.

Much exchange occurred between William, the driver, and the fort guard, in languages that resembled nothing of the Swahili she had grown to recognize. The fort guard inquired if they were clean; this was translated by William, who stumbled on his words trying to explain what was meant, until Thembi jumped in.

"He wants to know if we have any diseases. William has told him no for all of us."

Does rape count?

"Or if we're on any kind of medication."

Thembi, William, and Nona all shook their heads.

"And of course, for you and I, if either of us is menstruating? No, for me."

"Menstruating?"

"Okay, let me explain." Thembi began. "It's kind of like since we're about to embark on hallowed ground, and out of reverence to the ancestors, we are bound by honor to present in ourselves a cleanliness and purity in every respect."

To refer to a menstrual cycle as a thing clean or unclean was so old world and backward, but Nona wasn't the type to challenge these things.

"Well, I, I, I, I—"

"Are you?"

Nona hesitated.

"Hey," Thembi whispered, leaning in, "they'll smell it on you."

"Oh my God," Nona recoiled, voice high and tight. "Um, okay. Well, um, then, yeah. Damn it! What're the fucking—freaking—sorry—what are the chances? Does this mean we can't go in?"

Her reaction perplexed her. She hadn't been sure she even wanted to be here, but would also be damned to be turned away after working up the lather of *I can do this.* Every part of her was shaking and shifting from foot to foot, like someone on a coke high. She almost cried right on the spot at the idea of being turned away.

"No, no, no, no, no," Thembi assured.

"Not at all, Bride-sister," William inserted, overlapping. "It only means we have to get you a cleansing libation first. It's simply a matter of ceremony."

"It's just—it's an extra step, that's all," Thembi added. "Not a big deal."

"A cleansing ritual?" Nona whispered to Thembi. "What're they gonna do? Dip me in boiling water?"

The fort guard then rattled off some exclamation in his native Twi, and William translated.

"There is a witch doctor he knows in Sekondi, who can make and pour the libation."

"A witch doctor? Are you kidding me? I was making a joke."

"Sounds scarier than it is," said Thembi.

"Sounds like an Ed Wood movie," Nona whispered back to her. Thembi chuckled at Nona's attempt at levity, but was clearly not in the mood to make anything about this light.

"Sorry, I'm just nervous," Nona added.

"I know. Don't worry about it."

"Why am I so nervous?"

"It's deep. That's why."

The women sat on crates outside the fort as the men went off to find the witch doctor that would perform his ritual on Nona and her inconvenient menses. She could barely take being in her own skin, just standing, sitting, waiting, fanning herself, standing some more, pacing, slapping flies away, while on the other side of this formidable wall, she wildly imagined, were likely the shrouded, shrieking phantoms of some great-great-greats of hers, wondering why she'd bothered to come here at all to leer and gawk and ease her modern American guilt. If the men didn't return soon she would lose her nerve, if not her mind.

The sea was just beyond this parapet. The sea had always been able to calm her. Not today. And for the first time in weeks she was suddenly hyper-conscious again of the scars on her face and neck. She could feel the prickliness of the heat tickling the skin that had only recently healed. The scars had all but faded away, though there were traces on the skin that still required the nightly ritual of cocoa butter and sulfur.

They did finally see the men up the road. Nona ran to greet them just to keep body and mind moving. They hastened the rite, as dusk was beginning. The witch doctor was an old Ashanti medicine man with black skin and white hair, both of such severity as to remind one of a Charles White charcoal. He wore nothing about his old body except a waistcloth and sandals. This world in which she presently stood felt ancient, nothing at all like the city life of Accra or Dar that had been hers for the past several weeks. The old man said nothing to her. In fact, if he saw her at all it would have to be because eyes grew out of the top of his woolly head, for he never once even looked above the ground.

They followed him inside the gate of the old fort to an area with a dirt floor, and Nona breathed deeply. In the center of this foyer on the ground was an assemblage of small rocks arranged in a circular formation. The more inside this ritual they burrowed, the more she felt like Alice braving the rabbit hole.

The old Ashanti spoke in a high-pitched, rapid idiom, and she was reminded of Southern Black revivalists who spoke in tongues, and whom she and Thembi used to witness in horror as children spending summers with their Pentecostal grandparents in Opelika, Alabama.

William did his best to translate. What he couldn't catch, their guide from the city caught, as the two of them stumbled over one another to relate to Nona the old Ashanti's commands.

"—He requires five *sedes* per bottle—"

"—and he must have—"

"—that is to say, he must be paid up front before—"

"—before he can perform the cleansing ceremony."

Ah, there's the scam. And if I hadn't been on my period, then what would the charge have been for taking the infertile woman through?

She and Thembi rummaged through their purses, as she kept her sarcasm to herself, and tried hard to stop resisting and mistrusting everything. The old Ashanti proceeded to produce two bottles from a knapsack of something that resembled schnapps.

"He asks who is the unclean one," explained William, as the fort guard continued to confer with the witch doctor. Stepping forward to this command, Nona was suddenly Bert Lahr in Cowardly Lion clothing, clenching her coward's tail.

The old Ashanti directed Nona to stand in one spot next to the circle of rocks, as he and the fort guard took similar stances so as to create three points of a triangle around the outside of the circle. This struck Nona as awfully Masonic. Thembi, William, and their guide stood not far, watching.

For the next ten minutes, the old Ashanti witch doctor chanted indiscernible but musical words, as he periodically poured drops of his cryptic libation into the center of the circle. Nona was thankful it wasn't some witchly potion she was expected to drink. Later William explained that this was part of a prayer the old man spoke to the spirits of their enslaved ancestors, asking a pardon for the unclean one who wishes to pay her respect to their memory.

If I'm called unclean one more time...

When he had completed his prayer, the Ashanti stuffed his bottles back in his knapsack and mumbled something to the fort guard, then walked out and waited in the lorry until they were done with their visit. Never once did he look Nona's way or speak directly to her. He was in and out like a flash of light.

They were then escorted by the fort guard down a passage of dank hallways to a set of doors. The richly mineraled smell of soil was prevalent. Before they entered, it was explained that this room had been the holding place for the captured who were next to board the ships, that in many cases they'd been packed in like sardines; so tight was the squeeze of human bodies that if someone died he or she usually still remained in the standing position until the mass began to be loaded onto the planks. Nona's face grew prickly, as she listened to this unfolding. She kept glancing at Thembi, who looked appropriately somber but relatively unshaken. Nona couldn't seem to settle her breath. She shook her head as if shaking off beads of sweat.

The fort guard slid the huge metal door open onto a simple room of brick and mortar, no larger than a school auditorium. The far end of it contained another set of huge doors that opened directly onto the sea. It was explained that the slave ships would dock right outside this door and extend their planks against it. Everyone stepped inside.

There was something here. Perhaps it was guilt, or maybe she had just never left home and had never had to steel her spine, but the stink of fear began to perspire from her. She could smell her own armpits. Even the warm musk between her legs seemed to float up to hover around her head. She wanted to run from this place to a hot shower and scour this fear off of her forever. And she suddenly knew what it was that was here. The something.

One hundred and fifty years had passed since the last person had been thrown from this precipice, yet she realized in this instant, as she had become hyper aware of her own heightened olfactory senses, that what was *still here* was the smell.

It existed in the room even as they stood within it; the vague fetor of necrotic human flesh permeating these walls a century and a half later. Nona's eyes glassed and her lips pursed. Only in this instant did she realize just how indelicate her earlier joking had been, and while it had all been out of merely trying to calm her own nerves, there was no place for it. She placed her hand gently on her mouth, and no one said a word but stood quietly in this room. She wondered if they were all quietly waiting for some sound. She listened, herself. If the smell could still permeate this room, couldn't the tortured wails still be alive in these walls too?

Suddenly Thembi clutched her shoulders, as Nona found herself breathing hard and fast, and as she clung to Thembi's touch she wondered how on earth her sister could stand to make this trip more than once. They walked out of the room as Nona tried to nurse one clean, slow breath. There was more to see, but not for her, and once they were outside she broke into a full bawling. She leaned over, propping her hands on her knees, as though she needed to get blood rushed back to her head, and Thembi rubbed her back. She couldn't stop. She suddenly felt cold, and she shivered, though the temperature was easily a hundred.

"Jesus, why can't I stop? This is stupid."

She cried for everything. Things for which she wasn't even aware she was crying. Rape and injury. A man she wanted but ran from. A sheltered life that made her feel like a fraud of a writer.

Minutes passed in this deed, until she finally stood back up, done with tears, and climbed into the lorry. She gave her comrades only silence for the ride back to town, but would periodically squeeze Thembi's hand just to let her sister know that her silence wasn't ingratitude.

For days after, no matter what she and Thembi did, or where they went, Nona's hand continually clutched her sister's as they walked the streets of Ghana like two lovers. The more time Nona spent with her sister, the more she saw her sister walk upright in the world, a trick that was not always so easy for Nona, and the more she knew why Thembi continued to make the trek, herself, and insisted that Nona experience it too. Thembi knew that Nona had trials to confront, and needed fortifying. Thembi had been right about the tears. Each one shed seemed to lessen the weight between Nona's eyes just a bit at a time.

"It will threaten at first to devastate you, only then to make you grow ten feet tall."

Was it working? Was she growing? She almost looked down at her feet to see if the ground was fading distant beneath her.

TWENTY

Tensmith's wife was the one responsible for Daniel not getting evicted after his sporting match with her husband. He could only imagine that behind closed doors this little mousy housewife was a genuine ball-buster, and the old man a cowering puppy who cried, *"spank me, mum!"* before he went to bed each night. Thank God for small wonders.

He was still sleeping with Christianne, though less and less as weeks passed. She deserved better. But what she deserved he couldn't give her. He had become the official inexplicably aloof asshole boyfriend.

"What're you doin' with her, man," Arthur challenged one day, "when there's this other woman you been tellin' me about?"

"I know, mate. You're right."

"Do your soul a favor, Danny, and do right by 'em both."

"I know."

"Cuz your soul will pay you back in spades, if you don't."

Daniel was weary. They talked about his romantic dilemma every day, with Daniel curling into a corner, and at the end of each of those days no painting would get done.

He told Arthur everything about Nona. Everything except the rape. Arthur already lived with that demon. And Daniel knew, besides, that if Arthur ever found out, he would never have agreed to meet her. Because Daniel also knew that Arthur felt responsible for every rape ever committed in the world.

"Have a conscience, Danny. Do not play that game. Or somebody's gonna play it on you. Remember Chelsea?"

How could Arthur ask that horrible question? Chelsea was the woman Daniel had been seeing when he first met Arthur back in the early eighties. An actress. Beautiful and statuesque. From the same East End part of London as he. And a certified lunatic.

And like an obedient dog, Daniel went straight to the place of his past that Arthur had intended.

The twenty-six-year-old Daniel first met Chelsea when he and Tariq, his flatmate at the time, were living in a rented four-bedroom house inland of Venice Beach. She'd answered an ad for "roommates wanted." He and Tariq had studied all the applicants and, of course, after careful review, made their choices based on the best-looking women.

They finally welcomed to their humble abode Chelsea Carrier and Sandy Something. Sandy didn't stay long, so Daniel barely remembered her. In fact, the fourth room became the rotating wheel of endless flatmates in the five years that he and Tariq were there.

Within one week of meeting, he and Chelsea began sleeping together. Daniel seduced her at the kitchen sink one morning when everyone else was at work, and from that moment on they were inseparable. For four months they lived in bliss. They were both poor and struggling and therefore able to appreciate each other's plight. He was exhibiting primarily at coffeehouses and co-ops, if he was exhibiting at all. And she was active in a small theatre company, performing somewhere in the city fairly non-stop. There was, of course, the lovely convenience of being only a bedroom away, though they rarely slept apart. The ocean being a mere eight blocks from the house only added to the drug.

Then it happened. It occurred so many years ago now that he was a bit disoriented trying to piece it together in his present head. He remembered that the incident itself had been of no great importance, other than it being the launching pad into Hell.

The four flatmates had decided to throw a summer party of the Keg & Ten-foot Sandwich brand. Everyone that each of them had ever known attended, and there were scads new people to meet from every Bohemian Westside walk of life. The place got sort of ransacked but that was of no consequence, because the music was ear-splitting, which was most important.

Chelsea was living it up, as were they all, on tequila shooters and rails of coke, when she started sharing her illustrious hobbies with a small but captive audience. She bragged on about three-ways and four-ways; and the various ways in which she liked to shag; and what she would and wouldn't do (hint: there was nothing she wouldn't do); and how many women she'd been with versus how many men; and a drunken night of indiscretion as a teen with her brother; and on and on and fucking on.

Daniel was hardly the uptight sort; he didn't really give two shits about her past sexual exploits, and he'd certainly had ones almost as colorful. But when she started to describe, in graphic detail, the sex between her and him, and what she claimed were his peculiar fetishes, which got the room howling, he found himself standing against a distant wall with a pint in hand, fuming.

Chelsea clearly thought she was being witty and worldly and entertaining, but all she was doing was awakening the sick horniness of every male in the room. Ultimately she ended up puking and stumbling out of sight, on down the hall, and was quickly forgotten by her audience, who all went back to mingling and finding their hard-ons from some other unsuspecting female. Daniel was paralyzed with humiliation. Of course, he was also stoned, which probably heightened his paralysis to an even more Shakespearean sense of tragedy.

He couldn't really figure out why he cringed so, to hear her speak of sex that was more adventurous than he would ever see in his lifetime, and which was largely exaggerated anyway. What had he wanted from her? To be a shrinking wallflower? Someone who had everything to learn from him, and not the other way around? The very traits he had fallen for were her liberated woman-self, her beliefs that manners were a conceit invented to make sure women remained in their place, her rebellion against that.

He couldn't have been that unreasonable in his anger, could he? After all, she had violated their privacy — *his* privacy — all for the sake of what? Being thought of as hip and uninhibited? Having an audience? *Fucking insecure bird!*

As soon as consciousness and a large pot of coffee were hers the next day, he determined that he would speak to her on the matter.

That was the incident, of so many wretched years ago now, that had begun his descent into Hell. Of course he knew it couldn't compare to Arthur's Hell, but did Hells have to be compared to be legitimate?

He questioned Chelsea about her little theatrics the following evening, as she didn't awaken until after sundown the next day. Eighteen solid hours of unconsciousness was alarming. Her head was buried in her hands at the kitchen table when he lit into her.

"Would you like a review of your performance last night?" he asked calmly, with a smirk, on that hungover evening.

"What are you foaming at the mouth about?" she mumbled from beneath a shroud of fuzziness, which sent him instantly into a fury of sarcastic dramatics.

"Chelsea Carrier takes theatre to a whole new level of realism. She is riveting in the role of The Cunt. Her performance is so electrifying and true-to-form, her sexual prowess a bewildering tour de force, you'd almost think you were there in the bedroom with her. Wait a tick! You might well've been. It's the new wave of audience participation theatre! How cutting edge! How avant-garde!"

"Oh, stop with your bloody histrionics, Daniel! My God, you troglodyte! Should I wear a scarlet letter on my tit, as well? Look, if you can't take the heat, stay outta the fucking kitchen!"

"Ooohh! Missed your callin' in life, darlin'. You shoulda been a writer, what with all those luscious clichés at your fingertips. How about, *'you can't judge a book by its cover.'* Or better yet, *'an apple a day keeps the whore away!'*"

He definitely remembered the slap. It so stunned him, in fact, that without even consciously deciding to, he slapped back, almost on top of hers. It looked like a vaudeville routine.

Of course Sandy and Tariq were standing by, getting the show of a lifetime. Daniel hadn't even had the good taste to say, *"may I talk to you in the privacy of our bedroom, dear."* He'd wanted to embarrass her. He knew that now. He also now knew that nothing on this earth could ever embarrass Chelsea Carrier. She fed on drama.

Chelsea stormed out of the room, Sandy ran after her, Daniel started that way too, and Tariq jumped in front of him, hands out to block. It was a dizzying pandemonium.

"Oh, what is this!" Daniel spat. "You're treating me like I'm some menace to society. You think she needs protection from me?"

"Look, I know you're not that type, man, but I also know you're a little upset right now and we gotta keep the peace in this house. We can't afford these rents ourselves. AND—" Tariq added more succinctly, "you can't just go around slappin' back. It's a fine line, man."

"Oh, so now I'm not allowed to go near her, is that it? See, this is how shit like this gets taken way outta context! Sandy's probably in there right now sayin', *'look, honey, you need a counselor. Lemme call a doctor. You've been traumatized.'* This is bloody bullshit! Has anyone forgotten that I was cuffed first? She doesn't fuckin' hit like a girl. She fuckin' walloped me. Or is that all right because I'm JUST a man?"

"Look, do your men's liberation soapbox all you want. I'm just tryin' to keep the peace, okay? When you're calmer, then I'll leave you and Chelsea to beat the shit outta each other."

Tariq's comment was meant to inspire a chuckle from Daniel, but Daniel was beyond humor.

So there it was. The man/woman abyss. Tariq and Daniel in one part of the house, Sandy and Chelsea in another. Tension, tension, and more bloody tension. All he'd wanted was to have a nice little argument with his lady, kiss, make up, and disappear into the bedroom for two days. What he got instead was a greeting at his front door by L.A.'s finest.

He could not believe that he was being handcuffed on his own front porch and taken in for domestic abuse.

"This is insane!" he yelled to one of the officers, learning quickly that they don't much like it when you yell at them. But this was ridiculous; the slap he had given Chelsea was a stunner at best. It was a fucking reflex, for God's sake. Barely a brush. She, on the other hand, had given him a goddamned black eye.

Of course, his screaming, *"How could you do this?"* and her screaming back, *"You can't hit me like that and get away with it!"* only succeeded in bringing every neighbor out onto his front porch, mumbling *"crazy Brits"* as Daniel's head got violently shoved into the back seat of a squad car. He would later come to learn that his girlfriend had an appetite for scenes like that.

In the end, Chelsea decided not to file charges and, in fact, was the one who, ten hours later, came down to the station to bail him out. Contrition dripped from her face; just the right amount of wrinkle to her brow, the slight downturn of the mouth, and a ravenous embrace awaiting him as they let him go. He stood there baffled that this sudden tenderness was coming from the same woman who'd been responsible for his being there in the first place.

"How could you possibly think that I would ever try and hurt you?"

She was suddenly coy, and coy was just not Chelsea. She was the ballsiest woman he'd ever met. He barely recognized this one.

"Please forgive me," she cried.

Chels crying? It just didn't happen.

"I know you didn't mean to hurt me, Daniel. I guess it's just the little flinches that become yours when you've been through this before."

"What? What're you talking about?"

"And the slap I gave you—my God, look at your eye. I suppose that was just my defense mechanism."

"Christ, Chels, what're you saying? Who has ever hit you?"

"It's nothing."

"Chels!"

He was frustrated by her elusive act, and angry that there might be a history that his slap had re-opened for her.

"I guess I just never wanted to bring it up," she whimpered.

He grabbed her and hugged her close and hated himself.

"My God, honey, I'm so sorry! Listen—" he swore, holding her face in his hands, "—you don't EVER have to fear me, all right? This will never happen again!"

He tried everything in his power to let her know she could trust him. He begged her to talk about it. Not only right then, but for the remaining ten months of their relationship. He never succeeded. Every time he tried to bring it up, he would see that flinch, as if he'd just raised his hand again, which he never did. It frustrated him that he could find no way to comfort her.

He also began having his own plagues. He started doubting his respect for women, which was a doubt he never in his wildest imagination would've believed could ever exist.

And suddenly, as he presently relived that time in his life, he looked at Arthur.

"All right, I know I've not been a man with Christianne. I know I've never been anyone's Romeo. But *this thing* with Chelsea? From a fucking hundred years ago? That's just not me, damn it! Our whole dynamic has been defined by one crazy moment that I've never repeated in my life, to the point where you would draw back on that one to teach me some lesson about Chris? What the fuck, mate! I have never touched a woman before or since in any violent way. And this hitting-of-women psychosis, besides, is all about power. Hell, the thing I love most about women is *their* power! You know this about me."

"Who you tryin' to convince, Danny?"

"You're the one who's tryin' to compare this to that."

Daniel's voice was high and constricted.

"I'm sayin', what's the difference?" Arthur tried to clarify. "Whether you hit or whether you deceive?"

Who *was* he trying to convince? It would appear that Daniel was doing his fanciest footwork in front of the man who'd stood at the very threshold of woman-violence. And he knew that his argument held no water, besides, because he also knew that Arthur's experience with it had never been about power, but about utter loss.

He wanted to beg Arthur's forgiveness for his indelicacy, but they weren't even on *that* subject, and he had vowed years ago never to be the one to open that door.

"Actually that's not even what I'm tryin' to say," Arthur recalibrated. "I guess I'm sayin' that lovers treat each other so much worse than we ever would anyone else in our lives. There's just sump'n about sex, and the pull it has, and the swagger it gives us, that allows us to look our lover in the eye and pretty much say, *I've had your inmost self now. I no longer need to treat you with respect.'* And the minute that happens, man, you are on a bad road."

Daniel understood the sage's grace that Arthur's Hell had given him, and both delicately acknowledged the uncomfortable line between that Hell advancing Arthur to a place of redemption and it giving his terrible deed sanction. It was also all the push Daniel needed in order to go back to that painful time once more, snatch the covers off, and be reminded of the damage that can be done.

In those days following the slapping incident, Chelsea Carrier had Daniel doubting his sanity and his humanity, forging obsessed questions in his head of whether he was capable of that impulse ever again. For the remainder of their relationship, Daniel took up the blame for every ugliness that had ever occurred between them, neatly placing the source of all their problems on his single indiscretion, which had now come to be known as THE SLAP, as though it were the only in the world. It overrode all possibility that Chelsea could ever be the one responsible for anything. Inch by inch she succeeded in cutting him down until he was nothing but the shadow of himself.

He couldn't see this at the time, of course. He was of the belief that life was being made complete by this woman. He had asked Chelsea to marry him, she'd said yes, and for a brief while they were actually doing all right.

Then she had an affair. She didn't come clean with it, either. Daniel had to discover her in bed with the bloke.

Tariq had hinted at the signs, not wanting Daniel to make the biggest mistake of his life, but Daniel had refused to see it. He had convinced himself that Tariq had just been biased by that whole police business. And ultimately it was impossible for Daniel not to feel like the stupidest git alive when he discovered that the new flatmate, after Sandy Something, was the affair.

He'd done his best to be understanding. He'd spoken with Chelsea calmly about it, asked her if she was unhappy with their relationship, told her he understood if the affair had come out of the jitters of making a lifetime commitment. He said everything that was against his instincts to say. Of course he didn't understand! He wanted to pound the bloody walls! How could she do this to him? But with her past abuse looming in Daniel's consciousness, and THE SLAP looming on top of that, he feared any kind of conflict.

The minute Daniel cornered this tosser alone, however, it took Tariq, who seemed the only sane one in the house at that moment, to keep him from pounding the guy to a pulp. The prick was moved out by morning. Though apparently not before said prick managed to loot just about everything from under foot when the rest of the household was out.

Daniel and Chelsea had returned home later that evening to find their house ransacked, and that was all that was needed to finally awaken Daniel's rage. He tore the rest of the house apart. He punched a hole in the living room wall. He bashed the kitchen breakables. He could not believe all of this was happening to him at one time.

Chelsea stood by in shock, not so much at their vandalized living room, as at Daniel's explosion, so unlike the passive puppy he'd brilliantly become. She started screaming hysterically, as if he had time for that, and babbling on about how she'd hurt him once again, and she didn't mean it, and she always failed at relationships, and she loved him too much to let this go on, and she was a loser at life, and he deserved better than her, and blah, blah, blah. It was all a bit of a blur, after a fashion.

Before Daniel knew it, she had run to the bathroom, slammed the door, and swallowed a bottle of pills. He pounded and screamed for her to open up and wanted to die to think he'd driven her to that.

This was how his mind was working. *She* had had the affair, *her* lover had ripped him off of his entire possessions, but *Daniel* had been to blame. Chelsea was masterful.

Tariq arrived home just at the apex of their drama and helped him break down the bathroom door. Poor guy hadn't even been given the moment to react to his house being burgled before he was having to help Daniel in yet another domestic travesty.

Thankfully they managed to get Chelsea to an emergency room in plenty of time, and were fortunate that she hadn't taken enough pills to kill herself, only enough to wreck her stomach for awhile. Daniel thanked the doctors profusely, and found it odd that Tariq only stood with his arms folded, strangely unsympathetic.

"Do you know how easy it is to fake a suicide attempt?" Tariq asked him, one evening, later that week.

"Fake? What the fuck, mate?"

Daniel was appalled, and refused to hear what his friend had to say. And he still couldn't hear it on Chelsea's second attempt. This time it was slit wrists, although anyone knows you have to travel up the vein with the straightedge to effectively bleed to death. It didn't take anything as traumatic as an affair to prompt it, either. It was a silly argument over who contributed more money to the household. Past the first attempt, it always seemed to be trivialities that triggered it. How could anyone be that fragile?

Her third attempt. Her fourth. Each time Daniel's heart grew blacker. He told her she was killing him with this unrelenting self-mutilation. He tried to get her to tell him what could be so horrible that she no longer wanted to live. He begged her to open up, to get some counseling, to do something, anything, so that they could get back to the business of loving life and each other. Hell, they had a wedding to plan.

It was during that miserable time that he'd met Arthur at the theatre on Fifth and Western, where Chelsea had been doing a play. It was amazing she could even work in between the cutting and the clockwork emergency room visits. Tariq had done his best to convince Daniel that she was a sick seed. Harper had, too. But it was Arthur — king of fucked-up-ness and ultimate seer — who was finally able to open Daniel's eyes. He didn't shake Daniel's shoulders and beg him to *"...get the Hell out of there!"* or to *"...wake up and smell the coffee!"* or to *"...think straight, man!"* which was what everyone else was doing. He did no imploring. He simply told a prophecy. And the prophecy came true.

"One of these days you're gonna let all'is shit drive you to your own madness, man," he'd whispered in Daniel's ear that day. "And when you do, she won't be at the end'a that road to catch you, like you been catchin' her. Mark my words."

Daniel barely listened to Arthur that afternoon; in fact, never consciously recalled those words again until months later when he found his own stomach being pumped at County General.

Chelsea's suicide attempts hadn't ceased, and Daniel knew unequivocally that he could only hold them at bay for so long; that eventually he'd be worn down and she would succeed. And it would be his fault. This sick merry-go-round had managed to bleed every hope of happiness, every desire for life, every grace note of beauty right out of him. Even his shell had been worn away by her unyielding corrosion. He had become the invisible man, and he had truly meant to end his life.

He followed a bottle of whisky with a bottle of black shoe dye; maybe even a few other assorted potions from his medicine cabinet. This nice little cocktail did permanent damage to his stomach. He went into a full grand mal seizure, while his sweating pores oozed black crap, and his liver began the arduous process of an irreversible hardening.

At the brink of death, he was rushed to County. And as he lay in his sick bed, in a huge ward with ten other infirmed people, in the most depressing hospital on earth, fighting for his putrid life, Chelsea Carrier, his future bride, was on a plane to who-knew-where, never to be seen again.

Of course, in the proud tradition of her adulterous lover, she also cleaned their house out BUT GOOD.

Daniel's downtown loft held only silence, as he came back to the present from a burdened trip. No more was said between Arthur and him. They simply sat in the heat of the day. Daniel tried to slow his breath, which had begun to trill. It had not been a day of painting or collaborating, but of remembering. What he remembered most profoundly was that Arthur had foretold his future, and when that future became manifest, he was geared for it in a way he hadn't even been consciously aware, and probably wouldn't have survived had Arthur not been that little bird in his ear. Readying him.

"You saved my life back then," he offered to Arthur, breaking the silence, after recalling his life of sixteen years ago.

Arthur stared at him, but didn't respond, instead tapping out the butt of the spliff that they had been passing back and forth, stuffing the leftover roach in his jacket pocket, placing his hand on his friend's shoulder, and leaving Daniel alone to do some needed thinking.

Now that the memory of that time had been rudely shoved back into Daniel's thoughts, he thought it best to start reexamining his life. Arthur always seemed to have a knack for touching just the right nerve that would force clarity for Daniel. What Daniel started to realize was that he was rapidly losing his soul. By keeping Christianne as a toy on the side. By trying to determine how he could somehow slither his way into Nona's life instead of walking into it upright and honorably. And by abandoning all work in the process. He'd become no better than Chelsea, grand master of manipulation.

The only thing that truly had the potential to save his life again was the prospect of Nona Childe being a part of it. He knew as surely as he knew anything that in Nona lay the promise of something more meaningful.

TWENTY ONE

He consumed a great deal of alcohol in the nearly two months that Nona was away, and wallowed too much in repugnant memories of the past. He and Arthur spent many late nights at the Orchid Club, basking in the red glow of whisky and listening to Dorothy Favor, as her incredible voice sang songs of longing. Christianne had all but disappeared from his life after weeks of calculated distances on his part, during which time the job of collecting the rents was given to someone else and his own rent raised. She hadn't left angrily; just more from boredom, really. But she was definitely severing the ties, bit by bit. Daniel was the most passive fuck-wit he knew.

Nona never wrote as promised, and he was all but certain she was gone forever when one day she was suddenly a voice on his phone machine. An elixir, that voice: *"It's Nona. Remember me? Sorry, bad joke. I'm back. Give a call when you have a moment free from creating some brilliant thing. That is, if you haven't written me off completely."*

It nearly froze him to hear it, and though his life lately had been a certain shambles, and he was sure he looked a self-destructive mess, and though she should never see him this way, he promptly hopped in his car and headed out of Downtown and into the Westside.

He traveled the 10 Freeway during rush hour, which he'd quickly come to learn was pretty much any hour of the day in Los Angeles, headed north on the 405, which was even worse, did the beautiful drive across Sunset, though the sun was just to that point in the sphere that it gave painful glare, wound through a canyon of reds, browns, and yellows, during this last chapter of autumn, up to her Palisades retreat, pulled into her driveway, and caught a glimpse of her around the bend of her house, through a wooden gate that one only had to reach over to unlatch, making sure to open it as silently as possible, and through the acacia bushes that lined the side wall. He glimpsed the ocean's horizon in the distance. Its tranquil hum was worth the price of the property alone. He was beginning to understand why she loved it here.

She sat in a weather-worn Adirondack chair, facing the sea, bundled up and reading a magazine. He didn't immediately make his presence known, because he just needed to look at her for a moment, and remember what an incredible feeling she gave him when he was with her, and to be reminded that she was no Chelsea. This woman before him worshipped life. The rhythm of her breath, as she inhaled the ocean spray, said as much. She would never toy with her life, or anyone else's, in that perverse way that had been Chelsea's only gift. His too, he realized, as he thought about his treatment of Christianne.

She turned around, and a smile crept over her amazing face, larger than the moon and easily more vibrant. He smiled back, and thanked the ocean's breadth, which in this instant seemed the only thing wondrous enough to qualify as God, that she wasn't still angry with him.

She unwrapped her legs from the blanket and stood as he approached.

"So you're not angry with me?" she said.

"Me? Angry with you? Last I remember, it was the other way around."

"I know, I know," she offered, as she walked toward him. "It's just that I never called."

"It's all right."

He took her hands in his and perused that face that had been haunting him. He could tell she wanted to show him that her scars were gone. No more eye patch, and there was only the subtlest hint of asymmetry left over from the reconstructed jaw. But there it was. Her face. Not some pummeled sculpture from a rapist's fist, but the radiant smile he'd seen for the first time, almost a year ago now, in a grocery market. The one he'd been compelled to paint. The one he'd violated with his camera. The one she thought she'd lost.

"The journey was good to you. You look beautiful."

He wanted to be hurt that she'd ditched him for two wretched months without a word, and he sort of knew that the hurt was in his voice, but he wasn't about to give in to that. So he bucked up, smiled, and suddenly realized that he'd not yet kissed her lips in all this time of knowing her. He gave himself the permission now.

As he drew her close, her mouth parted slightly for him. It was a soft kiss, studied and artful, the kind that never wants to end. The kind that usually goes away after a relationship gets staid, and almost never comes back, replaced instead by the terse pecks of obligation.

Nona's own past with men included the belief that most didn't think much of kissing past the first one, because their only use for kissing was as the key inside. Once the door was unlocked, what further use did it serve? So, this being their first, and likely the best they would ever have, she relished in this moment and did her best to memorize it. It was the kind of kiss that alerts the rest of the body to get into action.

He boldly placed his hands on her backside and pulled her even more tightly against him, so that she could feel his arousal. After a minute — or ten, who knows? — she slipped her hand in his and led him over garden bricks, past wild orchids and horsetail bamboo and cassia trees, through her glass doors and up her stairs. There was the stupor of arousal about them both, and they floated inside like two drunks. To be led was such a turn-on. He was the one who had always done the leading, and now this woman told him with no words that it was finally all right. As they made their way to her bedroom, he found himself hyper aware of every stair creak and curtain flutter in this house he'd only visited once before. That was months ago. An eternity. He was so accustomed to "getting in and getting out," that this quaintly old-fashioned notion of courtship was oddly rousing.

As they entered her bedroom, he recognized that prior to her trip away a moment like this would have been impossible, with her likely wondering if her rapist wasn't out there somewhere, fitting nicely into society, being a good citizen and a terrific friend to all. And who was to say that she might not have even met this man again, and liked him, maybe brought him into her life, as she was doing now, not knowing that he was the one? She had to have been suspecting every male face that had come her way. And surely, at least in the beginning, Daniel had to have been thrust in that bunch, as well.

With her willingness to finally take him to her bed, perhaps it meant that she'd had a breakthrough of some sort. He wanted to assure her that she could have complete trust in him, that she could surrender wholly, and that he would never hurt her. He made sure to be as gentle as his roughened hands could manage.

As he cradled her waist and lay her down on her bed, he brazed his tongue against her lower lip before sliding it inside, and then sliding himself inside.

Daniel's instincts with sex had always been about feeding the visceral hunger with a rabid attack, then taxiing home. It took everything in him right now to move slowly, but he made himself do so until he knew that she and he, and not some wretched imagery, were the only two in the room.

For the first time in his life, sex wasn't about scoring, which frightened him, because he wasn't sure he was ready to lose the wall he'd built over the years against the sweet stink of gooey vulnerability. It was that stink that had his heart racing with the very idea of her; that suddenly had him believing he could paint again after weeks of impotency; that made this woman the crucial quotient to whether or not he could create, which was more than a little unnerving. All she had to do was walk out of his life again and he would be paralyzed mid-stroke, with the brush frozen in his hand, like some ridiculous, romantic-suffering Tin Woodsman.

When they finished, he dropped his sweating head on her pillow and thought about all that he had built his wall against for so many years, after being repeatedly hypnotized by women. Yet here he was, lying in her bed, pulse racing just to have her back in his life. Hypnotized yet again. He recognized this weird emotional incontinence he seemed to be suffering, but was too drunk with her to care.

Twenty two

The following days with Nona were stimulating. She told him everything of her remarkable and difficult African pilgrimage, and the needed time spent with her sister. And he told her about his newest project, confessing that he'd taken the liberty to include her in this bright idea without her permission.

"You'd better watch out for me. I'm sure to behave like a husband without benefit of a ring."

She laughed easily. "Are you kidding? I am honored. I can't tell you what it meant to be painted by you that first time. When I saw that portrait—I don't know—it made me feel as though I might actually live forever."

"Your writing is what'll make that happen."

She couldn't hear that.

"Seriously," she barreled right through, "everyone wonders at some point in their life what it must feel like to be a Mona Lisa, or Vermeer's girl with the pearl earring, or, or, or one of Van Gogh's crows, even. An insignificant flock of birds that inspired a stroke that is moving hearts to this day. That's what it means to be immortal. And I now actually have some inkling of what that feels like."

He watched her revel in the notion of beauty. She didn't drown in others' art, as he tended to do, as when he would listen to Billy Somebody and weep in his drink; she waded in it, like someone soothed by a mineral bath.

The day Nona and Arthur met was the day Daniel's ulcers kicked in. These two had each entrusted him with a secret, had sought out an ally, a comrade-in-arms. Daniel felt the betrayer of both their confidences merely by the act of an introduction.

"I've heard great things about you, Nona."

"The pleasure's mine."

At least she didn't say, *"Really? Cuz I haven't heard a word about you."* She had to be wondering why he'd never brought Arthur up, but she never asked.

He felt like the wicked puppet-master, willfully assembling this unnatural triangle to which he was the only one wise, and knowing that there was a tale from each that he could never tell the other.

Over the next several weeks, the three of them spent round-the-clock time together in the effort to create something. They were excited about this new project, and Daniel's flat became Headbanging Central, a vibrant, drunken roundtable, where many an evening was spent devouring bottles of wine and throwing ideas around the room like tennis balls. Sometimes, one of them might catch one and throw it back. Other times one might be hit in the head with it, only to retaliate with an idea of his or her own. They were merciless with each other. If an inspiration smelled like bullshit from someone, another would state it plainly. It was largely a growing trust that allowed them a liberation and frankness, but it was also partly their penchant for wine and grass.

Daniel couldn't believe how easily Nona and Arthur hit it off. It would've chilled him had he not been so grateful. Both were writing like mad scientists in some insane laboratory. They scribbled erratically in notebooks as Daniel sat back and watched them work, sometimes alone or they'd interact with each other. At times they wouldn't write at all. Or they'd bring in something they'd worked on at home and spin from there. And Daniel painted them, his exclusive subject-matter, with his own brand of madness. There were times when they wouldn't even sit for him and he'd simply paint off of what was in his head, because these two were stamped indelibly there.

Eventually a theme began to develop. As it did so, Daniel started gravitating toward certain hues while painting some Arthur mutation and certain other hues when creating some Nona thing. His original polar concept found itself smearing messily over the lines. Nona was no longer the exclusive embodiment of light, and Arthur dark. And it even showed in the writing each was producing. The more Daniel looked inside them, the more they all changed, the more that idea became a fascinating clutter.

As the weeks passed, fall turned to winter, and they did Christmas together, with a huge feast at Nona's place: Harper, Kai, Neville, Arthur's son, and the Dynamic Trio. But they could barely get through fruit cake, gifts, and holiday mania for jumping right back into the fray.

Of course, not every night was the Three Musketeers — the Three Furies — Julie, Linc, and Pete. Sometimes Arthur and Daniel would have sessions alone, or Nona and Daniel. At other times still, they got into mindsets where they wouldn't bother to speak to each other for days at a time.

On New Year's Eve, alone with Nona in his flat, after an exhilarating bout of lovemaking, sex, fucking — they called it everything, and they did everything; there was no more gild — Daniel watched her discover a gouache landscape that he was currently finishing.

"Is this part of our project?" she asked. He didn't answer her right away but allowed her to eye it, which she did, intensely, moving in circles around it, studying its lines from every angle. She stepped up close at one point, close enough to touch it with her nose. It was almost as if she were smelling it. She closed her eyes.

"This piece is so—" She searched for words that didn't come easily, like someone trying to describe the bouquet of an aged wine. "—serene. No, shit, serene isn't it. But it definitely doesn't fit with anything else I've seen of yours. Which is usually—I don't want to say harsh, but there is certainly an edge in the way you usually look at humanity in your work. This one is—" She sighed an exhaustive sigh. "There's something—I don't know, like, there's no edge. It's all surrender. Anyway, it doesn't matter. It's breathtaking."

He rather enjoyed her frustrated grab for words.

"Thank you," was all he said.

She referred to a landscape whose colors were warm and light. Soothing hues, the color relationships used often by the Impressionists, especially Degas. It was of a field that met with the edge of a lake. There were sparrows and hummingbirds in nearby pine and olive trees. In the distance of the field stood a person, small enough not to be detectable as either male or female, just a smudge from Daniel's brush was all it was, really. And the silhouetted figure was soaking in the sun and the tall surrounding grass.

His intention had been for it to evoke the sensory pleasure and sunlit freedom that first marked Impressionism. She was definitely right about it not reflecting his usual brand of sooty angst.

"I can't quite put my finger on it," she repeated, though clearly needing to.

"Look closer," he urged, though she was literally upon it already. "I mean, look deeper."

She couldn't see what he was trying to get her to see. He touched her shoulders, pulled her back from it, and told her to stay put. He then disappeared behind a partition and rummaged through one of his many junk-laden crates, until he came out with a photographic blow-up. This photo was exactly the same size as his landscape, 36" x 48", whose image had dissolved into an almost unrecognizable, out-of-focus haze from multiple enlargements.

He propped the photo on one of his easels right next to the landscape. The photo's image was printed vertically, as in a portrait, where the landscape's image was painted across the canvas horizontally.

The entire time that he was scampering about trying to set this up, Nona stood amused, laughing and wondering what the Hell he was doing.

When it was ready, he moved aside from his purposeful blocking of the photo, to reveal the unfortunate shot he'd snapped of her the day she'd left him. There before her, next to his landscape, which she loved, was her own larger-than-life image, a sullen face, ravaged, caked with scars and despair, a twisted mouth, a patched eye, a face from which she had long escaped, and gratefully. He knew he took a risk by showing her that he hadn't disposed of the film as he'd promised; that instead he'd developed it and blown it up. He watched her reaction, praying she would get it.

She didn't speak but stared at a ghost. He could see in her eyes that she didn't recognize the connection between the two. And he saw the confusion form in her rapidly reddening face, wondering what the Hell was up.

Come on, Nona! Look closer. I'm not the cad you think me. Just see it!

And then, as if she'd heard his very thoughts, a brilliant light suddenly clicked on behind those brilliant eyes. It was just a subtle shift in the face, but he saw it. Her mouth opened slowly, though no word escaped. Only the faintest utterance of a gasp. He finally breathed again and knew that he had done right to pursue the risky impulse.

"You do see it, don't you?" he asked.

Her response to his question was to walk up to it and lift the huge photo, tilting it on its side to lie horizontally like the landscape. Back and forth she stared from one to the other. He could see each discovery in her eyes as it occurred. The bridge of the lacerated nose in one becoming the lake eddy in the other. The hollowed shadow of the patched eye in the first becoming the hill and dale of a distant mountainside in the second. A barely distinguishable map of scar tissue and stitching in the photo's violated face becoming the complex network of trees and flora.

Her eyes glazed as she finally saw, lurking within the weaves of a peaceful meadow, her own tormented visage transformed.

Daniel tended to hate in women their easy penchant for crying at every turn, but with Nona it was different. She rarely whined because the world wasn't treating her right; that was his department. It was always the wonder of life at which she wept. And she could usually sweep him up with her, which he was learning to love.

She brought her hands up to her mouth and laughed in her tears.

"Oh my God. Oh my God," was what kept replaying. "You have no idea how angry I was."

"I think I have some idea."

She laughed an embarrassed laugh. "Yeah, of course you do. And look at what you've done. You've turned all that darkness into—" Then suddenly she was on a new tack. "Wait, had you planned this all along?"

"Okay, look, before you go any further, no, I had not. I was just exactly the very prick you almost called me that morning. I just, I dunno—I had to redeem myself with you. And I had to do it with this photo. To spin something beautiful out of all the Hell you'd been through this past year."

When she turned to look at it again, he walked up behind her and looked over her shoulder, to stare with her, eventually wrapping his arms full around her, and hoping that this might symbolize the demise of an old year, an old hurt.

"I told you there was still beauty in that face," he spoke softly in her ear. "And that the power was all yours. And there it is."

"Brilliant," she barely whispered.

"Not brilliant. Simple."

The ball dropped in Times Square on the television behind them, and

Nona clung to Daniel's embrace, as she continued to lose herself in the landscape, which, for Daniel, was only the very wrapping of her excellent self.

TWENTY THREE

Gentry Hall was a fly in Nona's ear day and night now. She couldn't blame the woman's panic. The editor had approved an outline Nona submitted over a year ago, an extension of the "artist compelled" theme of *Champion*, and was understandably expecting to see something soon. She hadn't wanted Nona to veer too far from the concept that had been introduced in the first book because *Champion* was now regarded as a sort of self-help cult phenomenon for artists, which made Nona nuts to keep hearing, as she wanted so badly to believe she was edgier than that. But Gentry Hall and the higher-ups were angling for a chicken-soup-blah-blah-for-the-blah-blah-blah-soul kind of *blah* explosion. Sure. Whatever. At this point, Nona was past mourning the loss of anything organic in this business.

But then she'd had the most uproarious year: Rape, Africa, two incredible men coming into her life, and bringing this incredible project with them. And she simply couldn't engage. She tried, but all she kept coming up with was crap. Frankly, she had plenty organic going on right here with Daniel and Arthur.

These were the two most fascinating men she'd ever met, and this project of Daniel's was turning out to be so invigorating that she wanted to devote her entire days and nights to it. They were each a puzzle that she felt compelled and excited to figure out, and there was simply no inspiration left over for a new novel.

She moaned endlessly to Daniel about her dry spell and asked him if he would mind reading what she'd drafted so far and give her his honest feedback. He agreed in a sort of vague way, but she knew this project of his was all-consuming.

She and Arthur were currently being posed for a canvas. Daniel had mapped out a corner of his studio and had shoved everything aside, asking them both to stand against a wall. He had her leaning into a windowsill glancing outward, while Arthur sat in a chair almost against her but looking in the opposite direction. It was a composition that was intended to split the focal point from a natural center. Daniel then marked with chalk their exact poses and location so that everyday they could resume their places. He warned them to wear clothing they wouldn't mind losing to the paint, which had Nona envisioning him flailing paintbrushes around like some insane orchestra conductor.

Then one day he changed his mind and told them he'd rather they were nude. They posed for this particular canvas for weeks before he painted a single stroke. The daily routine became religious. Daniel would pace the room and study them. They were allowed to write if they wanted, even scribble on the wall near them, which one of them might periodically do, but they were always bound to return to their original poses. Then Daniel would creep over and caress Nona's head, or lean in to confer some furtive thing to Arthur, and the hushed mumbling would commence. Daniel played endless Maria Callas as he posed them, taking care in handling an arm here, a leg there, and then would lean back to assess, like some intense sculptor. The way he might stare at them for hours on end unnerved Nona at first, but Arthur had already retreated to his world and largely ignored Daniel's indulgent voyeurism. Tons of Polaroids were snapped for compositional study, and Daniel hung them everywhere.

When Daniel finally did get started, after weeks in this ritual, and to Nona's amazement, she discovered that she and Arthur weren't posing for a canvas at all. They *were* the canvas. As was the wall adjacent to them, the window she was glancing out of, the chair Arthur was sitting in.

After a warning that morning to "urinate now, or forever hold your piss," Daniel began flinging paint like a wild man, or meticulously applying it like a surgeon, depending on the time of day or the pot he'd smoked. He shoved the junk that surrounded them up against them and the wall in one tempestuous swoop. There were piles of paper, kindling, books, magazines, laundry, tubes of paint, unstretched canvases, a manikin's arm, or old album covers that littered and climbed up around them. Daniel painted on all of it, every scrap, every crevice, until an insane circus of colors blended the junk right into Arthur and Nona and beyond them, onto the wall. Their very naked bodies were painted on and became camouflaged in the landscape of junk and wall and window. If a portion of the wall was painted blue, so was an arm that might be leaned against it. If a nearby canvas was presently being bombarded with furious multicolor, the colors would extend beyond the edges of the canvas, onto the wall, or Arthur, or Nona. This was a more deranged offering than anything Nona had ever seen by Jackson Pollock.

This session took an unbroken eighteen hours, with Arthur and Nona never leaving their spot, perhaps allowed to stretch a leg or two, or periodically being fed pizza slices. Standing still that long was easily the most physically challenging thing Nona had ever encountered. A muscle in her calf knotted itself into a painful spasm at one point, and she had to excuse herself to everyone and pound it out with her fist. Her body screamed to move. Arthur appeared unusually unfazed by the constraints.

At the end of it all, Daniel set up his tripod, adjusted his light screens back and forth until they were just so, positioned lights, clicked meters beside each of their heads, and eventually started shooting his Hasselblad on the sight.

During this entire holy madness, holier than anything within the walls of a temple, Nona was given ample opportunity to ponder Daniel's old friend, and her new one. Arthur was the quintessential derelict, a venerated member of Bukowski's and Waits's L.A. Only minutes before she'd met him Daniel had quickly, in a whisper, informed her that Arthur shot heroin. It must've been some kind of warning; as in, *"Beware! This movie contains some violence and nudity."* But it wasn't until she and Arthur had begun to undress for this new creation, and she'd seen the dark track marks on his forearms, between his fingers and toes, his neck, everywhere, that she was truly faced with it. It frightened her.

Her own body contained a tattoo of the Hindu ohm symbol on the small of her back and a fairly intricate Marquesan tribal crawling up her left arm that she'd had done at Venice Beach. She couldn't even claim an adventure in the Marquesas Islands as her story behind it. Still, she'd always considered the tattoos her wild trophies of dissent. But she was a child. Here before her was true anarchy.

She couldn't help but surmise that Arthur's ease with sitting still all these hours, when she was restless and uncomfortable beyond measure, had to be from the years of drug use that rendered his body so adept at playing dead.

The better they got to know each other, the quicker she learned to recognize the floating absence that told her that Arthur had just fixed (which he clearly had to have done just before this particular eighteen-hour session), or the jittery constitution that told her he needed to. He never really spoke of his habit, but he also never tried to hide it. When Daniel wanted to photograph his arms, Arthur willingly stretched them forward before the request was even finished.

She knew there were those who would find it strange to claim, but she found Arthur to be purity. He hid nothing and was ashamed of nothing. Not like her, hiding the scars of her face and her soul, walking through her life like some shrouded Afghani woman, which she had certainly done for a long time after the rape. One could surely take a lesson from the naked being who stood before her with every scar of his incredibly difficult life bare for the world to judge. Arthur didn't care who judged him. And when she first saw those scars, she wanted to weep that he had chosen that path.

What she learned quickly about Arthur was that he had the hardest time reconciling God in his life. And he vented those frustrations every day that he breathed, pontificating constantly on either the utter myth or supreme truth of God, depending on his mood. And each extreme would only send him deeper into the forest of his conflict.

He was remarkably genteel of heart. Yes, his language was laced with loads of crude expletives at every waking moment, but she rather found that intoxicating. And the intent behind was never the instinct of hate nor the impulse of violence. The strangest of all wonders was that his crude language was often, and effortlessly, interwoven with some scholarly thing you would never expect to hear in the same sentence, and each was spoken with equal aplomb.

He loved his son, Lorca, more than anything in the world. Everything in Arthur's life, in fact, except for the heroin, which seemed to be for the purpose of nursing some terrible sore, was for that boy. Lorca lived with his mother, yet there was no more hands-on a father than Arthur.

Gnarly dreadlocks, slight lisp, and a ghastly melancholy behind hazel eyes made Arthur's a most alluring face. And like all men with alluring faces, who were always the first to point out some remarkable fascination in others that no one else could see, Arthur had stared into Nona's eyes the moment they'd met and had warned her that she could put a spell on the innocent with those eyes. Arthur's severe carriage, and blunt way with words toward a perfect stranger, spoke mountains about this tumultuous life. But Nona was the one under a spell, and eventually came to learn that there was nothing to be afraid of in Arthur Hughes Dufresne.

These were rich days, filled with the new company of thrilling artists and blossoming friendships and stimulating love affairs and the effort to create something great. She and Daniel only grew closer. She relished watching his genius blossom, and snuggled comfortably in the most exhilarating relationship she'd ever had. They finished each night of their lives with lovemaking and started each new day with some creative venture.

The only kink left, which was no small kink, was the book dilemma. She had been predictably stricken with the one-trick-pony syndrome. She didn't seem to have a second book in her, and was scared to death to let on to her editor. All she wanted to do was give everything to Arthur and Daniel. She wanted to write about their incredible lives, and tell her editor, *"Forget the outline I sent. Have I got a couple of compelling life stories for you!"* But Gentry Hall would only think her insane and drop her without a warning. And the woman would be right to do so.

As far as Nona knew, Daniel still hadn't read the pages she'd given him. And every day that she arrived at his studio and saw it still unopened on his worktable, the pang of rejection hit.

As did a long ago fantasy: Nona's mother had taken thirteen-year-old Nona to see the movie *Julia*, about the writer Lillian Hellman. Child Nona had never heard of Hellman or Dashiell Hammett, much less read them, but the scene that stole her heart was a moment where Dashiell reads a draft of something Lillian has written. Lillian trusts him because he is a fellow artist. Even at the age of thirteen, Nona couldn't have imagined Lillian giving a first draft, the most fragile of flowers, to a husband who was, say, a banker or a salesman, someone whose job it was *not* to probe and derail the literary conceit. The banker or salesman would simply say, *"I don't like it,"* or perhaps even, *"I don't get it."* But only when Dashiell says, *"it's crap!"* does it resonate with meaning for Lillian. She accepts his indictment because she knows that he recognizes what she is truly capable of. Indeed, he is utterly in love with and is carrying on the most torrid of affairs with what she is capable of. Would the banker or the salesman know what she was capable of?

Even at thirteen, Nona dreamed about how remarkable it would be to have the kind of love with someone where even their *"it's crap!"* was fortified with the richest of minerals, the most generous of gifts, the purest expression of love. She wondered with some longing that day, as young girls will, if there would ever be a Dashiell in her life. And today felt like a slap in the face of that fantasy.

Daniel had always been such a great listener and so genuinely compassionate about her dilemma that his strangely contradictory ignoring of her pages magnified even more. She knew he was entrenched in his project, and perhaps he was the type of artist who abandoned every other thing in his life until a piece was completed. But after months of having it sit on his worktable, she was baffled and irked.

"Do you ever plan on taking a look at my pages?" she asked, one night in bed. "Or should I just ask somebody else?"

"What?" he returned, puzzled.

"I don't understand why getting you to read this thing has been like pulling teeth. As much as you say you love my writing."

There suddenly came over his face a stunned take.

"And every time I see it lying there, untouched, I just…aagghhh! Maybe this wouldn't feel so dismissive if I thought you didn't think all that much of my writing in the first place. But after how you just go on and on and on about *Champion*, this feels like a cruel tease."

"Are you kidding me? I kinda have a lot on my plate right now."

"That's not it, Daniel, and you know it. You've always got a book going, even at your busiest. Even at your most insane. You're a man who can't NOT read. That's what I love best about you."

"Darlin'…"

"No, no, don't darling me. You're always going on about what an incredible writer I am, and yet I can't seem to bribe you to read a few measly pages. Are you just bullshitting me? Telling me you think I'm good when, really, you just could not give a shit?"

"God, no!" he burst back. "How can you think that? Christ, if you only realized how off base you are."

"Then tell me how off base I am. I mean, goddamn it, Daniel, I am miserable over this whole thing. I can't seem to get anything out that's good. I'm even halfway trying to find a way to manipulate the prose I'm writing for your project to be something I could possibly spin into a sequel to *Champion*, which—yuck!—a sequel is all my editor is interested in. And then, of course, the problem with that is that I don't like coming from such a calculated angle in the first place. I want our project to be our project, and my book to be its own thing. Except that all I seem to have in me these days is you guys. And I need your help to tell me if I have a prayer of writing anything other than my current Daniel/Arthur obsession. Because, I'm afraid I'm gonna lose my book deal. And I would never have inflicted this on you if I'd thought this would be such a hassle. Besides, I kinda thought, you know, how cool is this relationship between two artists who are deeply mired in each other's art? I mean, I know I'm a silly romantic, but I'm doing your project. And I don't mean that in a *'you owe me'* kind of way. Believe me, I'm honored to be a part. Look, I only asked you because I thought you loved my writing, and I could use the feedback. Tell me this isn't worth your time, and I won't ever inflict this on you again. Just don't play me, because I don't have time to waste."

"Don't play you? Bloody Hell, woman, slow the fuck down. There's no plot to undermine you—"

"Just don't keep telling me you love my writing!"

"I'd be a happier man if I didn't love your writing! All right? Does that do it for you?"

Silence suddenly blew in the door. It didn't belong here now. This was a fight between a man and a woman. Silence had no place.

What did he mean by THAT?

The puzzled female brow surely tipped it, for Daniel suddenly poured his own ire.

"I wish I hadn't been as affected by *Champion* as I was, all right? I'd be a less tormented human being today. That's for bloody sure. Don't you get it? This has nothing to do with me not loving your writing, or taking you for granted, or whatever ridiculous thing you've drummed up. I can't read what you write! There it is. Confessions of a coward. And I'm sorry that I wasn't upfront with you in the first place, and that I've given you the runaround, especially considering the time you've devoted to my thing. But, darlin', what you write flattens me. And d'you realize how difficult this is to even 'fess up to? I'm not sure I wanna know what's scribbled on those pages, wondering whose life is gonna be the parable this time. Because mine was with your last book. You didn't even know me, Nona, and your book managed to nail me. Fucking warts and all—"

As he stood there claiming that *Champion* had chillingly spelled out his life, she wondered if it could actually be true. Was there some cosmic force that had connected them long before they'd ever met? After all, this was Leviticus Rankin's grandson. Or did the tortured simply read their stumbles into every nook and cranny of every artistic work, as a simple matter of tortured course?

"—Only a great writer can be as lethal as you've been, and you're tormenting over whether you've still got it." He laughed. "I wish I had your dilemma—"

What the Hell is he talking about now?

"—So the Muse isn't working for you today," he continued. "How about this? She doesn't work for me most days of my life."

The king of self-pity pranced about the room, huffing and puffing. His art was really so extraordinary that she was baffled any human being could be as self-effacing as this man, who had critics and dealers buzzing like bees over his work.

"Okay, first of all you're insane about the Muse not working for you, but we'll get back to that. How exactly does my book flatten you, Daniel? Tell me. You say I wrote about your life, and you're right, because I wrote about a genius. So—what?—being a genius makes you miserable? Cuz—then—darlin'—I wish I had YOUR dilemma."

"Goddamn it, I'm not Champion, Nona! Don't you get that?"

He stared at her. Waiting to see if she really didn't get it? What was she supposed to be getting?

He continued his rant. "I orchestrate and manipulate my life every day in the pathetic hope that some tangible thing might spur me on toward something great. And the only thing I achieve instead is attaching myself, like a leech, to the greatness in others. Sound familiar? That's exactly what your Will Speck does. Even these—" Daniel spat, grabbing hold of several of his new canvases, "—these convolutions I have the nerve to call paintings. I told myself that if I could bring two great artists together to collaborate with me on some expression, then maybe there'd be a chance they would uplift me and make me rise to the occasion. Raise the bar for me. Christ, what do you think I fell in love with, Nona? A pretty face? A tight ass? Sweetie, if you hadn't been as brilliant as you are, I couldn't have given two shits about giving you the time of day. Love is not what I was after. I've been too fucking desperate in my life to contribute something of value before I die, to have time for that. You were gonna be great to fuck, sweetie, but never to love."

TWENTY FOUR

Now, *that* would've merited a slap.   That was easily as horrible as anything he'd ever uttered to Chelsea in their many fights.   And perhaps if he hadn't KO'd her so effectively, Nona might well have slapped him.   But all she did was stare, open-mouthed, floored by his easy knack for prickdom.

She wasn't the only one floored.   Daniel hadn't vented this kind of humiliation in years. He steeped in his fumes, though it was only at himself that he fumed, and pounded fists on a nearby table. At that, Nona headed for his worktable, snatched up her folder of pages, and went for the lift. It was all he could do to keep from falling apart at the prospect of her walking out on him again, this time perhaps for good.

"Nona. Nona. No, you don't understand what I'm saying," he said, beating her to the lift and holding out his hand for her to listen. "I do love you. That's just it. Whatever other idiotic thing I've just said, you must know that. What I was saying—God knows the last thing I wanted was to fall in love. My whole take on love was that it was the surest way to my demise.   And this, you have to understand, this is based on a whole ridiculous history that you don't even want to know about. But you caught me off guard by writing that book and then entering my life."

"You entered MY life," she bit.

"Yes, I did. You're right."

"I was minding my own business."

"Yeah, yeah, fair enough, fair enough. But when I did enter it, Nona, I fell. I fell so ridiculously hard that I couldn't keep from loving you if I tried. And believe me when I tell you, I did try. Because the last time I was in love was a very fucked-up time in my life."

She was hurt. He could see it in her face. No words he uttered were about to change that. But she was calm. Not like the searing inferno of her crass and errant lover.

"Tell me, Daniel, where does *'great to fuck, but never to love'* fall, in all this romantic professing?"

Only hearts that broken recalled every syllable and sigh like a dictograph.

"All I meant was that of course I was attracted to you. Of course I wanted to get you into bed. What bloke wouldn't? I just hadn't bargained on falling in love with you."

"Well, then, thank God for my brilliance, as you put it, or I wouldn't've stood a chance."

"No," he barely muttered, fearing that he was losing her. "That was just me being cruel."

"No, Daniel. That was you being honest."

"You want honest? Here it is. I loved *and* resented your talent. D'you remember your reaction when I snapped your photo that day? You said you hated that your most intimate self had been exposed. Well I, likewise, hated that you seemed to know every ugly blemish of my life's dynamic before you'd even met me, which is all right there in your book. You see? That's what I felt like. Like I was naked and found out. That's what your book did to me. It gave me away—"

"My book is fiction!"

"It's a fucking mirror! That's what a great writer does. And that's why I hated falling in love with you. It made me much more vulnerable than I have ever chosen to be with any woman." He laughed bitterly at his life. "And yet as much as I suffered by it, it was also exhilarating. I mean, to see words on a page portray the kind of internal compulsion that is everything we are made of. The woman behind all that...well, she must've been something amazing, I figured. And it turns out, she is. How do you not fall in love with her?"

She gazed at him, as he blocked the elevator like a spoiled child. It was a doleful gaze.

"What I said before is the truth, Nona. Love was not what I was after. But it found me anyway. Against all my best laid plans."

She stared at the lift just over his shoulder. Considering. He saw it in her eyes. Only then did he have the courage to walk away from the lift, giving her the way out, if it was to be. He'd made his closing argument; the rest was up to her. He wandered amid the debris of his flat with a nervous aimlessness. He couldn't look at her for some time. When he finally did, she still stared away.

"You left me once before," he tossed out, behind her. "And it nearly wrecked me."

No, *that* was his closing argument. Nice and manipulative. He wasn't about to play this game fairly.

She finally turned around, and he saw every thought and consideration clearly in her eyes. She knew he meant to hook her with that comment, and she could forgive him that, but probably not much more. She walked toward him and gently patted her hands against his chest, wearily leaning her head against him. His desperate arms wrapped themselves around her frame. He knew she wasn't happy. He knew there would be more days like this, and he knew she knew it too. But he'd meant what he said. He was here for the duration and would do everything in his power to throw less of his afflictions her way.

The next morning he sat up in bed, pensively, after a night of fitful dreaming. He stirred her too. She just sighed his way and rolled over to sleep more, but he was plagued. Was he chopping her down out of his own narcissistic wallowing? He had shoved Champion in her face, as though the fault were somehow hers that he had been so agonized by her fictitious artist. It was just that Nona Childe was a sorceress for certain, and his life was being mapped out daily by her magical arts. No matter. He couldn't keep letting that divide them. She was the real thing, and he needed to celebrate that, not use it against her. Especially since it was the very thing that had drawn him to her in the first place. She came too close to walking out of his life for a second time, and suddenly the thought brushed past him.

"Marry me."

She opened her eyes, shifted to sit up, with the look of first-morning fuzziness about her, and stared his way.

"What?"

"Whaddaya say?"

He smiled like that schoolboy he seemed to revisit a bit lately.

She pondered his question, his uncharacteristic buoyancy, especially first thing in the morning, and his ridiculous grin. Her eyes did that pull-open, struggle-&-adjust thing, as if she'd just been struck with a baseball bat.

"Could we maybe get some coffee first?" she spilled.

He blurted an obnoxious, knee-jerk laugh, probably trying too hard to "get" her playful comeback, because it didn't really sound all that playful. And suddenly he feared her barely courteous non sequitur.

"Daniel," she sighed.

Here it comes.

"Do you realize what you sound like, asking me to marry you after the fight we've had? I mean, it's only our first one."

"Second, actually."

"Oh...Yeah." She finally sat up. "Well, guess what? There will be others. You don't have to make up for every quarrel we ever have with such a grand gesture."

"This is not about what happened last night."

"Isn't it? Come on, then, why? I mean, your timing."

He'd often been accused of burying troubles with romance. When life gets too creepy, just fall into bed and forget the whole thing. But he was showing her that he wasn't nearly as shallow as that. He wasn't trying to seduce her. He was making a commitment to her. And for just one second he suffered the pang of a miserable flashback. It was, after all, his second proposal this lifetime, wasn't it? Yet all he had to do was to look in her eyes to remind him that this woman was no Chelsea. This woman celebrated life, and might help him to do the same. She was his certain salvation.

"What are you afraid of?" he asked.

"Daniel, I can't pretend it hasn't run through my mind. Of course it runs through my mind. I love you. I think we have this remarkable thing. It's just—"

Christ, is she turning me down? No, no, no, keep on the remarkable tack!

"—marriage isn't meant to be used as a refuge from the world. Whatever problems we may ever have are not gonna get fixed just by saying *I do.*"

"I want to spend the rest of my life with you, Nona."

He saw a softening of her eyes at the pronouncement. He got the feeling no one had ever said those words to her.

"I want that, too," she said, but in that manner that almost begs a way out.

What was she trying to do to him? He knew she loved him. Why then was this proposal so inconsiderable for her? Had it to do with the rape? Didn't she know by now that she could trust him to protect her? To celebrate her?

Oh, who was he kidding? He realized the second those words spilled from his thoughts that he was unprepared to offer her his unchafed self. Last night had certainly been no shining example of a nurturing lover.

But diving into the deep end of domesticity was sure to drown out the screaming phantoms in his head. Didn't she realize that? His happiness relied on her — his ability to paint — escaping the dungeon of his mad head — becoming a less ornery creature — all of these would rely on her. Otherwise, he was certain to slip into the musty well of cantankerousness, which had been quickly becoming his lot before he'd met her.

"You have to say yes, love."

TWENTY FIVE

As if the crucial part of our lives begins the day we're married, Nona's and Daniel's started with a bang, on the morning after their wedding night, which incidentally was not the wedding night his bride had assuredly awaited all her life.

Daniel had successfully convinced her that they were made for each other, that art was their whole lives, and he'd asked her how many couples could claim sharing that. He had painted a glorious picture of traveling the world and experiencing new horizons together, painting and writing everything they encountered like two unstoppable forces of nature. They'd be Tracy & Hepburn, Rivera & Kahlo, Hammett & Hellman, take your pick. They'd live rich lives, create always, and love each other with a vengeance. He knew he could reel her in with that one, because she was a sucker for a romantic play.

And his way of thanking her for finally saying yes was to be a drunken groom.

They'd all consumed their fair share of alcohol at the reception, but Daniel's consumption was award-winning. The truth was, Daniel Cross drank too much. Always had. He came from a family of drinkers. Franklin and Camilla Cross had imbibed from morning until night for as long as he could remember, and by the ripe old age of twelve, he, himself, was appreciating the bouquet of a good, stiff ale.

Nona had to pour him into bed, cummerbund turned backwards, bow tie long lost, morning coat in much need of repair before returning it to the rental shop, and body and mind wasted beyond reform. He vaguely recalled her pulling the covers back on her king-sized bed, which was now their king-sized bed, in that master bedroom of hers, which was now their master bedroom, and feeling guilty about living in that kind of luxury, which Nona never considered especially opulent, but then she grew up in the tidy Santa Monica Mountains and went to high school with future movie stars. She would never know what it was like to call Bromley Hall her home. Or what it meant to have her family name emblazoned on the official homeless registry. Or to have to stand in a soup line for a meal.

It had never even entered his mind that the most logical place for them to live, now that they were married, would be her ocean-viewed sprawl. Moving into his downtown flat was out of the question. That place was a Hellhole. And he could never get work accomplished in that scenario besides. Her suggestion for them to live in her home yet still keep up the rent on the Santee flat and use it only as Daniel's workspace was ideal, but it so unsettled him that she and he would have essentially two homes at their disposal, one of which was a two-story, four-bedroom, sunlit confection, with a koi pond, a wine cellar, an office for her and two guest bedrooms. Christ, who the fuck invented that concept? Guest bedroom? He wanted to say, *"Hey, love of my life, Arthur lives alone in a goddamned hole on Figueroa. Let's give him a guest bedroom, shall we?"* Or, *"Your best friend, Kai, just had her apartment turned into a condo, and she's crying the blues over having to move and deal with another first and last and security deposit. Why isn't she being offered one of the guest bedrooms?"*

His mind flooded itself with the above drunken clutter the minute Nona helped him into bed. And it was some pretty ill-tempered pondering, which he tended to acquire when he was pissed. Nona was the most giving woman he'd ever known, and if any one of those people, plus a thousand more, ever came to her door weeping, she'd welcome them with open arms. Who was he to suggest that she should go out there in the world and be everyone's savior just because she had means? They were her means, hard-earned.

And he knew this house wasn't just a house. It was her family home. It contained her lifetime memories. She clung to it out of familial ties, not material ones. There was actually nothing in her entire existence that disgusted him, yet he found himself blathering on, in his slurred stupor, about conspicuous consumption, and how vile it was that they'd spent so many thousands of dollars on a wedding, and poor little rich kids *this*, and he didn't want to play that game, and they could suck his cock *that*, and how out of touch the wealthy were with the rest of the world.

"Of course, you are the exception, my darling," he'd slobbered patronizingly. He was, frankly, surprised she didn't leave him that second.

Daniel could be so easily soured when he was drunk. Even easier soured when money was the topic. His parents had crapped theirs away so early in the game that they were either homeless, living at Aunt Beryl's, or holed up at the dubious Bromley Hall. He had never known any other life back in England and hadn't really known much better on this side of the pond until his recent spate of career ascension, which he also knew could be snatched from him at any moment.

There was just something bitter tasting about being suddenly cozy and comfortable. And the newly marrieds were comfortable for sure. Nona had a bestseller under her belt, and a substantial advance on her second book. And Daniel's own work had officially moved itself, due to his catalogue and LACMA future, into the five-digit bracket. A very renowned filmmaker was now the proud owner of a Cross original. It seemed to be some insane throwback to the Reagan eighties, when art was selling for ridiculous amounts of money. And Daniel couldn't even bother to care.

He had wanted so badly to make love to his wife on their wedding night, yet all he did instead was slug into bed. He sweated so horribly from the booze that he soaked the sheets and Nona ended up sleeping in one of the guest bedrooms. *Ah, so that's what guest bedrooms are for — for the event of drunken husbands.*

He awakened to the shaft of daylight shooting through the window. He thought to himself how violent the morning was, not to courteously creep upon him, until he realized that morning was not the villain. The clock on the wall said four p.m. and his mind said *bloody-fucking-Hell!* Legs and lower back ached horribly, head spun like a top, and there was a damp cloth lying tossed beside him, evidently placed on his forehead during his unconsciousness by his bride.

He arose and tiptoed cautiously down the staircase, looking everywhere for Nona, though he couldn't really call out her name without too much pounding misery. He heedfully floated through each room, unsuccessfully searching her out.

After several painful minutes, it became evident that he was alone. The house was still and perfect. She had worked hard to make these walls and the contents therein work for her, state her, be there for her when the world got complicated. This place was her sanctuary, her calming haven in which to retreat when the chaos outside grew great, and which painted itself familiar with all her markings. The art on the walls. The books on the shelves. Her Turkish rugs and Moroccan hallway tiles. Even her Hallet & Davis grand piano that sat in the picture window alcove, and where she would periodically sit, and lay her hands on the keys, and close her eyes, and pretend to be her mother.

"If I put this thing in the *Recycler* for free no one would answer the ad," she would tease. "It isn't worth much. It's certainly no Bösendorfer. But it's my mother's, and I'll always treasure it."

He remembered smiling secretly when she'd said that. She could've said *it's no Steinway* in making her joke, but she didn't. She recalled a piano that was an intimate character from Daniel's past, and she didn't even know it.

So the story goes that a Bösendorfer had once been purchased from a celebrated opera singer by Daniel's great-grandfather for his great-grandmother, who, herself, had been a gifted coloratura. Why it ever got handed down to Daniel's irreverent mother he would never understand. Camilla Cross never held anything precious in her life except a bottle of rye. And sure enough, Daniel's great-grandmother's Bösendorfer was turned over to their landlord, in remittance for past rents, who surely turned around and sold it for his own ticket out of Hell.

Nona didn't play, but Daniel understood her love for the heirloom, though the instrument itself was a rickety old box that couldn't hold a tuning. She would tell him that she could hear her mother's voice in the resonant timbre of a note struck. Whose voice would he hear had he the means to strike a key on Anna Rankin's Bösendorfer?

He looked around the house, which held all of Nona's past in it, and envied her still-intact link to Childe history. He knew nothing at all about the Rankins or the Crosses except that Franklin Cross once asked Camilla Rankin to marry him, and from that union were born two boys, Duncan and Daniel, and they'd pretty much hated each other ever since.

He sat down at Nona's piano, hangover ripping through him, and lowered his head onto the keys, begging his headache to go away. A soft drone that was oddly comforting, cocooning, vibrated the piano, and he wondered where his wife was. *My wife.* He might've remembered nothing much fond about the Rankins or the Crosses, but he had a new family now. Nona was all the family he would ever need, if she hadn't already left him for being a drunken sot.

Suddenly he heard her car in the driveway, and seconds later the front door burst opened, and his agitated bride startled him as much as he startled her. She agitatedly flung her purse onto the nearby sofa.

"What's the matter?" he asked, though his headache begged for quiet.

"I just came from Arthur's. God, I thought he was dying—I mean— on the phone he, he sounded so—and, and—"

She was hysterical. Or else his hangover made it all seem the more befuddled. He could only make out that she'd finally experienced an Arthur Heroin Episode. He had spun every wheel possible to keep her from ever witnessing such, but day-in, day-out contact brings inevitability.

"It's all right. Everything's gonna be all right."

Why did people always promise that, he suddenly wondered, feeling insufficient to comfort her?

"He called this morning. But I told him you were asleep—"

She was too polite to say *"out cold."*

"—I asked him the matter and offered to help. But he said no thanks, that he needed you. And when I told him that wasn't, um, uh, possible—"

Bless her heart.

"—he slammed the phone down, which scared me so badly that I just grabbed my keys and drove over there."

Some honeymoon morning, she must've been thinking. Here she should be toasting over Kir Royales and Eggs Florentine with her new husband, who shouldn't be out cold from alcohol poisoning. Instead she's running to the rescue of her husband's equally fucked-up friend, never even realizing that she's about to walk in on her first dope fix.

"I didn't even knock, you know, because he just sounded so frantic on the phone," she stumbled in hysterics. "I didn't know what was wrong. I thought he was having a heart attack or something, and I just thought—I don't know what I thought. He just—he sounded like he was dying! It never even entered my mind that it—oh God, I feel like an idiot!"

"Sshhh. You're not an idiot," he said, holding her at her mother's piano. But she wouldn't be held long. She was wired, fidgety, repeatedly wiping her palms on her sweat pants, and struggling to process all that had unfolded.

TWENTY SIX

Arthur lived above Greater Faithful Baptist Church, a tiny storefront on the corner of Figueroa and Martin Luther King Jr. Boulevard in South Central Los Angeles. The sturdy working class lived in this part of town. So did crack whores and gang thugs. The urban decay was even worse the further south and east you got, but Exposition Park was the beginning of it, even while, with great, beautiful, perverse irony, housing the largest complex of educational museums the city boasted and one of the richest universities in the country.

It being Sunday, Nona circled the block several frustrated times before she could find parking. Hastening up the street to where women in white frocks and men in dark suits littered the sidewalk outside of Greater Faithful, she pardoned her way through the crowd and entered the side door, which lead upstairs.

She found Arthur's door opened to a tiny sliver and bounded into his one-room apartment to find him and another man cooking up heroin on the coffee table. She assumed it was heroin, since that was Arthur's particular habit, but she'd never seen anything like it before, other than in movies.

She fell back against the door startled, both men instantly shooting looks her way.

"Shit, girl, get the fuck out!" Arthur yelled, in a voice that didn't belong to him. He was sweaty and lit. "What the fuck!"

"Man, what is this shit?" bit the other one, a jogging-suit-clad gentleman who donned a crisp Lakers cap.

"Ignore her, man, she's just family. Get the fuck out, Nona!"

She could only whimper a traumatized *no* but nothing more, because she was afraid of this other man, whoever he was, and knew that he would not be patient with the pleadings of some bitch, which surely, to him, she was.

Poetic, she thought, that Arthur could call her family even as he was violently yelling at her to *"get the fuck out!"* But he could barely keep to the business of getting her out, so intent was he on this other business of cooking up his white powder in his little spoon.

He began tightening a surgical tube around his arm, fumbling agitatedly and yanking one end with his teeth. All she could do was remain glued to the far wall beside the front door. The reality of what she was witnessing socked her with its fist, and she felt her armpits moisten and her skin pimple, as she watched him fill up a hypodermic with the newly viscous fluid. Her presence was instantly forgotten.

He then found a vein, closed his eyes, and mainlined.

She stared at the hypodermic as though it were the only thing in the room. Her head cocked to one side in a pointed glare to see Arthur's dark blood slowly swoosh and dance with the deadly liquor. The red and clear mixed and swirled together inside that tiny plastic vial with a movement that could almost be called sensual, if one could be aroused by such things. But she felt as though her very spirit had just been emptied from her.

Even as she stood presently in her own living room, hours later, safe, away from that oddly stirring horror, and facing her new husband who had vowed to love, cherish, and protect her, she felt the spirit pour from her again.

"And then the guy in the Lakers cap grabbed a wad of bills from the coffee table, said his little business goodbye to Arthur, who was already way gone by that point, and left. Didn't even look my way. And then there was just Art and me. Alone in that room. And everything that had been a fucking frenzy only seconds before was this instant silence and stillness. And I just stood there. I couldn't move. I just stared at this stranger, whose body may've been in that room with me, but the rest of him was somewhere else."

She looked Daniel's way, but he offered nothing. He looked as shaken as she felt. Yes, she had known from the beginning that Arthur was a user, but the Arthur she had come to know was a quiet spirit who wrote words like Byron, loved his son, and possessed an infectious smile. The Arthur she had come to know would, on a moment's whim, gather everyone in the room and head them all down to the Watts Towers at midnight, because it was religion to him. To breathe in the power of that artful monument, in the middle of that ravaged neighborhood, during the pitch hours when the gang roaches were crawling on every corner. Because, for Arthur, it wasn't about seeing the intricate mosaic of tiles and bric-a-brac. It was about connecting to its sweat and blood, heart valve to heart valve. The Arthur she knew was, in spite of his particular affliction, the absolute affirmation of beauty and life.

But this morning's witness, whether she liked it or not, was the hidden ritual that had been commanding his other life for years, a life that few had ever been allowed to see.

Time felt dead. Not only as she spoke to her husband presently, but at that earlier moment, standing in Arthur's apartment and watching him, unable to move from her spot.

She was back there again, with her sweaty palms plastered to Arthur's walls for what seemed a sentenced eternity. At that sweaty moment, she began faintly hearing the muffled thump of pious revelry in the storefront church below, and the sermonizing of its preacher, whose alluring voice mountained and valleyed as it sailed through dead air. A warmly familiar remembrance from childhood. An organ revved beneath tambourines, and clapping hands, and the foot-stomping and joyful noise of a woman feeling the spirit of the Lord, which only aroused the preacher to greater volume and the congregation to wilder pandemonium. It fed on itself, which had always been her fascination as a girl. And then the swell of a choir sprayed the air with a rapturous plea that sent a creeping hand up her spine.

She squeezed her eyes as tightly shut as she could manage without bursting a vein when the words of their gospel, calling for Heaven and having no further use for this world, a hymn known to her from her own girlhood churchgoing, began to fill up her ears.

She wondered if Arthur wasn't hearing them too and perhaps whispering a secret *"amen."* Had he done it? Achieved Heaven? With his head bobbing, and his mouth slobbering and crusty, and his nose running, and his eyes empty and lost?

She wasn't sure how many minutes — hours? — had passed by the time the hum from the church dissolved into the gentle murmur of a congregation dispersing, but silence had again permeated the room, and Arthur finally looked her way.

The world spun fast on its heels and swirled around them in a dizzying, neon flurry, when she suddenly met the leopard's eyes and they sharply gleaned each other's wit.

"You shoon be 'ere, Li'l Wing," he slurred in a stuporous fog, consonants barely consonants. The only comfort that was strong enough to step out from the fear was hearing the familiar way he had nicknamed her Little Wing, after the Hendrix tune. It was a balm.

"Nona," Daniel's voice suddenly interrupted.

Another balm.

"I'm so sorry you had to see that."

As she came out of her reverie and stared at her husband, it suddenly dawned on her that Daniel was someone who aided Arthur in his desperate moments.

Before she could allow him to continue, she bit, "No!"

She shoved a finger in her new husband's face, as he battled a stupendous hangover.

"Why was he calling you, anyway, Daniel? What exactly was he looking for? Do you give him money for his habit? Or maybe you just buy the stuff for him. Or do you actually give him the injection? Cuz he looked like he was pretty accustomed to having some help."

She practically demanded to see Daniel's arms, until she realized that she was losing her mind to have completely abandoned all faith in the man she'd married less than twenty-four hours ago.

"All right, calm down," he finally uttered, jumping in and inserting a rebuttal into the one-second space of silence she'd been kind enough to allow him. "First of all, do you have any idea what happens if a man who needs heroin can't get it? I'm just there—obviously when I'm more capable—to make sure no cars get stolen and no houses get broken into."

She recoiled at this picture Daniel was painting.

"Nona, he is the same man today you've known all along," he pled passionately, if quietly. "Capable of the most incredibly loving deeds. It's the heroin that's a different animal. But you might as well know what IT is capable of. All right? I am his friend—"

She shook her head in determined denial.

"Listen to me, Nona, I am his friend—"

"Then stop! Stop helping him!"

"Do you want him to mug some old lady? He'll do it! D'you

understand me?"

Her mouth fell open with a dead thud, like Rod Steiger's silent cry in *The Pawnbroker*. Daniel's hands came up to hold her shoulders.

"Nona."

She got up and moved away from Daniel, shaken at what she was being asked to envision.

"Listen, I know you don't wanna hear this, but you have to know. For the most part, he's pretty good at getting what he needs. The stuff he publishes gives him some income, and he always keeps an odd job here and there, but once in awhile he just finds himself with no means till the next check comes in, and if he can't get what he needs a fucking monster comes out, you can be sure."

"How can he live that way?"

"He just does. All right? People do it all the time. I realize not in your world—"

What the fuck does that mean? Nona's face betrayed her wound.

"I'm sorry—I'm not trying to suggest—look, that's just the life of a junkie, all right? Don't you think that in nearly twenty years of knowing him I haven't already exhausted every effort to shake some sense into him? It's so much deeper than you or I can ever know."

And though she heard these words clearly, something told her that Daniel knew just exactly how deep that wound was, to the inch, but would not give it. Meanwhile, she searched foolishly for the win to this argument, for a way to rescue Arthur from himself. They both loved him, but Daniel had long ago resolved his feelings on the subject; hers were just beginning.

"If you can't accept what he is, Nona, if you choose not to be a part of his life, I respect that. He'll even respect that. But I have chosen to be a part of his life. He's my friend. He's more than a friend. He's…he's my brother. If I can't offer him health, I can at least offer him sanctuary. I can keep him from lashing out at the world."

"But, but, I mean—" she stuttered, "—what if you simply said no? What if you just weren't there for him one day? Like today. At least you didn't contribute to the awful fucking thing this morning."

"And he found the means anyway, didn't he?"

"Yes, but at least you weren't a part of it."

"Well, bully for me. Now I can live with myself, can't I? I can sleep at night with a clear conscience. And Arthur's still a junkie. What's important here? My salvation? Or his?"

Everything drained from her as she realized there was no win to this argument. To even call what they were doing an argument didn't fit, since they were on the same side of this thing.

"We can't save him, Nona," Daniel uttered. "We can only help make life a little more bearable for all involved. If we suddenly start this campaign to try and get him to kick, he'll only pick up and disappear from our lives."

She glared numbly at the floor, and was suddenly aware of what she looked like. Wrapped from head to toe in flannel sweat pants, an oversized sweater, and her winter mukluks with the pant legs haphazardly tucked half in, half out, face cold and clammy, mouth sour, crust in the corners of her eyes, hands shaking like an alcoholic's. She didn't want to hear anymore, but Daniel would continue.

"He is the same man today that you knew and loved yesterday, Nona. What you saw this morning happens every morning of his life, more or less. No tragedy has occurred today that hadn't already been set in place years ago. And yet he still smiles. And loves Lorca. And writes glorious words. And is awed at the beauty of life. And has valiant integrity. All of those things we've loved about him are still him."

As he spoke, he held his temples and rubbed them to battle his hangover. He was really in no condition to deal with a traumatized bride. Yet he'd done so, or had at least tried. She could see that. And appreciated it. Sort of. But a melancholy had struck her, rendering her incapable of much else. She walked upstairs during his monologue, defeated. There really was no more he could offer.

"Nona..............Nona...............Nona........."

She left him behind, as she closed herself in their bedroom, pulled the covers back on their bed, and climbed inside. She wept and stayed bundled for days. Like someone in mourning.

TWENTY SEVEN

For the next eight days Nona hibernated, but Daniel could never tell Arthur that. His new bride and dearest brother had gone a bitter round in a chapter out of life's melodrama they could've done without, while he'd been busy sleeping off a good one.

"She okay?" Arthur asked the following day at the Santee flat, hoping Nona wouldn't be there, and profusely begging Daniel's forgiveness for having ever subjected her to any of it.

"Well, I mean, Art, she was gonna have to face it some day, right?"

Daniel hated every part of it, but he knew Arthur already knew that. It was time to move forward.

During Nona's hibernation, Daniel told Arthur that she was under the weather and wouldn't be joining them for a bit. He doubted Arthur believed him, but Arthur didn't challenge him on it, and they ended up having their most intense sessions yet.

On one remarkable night's session, Arthur rambled on in that stream-of-consciousness way that always knocked Daniel on his ass. Arthur brought no notebooks to scribble words or ideas on, as he usually did. This wasn't for that. He simply paced the floor while Daniel worked on a mural-sized canvas and talked as though no one was in the room but him.

Nothing was terribly coherent. It was mainly a soliloquy of mumbles, like something you'd hear from the homeless bloke who hangs out in front of the local liquor store. Except that every once in awhile Daniel would catch words like *penance* and *purging* and *sangfroid* and vague utterances about the ugliness of syringe to vein, and never wanting Nona to be so chilled. At one juncture Arthur almost broke down. Daniel knew he needed to get the Hell gone soon and to his fix.

If only there'd been a way to package that wave and place it in the center of what they were creating. It was powerful. He then suddenly jolted himself with disgust at his instinct to regard Arthur's struggle as

THE ASSASSINATION OF GABRIEL CHAMPION 175

garden fodder. At that point, it was time to pack it in for the night.

Every evening at home, during the hibernation week, Daniel held Nona as tenderly as he was capable. They'd curl up in front of the television. They'd cook. She never left the house. And all along, Daniel wondered if the day would ever come for her and Arthur to face each other again, or if that fateful morning had marked the end for them. These two people whom Daniel loved the most seemed to have a penchant for landing on opposite ends of some insane teeter-totter, and it would seem that he was the faulted link.

He tried to assure Arthur that Nona hadn't been traumatized, only slightly shaken, but if Arthur could see her now he'd know differently. Daniel simply did not want to invite the notion that Arthur had once again wrecked a woman, because if Arthur kept that one in his brain long enough it would kill him. What Daniel wanted to say was, *"Hey mate, Nona was not the victim here. She was just the unfortunate witness to the pillaging you commit on yourself every day."* Frankly, he was just too weary to go there.

Instead Daniel offered, "Hey, mate, don't worry. She'll get past it."

On day-eight of this hibernation, he came home from a chain-smoked evening of painting and scrapping. Nothing had worked on this particular evening, as his huge garbage bins quickly got filled with the remnants of his flustered head, or his canvases got re-covered with a gesso primer. When he walked in the front door, he found Nona standing at the floor-to-ceiling picture window, wine glass in hand, television blaring yet being paid no mind, and her with a fidgety energy he thought he might never see again. It wasn't the zombie that had been floating from kitchen to living room to bedroom for the past eight days, but it was definitely an IT. As she paced the hardwood floors, hers was the next stream-of-consciousness he got to witness.

"I've never seen anything my whole life," she ranted, without even a hello. "Shit goes on in this world every fucking day, and it's way beyond me. Even my sister's had more life experiences than me. My *little* sister, who had to orchestrate and walk me through my own trials, who had life lessons to offer *me*. Not the other way around. How pathetic is that? You know what's hilarious? Look at what a joke even this rape thing has turned out to be."

"A joke? Nona, please—"

"Are you kidding me? I've been so goddamned sheltered my whole life that I've even been sheltered from that. My mind's a total blank on the subject. How perfectly convenient!"

"Nona, you know better than that. Your mind's not a blank because you've been protected and pampered by some kind of cosmic silver spoon, or whatever you've conjured up. Your mind's a blank because there's been trauma and repression. I hardly call that being sheltered."

"Yeah, whatever. Well, guess what? I welcome what I saw the other day at Arthur's place. I refuse to let it take me under. This is life! Goddamn it! Of which I have to periodically remind myself, THE WRITER. God, what a joke! That I even call myself a writer when this can shock the shit outta me and lay me out for days! How did I get so fucking fragile? Well, it's time the naïve little girl grew up, don't you think? Time that I actually lived a life that informs my art? Gee, what a concept!"

She looked at him in an exhausted finale to her soliloquy.

"Don't do this," he whispered.

"Do what?" she bit, still pacing.

"To belittle your writing is to belittle everyone who was ever moved by it," he tried to offer. "You're right, what you saw the other morning happens all over the world, along with all the other crises of the human condition. But don't crucify yourself because you weren't so wise as to be callous to it. Don't resent your life because it's been a good one and with a minimum of quandaries. Thank your lucky stars for that."

She stared at him, searching desperately for her solid ground, wondering if it existed in the fortunate life she'd led, or in the gritty life she was feeling she should've led. She used to say to him, "no one would ever write my life story, cuz it would be a book of blank pages," then snore sarcastically and laugh. She was feeling fairly insignificant right about now. She was anything but, though you couldn't tell her that today.

"Is Arthur okay?" she asked, giving up the volley.

"Yes. Are you?"

"Yeah. Sure."

Daniel could only cock his head in exhaustion from the web he'd spun. He could now count on his wife to lie and hide and self-berate. She used to ask him constantly why he never kept a diary. She would say that diaries were the healers of man's wounds and that his own tortured artist self might benefit from being able to write 'fuck the world' on a page once in awhile.

"Words are your thing," he remembered telling her when she tried to sell him on the idea. "If painting can't get out all I need it to get out, then I've no business doing it."

"You know the funny thing about art, though?" she'd given back. He remembered loving that she was about to give him some freshly scrubbed pearl. "The offering isn't only to serve the taker, Daniel, but the giver, as well. You're the most gifted painter I know living today. You serve me, and everyone who knows your art, abundantly. But I don't think painting has served you. You're so busy feeding everyone else that you forget to allow it to bring you joy." Or something like.

The woman who once uttered that sentiment was the woman who used to get aroused by the mere contemplation of beauty. She smiled most days and was charmed by his brooding artist temperament, but wanted to save him, anyway, and pull him up there with her to utopia. That was the old Nona.

Live in the company of Daniel Cross for a solid year and you, too, can trade in your bliss for a life wrinkle-browed and tormented.

As he watched her pace the floor this day, having emerged from an eight-day gloom, deriding everything she'd ever written and sounding a little too frighteningly like him, he thought to himself, *Great, Daniel, maybe you do need to keep a diary. So you can give yourself some ease, and so you can push that vibrant woman back up there where she was when you met her.*

TWENTY EIGHT

When she'd asked Daniel why he hadn't arranged to have his parents flown in from London for their wedding, he'd tossed off rather evasively that there was no relationship left between them, which was why he'd left England in the first place. So it seemed that she was likely never to meet Daniel's mother, Camilla, the only daughter of Leviticus Rankin; or his father, Franklin, a publican from the East End. Nona had only heard bits and pieces. Bits and pieces, it seemed, was all she'd ever learn.

They had taken their vows in a peaceful ceremony in her own mother and father's backyard, waves crashing below them on a perfectly sun-drenched spring day, the scent of snapdragons and peonies in the air, all their loved ones in attendance, including the very special surprise of Thembi and William, all the way from Nigeria, who'd brought with them white Kanga silk for Nona to wear on her bridal day.

Every word uttered from the Justice's mouth stamped boldly on Nona's chest. She was not only vowing her earthly life to Daniel, body and soul, she was vowing it in the witness of God and State. She was promising to have and to hold, from that day forward, and to be had and held; to forsake all others in the good times and the bad; to be there for each other, no matter how bad the shit got. And it was up to her and Daniel to make sure it didn't get rank.

She'd known there would be much turbulence in a future with this man. Their relationship was sure to be one herky-jerky roller coaster ride of unbelievable highs and challenging lows. Frankly, it's what had always been most thrilling about him. If only Daniel's failure to read her new pages had been the worst thing she could expect. And in less than twelve hours after they'd said "I do," she had definitely gotten her first hint that it wouldn't even remotely be.

Between her new husband and his dearest friend, she had her hands full. After that fateful Arthur morning, she had, at first, feared she'd been shoved dangerously toward some sort of breakdown. Then she woke up. She knew that things in her life would have to change if she was truly going to be the artist she wanted to be. She had to decide if these two galvanizing men in her life were going to be her madness or her salvation. And she gullibly believed that the answer was as simple as merely picking one. Instead, over the next few months, she found herself floating in between those two potentials in a kind of delirious, nausea-spurring limbo.

She and Arthur had made their peace only shortly after the incident, as though there were really any to make. It happened one night at Santee about a week and a half later. Arthur walked in the room, and Daniel left immediately to give them privacy, though it hadn't been necessary. No words were spoken; the apology from both implied. They simply hugged. But from that day forward, whenever Arthur's eyes locked with hers, there was a new intimacy between them. She had seen his most private act. She felt like the dirty adulteress, and he her guilty lover.

It also did something else very interesting; it began to shift her fascination. Daniel had always been a gorgeous intrigue, dominating the pages of her diary for more than a year now; she would certainly use a lot of that for this project. But it was Arthur who began to change her and make her see the world differently. From that fateful morning on, he had lodged himself squarely between her eyes.

Daniel had named the project *Murmuration*, and during the months of creating for the series, Nona ended up writing volumes about Arthur's heroin use. She couldn't dump words onto paper fast enough to keep up with everything that was reeling in her head. And Arthur didn't seem to care that his gnarled life might possibly end up spread out for the world to scrutinize next to some abstract conjuring of Daniel's in some art gallery. One would almost swear that he invited public flogging. He seemed to live to pay penance for a regretful life.

When it hit her one day how exploitive this felt, she tried to change her mind about using what she'd written, but he wouldn't let her.

"The world is an artist's canvas. And I'm a part'a this world."

Arthur saw himself as a lesson to be learned. There seemed to be absolutely no ego involved. And she flashed with a moment's shame on her reactive explosion to the photo that Daniel had snapped of her that day in his loft, almost a year ago now, when her face was still healing and she was hiding from the world. The one Daniel ultimately transformed into a breathtaking landscape. She realized just how much babysitting she needed, and just how high the people in her life seemed willing to jump to appease the baby. There were lessons to be learned from Arthur Hughes Dufresne, to be sure, and she was eating it up as if she'd been starved for thirty-three years.

What was exhilarating to her was that this man could routinely spend a night in Parker Center or the Van Nuys station if he was found holding, or he could be discovered in front of his apartment stoop passed out and foaming at the mouth, like all the winos stepped over with disgust. Yet it never stopped people from loving the work of this underground enigma, or following him around town to hear him read in a coffeehouse somewhere. He riveted people, and perhaps even more so because he was such a bleak presence.

Arthur was already a published poet, with a good couple of hundred pieces over a thirty-year span littering the market of journals and quarterlies and chapbooks. His first published poem was a contest winner in a local Inglewood periodical, and was on a page of its own right next to a Ralph Ellison byline. 1967. After that, he served a short tour of duty in Viet Nam; came back a heroin addict; wrote for the Black Panthers's L.A. branch pamphlet in between gun-running in his '62 Buick from their 103rd & Grape Street headquarters; ran for L.A.'s ninth-district council seat in '79; and lived, for a brief time, on Alice Coltrane's ashram in the Topanga mountains. He was fifty-something years old, but would never say exactly. Nona got the feeling he wasn't sure himself. This was the poet she knew as Arthur Hughes Dufresne.

He had always survived by his wits, though she'd often wondered how, knowing the life he'd led. Now, after seeing him disappear from the world as effortlessly as he had that day in his apartment, after watching his spirit literally lift itself out of his body and float away, only to return later, but always forever changed, she knew exactly how. On the page, he was slowly becoming an epic.

Murmuration's catalogue was slated to hit the LACMA gift shop, followed by the major retailers, in about sixteen months, to coincide with the Benton Gallery exhibit. Benton was the Museum's off-site experimental space, and was Harper's biggest triumph to date. Daniel's name in trendy, hi-tech splendor would emblazon the windows of Benton, with Nona's and Arthur's to follow. And monographs on them all would be available on parchment handouts upon first entering the exhibit.

Celebrated multi-media painter, Daniel Cross!
Bestselling author, Nona Childe!
Underground poet legend, Arthur Hughes Dufresne!

It was all a bit of slick Hollywood show, of which Daniel had absolutely no interest, but at which Harper was superb. Nona was accustomed to hype, having marketed her book all the way to the New York Times list.

They had a little over a year to get this thing completed, and she found herself overwhelmed. The writing she was doing for *Murmuration* was coming along. She didn't know if it was good, but it was at least pouring forth organically. Producing chapters for a new book was another story altogether. She had nothing. Only the scribbled head trip of a woman shaken by rape, newly driven by heroin witnesses, facing a spiritual awakening head on, and juggling frantic phone calls, faxes, and emails from her editor, politely demanding to see pages. She was also working nonstop with Harper on the publicity for *Murmuration*, and trying to nurture a fastidious temperamental-artist-of-a-husband to boot.

Many of hers and Arthur's pieces had already been submitted to the publisher and the lithographer, though they were still writing. The idea was to have passages mounted on a wall in bold typeface along with the canvases. And Daniel had employed Tariq, an old friend of his, to assist him in photographing the completed canvases, creating the transparencies to be deliverable to the publishers, and developing the film of his photographic works. Daniel's color plates were finally at the printers, and there was much business to assemble, from typeset approvals for the catalogue, to copyrights, to meetings with publishing house design consultants. And as much as Daniel preferred to hide under the table from these people, he couldn't let Harper do all the work if he wanted this project to be exactly as it should be. So for the next several months, he had to be the businessman, taking meeting after meeting and swimming in the headache of it all.

He proved no angel. He obsessively went back to change a canvas, here and there, over and over and over again, even though the color plates had already been completed. He complained in his meetings with Dugnac, and the County Museum people, and the underwriters, and the lawyers. He became a nightmare for the publishers, the sponsors, the lithographers. It was Harper, consummate businesswoman that she was, and in her natural element, who was Daniel's only hope for cutting the deals that could make him huge.

One day, about six months into this, Harper took him by the hand and got him on a plane to New York to personally meet with the publishers. Her agenda was to get them to reassure Daniel that his vision would never be compromised, and his agenda was to personally hand them new transparencies, along with his grocery list of printing demands, as if they could just effortlessly toss all prior costly work and start from scratch.

During the week that Daniel was gone, Nona realized that it was the first solitude she'd had for over a year. She always missed her husband whenever he wasn't immediately in the room with her, but there did seem to be a long, l o n g , L O N G breath exhaled when she waved goodbye to him from the airport window.

One evening over dinner at Nona's favorite Tibetan restaurant in Pasadena's Old Town, she had Kai begging her to spill more about Arthur. The two had barely spent any time together since the *Murmuration* project had gotten underway, and since Kai had also been busy launching another performance piece, this one a kind of sound sculpture installation at Union Station. Now that Nona had a week alone, she luxuriated in the company of her girlhood friend, and the buoyancy that always accompanied it.

"Oh God, that sound is in your voice," Nona teased with a groan, but knew she could never lead any girlfriend of hers to Arthur's slaughter. He would eat Kai alive without lifting a finger. They were a pretty pitiful pair of unworldly Black chicks, living behind the mask of having been around a block or two. If Kai knew half of what Nona knew about Arthur, she'd shiver and run home to her minister father.

"You don't want to get involved with Arthur. He's pretty dark."

"I like 'em dark," Kai purred with a wink.

Nona rolled her eyes. "I'm tellin' you. He scares the shit outta me half the time."

"Yeah, well, it's easy to scare the shit outta you, Little Miss Sheltered. If I recall correctly, the first time a boy slipped you the tongue you ran home thinkin' you were knocked up." Kai could barely spit it out for laughing. Nona laughed, too, but felt just the faintest sting from the Little Miss Sheltered comment.

"See, that's what growing up in tidy Ronald Reagan Land will do to you," Kai resumed. "Now if you had come from Compton like me, o-KAY? If you knew *wha' wuz up*—"

"Oh, no you did not!" Nona squealed in pretend mortification, and just about coughing up her soup. "You left Compton dragging your dirty li'l diapers behind you, Miss Thing. But you are gonna sit there and try to make somebody think that bein' born somewhere off Alondra is your passport to street smarts, and that you are ace-boon-tight with the Crips and the Bloods. Sell it elsewhere, IRENE!"

They made each other laugh easily. They rolled their necks. They snapped their fingers. They loved playing the hood-brats, which were endearments the two of them alone could share, because the truth was they'd never been a part of that world.

"Crips and Bloods?" Kai repeated, shaking her head. "Girl, what decade are you visiting?"

"What are you talkin' about? The Crips and the Bloods still exist."

"They do not."

"They do too."

"They do NOT."

"They do TOO."

Neither had a clue.

"Don't change the subject. We were talking about Arthur, and that is one sexy man."

Arthur may have danced the Stumbling Stupor often, and for certain had something eternally bleak behind his eyes, but he did have the most beautiful face, chiseled and creased with electrifying life.

Kai rambled on this temperate evening, as the two finished dinner and strolled through Old Town, passing street musicians and shoppers and horse-drawn carriages-for-hire, belching their satisfying meal, and blooming in each other's presence. They'd spent the day at the Norton Simon, which begins the strip on its west end, filling themselves up on Rodin's bronze sculptures and copious helpings of Impressionists and Asian artifacts, and now they laughed together and Nona teased Kai that just last week the girl was head over heels for a saxophone player she'd met at the Bodhi Tree Bookstore. That was Kai. She seized life, and made Nona smile easily. This evening needed to be kept light, as the past year had been anything but. Though, what Nona really wanted to do was grab Kai's shoulders, and shake her, and warn her to get Arthur Hughes Dufresne out of her head.

TWENTY NINE

Get him out of your head, my friend.

"Here's a dream for you, Little Wing," Arthur began. "Eternal Life Baptist Church. Usual Sunday morning. I'm maybe six years old, and I walk into the sanctuary with my mother and father. Now, Reverend Wiggins is this flamboyant, peacocking, cake-walking, gyrating minstrel show, and he's breathing fire and brimstone down every man's pants and up every woman's skirt. Ushers are passing out fans that advertise funeral homes to all these old ladies who are too fat to be out in this heat. Even in my dream, I can feel the heat. All the deaconesses in their starched white uniforms, looking like nurses for the Red Cross, are sitting neatly in the front row. And all the dapper deacons are lined up against the pulpit in pristine suits, like something out of the Fruit of Islam.

"And the whole dream is in slow motion. I sit down in the front row, barely three feet tall, in my tidy little suit and bow tie, and my Quo Vadis haircut, and my Vaselined face. And my mother's sitting next to me, smelling like Noxzema in her white deaconess dress. And I've got my Bible in my hand with my name inscribed, and I'm holding my mother's big hand, which is all sweaty, and she's squeezing tight. I can feel all the rings on her fingers gashing into my tiny hand.

"Now, Reverend Wiggins, you see, is thundering, towering over me, taller than the fucking church steeple. And he's pointing his finger straight at me. And that finger, man, is bigger'n he is. And he starts saying, *'You done did yo mama wrong, li'l man, and now she's gone. You done broke her heart!'*

"And I'm confused, cuz my mother's right there with me, squeezing my hand. So, I don't know what he's talking about. And then I look up, and sure enough she IS gone. What the fuck? And I'm darting my head all around yelling, *'Mama! Mama!'* until I see her lying in a casket at the altar. And—I mean—it's like, theatre, man, this shaft of spotlight, just flooding down on her. And there's all this red carpet that spreads out around it, with mountains of white carnations everywhere. And, man, I gag at the smell of carnations because they make me think of death. My father once forced my face down onto my grandmother—this is not part of the dream—to kiss her when she was lying in state at Angelus Funeral Home, after she'd been all dolled up by the morticians. And her face felt waxy on my lips, and it just crawled up my spine, and I just, I just, I can't stand the smell of carnations anymore.

"So, anyway, there's my mother's casket. And I start screaming, *'Nooooo!!!'* I'm begging her to come back to me. And I just know that my father's gonna do the same thing again and force my head down there and make me kiss her cold, waxy face. And sure enough, he starts shoving my greasy head down in there. And right at that instant, this huge Browning 9-millimeter suddenly grows outta my right arm. An extension of me. And I just haul off and splatter the whole goddamn congregation of Eternal Life Baptist Church to the bloody fucking winds.

"And you can't even see all the blood that's oozing from the carnage, because it just blends right into the red carpet. And all the time I'm screaming, *'Mama, please come back to me! Please, don't leave me here alone.'*

"And I'm trying to find the man who called himself my father, the great Deacon Taylor, cuz all I wanna fucking do is pop a cap in his ass. But I can't find him anywhere, so I nail everybody else instead. Even the innocent. And in my dream, I've got no remorse. Which frightens me.

"Then suddenly, quiet. It's all gone. Everything. There's nothing. Just silence. Emptiness. Bodies on top of bodies, sprawled out all over the carpeted pulpit, like some holocaust nightmare. And my father, he's just disappeared, man. I cannot find the great Deacon Taylor anywhere. So I forget him for the moment, and step over all the bodies, and walk over to my mother's remains, and stare at that stranger in that box, face swollen and misshapen from all that embalming fluid, mouth plastered on her face like some wet, smeared sculpture. Her hands wrinkled and still. So still. I can't believe how still they are. Those same hands that held my little ones, squeezing the life out of 'em. Those same hands that whupped me a hundred times and held me a hundred more. Those same hands that came up to cover her frightened face the first time she found out what my father'd been doing to me. Those hands are holding a corsage of carnations.

And when I catch a whiff, I start to gag. Cuz I can't stand the smell of carnations. And I stare at those closed eyes, and beg 'em to open. *Just open up and look at me!'*

"All of a sudden, the wig on her dead head moves. It shifts or… sump'n, I don't know…but it scares the shit outta me. I'm thinking, fuck man, she's not dead! And they've stuffed her with all that embalming shit! And I start calling for her. But I know it's not her. I'm just confused, you know. It's just her shell. And I've actually seen them embalm corpses before, because my father used to make me come to work with him if there was no school.

"And I know that inside that body, whose wig is shifting and scaring the crap outta me, that her brain is no longer there, or her liver or spleen. Or her beautiful, sad heart. Gone, all gone. And the woman too. Her soul, you know. It's no longer with her. But I want it to be with me.

"And as I'm standing there watching this wig shift, I'm trying to reason with myself that dead bodies can't just get up and walk around. And I try telling myself this, even as I see her body start to rise from that fucking coffin, and I'm, like, mu-tha-fuck! What the fuck is this voodoo shit! And I'm screaming my ass off. Until I see HIM.

"It's him making my mother's body rise. Him hiding under her, inside that coffin, so that I couldn't find him and kill him. And you are never supposed to disturb the dead. It's disrespectful. He used to say that to me all the time when he'd come home from the mortuary with that god-awful smell of formaldehyde on his skin. And here he is, disturbing my mother's state.

"And I hate that mother-fucker even more than I ever have before. This man who called himself my father, whose name is Taylor. My mother is a Dufresne from Metairie. Beautiful Creole woman with a stark white braid down her back that she used to wind around the back of her head and secure with bobby pins. And I no longer go by my father's name.

"And I see him come up from underneath her corpse and watch her body flop this way and that. Which he could not give a shit about, cuz he just wants to use her as a shield. But I'm faster. I lift that semi-automatic rifle, which is bigger than me. But in this dream, see, it doesn't even resemble a rifle, it's just this deformed extension of my own flesh and bone and cartilage. And I cock it and unload. Slowly at first, bit by bit. I want him to suffer. I cock it and unload. Cock it and unload. And each time some screaming, cursing, shouting part of my father goes down in a flurry of exploded flesh and pink rain.

"And I just stare at him, as his whole body disassembles. The man who sired me, the man who raised me and gave me his name, the man who punished me with lashes for wetting the bed. And I blow that mother-fucker to the fucking winds.

"And just as surely as he goes down, my mother begins to rise up from her casket. But this time she's full again. With liver and spleen and blood and heart. Alive. Eyes open. Looking at me. And I'm so happy that I don't know what to do with myself. And we romp and celebrate, and she dances with my father's head on a platter, like Salomé. And I sit back and watch, pleased with myself, just drinking Mother's Pride orange soda like a drunkard, which my father never let me do. And when my mother and I are done reveling, I blow her away too."

Arthur stopped to take a breath. Nona had stopped breathing. When she suddenly realized it, she took a scoop of it up into her. Daniel was still in New York, and she and Arthur had gone to a play and had ended the evening at Chateau Palisades, a cute name Daniel had given her house. They were smoking pot and going where pot takes you.

All she could think about in this instant was Kai's infatuation, and (foolishly believing in an ounce more worldliness than her friend) that tales like this, even if just a dream, would eat a sweet bird of light like Kai alive.

The wilder Arthur's tales got, the wilder Nona's images got, surely pot-induced. Even being marijuana-saturated, however, Arthur did not possess the bloodshot, distanced haze that usually existed in stoned eyes. He was alert when he told this one.

"I mean, it's pretty fucking textbook, what it means. With my father gone, my mother could have a rebirth, maybe me too, blah, blah, blah, what-the-fuck-ever. But the part where I blow HER away...man, I just don't know what that means, because I loved her so. But I keep having this same dream. It keeps starting out with Deacon and Deaconess Taylor quite alive and doing their church duties. And little Arthur Taylor is just sitting in the front pew with his shiny face and obedient smile.

"And this is the part of the dream that comes and goes. It doesn't occur every time. But sometimes when I get to the part where he's bleeding like a gutted pig, this sense memory hits, like maybe that's the purpose of the dream. To get me to this place where, where...I'm meant to NOT forget? And it regards the first time I ever saw my father bleed."

"The first time you saw him bleed?" Nona asked, envisioning some disturbing ghetto scenario of neighborhood disputes and gunshots that children should never witness.

"I don't remember how old I was, six or seven—same age as in the dream—guess that makes sense—but anyway, I had wet the bed. And my father, the great and pious Deacon Taylor, came in to beat me. This was routine for bed-wetting. Obviously it proved an effective solution to the problem, since I wet the bed till I was thirteen years old. But the beatings stopped at that age, too, because by then I was big enough to kick his ass.

"So this particular night he came in with the belt, stripped me naked, threw me over on my stomach, beat me standard. Now, usually when he was done, he would hold my face down on the bed till I stopped crying. Then when I'd calm down, he'd release me and walk out.

"Only, this time, instead of releasing me and walking out, he throws me back over the other way, face up, and holds me down just below my tiny Adam's apple with his left hand. Then his right hand disappears inside the zipper of his pants, and out comes this huge cock.

"Of course, I don't know it's a cock at the time. I'm, like, fucking six or whatever. But I remember thinking so clearly, *'My God, what is this thing?'* And I was frightened for my father, you know, because I thought that maybe he'd developed one of those growths, like the ones my mother used to get on her face. You know, those, they're like moles or skin tags that kind of protrude from the face. My mother's face was swarmed with them. I used to tell her she looked like a chocolate chip cookie. And what she would do was tie a piece of sewing thread around them and just let them fall off weeks later. But they would always grow back, you know, because my mother, she just, she had a penchant for that condition.

"So, see, I was afraid for my father, cuz my mother'd never had one that big before. And I thought maybe it would kill him. And I never put it together that it was the same thing as what I had between my legs. Cuz, at six years old, all I knew was that mine was for peeing and was this soft, little, shriveled nub. My father's was no nub. That was what made me certain he was suffering some kind of disease or abnormality. His was large and straight and thick and hard, and he held it tight, the way my mother used to hold my hand, and I thought that surely his wedding ring would hurt it the way my mother's rings used to hurt my hand.

"And I cried for my father, because I knew in my heart that he had to be in pain. I mean, this huge, monstrous thing that he was desperately trying to yank off, or get rid of, or beat into submission, or something, I couldn't tell, was surely causing him grief, because his face was suddenly this face of great agony, and his voice moaned this guttural yowl. And when all this happened, his left hand, already fastened around my neck, just grew tighter. And I almost lost consciousness, watching him wrestle with that monster, until it suddenly started to bleed.

"Only, this was blood like I'd never seen blood. Because, of course, it wasn't blood. And I almost had a little six-year-old heart attack to think that my father was being attacked my some alien fucking something, whose blood wasn't even red. And then, just as heartlessly as the thing had attacked him, it was done with him. He was all of a sudden calm. And he wiped off the bits of that alien blood that had fallen on my stomach, and stumbled out. And that was the end of that night. But only that one."

When Arthur saw that Nona was breathing fitfully, he looked away from her. But not before she'd had the chance to see the ire in his granite face. It was an old, dead ire, faded and ghostly any longer, but still there, embers, just waiting for the last of itself to finally burn out.

"Oh Arthur," she whispered, barely able to hold tears off, but holding. Her voice was an unintentional crackle. She cleared her throat and leaned in to put a hand on his shoulder, but he put his own up to stop her.

"No, no, no. I didn't tell you this story for pity."

"It's not pity."

She stared at this perpetually self-denying, self-mortifying man and watched him stare out of her window.

"Why did you tell it to me then?"

A good minute passed.

"I don't know."

She sighed.

"Why don't you ever let anyone comfort you?"

"I've already got too many addictions, Little Wing, which may still take me down some day. Last thing I need is to start feeling too good in somebody's embrace, and then get to that point where I have to have that goodness every day or I'll die. I'm already intimately acquainted with that brand of desperation."

At simply the allusion to his addiction, an allusion that in his sober state he would never have allowed after that morning in his apartment, she suddenly felt vile and complicit for sharing a joint with him.

"What do you think saved you, Arthur?" she asked, stamping out her guilty roach.

"Saved me?"

"Well, I mean, obviously you weren't saved from your father's sickness. But, I guess I mean from letting it become your sickness."

"You think I've been saved?"

"Well, Art, come on, you certainly didn't become a nut job who shoots up post offices and ends up on the eleven o'clock news. You became a poet, for God's sake. You're a man of elevated thought. You're raising a son with love and reverence and nurturing. You're not following in Daddy's footsteps and molesting Lorca. Forgive me for presuming, but I happen to believe that art is what saved you. I guess I was just hoping to hear you say it. Because I think it would comfort you to be able to acknowledge that. Especially since you won't let anyone else comfort you."

He smiled. "Look at you. Always marveling at the wonders of life. Always trying to put a poetic spin on everything."

"I know you find me precious—"

"No, I'm serious. The world's a better place because of people like you, Nona. Believe it or not, I do find comfort in that."

"But you're missing my point. It's your own self that you should be able to find comfort in. Not whatever spin I put on it. Look at what you've been through, and yet you grew up and became this extraordinary poet, Arthur, not someone who destroys people's lives the way your father tried."

He looked at her directly. Stared. Dreadful melancholy lurked in his eyes. He took a deep drag off his tweezered roach. Held it in his lungs. Looked away again. And with his breath held, uttered:

"I've had my moments."

THIRTY

Daniel arrived home on a red-eye from JFK after having been gone for two weeks and quietly tiptoed into their bedroom somewhere around dawn, careful not to wake her.   When he saw her lying naked and sleeping soundly, with the blankets jostled about her, he leaned over and placed a kiss on her exposed breast.   The nipple was soft but quickly hardened, and the flesh goose-bumped. She never stirred.

He missed his wife, as he stared at her still face on this dark orange morning.   The birds had already begun their daybreak sounds.   She was deeply into a slumber, like someone just coming off a cocaine weekend, and he knew that he, and his life, and those who lived in it, had been lately sending her through the wringer. Who wouldn't sleep like the dead after all he'd put her through?

He wanted to hold this fragile gem in his arms and give her better than he had so far, but he wasn't sure he knew how. As he stared at her, paying particular attention to the closed eyelids, whose eyes beneath danced about furiously, he knew she was dreaming.

On the floor beside her lay her diary, obviously dropped from her hand when she'd fallen asleep. He knew he shouldn't, but he quietly picked it up and glanced over the opened page, as pitifully as the jealous lover who searches rashly for clues of adultery. It wasn't adultery, though, that he sought out, but signs of her weariness of him.

I've come to learn that there is an enigma to Arthur that will always exist. He never gives much, but always just enough to completely change one's life. At least my life. Being in a room with him is like being in the presence of some wise, old seer. He spins tales that take one into the darkest, thickest jungles. I once commented to him that Joseph Conrad could learn a lot from Arthur Hughes Dufresne, but he only laughed and said, "Well, I've never sailed up the Congo, but I have been to Eternal Life Baptist Church, and that's easily as scary."

Two nights ago was one of those sessions. We talked until the sun came up, and when it was time for him to leave I didn't want him to go because the ritual I knew he did alone in his apartment gave me hives to picture, and I knew he was on his way to it. But Daniel is right. We can't be his babysitters. Arthur is no baby. And in truth, rusty old cockroach that he is, he'll surely outlive us all.

When I went to bed that night, I slept fitfully and dreamt of my invisible rapist again. It is almost two years now since the crime, and I fear he will continue to interrupt my sleep until the day I can put a face to him. Now I have Arthur's father (HIS rapist) to violate my dreams and cannot help but reflect that a world of proper eunuchs might not be such a bad idea. That thought, however, is only a passing whim. I'm simply now in a position to recognize fully the power of man's carnal instinct for wonderful AND horrific deeds, and cannot help but wonder how the world has gotten so bent that it

seems to be more increasingly used for the latter. I
have decided that if I have to dis

And that was it. She didn't even finish the word. Dis...? Discover what? That if she had to discover one more person who'd been a victim of sexual violence she'd go mad? Or was the word even going to be *discover*? What else could it be? *I have decided that if I have to...dispel? dispose? disown? disengage? disappoint?*

It was fruitless. Besides being what he deserved for sticking his prying nose where it didn't belong.

So, Arthur told her about his father's molestation, did he? Just exactly how many more times was Arthur planning to shake her world?

He couldn't love a brother more, but he had the feeling he was going to be forced to tell Arthur a thing or two about what should be spilled and what should be kept to oneself. Because, for as dark and brooding as Nona had always claimed her husband to be, Daniel knew he was just a hazy gray compared to the murky Arthur. And he wondered if his new job now wasn't to make sure that Arthur's battery-acid life didn't rub off on his wife.

He looked into the fragile face that slept before him and assessed their first year together. Her words had aroused him the first time he'd read them, and the woman herself had done the same the first time he'd laid eyes on her. Now she was his, an angel sleeping in the bed they shared. It had been a tumultuous first year but never dispassionate. Daniel was painting like a madman with her in his life, and to have her be a part of his work was more than he could ever have imagined in his perfect daydream. She was writing incredible prose for *Murmuration*, passages that were powerfully fortified with rich minerals. He knew he hadn't been helpful to her with her current book dilemma. It was now a sore subject between them, which he had never intended. But she had to know that she was still a gifted writer. He knew she'd get past this particular block.

He continued to stare at her this early morning, eyes closed, mouth slightly parted, the faint snoring he'd come to tease. She was his whole life, and he beseeched earnestly now that if God really did exist, and if he, Daniel, was just being stupid and pig-headed, then may his stubborn atheist ways please be forgiven and this one prayer answered: *Don't let me fuck up and drag her into my turmoil of a head. Don't let me stain her heart with moroseness, as I fear I've begun to do. Don't let me drive away the very spirit with which I fell in love. A-Fucking-Men.*

While in New York, he'd started, as she had suggested, keeping a diary. This was his attempt to fix whatever sores were between them. Alone at night, or when he'd just come back from some high-powered dinner at Elaine's or the Rainbow Room with Harper and her art publishing cronies, or when he'd taken off on a subway alone for Battery Park, he'd made a few silly efforts to scribble his thoughts:

9 / 15.   I miss Nona. I'm riding this subway. Thinking of going up to Harlem to find some music.

9 / 16.   The ~~word~~ world is fucked up, and so am I.

9 / 18.   I want to photograph Nona's ~~breasts~~ breasts when I get home. Have a new color reversal process I'd like to try out.

9 / 19.   ~~I'm horny. I'm the only one on this train tonight. Wonder if I could get away with wanking off.~~ Fuck. Who cares about that? Not even me. Boring!

9 / 20. Need to call Tensmith in the morning and have him contact Nona for the rent money I left with her.

9 / 22. Go to Whitney tomorrow.

He was no good at keeping a diary. It always started off as his thoughts, and inevitably evolved into his "to do" memo. Diary as grocery list.

Fuck-wit!

Frankly he was too overwhelmed with demands from the publishing front to be able to focus in and jot anything down of worth. Of course, Nona would say that that's exactly the time when jotting something down is the most helpful. But what was there to write? That the money people were all pricks and imbeciles? That he was not about to let them make T-shirts and coffee mugs out of his canvases? What next? The Daniel Cross action figure to go next to the Van Gogh lunch pail? This whole project was outgrowing its own heart insidiously, and it was only a testament to Harper's great spirit that she'd been able to keep the publishers, the investors, and Benton from bailing on the project altogether; or him from reaching across some linen-draped dinner table and strangling some suited exec who knew nothing about art but was about to determine his fate.

I guess I could've written that.

Oh well. Words were her thing. Now that he was home, he was just happy to get back to work, hold his wife, and remind himself of what was important.

Over the next several months, everyone worked diligently on the final details for *Murmuration*, but Daniel began to worry about Nona. The custom of them all hanging out together after their day's work grew less and less frequent. Traditionally, they would wrap up their business for that day, and do the Orchid Club or the Factory for some music and a drink and a late dinner. And ordinarily, they'd all be so wound up that it would be a welcomed tonic to their hard day. But lately Nona had been declining and heading home early, leaving Arthur and him to do their guy thing. It was probably best. She seemed angry these days. Though at what, she could never articulate. She just withdrew.

By now he knew all of her little idiosyncrasies. When she wanted to disappear from the world, she socialized with friends less and listened to music more. The wilder the music, the better it worked for her. She'd close herself in her office and pace the floors, while Ornette Coleman or Pharoah Sanders screamed against the walls of Chateau Palisades. They blasted their exorcisms out on their horns and seemed to give her some kind of orgiastic release, which kept her with it all day long, sometimes not even coming out to eat a meal. She'd become obsessed.

She went to jazz clubs alone. If there was some new, local, kick-ass tenor player who reminded her of Coltrane, or some prodigy piano player who was the next McCoy Tyner, and who had a self-produced CD to sell at the door, she was there and she bought it. She made him listen to everything she brought home, when he was usually too busy trying to put their Benton show together.

She decided on her own one night that Dorothy Favor was the lost gem who should be discovered, and that the world was a sad and sinful place for not bringing this singer the acclaim she deserved. No one had to tell him how incredible Dorothy Favor was. He'd painted her, for Christ's sake. But suddenly Nona was at the Orchid every night, whenever he and Arthur were *not* there, drinking martinis and clapping louder than the rest of the room when Dorothy would come to the close of any song. This was Nona's statement to the world, or at least to the lowly barflies, that she was the only one who appreciated this miracle in heels, and *"isn't that a fucking shame?"*

All he could do was watch her evolve into this reamer of the world's asshole for some general crime he couldn't identify. He begged her to talk to him, but she would say there was nothing to talk about.

"About what, Daniel? Talk is stupid. This whole self-help crap of talking everything to death is just so laughable. We're a generation of whiny babies. Let's just create, goddamn it! Before life ends and we have no legacy to leave behind!"

And then he realized that though she had seemingly put Arthur's episode behind her, because they were getting along like best chums, this was that. She wasn't angry, at all. She was revved up.

There was a new lust about her, but it wasn't a good one. Music got louder. She gave and got sex as though she might die to be denied it. There was a frenzied desperation to everything now. And the drinking. Five or six martinis at the Orchid Club, and she was there practically every night. She often taxied home. Of course, that pace was nothing to an old pisser like himself, but Nona had always been a light sipper at best. This was a woman who could get giggly from a white wine spritzer.

For a moment there, one day, she got him seriously worried when she added a swig of his rotgut liquor to a protein shake she was blending up.

"Just to give it a bite."

To give it a bite? Christ! In that one fucked-up second, she was Daniel's mother. His slip-wearing, curlers-in-the-hair, grimy-stockinged lush of a mother, who had started adding brandy to her tea for menstrual cramps some time during his boyhood, then moved up to brandy without the tea, and on and on.

Franklin and Camilla Cross had been a charismatic duo. Every night of Daniel's boyhood seemed to be a race between his parents to see who could get the drunkest. Of course, whoever succeeded was the one who could more successfully beat the crap out of the other.

Daniel's mother had been a tough old broad in her day. She seemed, in his boyhood mind, to have the strength of ten men when she was sufficiently tanked and reeking, which he just about prayed for each night. Because if she was drunk enough to let the brute out, was his adolescent thinking, then perhaps his father wouldn't bash her head in. The old man actually feared her in that state. Drunkenness was, in a sense, her safe haven. On the other hand, if his father was the one to beat her to the drunk-punch, then a couple of black eyes and a busted lip on her once-comely face could be pretty much assured.

Daniel's father had certainly not been immune to receiving abuse, either. Once, she pulled his own gun on him, and, after giving him a shit-in-his-pants scare, proceeded to parade through the neighborhood in her brassiere and a girdle, gun prominently propped inside her cleavage, yelling: *'I'm gonna kill the fucker soon! And I just want ya' all to know it, so you can be sure just where to send the bobbies. Send 'em to me!'*

Moments like those, which seemed to exist their whole lives, always drove Daniel and his older brother, Duncan, away for as long as they could get away with it. The nausea in their guts would swell up whenever their mother went on her public tirades. And they could never keep chums long because their mother was the neighborhood clown. He and Duncan usually ended up beating the tar out of a bloke for making her the punch line to some lewd joke.

They might stay away three, four days sometimes, sleeping in condemned houses, which London was full of, and generally fending for themselves. Their absences, even at the ages of ten and fourteen, were rarely of any particular concern to their parents, because Franklin and Camilla were usually much too preoccupied with making themselves each the dramatic victim of the other.

He gave his parents one thing, though. They fucked as ravenously as they fought. And this was where he had started to see the flash of his mother, Camilla Rankin Cross, in his wife, Nona Childe Cross. That nausea in his gut from boyhood was suddenly with him again, as he watched Nona lace her protein shakes with an 80-proof kick and beg him to fuck her up against a wall. Not that he ever minded any kind of amped-up sex, but it was all amped up. And he swore he would not let them become another Franklin and Camilla.

The subject had thrust him into thoughts quite a bit lately of the great escape from his boyhood, and the vow that he would never return to it. Nona had been his assurance of that vow, because she had a calling on this earth that was meaningful.

He'd always hoped his mother would find her calling. He spent most of his youth pondering how she'd gotten so far away from her own childhood, having grown up in Leviticus Rankin's home, which had been a home filled with the pursuance of great things. Instead, their existence as a family ended up with them being kicked out of every council house throughout the East End. He and Duncan had to make new friends at every turn, and found their secret second home in the abandoned Victorian houses in the Tower Hamlets.

Duncan had taught little brother Daniel the ways of survival early on. They smoked cigarettes, drank rye, played hard in the abandoned slums that were soon to be torn down in order to make room for tower blocks, broke into shops and warehouses, and established, with two other primary school chums, a black market in their neighborhood. Every adult knew whom to come to for any particular need. Bicycles, toys, cigarettes, beer, building materials. Duncan and Daniel could get it for you cheap, because they were great thieves.

They were the equivalent to what Americans call White Trash, though they were actually racial mutts, just like their neighborhood, which was a colorful mixture of Blacks, Irish, Gypsies, Jews, and Indians. But they were the soul of White Trash and were the anointed kings of their slum hill.

They broke the doors down on condemned houses and for angry sport smashed up the televisions and pianos that were often left behind. Or if there was anything of great value left there, they confiscated it and hid it in the air-raid shelters, which still existed in the backyards of these homes, slowly building up the inventory for their business.

Lead piping and copper wiring were always a valuable sell and were how they made their best money. They ripped them out of the walls and ceilings and offered them up on the street at a steal of a price. They were, of course, completely prepared to heap violence on any adult who made his attempts to do his own thieving on these slums, which they had claimed as their own. And all they had to do to instill effective fear was to offer the community one single example of their commitment to this notion.

So one night they pummeled a bum with their lead pipes for attempting to sleep off his drunk in the hearth of one of their houses. To this day, Daniel didn't know if they killed him. They hid on the roof, watching the ruckus below, as the wagon arrived to lug the guts from the street.

From that moment forth, no one came near the houses the brothers claimed. But if you were a faithful customer, and didn't try to con their prices down, in that condescending manner that adults love to use with youngsters, they treated you well.

He and Duncan learned how to drink early on, growing up in pubs for most of their boyhood. Their father had been a publican, and their mother had never been much on guidance to keep them out of that environment.

When Daniel's father wasn't drinking, he was actually good at his business. But ultimately the old man's alcoholism got the best of him, he lost his pub for it, and the family ended up in Bromley Hall, a sort of storage facility for the homeless. In many ways, Bromley Hall was the beginning of the end of Daniel's boyhood. He lost his virginity there. His mother lost her sanity there. His father lost his soul there. And poor big brother, Duncan, lost his life there.

Daniel watched his older brother get beaten to death one night by drugged-out hooligans, much in the same fashion that they'd beaten up the old hobo. He looked on numbly from a distance as the coroner's truck took his brother's young body away and witnessed his fair mother completely lose her mind from that day forth, while his father, a handsome man of Black and Gypsy blood, managed to find his solace in a string of whores.

After Duncan's death, and as Daniel watched their mother's mind wither away, he wondered if Camilla might not have been able to save herself from her break had she been given a passion, something to believe in. But nothing had ever stirred her. Not art, or politics, or science, or philosophy, or adventures.

He used to have a recurring daydream, and it was even more vivid after Duncan's death, of his mother in some great uniform: Doctor Camilla Cross. Captain Camilla Cross. The renowned barrister Camilla Cross! Camilla Cross, the great poet laureate! The Right Honorable Baroness! The Grand Diva! Camilla Cross scales Mount Everest! And oh, the myriad others.

His mother could've been something great, but she chose nothing instead. So when Duncan's death threatened to put her over the edge, she had nothing to bring her back, nothing worth fighting for. Only a husband who drank and caroused. And one remaining son who withdrew and would speak to no one. Not exactly a precious life worth staying sane for. So she didn't. She happily retreated to her madness. And it was during that time that she crazily amped up her routines of parading the streets in a brassiere and girdle, brandishing her husband's gun and dramatic soliloquies, and being picked up daily by the authorities.

It hadn't always been that way. When his father first met his mother, a fair-haired Jewish beauty who smelled of White Shoulders Perfume and typed in a secretarial pool in an office where his father had worked as a janitor, so the story goes, Franklin completely lost his head and fell deliriously in love with the fetching Miss Rankin. It was dangerous in those days for a colored man to call upon a fair beauty. And he was only partly colored at that; the other part of him was gypsy, which was just as bad. She, especially, received ridicule and harassment for consorting with someone with *"a touch o' the tar brush"* about them, but withstood it, which was the best of it, the most romantic. It wasn't easy for either of them, and ultimately they were both driven to their drinking descent.

Daniel had never especially liked his father through most of his boyhood. He'd always blamed the old man for beginning the spiral. But when his mother became a loon, he and his father found themselves banding together in an effort to keep each other sane. He finally began to see just how difficult his father's life had been, having grown up a racial mutt in Whitechapel.

Eventually he and his father started drinking and womanizing together. Daniel was twelve. They philosophized heavily and often on the state of Daniel's mother, and he saw the agony in his father's face that she was lost to him. To them.

Franklin cried nightly in his whisky, and Camilla repeatedly injured him with frying pans and broom handles. He stopped keeping bullets in his gun, because he knew she might kill him some day, given the chance. And he grew passive; he allowed the abuse. They used to beat the crap out of each other, and now she beat it out of him exclusively. And he was only a marvel at withstanding it all because of a slow drag from his fag, a deep drowning in his rye, and the burying of his tortured face in a set of whorish breasts.

Franklin took Daniel to whorehouses with him regularly, and that was Daniel's existence until his sixteenth birthday when he was old enough to get the Hell out of England.

Today Nona Childe was in Daniel's life largely because she was nothing like his mother. This beautiful woman he called wife had a purpose. She could withstand all manner of tragedy if she had to, because her life had meaning. She was what Camilla Cross could've been. And Daniel clung to that, as though perhaps he might still be able to will the course of his mother's tragic life to a different path merely by his association with someone like Nona. Nona had become his assured escape from a fruitless existence. And the two of them, as the zealous purveyors of some artful purpose, would live a valuable life and never turn into Franklin and Camilla. So, he couldn't very well let her become the drinking genius he was. Because he couldn't let them become the battered ghosts of his lushed mother and father.

THIRTY ONE

"I'll have a martini please."

"Shall I start a tab?" the girl asked, curtly.

"Yes, thanks."

Otto's only waitress in this tiny bar took Nona's order quickly and hustled on to the next table. Nona sat in the Orchid Club on this rainy fall evening, which only seemed to feed the mood. It was like what she'd always envisioned down some dark alleyway in Paris; a place she'd never been but had always fixated on. A winding staircase led one down below the ground to find this moody, brick-walled basement, in a part of town adjacent to Little Tokyo. It was dark, and neon blue, and irresistible.

The first time Daniel had brought her here to listen to Dorothy Favor, and the songstress walked out from beyond the curtain to step behind a microphone, Nona remembered thinking how much Dorothy reminded her of her mother Ruby Chancelor Childe, known simply as the songstress Ruby Chan. It had been a brilliant, somber reminder.

The Orchid Club had always been Daniel's lair. He'd been coming here for years, listening to Dorothy, or Neville's trio on Wednesday nights, or the Billy Somebody he always talked about; and ordering his regular from Otto, the German bartender and owner, who loved debating with Daniel the impact of Dadaism on world culture.

After that first night, the Orchid was always Nona's suggestion for a place to go, and for awhile it had even become the site of their own Vicious Circle. Daniel, Arthur, Harper, Neville, Kai, and Nona had established their roundtable at the Orchid, and had spent many an evening eating, drinking, lobbing quips, which would invariably end up in a Kai performance piece, and arguing art and the social order.

On those evenings, Dorothy Favor never joined them. Instead, the songstress would head to the bar, usually with her husband Nick. And while Daniel was always raving about Billy Somebody, Nona was convinced that Dorothy's husband was the best piano she'd heard in this town. Just another enthralling artistic debate with Daniel. Other than a brief introduction that first night, it didn't seem likely that Nona would ever get to know Dorothy, as long as the gang was in tow. Not to mention Nona always got the vague feeling, anyway, that Daniel was much more satisfied keeping Dorothy a marvelous fable. But Nona wanted to connect with the woman who evoked Ruby Chan. So tonight she came here alone. She took a small table near the back of the room, ordered a drink, and was reading her New Yorker by candlelight when the first set finally began.

When it did, Nona immediately closed her magazine and her eyes, lest too much sensory overload occur and she begin to lose her mind thinking her mother was back with her. When Dorothy Favor began some Ellington, however, Nona's eyelids found their way back up, and she became obsessed with watching Dorothy's lips slowly purse and stretch to form words, the head tilt gently to one side, the eyelids slink down over coal black eyes, the expressive hand grope the microphone, and the way Dorothy would periodically wipe her thumb across the ball of it whenever she'd get just a little too close with her blood-red lipstick. Dorothy's voice was deep and rich. Not pure, not clean. But like smoke and abuse and pain.

Actually, as she proceeded to deconstruct this siren, Nona realized that Dorothy Favor and Ruby Chan didn't have similar voices at all. Dorothy's was a bit of a mottled lemon, aged and run through the mill a bit, cracked with world-weariness and seasoned to perfection, like Billie in Billie's day, where Ruby's had always been more of a sweet and velvety Sarah Vaughan peach. It was the soul inside each, which was so like the other's, that merited the comparison. Both were rich with pathos and depth, and able to soothe like a balm.

Nona's mother had done the bulk of her singing in Paris nightspots in the 1950s. She used to tell Nona all about the Slow Club, which had been her room on the Rue du Rivoli, half a block from the Louvre. It, just like the Orchid Club, took one into it by way of a winding staircase. And it, also like, and by her mother's description, was dark and blue and irresistible.

The Dorothy Dandridge look-alike, who stunned men with her sleepy eyes, crooked smile, and unnervingly erotic vibrato, had snagged Nona's father by the very sound of her voice. They'd met when they were both living in Paris and working in Jimmy Freisen's Big Band at the Opal Room on the Rive Gauche. Nelson Childe had held the second trumpet chair and Ruby Chan was the piano player, until one day everyone discovered Ruby could sing like a lark and Jimmy promptly placed her out front.

She was gorgeous and charismatic, and being the only woman player in a traditionally male big band, the crowds would go nuts for Ruby. So when she got moved up front to take her female place behind the microphone and leave the piano chores to a man, she objected, stating that now Jimmy Freisen's Big Band was no different from all the others. Ruby loved the piano. It broke her heart not to play anymore. And when her objections were viewed as difficult, she was promptly booted out of Jimmy Freisen's Big Band.

So the story goes, at the very instant of her dismissal, during a rehearsal one evening, Ruby sashayed right out of the Opal Room, swayed her hips on down the street to the Slow Club, walked prominently in, and asked to sing and play for the management. They loved her. Probably more for her honey brown complexion, shapely figure, and sassy smirk, than for her music. But a job was a job, she figured, and she'd get it how she could and make them love the music later. She was given a single weekend at first, but had the audience so on its swinging feet that management asked her back for another weekend. And another after that, and another after that. Until she looked up one day and had been there a solid year.

Meanwhile, Nelson continued to be a sideman with Jimmy's headlining razzle-dazzle band. And for a time, life was a dream for Nelson and Ruby, living in Paris, working the clubs, rendezvousing after gigs. He'd drift by to watch her swing the house after he'd swung his own down the street, and afterwards they'd walk romantically along the Seine.

It all began to dismantle soon enough, however, when Jimmy Freisen's Big Band finally came to the close of its Opal Room contract and Jimmy booked them back in the States. Nelson asked Ruby to marry him, and she happily agreed until she realized that he was asking her to leave Paris. Ruby adored Paris. To her thinking, it was the one place a Negro woman could be revered. And in the late fifties, Los Angeles was not about to offer her anything nearly as gratifying as the life she was living there. She tried to persuade Nelson to leave Jimmy Freisen, but he delicately reminded her, in an effort not to dash her *vie en rose* look at Paris, that life for him would not be nearly as easy there as it was for her. And though what he implied was some kind of claim of racism *(a Negro woman is one thing, a Negro man quite another)*, Ruby knew the truth. Charlie Parker had been hailed in Paris. Sydney Bechet had been hailed there too. Nona's father, Nelson Childe, was an average trumpeter at best. Not nearly as gifted a musician as Ruby. The reality was that Ruby Chan would always get work but Nelson Childe might not, and he'd best go where it was insured.

Ruby ultimately accepted Nelson's proposal, but it was bittersweet. She hated having to say goodbye to one love in order to accommodate another. And three short weeks later, they were married and on a plane back to America.

Nona didn't have nearly as many personal memories of her father, mainly stories, because he'd died when she was a girl. But her mother had died only a few years ago, cancer, so she missed Ruby with a knot in her gut, and had repeatedly shared her fantasy with Daniel of the two of them some day going to the city of her parents' romance. Until such time, she stared at her mother's reminder, the beautiful Dorothy, who, after her first set, swayed over to the bar with a lazy gait, and haunted this place and Nona.

Dorothy was slow-moving, and she smoked Tiparillos (boldly ignoring the new smoking laws) and drank Sloe Gin Fizzes as if she'd invented them. Nona's mother used to drink Sloe Gins. And also boldly defied convention. And with each sweep of the hand, or turn of the head, Dorothy Favor absolutely evoked Ruby Chan.

Nona shyly nodded at Dorothy from her seat, who returned the courtesy with a smile. Nona's whole reason for coming here had been to connect, yet she found herself unable to move. Maybe Daniel was right. Maybe keeping Dorothy a marvelous fable was the best way for Nona to get what she wanted from the songstress. That way, she couldn't possibly be disappointed.

Or she was just a coward.

When Dorothy's break was done and she stepped back up to the microphone and started in with her trio on *I'll Be Seeing You*, Nona was spooked to have this sublime chanteuse know exactly the song to sing at this precise instant. For Nona was, indeed, seeing her mother in all the old familiar places.

    She hummed it the whole way home.

THIRTY TWO

"She's withdrawn these days," Daniel whined over too many scotches at the Dresden Room. The claustrophobic ambiance of new hipsters, white vinyl booths, cork and rock walls, and quirkily delivered lounge music enveloped Arthur and him like a Frank & Sammy fog.

Through the years, Daniel and Arthur had nursed each other's heart wounds and propped each other up, as they'd both come from a bleak and imprisoning childhood and had escaped each only by benefit of an artful world. Beauty always lifted them out of the bog, but something else could always be counted on to yank them back in.

"It's not like there's no life in her," Daniel continued to slur. "There's a whole lot in her, but it's a scary amount. If there can be such a thing. It's not *her*, you know what I mean? It's like, she's tryin' to bite the heads off chickens or…somethin'…just so she can say, *'Well, I've had that experience.'* She's operating like someone perpetually stoned. It's all party, party, party."

"Only, she's not partyin' with us," added Arthur.

"Right. A party of one. I'm worried."

"Maybe it *is* us."

"How do you mean?"

"Right now she's feelin' like a daredevil. She wants to walk to the edge of the cliff, hang one foot over, close her eyes, and dare fate. She thinks that if she can feel that rush, then maybe she can create sump'n better. Be a more profound writer."

"She's already a profound writer."

"Of course she is. Follow what I'm sayin', Danny. You know how Nona's mind works. She marvels at every little thing around her. And she's had a pretty comfortable life, right? One she kinda feels a little guilty about. Like, you know, how's that gonna possibly fuel her art? Yadda, yadda, yadda. And by the way, you callin' her crib Chateau Palisades doesn't help."

"I know," Daniel lamented, feeling every bit the insensitive lout.

"You know that she has started callin' her own home, a place she's always regarded as her sanctuary, Chateau Palisades, in the same condescending way."

"I know! I'm an asshole!"

"In any case, all of a sudden you come into the picture. Then me. And look at us, and the shit that we come from. So the next place her mind goes is that she wonders what takes man into his darkness. She sees you rail against the world and go get fucked-up, or smash up windows, or whatever the fuck you do when you're in that headspace. Or she sees me, like she saw me that day in my crib, which, again, man, I cannot apologize enough for—"

Daniel just waved it away. Old news. Apology long ago accepted. Next.

"Anyway, she asks us both why we go to those places. Only, she doesn't really ask *us*. Cuz see, she does all this marvelin' in a little vacuum. And she gives herself an answer that's much more profound than the truth is. She tells herself that anger and hunger and extremity and pain are what take us there, and that from outta all'at shit we seem to create these beautiful things. When the truth is, home's, you and me just a couple'a fucked-up mu-fuckas."

They both chuckled. But it was burdened.

"That we're also artists is purely incidental."

They clinked their glasses and toasted two *fucked-up mu-fuckas*.

"She's lookin' to put some shit in her life, man," Arthur gave somberly. "Don't let her do it."

Shit in her life. Great. Here Daniel was searching desperately to clean the shit out of his, and his wife was looking to find some and wallow deep. He wondered if he should suggest to her that maybe she was trying to orchestrate her life to fit some idealized notion of romantic suffering.

Hell, maybe he needed to say it to himself. Because the truth was, he loathed living in their rock star house, with their much breathing space and their aroma of the sea. And he told himself he loathed it because there were people sleeping in the streets, but maybe he only really loathed it because to like it too much might just take away whatever hunger he had in him to keep painting. Maybe they were both on their way to certain danger; trying to manipulate a mood in their lives to keep forever teetering just on the scarier side of safe.

And why was it that just at the moment of some ease in his life, there always seemed to be some new kink to comb out? Thanks to Harper, everything was going brilliantly toward the opening. The prototype for the catalogue had finally been approved, the galley proofs were in, the templates laid, the printing begun. It would be a hardcover volume of color plates and photographs, and Arthur's and Nona's prose. A huge thing, too. Ten inches by twelve inches. And a little over six-hundred pages. Each piece would be linked to a passage of prose, which would be linked to another piece, which was largely some study of Daniel's two muses. The design layout was beautiful. Dugnac was already generating interest in Marseille, New York, and London by sending their galleries advance copies of the catalogue. It was going splendidly. Yet he couldn't even revel in any of it, for worrying about his wife.

He also couldn't help wondering, at the mention of London, if this hardcover art book with his name emblazoned on the front might not just cross the path of his mother and father, whom he'd not seen or spoken to in thirty years.

It was only a passing thought, but his drunken head ached as he said goodbye to Arthur and drove by Braille down Vermont to the freeway and east into downtown, stumbled up to his studio, overwhelmed by his life, which screamed to be simpler but never would be, and itchy to paint. Or at least itchy to be itchy.

He stepped into his flat somewhere around three in the morning and for a time simply sat in the dark listening to a Keith Jarrett recording. The street lamp below glared steel blue light into the room, and all he could see were the exaggerated shadows of his painterly junk, barrels and table tops filled and cluttered.

The easels, though, were all empty. The pieces for *Murmuration* were already out of his hands and mounted on the walls of the Benton Gallery, darkened this time of night, awaiting some grand significance toward his anticipated acclaim. About to determine his fate in ways for which he was surely unprepared.

Keith Jarrett was trying hard to soothe Daniel's roiling head. Jarrett's piano was lovely and tender this night, while Daniel was drunk and untender, which made them, really, the perfect pair. The piece that was playing was so slow you could barely hear the time. There was ridiculous space to roam in between each pianistic offering. Here was a musician unafraid of a tempo this slow. He didn't need to fill every bit of silence with gaudy arpeggios. He let it breathe. And so he begged it of Daniel, who could almost hear Jarrett's voice through that piano whispering, "Breathe, Daniel. Breathe, Daniel. Breathe, Daniel."

Damn it! I'm trying!

THIRTY THREE

Something strange and exhilarating was starting to take over her life, and it was all because of Daniel. From the moment she first locked eyes with this passionate force of nature, he had shaken up her neatly planned existence and awakened in her the daring to really live, to close her eyes and dive in, to wear no life jacket but welcome the turbulent waters. Just as her mother had always done. And then, just to complete the lesson, he promptly introduced her to Arthur Hughes Dufresne, and it was *that* times ten.

She believed she was a talented enough writer. She'd always had a knack for adventures, for spinning a tale and examining the human condition. But the safe hallways of academia and the burying of her nose in other writers' books had been her only experience. She'd never really stepped out into this world. No sashaying of sassy hips down a Parisian street for the sheltered and frightened daughter of the larger-than-life Ruby Chan.

Until recently, a self-disgust had been creeping up, perhaps years in the deed, as she could never resist comparisons between her life and that of the people around her. How disgusted she'd been on that first date to confide in Daniel that she'd never been out of the country. Africa had certainly checked that claim off the list. But how many others would need checking off to deem her worthy? She had spent her entire life walking skittishly through it, apologizing for everything, and ensuring never to rock any boats. And on those rare occasions when she'd inadvertently do so, she would wield the hammer ferociously to stamp out the offense. The example that, to this day, made her slap her forehead was the time she bought a sweatshirt on Venice Beach when she was a teen, that had scrawled on the front: *God is dead – Nietzsche. Nietzsche is dead – God.* She'd found the jest cleverly mischievous, and had had fun with the impulse purchase, yet the first time she wore it out in public and got disgusted stares from those who didn't get the twist, off it went to the Goodwill. She'd been mortified to have garnered the disapproval of strangers.

These days she felt different. These days she dared anyone to look at her twice. Senses were sharper. Food tasted better. Colors were brighter. Smells were thicker. Sex made her explode. She was lustful about the world around her for the first time ever, and itchy for a fight.

Of course, she tried giddily to share all of this with Daniel, but the fate of *Murmuration* was too much on his mind right now. Instead, she frequently wrote Mrs. Wenda in Tanzania, and would await letters back as if they were the sweepstakes. Mrs. Wenda was a woman who had known a huge life. She, like Nona's mother, had fulfilled every impulse for which her soul had ever yearned, and in her late seventies there were still horizons to conquer. Right after Nona had left Tanzania, in fact, Mrs. Wenda had taken a job writing for a local radio show, documenting the continual unrest in Burundi and Rwanda, and keeping the Tanzanian citizens abreast of guerrilla activity. Remarkable.

Nona always had Kai to talk to, of course, but Mrs. Wenda, who was living life just about as large as it got, was exactly what Nona needed right now for inspiration and counsel.

Mrs. Wenda listened patiently to all of Nona's ramblings about mother and father *this*, and Dorothy Favor *that*, and the two brilliant men she was surrounded by these days. And Mrs. Wenda alone, in a recent letter, led Nona to her most liberating epiphany.

```
Dear friend,
     The fact that you are, in this era of your
life, meeting so many remarkable people cannot
have been accident. It seems to me that the goal
in getting past this rape was never about
getting even; or necessarily even remembering
his face, a face that, once remembered, would
never leave you; or even to have him found and
incarcerated. The real goal has always been to
allow his deed, however threatening it was, to
steel you and to wake you up. Your eyes see
```

differently now. As they should.

Perhaps it is that difference that has allowed you to see these extraordinary people coming into your life, and to be able to welcome them. Perhaps it was not possible for your husband and your husband's friends to be noticed by you before. You were close to death, my dear. When we are lucky enough to survive that, it opens the eyes so much wider and makes life's colors so much more startling, does it not?

Yours,

Mrs. Wenda

The woman was right. It did not serve Nona to denigrate herself for being pampered, and for using even her repression of the rape as a weapon in the case. Or maybe her need to remember had been even more sinister than that. Had she only been resentful of not remembering it because then it would mean that she couldn't exploit the experience as fodder for her writing? Was she trying to use this rape as a bargaining chip? *Hey Rape, I'll allow you to traumatize me, but only if I can get some really powerful art out of the deal.*

She grew queasy at the notion, refused to believe that such an instinct could live in her, and determined to shake it off by embracing the idea instead that she had the chance to accomplish a much greater goal. To make flesh a remarkable reaffirmation, to seize everything, the inspirations of her husband and friends, memories of old familial longings, and great, big, loud life, which, according to the wisest woman she'd ever met, was far more victorious than constant self-castigation and using her rapist the way he had used her.

THIRTY FOUR

The holidays came and went without event, as everyone was much too busy frenzying over the January opening, and the Crosses found themselves on the eve of *Murmuration* being taken on an adventure by Arthur. Daniel could've killed him for the distraction. It had, after all, only taken the past two years of Daniel's life to prepare for this night, a night that was surely to give him a brand new set of ulcers, and the last thing he needed was to have his attention diverted and his focus lost.

But Arthur had a knack for unexpected gifts. The kind that knock you off your balance and force you to look at your life in a whole new way. So Daniel decided to trust him, and hoped that whatever it was might just bridge the gap that had been steadily growing between his wife and him. Curiously, Nona didn't feel it. She was much too busy bounding through her life like a terminal patient who's been told she's miraculously cured. Except that the farther upward she leapt, the farther away from him she flew. And only the earthbound one can ever really sense the gap.

Arthur took them to a coffeehouse, which wasn't unlike every other coffeehouse they'd ever haunted, as was the obligation of their kind; their kind being the arty, fringe, miserably hip breed. This one, called the Talking Drum, was in Leimert Park, and was reputed to have the best coffee anywhere, though tonight Daniel was more interested in a stiff drink. The gang tonight was Nona, Arthur, Kai, and him.

All Arthur had said was that he was taking them to what he called his religion and that there was no need for further explanation. As they parked the car and headed on foot up Degnan, Daniel suddenly heard the faint murmur of drums from some distant place. He wasn't sure if anyone else heard it, or if it was in his head.

For a moment he seriously thought of abandoning the group and sneaking off to find this primal sound, this force that seemed tribal and was calling his name, when suddenly he looked up and realized that it was the very source of their destination. He'd entered upon his first drum circle. Arthur put his hand up when Nona started to ask something.

"No questions yet. Just be present."

Daniel had never heard of a drum circle before, but when he stepped across the threshold he felt anointed. He couldn't have articulated what it was, the moment, the feeling. It wasn't exactly quantifiable. Actually, he was getting much better at this diary thing, so perhaps he would attempt to capture it with words later.

There must've been thirty drummers sitting in a huge circle in the center of the room. The hum was what first hit Daniel. Except that it wasn't exactly a hum. An indescribable energy hovered over the circle from the hum — damn it, he kept going back to that word — of rhythms being beaten out. It was an almost electrical force, which could literally have carried him up and over the crowd to the back of the room had it wanted. This current was thick enough to be almost visible. It sent a chill through him. The men and women in this circle held in their laps, or between their legs, or in front of them, some oddly shaped drum, gourd, vessel, thing. And the configuration of drummers was as diverse as the drums themselves.

Playing a giant pow-wow drum with the palms of his hands was an ancient African-American man, with his mile-high, snow-white hair stuffed under a grubby knitted beanie, and who smelled of patchouli and sweat. A young White kid, whose blond hair, and even his beard, had been rendered dreadlocked, twirled and swirled and bowed a spindly gourd called a waterphone, which created a kind of unearthly cry, like that of a woman wounded. Daniel had never heard such a sound come from a little coconut. A pierced-lipped beauty danced in the center of the circle so freely and un-self-consciously that she might've even forgotten she was in a room with a hundred people. Her eyes were closed, as the world in which everyone lived at this moment was clearly their own, yet undeniably communal. There was an ancient African woman, easily ninety years old, who burned sage and placed the visible stream of its aroma over everyone's head as she walked in a kind of sliding shuffle from person to person. This rite she performed, Arthur explained, was to cleanse the cluttered heads. There was

Stanley, who had once belonged to a Chicano gang from Pico Rivera, and who was tattoo-covered and struggle-burdened.

The tattoo part of the story was before Daniel's very eyes, and the gang part whispered to him by Arthur. But the struggle-burdened part was purely Daniel, who could never resist tacking a story onto everyone he ever encountered within seconds.

The tattooed Stanley was an older gentleman, whose son, according to Arthur, was presently lost to the Cholos, and who, himself, had been a second-generation Los Angeles gangster.

This Stanley stood in the middle of the circle with the dancing beauty and virulently struck a single steady pound onto the stretched head of a large djembe. He was angry and poetic and dapper and stylish, and Daniel came to realize that this man's pose and stance were as important as the striking of his instrument. He stood taller than his 5'7 stature. This drumming meant something to him. To them all. Daniel didn't know what, yet, but he knew he was on his way to finding out.

On a nearby table outside of the circle were udu drums, and tambourines, and quicas, and shakérés, and tsuzumis from Japan, and darabukas from India, and djembes from West Africa, and finger cymbals, and bongos, and rainsticks. A woman standing nearby had pointed each one out when she noticed Daniel staring at the table. Arthur left them fascinated and silent and contemplative each, and joined the circle.

Apparently anyone could join; drummer or no. And Daniel quickly came to realize that this happening was something more than musical for its participants. This was no elite jam session where only heavyweight percussion cats could participate. This was humbler than that. A housewife, clearly a housewife, had grabbed a tambourine and joined in. Children with triangles and maracas and homespun drums made from Quaker Oats boxes joined in. And even percussionists of great musical weight and lineage joined in. Nona was the one to point out the notables.

Daniel, Nona, and Kai stood back and observed Arthur, who was quickly entrenched in the music with a drum handed to him by the older Black man, who appeared to be the designated Elder of this group. Not in any official way was this man designated; there was simply an inherent energy center in the room that seemed to originate from the spot right between this man's old eyes. That he was the Elder of this group was purely an understanding.

It didn't take long before Kai, naturally in her element, was in the middle of the circle, dancing and reveling with the pierced-lipped beauty and beckoning for Daniel and Nona to join. Nona, like Daniel, was more hesitant. She simply closed her eyes and began to hum faintly. And Nona was no singer. His wife was so self-conscious about her thin, reedy voice that she didn't even allow herself to hum around the house if Daniel was there. Now she stood in this room of a hundred people and hopped a ride on that current without even realizing she'd done so.

Forty-five solid minutes must've liberally passed before any drumming stopped. When it did, clearly not the end of the evening, it was a kind of abrupt and unnatural ceasing initiated by the Elder.

"People, please. People, please!"

Everyone in the room hushed as the Elder commanded the floor from his throne behind the pow-wow drum, and Daniel suddenly noticed the heat and sweat that had thickened the air.

"I must tell you all in good frankness, people, that the Devil is in this room tonight. And I mean not to trip you up with hackneyed Christian tripe, but perhaps it will wake you up if I throw that out. What's happening tonight, my friends? Is ego finally getting to us? Are we trying to out-play the brother or sister next to us?"

The question was rhetorical. Or maybe not, considering the long pause that followed. This suddenly felt like a hand-slapping, and Daniel was just glad he hadn't participated. Had Arthur brought them to fucking church?

"We are not clicking tonight as we have in the past. There are nights here, family, when I reach a transcendent state. And I know others of you do, as well. Likewise, I mean not to trip you up with hackneyed New Age tripe, but there have been nights when I have been literally lifted out of myself. Tonight that's not happening."

Daniel waited for this old man's angle. Having lived through the whole est/Lifespring era, his radar for cults was fairly keen.

"I'll tell you something, people, I do this drumming thing for a living. But I'm not here to recite my résumé. I come here every Thursday night and haul my gear down those steps, and I'm not a young man anymore, and nobody's paying me to be here. Yet I'm here. For one purpose only. To draw up the Spirit, yours and mine, through that cement floor, and make it swim around us, so we can bathe in it. And I don't know what God is, man, I gave up religion long ago. But I do know what Spirit is. And I know that Spirit, if it can be faced and dealt with, is the answer to all God questions. It lives in every nook and cranny in this room and in our bodies and souls, but can easily lie dormant. Yet it can be beckoned by the striking of the drum. If there are any doubters in here, I beg you to ask an Eskimo shaman or an Oshogbo drummer. Ask any tribesman. And we are a tribe here, people. Are we not?"

Daniel glanced around to see if anyone was actually intending to answer, or to murmur *hallelujahs*. No one did.

"Tonight, however, we're letting the world get in our way. Are we making music? Because it doesn't sound like music to me. It sounds like noise. We're all trying to out-volume each other. Why, this sister over here is doing her best to lay down a pattern and all we're doing is trampling her. We're not making music *with* her. We are burying her."

Daniel's eyes darted over to the woman in question, who sat with her head lowered, as if in deference to some great Sermon on the Mount.

"This man over here brought his shakuhachi in tonight. This is his offering to the drum circle, and you can't even hear the brother's flute, man. He's blowing his tail off, and nobody can hear him. What's wrong with that? And what's with this rushing? You people have some place to be? If you can't lock into a rhythm, if you're playing a tempo that's three times faster when you finished from where you started, something is wrong, my friends. You are not listening to each other. You are not listening to yourselves. And if you are not listening, then how will you know when the Spirit has arrived? For, you will not have heard it coming."

At this point, there were faintly audible huzzahs from the crowd, which clearly inferred that this old man was onto something. Daniel remained pensive.

"This is no bullshit, people. This is life and death for me. This is where I come instead of church, where all people do is ask me for my money and tell me what Hell's going to look like when I get there. So I am not here to waste my time by playing with people who are only here to stroke themselves. This is a shared offering. We don't come here to take, like you do in church. In church, you take the message the preacher has to shove down your throat, you take the communion, the wafer, the wine, the body of Christ. You take it whether you want it or not. Here, we give. We give of our hearts. We give our gifts. We give our love, to ourselves, to each other, and to the Spirit. We are altruists.

"To those of you here for the first time, we ask you for no money, nor any confession. We only welcome you to join our circle and help us draw up the Spirit. And perhaps patronize the establishment a little by buying a tea or a muffin, since they have been kind enough to allow us this space. Let me tell you something about the Spirit, people. It loves beauty. It loves music and dancing and joyous song. And I don't know about you, but that's what I'm trying to make here. The Spirit, however, does not like noise, and it does not like abuse. Now, I'm not pointing any fingers, but some of you brothers are beating your women! Oh, you look puzzled when I say that? And, of course, every one of you is glancing at the brother beside him. Well, you hear what I say now. A drum is a woman. I was playing drums before any of you were born. I'm ninety-four years old, and I've been playing drums for ninety-FIVE years. Yes, family, because I was playing in my good mother's womb!"

There were hoots of praise from a few bold ones, but most of the room just stared dumbfounded and frightened of this old guru.

"I repeat. A drum is a woman. And you had better treat her right. You'd better caress her and entice her to sing, because right now all you're doing is beating your woman, and she is very angry! That's why she's rushing all over the place. That's why she can't keep a steady tempo. She wants to get the Hell out of here and away from you. And that's why she's screaming so loud. So caress your woman. Don't beat her. And let's try this again."

Before he'd barely come off of his last word, his old hands had placed themselves once again on his drum, with everyone else to follow his lead, slowly, one by one.

Daniel had to admit, as he tried to burrow behind this old man's eyes, that he'd been given a proper chill. And that just wasn't Daniel. Nona was easily swept, so taken was she by the wonders of life and the occasional Elmer Gantry, but Daniel had been too long jaded, too old, too bitter. He rolled his eyes at everything. What this old man spoke of, however, was about purity of intention. And that would always resonate with Daniel. And he now knew why Arthur came here. He also knew in this instant what that lifeline was that had kept Arthur alive when everything else should've done him in years ago.

Arthur had always searched for God. Or battled with God. Or cursed God. Or denied God. Tonight, as Daniel watched him pick up the waterphone, long abandoned now by the blond kid, and close his eyes, and rub it slowly, and call upon that eerie womanly sigh, he saw Arthur connect with the divine.

He had to admit, once the circle began again, there was a difference. The music was glorious. He'd thought so before, but it truly was now. And, again, he couldn't quantify the difference if asked. Either he was just highly suggestible tonight, or it truly was a perfect illustration of the radiant abstract.

Hundreds of drums with intricate patterns and widely diverse cultural influences worked together to sing together. Daniel was tickled to see a smile on the old man's face creep upon him. It made Daniel smile. And it even made him do something crazy. The act was upon him before he could realize it to stop it. He picked up a small drum, and he joined the circle. And Daniel Cross had no sense of rhythm whatsoever. Not even his father — the Black man! — the Gypsy! — had been able to give him that. But it couldn't, nor did it, matter here tonight. He was rapturously carried along by the strength of the mass and delirious in his goofy romp.

Was he drawing out any spirit? Who the Hell knew? But he was being rectified and purified. It was better than a colonic. He was downright childlike, bobbing head to and fro, thrusting shoulders up and down. One might almost be able to say that he was dancing. And Daniel Cross just didn't dance. His wife couldn't even get him to dance at their wedding. Slow dancing sure, as they'd done on their first date, or if he was drunk enough. But on this night, he'd been caught.

For hours this music never abated. He was drenched in sweat, his wavy locks pasted to his neck and forehead and the side of his cheek, hands hot and glowing from having been struck against hide for hours on end. Once in awhile he'd come back to the world, in between long stretches of having utterly left his body, and glance up to see Arthur, as lost in his own reveling. Daniel watched Arthur caress that waterphone and twirl and bow it with the caution of a surgeon. Arthur cleaved unto it, as though to lose it would be to lose everything, and he drew in its eerie cry, that cry that sounded like a woman. Daniel could tell that Arthur was exorcising demons again, for he knew that in the sound of that waterphone Arthur heard Ophelia's wails. He probably used it to talk to her and implore her forgiveness. To tell her that he loved her still, and would give his own life if only she would give him the sign.

Maybe Daniel didn't read any of that in Arthur's face. Maybe he just reveled in melodramas. But he knew his friend well, and he knew that Arthur was seeking to make his peace through these drum circles. They both knew each other damned well, actually, which was why Daniel had allowed himself, bitching and moaning, of course, to trust that Arthur had had a master plan in bringing them all here the night before a very huge day. Arthur knew that there was nothing that could take it off Daniel's mind tonight, if not this.

THIS was magnificent.

Another glance up, some time later, and Daniel saw Nona and Kai dancing in the center of the circle, eyes closed, shining with sweat, floating above the world, unconcerned with a thing, connecting to each other in a way at which only women were gifted, and which they never confused with anything sexual, as men always did.

As the evening took everyone to a higher plane, it was ultimately stopped by the proprietors of the Talking Drum, claiming regrettably to have to close up shop. This pass could've lasted until daybreak had logistics not been in the way. They slowed it down, en masse, ritarded the tempo, lowered the dynamic, resolved it to a low drone, and finally faded out this sublime experience.

Daniel wasn't the huggy, feely sort, but he enjoyed watching it happen between everyone else, as he philosophized for one brief moment on the people who had been assembled here tonight, and apparently every Thursday night. All with different stories and agendas. All gathered here together for one lovely goal. To discover something greater than themselves.

He was contemplative on the drive home, as his head spun with the events of this evening. To have Nona with him as he discovered this drum circle was perfection. She was the light and weightless wonderer of life. It was the grounded source.

As he sat behind the wheel, he flashed on the image of Nona dancing in the center of the circle, awash in passion and perspiration. Watching her legs slide against each other under her skirt. Catching the sight of erect protrusions from her chest against the cotton of her blouse. Glimpsing her panting breath, mouth open, eyes squeezed tight, as they did during orgasms. He always watched her during her climaxes, even if he was coming at the same time. His eyes would remain fixed on her wonderfully tortured face. Tonight she had danced and drummed as though she were making love. He had wanted to lay her down right there on that floor in front of a hundred people and ravish her.

And after sweating in the drum circle to save his soul, a soul he didn't even believe in, he only wanted now to sweat in abandoning it. With one hand steering the car, he gently sneaked his other up her skirt and touched what he knew would be ready for him. Instinctively, as his hand slid upward, her legs closed on it, to pin it in, and her own hands clasped around his wrist. She helped him to fondle her as they soared west across the 10 Freeway. And though it was the heart of winter, it was also Los Angeles, so it was one of those warm, windy nights, with Dexter Gordon on the radio. And he'd just come from one of the most invigorating experiences of his life. And his wife was sexy. And the stars could not have been better aligned.

On the shoulder of the freeway he pulled over, a dangerous choice anyway you looked at it, but it was past two in the morning and so only sparsely trafficked. There was something irresistibly juvenile and titillating in the risky impulse. They were only about twenty minutes away from their comfy home, where they had the safe freedom to be intimate wherever they wished. But like two school kids, they wrestled with steering wheels and stick shifts, tangling themselves in each other amid seventy-mile-per-hour surroundings.

He knew she'd be game. She was game for anything these days. And though this new aggressiveness had concerned him at first, he had to confess that after a fashion she only reeled him in.

He sank down in his car seat, as she straddled atop him. The most surprising of all notions was that this woman wrapped around him was not some whore he'd bought, or some one-night stand he'd picked up in a bar, or even some girlfriend he'd only wanted to shag but never get to know. *Those are the women who get your cock hard. Not wives.* Yet he was crazy in love and lust with this woman with whom he was commanded, by law and moral code, to indulge in just this very carnal thing he had in mind.

Her hard nipples, which his fingers delicately pinched, and the wetness between her legs, where he feverishly slid in and out, were all his.

When they finished, out of breath and smelling like each other, they drove home in silence. Twenty minutes later they got out of the car, opened the front door, and walked upstairs to their bedroom with not a word spoken. He grabbed her and slipped his tongue against hers once more, catching her lip between his teeth and biting it gently. The softness of her mouth threatened to arouse him again, but they were both exhausted, and they promptly climbed into bed and fell asleep, as full from the wonders of a strange life as from the puerile car sex.

Nona slept effortlessly this night, and in general, of late, seemed to possess a new composure. He knew it was her letters to and from her friend in Africa, which she'd briefly shared with him. She was in the midst of a victorious breakthrough, after a long and difficult battle. As he lay in bed, with her comely face resting against the crook of his arm, he comforted in the notion of her happiness.

He, however, was suffering some fidgety restlessness that eventually got him up to scribble in his notebook. Nona would smile to know that he was beginning to see the merits of journal keeping. And tonight it would get its scribbled fill, because he could not, for the life of him, get those drums out of his head.

THIRTY FIVE

Murmuration.

It seemed as though he'd been preparing for this large, looming animal his entire life, yet it had actually only been two years out of a tedious forty-five. He was tempted to think it might change his life. He'd certainly been teased with the hype of it all: Michel Dugnac! June Steele! A book! If this all went well, then, according to his teasers, New York, London, and Marseille were virtually guaranteed.

He paced and chain-smoked through most of the day, declining brunch at the Four Seasons with Nona, Harper, and Kai, and instead awaited the eleventh-hour delivery of the art books to the gallery. There were handlers hired to take care of all that, but Daniel wouldn't have been Daniel if he couldn't butt his nose in everyone's business, and he couldn't wait until tonight, besides, to see the book.

As he ripped open one of the boxes, he lifted the handsome coffee table book out, with the piece merely labeled *Untitled* as its cover. It was a photographic tableau, camouflaging a nude Arthur and Nona into a portrait of his chaos of a workspace. Harper thought it would be the perfect piece for the cover, since it not only portrayed Daniel's subjects but his studio, as well, which had always been a virtually untouchable lair, except for intimates.

"The viewer feels as though he gets the chance to be inside Daniel Cross's private life just a bit," had been her rationale. Daniel didn't care. He liked this piece.

The predominant hue was cobalt, but then avalanched into a deluge of furious color and junk that seemed to swell upon Arthur and Nona, as if they were stained, bled upon, by the junk of this world; yet also, in a sense, cocooned by it. And in being cocooned, were gestated and transformed.

He stared at it now, realizing just how much his thoughts on rape and loss and redemption had become a driving force in all of his recent work. Behind every expression lurked the nocturnal phenomenon of the breach. It leapt off the very cover. The two figures in this portrait weren't even his friend and his wife any longer; they had transcended those roles. He stared at two strangers. Two abstracts. To be interpreted, and debated, and reckoned with. Naked. Literally, of course. But, as well, in a symbolic way to which he was the only one wise. In all of the thousands of works he'd created in his nearly thirty years of painting, it counted as the first that he'd been unable to title, and only now did he realize why.

When the evening finally did arrive, and as Benton's lights shined brightly onto Rodeo Drive with their three names, everyone was in attendance. Artists, critics, philanthropists, movie stars, curators, press, intending to snack on Beluga from L'Orangerie, sip champagne from the Krug Vineyards, hobnob with their Prada-appareled brethren, and render their verdict on his life.

And none of this brouhaha, however ephemeral, was because of any weight he could claim but because Harper Levy knew how to get things done. She was in her greatest element, giving the firmest handshake in the room and feeling deservedly proud. She'd worked harder than anyone to make sure this evening would be significant.

Before Daniel had met Harper, he'd never known what it felt like to have someone believe in him. She was there for him during the co-op days, and during the days of no showings at all. She was there during the era of Chelsea, and had been on hand in the hospital when he'd tried to end his life. She'd found him living on the street as a young twenty-something, hustling people to buy his wallet-sized sketches, and she'd taken him in and encouraged him to further develop his talents. She was the one who had turned him on to *Champion*, and was the first person he'd excitedly told about meeting the author of that book. And tonight he watched her oversee a splendid effort.

And then there were Nona and Arthur. He was so humbled to be a part of this venture with two such remarkable individuals as his wife and his brother of the spirit. Their essence was everywhere this evening, larger than their own lives, seeping from the cracks in the walls, lurking about every room, haunting every canvas. Their prose was unequaled.

Daniel had tried hard to be worthy of them, and the effort had almost succeeded in besting him. And for just one instant he reflected on the reputation of artists: All nuts, or so it is said. Or did they merely wish to be? Were they truly incapable of connecting the dots of their sanity because they were too overloaded with resplendent fancy? Or was it just irresistibly fashionable to be so left of the middle? He was beginning to wonder if they weren't all cons and swindlers, himself included, staging lunacies not because of any higher calling, but because of the hunger for attention. What was, after all, so alluring about being wrinkle-browed? Besides the women he could bed?

In the past, he would approach these openings either indifferently or with his brooding cap on, wondering if that was all there was, always suspecting someone's compliment of his work as ulterior, always doubting that there was any inherent good or beauty in anything. Always suffering. Always Hamlet.

Tonight, as he began to suspect his own breed, and which almost had a wink to it, he actually worked the room, and shook hands, and greeted, and periodically glanced up to see some labor that had begun its life in his flat, and felt unbeaten. No, it was better than that. He felt valid.

Having Nona and Arthur by his side was surely the best of it, but it was also that some of the drummers from the night before had agreed to come down, a last minute inspiration, to begin a circle right in the center of the Benton Gallery. Red Carpet meets Haight-Ashbury. Just the kind of peculiar marriage that had always fed Daniel's temperament. All of the people he loved were here, and they were genuinely making him feel that there might actually be something inherently good or beautiful in this world.

"Hello, Daniel."

He spun around to find Christianne Tensmith standing before him with a glass of champagne raised.

"Chris," he practically fumbled. It had been a good two years since he'd unceremoniously exited her life.

"It's wonderful work," she said. "All of it. Better than ever. You're really coming into your voice, aren't you? There's no pretension in it. I mean, not that there ever was, but—"

"Em—I—I—thank you. What a surprise. I—I—"

" 'Course, still no portrait of me anywhere," she joked sweetly.

He laughed nervously.

"I can't wait to show Daddy the review in tomorrow morning's paper, which I know is going to be killer. And which might actually kill HIM."

They both chuckled.

"So—how've you been?" Daniel asked. "I mean—"

"I don't want to keep you. I just wanted to let you know that I would not have missed this for the world. Congrats, Daniel."

She leaned up to kiss his cheek, and walked away.

He stood stunned, chest thumping. He hadn't expected the ghosts of Daniel Past to come haunting. If Chelsea Carrier showed up, he'd have to scrounge himself up another bottle of shoe dye.

He watched Christianne walk away and wondered if he hadn't misjudged her all of these years, chalking her up to vapidity, like the snob he could be. Tonight she was quite refined. And apparently not hating him any longer for the way he'd spinelessly cowered out of their relationship. She never even made trouble for him about staying in his flat. Wonders would never cease.

Should he run after her and apologize once more for the prick he'd been?

He decided to meet and greet instead.

Alas, cowards, as well, never cease.

After enough handshaking and photos taken to qualify him for election, which lasted a solid two hours, he finally took a moment alone to regard his canvases, to assess his life in this body of work, and to wonder if anywhere in any canvas he'd ever painted might there not be traces of his estranged mother and father. For the first time in years he wondered where they were and if they were still alive. He came frightfully close to wishing that they could see what he'd tried to do with his life.

As he pondered thoughts he hadn't in some time, a creeping sensation began to take over him. Tonight he felt uncharacteristically sentimental. Probably just too exhausted any longer to be so perpetually and fashionably in a huff.

He couldn't help but feel that the spirit the old man had spoken of last night had indeed entered the room and somehow blessed his work. Because for the first time in his life he didn't despise himself, as he usually did, and he didn't get drunk, as he usually did. Tonight he soberly relished in his burgeoning success and was just thankful no mirrors were around, as he would surely not have recognized his own face. He had Nona to thank for that one, as he watched her in the distance, shaking hands, wowing the paparazzi, loving life, eating this evening up, and apparently teaching him a few life lessons.

His wife found joy easily within every crevice that held an enticement. For a time he'd been worried. But tonight she was truly happy, he noted, as he watched her float through the space with a peaceful confidence. It was important that this night be a good one for her, too, since there'd been a history of her doubting her own worth with what he knew was a frustrating writer's block. On this night her luminous smile lit the place up, brighter than the marquee lights of Rodeo Drive. She even threatened to sweep him up with her in that joyful tide.

With his new gleam, he geared himself for the firing squad of critics, and felt invincible. He already had a history with some of them, the ones who had traditionally found his work too bleak for their tastes, too self-indulgent, too something. Of course, they were all in attendance and were the first in line to tell him what they thought. But most, tonight, seemed to laud his portrayals of the already acclaimed Nona Childe and the soon-to-be acclaimed Arthur Hughes Dufresne. Not to mention, both possessed such stunning visages that could be molded and shaped into practically any perversion and still remain stunning.

Aside from the New York, Paris, and London art media, the literary world was also in attendance. They gobbled Nona up with their accolades, reminding her that she was special, a task at which he'd lately failed.

They asked her a deluge of questions on why she would indulge in such a risky art house venture, after having taken the mainstream by storm. Mainstream? They considered *The Assassination of Gabriel Champion* mainstream, did they?

She was exquisitely playful in her replies. When one queried, "Why this involvement with such an unstable, albeit titillating, avant-garde, after nestling comfortably in the commercial book market?" she responded with a smile, "Why, to fix that very problem."

THIRTY SIX

When they questioned her involvement in this vanguard project, Nona was perplexed with all the allusions that her alliance with this show might've been ill-advised, until she realized it was the critics' job to court agitation. Made good copy. They were actually eating the exhibit up, so she decided to just have fun by playing feisty.

As the sun set, and she finally stopped for one moment to take a swig of champagne and a deep breath, she and Kai watched Arthur in the distance. With his signature dreadlocks an unusually majestic, lawless crown of tentacles, Arthur wore a threadbare suit jacket, a pair of pants that did not belong to the jacket, and a wrinkled, out-of-date necktie. Nothing of the ensemble was sharp, but neither was it exactly awful. It existed just somewhere in the intoxicated vicinity of romantic struggle. Nona couldn't help but attach a trendy sartorial statement to Arthur's utter lack of it. After tonight, all the young poets would soon start sporting their fringe-existence duds, all because the new bard of South Central had set a tone, and a new hobo chic would be born.

Arthur had started the evening off happy. This would be the night that would give him the chance to show his son what he'd accomplished. If this night was for anyone, on Arthur's own personal agenda, it was for Lorca.

What he'd created to show his son, to show the world, was extraordinary. Nona had always felt that there was something feral and hallucinatory in Arthur's words. She'd earlier overheard a reporter dictating into a tiny machine: "Arthur Hughes Dufresne writes poetry for a cataclysmic world, as though he is perpetually on the verge of hysteria or some quiet, warring mania, all toward a violent resuscitation of heart and lungs." And all Nona could think at that eavesdropping was, *amen.*

Then there were the cloying ones.

"Mister Dufresne," offered one reporter, with a mic stuck in Arthur's face, "you seem to write in a manner that is at once a kind of stream-of-consciousness, urban speak, while at the same time a cunning philological wordplay. A bit reminiscent of Stoppard—"

"A kind of homeboy-from-the-hood Stoppard, if you will—" interrupted another, feeling droll.

No one actually gave Arthur the chance to respond, as they were much more interested in the sound of their own voices. The ingratiating nature of these admirers made Nona cringe, especially in offering their patronizations with accents on the words *homeboy* and *hood*, as if to assure that they could hang with the Blackest and street-smartest of them. She and Kai had been rolling their eyes and giggling together at the ridiculousness, and were on top of the world to be able to watch their friend being lauded and cooed over, even if it was by idiots.

Arthur could care less that he was even the topic of conversation, as he had one eye and ear cocked obligatorily to the cooing and the other searching eagerly around the room for his son's arrival.

That the drum circle, which they'd all discovered the night before, would recreate itself on this opening was truly the ring on the finger of a long, difficult, and thrilling romance.

At various junctures in the evening, between contemplating a piece and the whispered chatter that always accompanied such, people would come and go from the circle. Some would join in, retreat. It would grow and shrink. It was a thriving animal that kept itself alive the entire evening, and was becoming as much the thing to do as the partaking of champagne and aged Brie.

The night was working, and it was all thanks to her husband. Arthur's brilliance notwithstanding, the work that Daniel had created for this exhibit was the most powerful body of work that she could remember seeing from any contemporary artist since…well, she always instinctively went back to her beloved Basquiat. Her scope as an art lover wasn't nearly that singular, but her affinity was directly proportional to her collectorship. There was no other "important" artist that she'd ever owned, and this work before her tonight was genuinely reminiscent of artists past who had blown onto the art scene and changed the game. Tonight people were gasping at and dissecting the colors and the textures and the breadth and the swirls and the bold flashes that were leaping off the canvases.

Daniel was being compared to the new wave of New York modernists, for attempting to turn medium on its ear. That was the very least of it, she thought. Daniel was reinventing art. On this unforgettable evening, Daniel was as close to God as any mortal force that had ever breezed past her heart.

While most of the critics tonight were jumping through hoops to claim Daniel as their own personal discovery, and to drool over his severe, exaggerated, almost tormented depictions of humanity, some found his work unappetizing. One critic observed rather coolly: "As subjects, Dufresne and Childe are being turned inside out in these pieces. The viewer isn't being shown their souls, as much as their symbolic bowel movements."

Wow! Did she and Arthur really seem just that naked and blemished to this uncomfortable critic? Did they make him just that fidgety in his seat? And if the answer was *yes*, then as far as she was concerned Daniel had done his job superbly.

"What irony, if any, are you offering with all of this darkness?" this particular critic had earlier asked Daniel, displaying quotation signs with his fingers around the word *darkness*.

What were the quote signs for, Nona wondered? Did he mean that Daniel played at darkness without actually achieving it? Did he mean that Daniel achieved it, and he wondered the importance of that? Was he saying that Daniel was finding trendy vogue in the darkness label?

She was annoyed, and wanted Daniel to fight back with something pithy and effortlessly smart-assed, as she'd been doing, but Daniel never answered questions like that. You were either moved by his work or you weren't. And if you weren't, he didn't bother spinning his wheels trying to defend or bring you around. He would gracefully, if he could, accept your distaste for it and still agree to be your friend.

She was more in love with him and his Fuck-The-World creed tonight than ever before. It was the F-T-W of a man who cared about stimulating the world, about egging on the mind, and the heart, and the soul. And he was her husband.

For the life of her, she couldn't get the smile off her face.

THIRTY SEVEN

They were all buzzing, Daniel took notice. About him. About Nona and Arthur. Even the ones who showed their distaste seemed ecstatic to be a witness to this happening. And if they gobbled Nona up, they resolutely turned cartwheels over the undiscovered, disheveled genius, Arthur Hughes Dufresne, who could care less about them.

Arthur had become nervous and fidgety. He had started out feeling proud of this evening, even buoyant, though Daniel knew he was much more at home swilling a 40-ounce and deconstructing literary criticism or playing a hand of Bid Whist. Still, this night had been as important to Arthur as to himself. And all Daniel could see at this point in the evening was Arthur doing his best to put on a polite front, but beginning to seethe because Sonja had yet to show up with his son.

Sonja was on a fairly new jag these days of discrediting Arthur in the courts with regard to his parental rights. They had always co-parented without much incident, but she had recently made the announcement that she wanted to move back home to D.C. to get help from her family. Arthur knew he would never see his son again if that move happened, and after imploring her not to, and his pleas ignored, he decided to take her to court. And though she had promised to bring Lorca to the opening tonight, he also knew she was on a sudden warpath after the summons, maligning his name to the courts and their son, calling him a worthless father and drug addict. Drug addict, yes, unfortunately, but worthless father? There was no more dedicated or conscientious a father in the world than Arthur.

At twelve years old, Lorca was already an avid reader and a hungry learner, who would regularly challenge Arthur to some philosophical match on whether or not the ghost of Hamlet's father really symbolized the Devil. Or whether rap was any less significant a music form than jazz. Or whether Martin and Malcolm *really* took opposite approaches to the Civil Rights

Movement. The kid was inquisitive and wide-eyed and amazing.

And this itchy wonder in Lorca's head was all Arthur's doing. Sonja barely picked up a book that wasn't either the Bible or some Hollywood tell-all. She was a paradoxical woman who'd gotten pregnant with Arthur's child, though she'd been married to someone else at the time, and when asked by her sister-in-law why she hadn't used birth control, if not discretion, had answered, indignantly: *"It's against my religion!"*

Daniel didn't much like Sonja.

But tonight she'd promised to put the weapons down and bring Lorca to the opening, so that the boy could read his father's works, and see his father respected, and take home his own copy of *Murmuration* with his father's name boldly stamped on the cover. And so far this evening, she and Lorca were nowhere to be found.

Arthur never drummed once tonight, and this really should've been Daniel's first clue that he was in trouble. Art was the one, above any of them, who had been the most connected to the drum circle experience. Tonight he was as disconnected from it as by any gulf Daniel had ever seen.

By the time the night was nearing its end, there still was no sign of Lorca and Sonja. The event was being considered a success — indeed they'd all felt it — yet all that could be mustered from Arthur was thinly disguised despair.

"I can't believe she didn't bring him," Arthur muttered at one passing, fury low and simmering, but quickly rising. The quickly rising part worried Daniel.

A few minutes later Nona came running over, quietly panicked.

"Arthur just bolted outta here," she whispered confused, amidst the mingling crowd. "What is going on?"

"Shit!" was all Daniel could utter.

He knew Arthur was on a hostile course, but he never imagined Arthur would choose this moment to take care of business. And knowing Arthur's dark place as he did, Daniel felt a chill claw at his neck.

"He's on his way to Sonja's," Daniel warned. "We can't let there be a scene in front of Lorca."

"What do we do?" Nona asked, alarmed.

"We have to go after him."

"Right now!?"

All three artists suddenly exiting their own opening, especially one as high profile as this, was not a concept Nona was digesting well. But Daniel could give two shits about causing a scene. Arthur was in trouble, and Sonja was about to be. And he loathed his instinct — that perhaps for all these years he actually did still see the murderer in Arthur. He suddenly felt unworthy of Arthur's friendship.

He and Nona whispered to Harper that there was an emergency and to please buffer any possible questions of their whereabouts to the remaining guests, which, fortunately at this hour, weren't that many. And they bolted, as Arthur had bolted.

When they arrived forty-five minutes later at Sonja's front door in South Central, Arthur was fairly banging it down. He'd been pounding for some minutes, yelling for her to *"open up, or else!"* His rage was in full gear now. And there really is nothing quite so powerful and awe-spurring as the rage of a Black man; his voice is somehow deeper, his sense of doom intrinsic, even poetic.

Before Daniel and Nona had even approached the front steps, Arthur had managed to break a window, reach in, and unlock the door, but not before bloodying his hand. They were quickly on his heels, as he stumbled into the living room to find it empty of all furniture. The sight of the naked room slapped them all in the face, as Arthur stopped dead in a stunned dawning.

"No, no, no, no, no," he whispered in a swelling frenzy. He ran to the kitchen, the bedrooms, he flung open closet doors. Empty, all empty. Nona's hands came up to her aghast mouth, and Daniel held her, as each knew what was unfolding before their eyes.

"GODDAMN IT!" Arthur roared, as neighbors began to spill out of their homes, in gossipy wonder.

"Noooo!!! You fucking cunt! You goddamn fucking cunt!" He put his fist through the bathroom door. Daniel tried to stop his ravings, but Arthur could only look his way in terrified disbelief.

"She took him! She took him from me!"

Arthur's hands came up to his temples, as he squeezed his eyes shut to bear the weight of what he knew he had to face: #1) Sonja had gone. #2) She had taken his son with her. #3) They had no intentions of being found.

His breathing grew labored, and the sweat of his head poured profusely. He grabbed the wall phone, almost pulling it off the wall, and furiously punched numbers on it, not even entertaining the possibility that the service might've already been disconnected. Or refusing to entertain it, as that would mean the cruel reality of a plan in action for some time.

Daniel watched him cautiously to make sure he didn't injure himself further. Nona was too afraid to advance. Instead Daniel had her walk back out to calm the approaching neighbors and to see if she could find out any information on Sonja's and Lorca's whereabouts.

Over his shoulder, Daniel could hear a neighbor explaining to Nona that Sonja had made her hasty escape with Lorca sometime that afternoon with the help of eight or nine muscular cousins who'd moved furniture and boxes quickly into several cars and pickups.

"She did not come here, Arthur, I swear!" pled a female voice through the receiver. Turns out, there was little consolation in there still being phone service. Everything seemed to be a symbol that carried with it the promise of great meaning, only to deliver no meaning at all.

"Then where the fuck is she!" Arthur yelled, as much to the phone itself as to Sonja's distraught mother on the other end. "Listen, Etta, I will come there myself and END YOU, if you don't tell me where she went with my son!"

Arthur was a dragon. Daniel was grateful Nona was outside and away from this witness, because he saw the Devil form in Arthur this night, as on one unspeakable night of twenty-eight years ago. This night, as on that one, Arthur was absolutely capable of murder. He was fully prepared to give this old woman heart failure with his threats if she didn't cooperate, and if that failed he was just as prepared to hop a plane to D.C. to put an end to her in person.

Suddenly, amidst all the riotous confusion, there emerged a kind of defeated collapse that curtly peered out from the frenzy. It was so brief that if Daniel had blinked he'd surely have missed it. He saw Arthur's heart fold up and begin to die. Arthur begged the old woman to tell him where they'd gone. But there was no more cock-strutting. Only desperate pleas. At this moment, Arthur must've felt less than a man. And only another man, Daniel thought as he watched his friend, could truly know that hollowness so intimately.

Then, in a second instant, the frantic pandemonium was back in full force. Arthur slammed the receiver onto its base, splintering the chrome and plastic. He pounded it again and again until there was nothing left of it and spurts of blood shot from his hand. His fingers would not unhinge themselves from the mangled receiver. Daniel tried to grab him and hold him still.

"Look! We can find them. We just have to put our heads together. We just have to calm down and not be rash. We can use this against her. This is kidnapping! I mean, taking a child from his father when there are still custodial rights? There's got to be something that protects you. We'll just…we'll just look into it. We'll find out what we need to."

Arthur just kept repeating "I can't believe she did this!" as he madly paced the empty house. He could barely focus in to listen to Daniel.

Daniel knew Arthur needed to fix, and even as much as he loathed the idea, and knew his wife would never approve, he would personally take Arthur to the deed, so that the mad dog could be tempered.

THIRTY EIGHT

Why did Sonja's have to be the only house on this block that didn't have security bars on the windows and doors, Nona wondered, so that Arthur could've been dissuaded from this destructive course? Instead, here they were. Burglars officially.

As she attempted to gather information from a neighbor, another interrupted the conversation loudly.

"Who the Hell y'all think y'all is, comin' up in'is neighborhood like some mu-fuckin' caped crusaders, thinkin' y'all gon' save somebody? That niggah ain't nut'n but a loser crackhead, and it's 'bout time Sonja finally got up off her ass and got the Hell outta here with that boy. Ain't nobody cooperatin' wit'chall! Like, y'all got a badge or sump'n. Shit, y'all better git the fuck on outta here, befo' the REAL badges show up, cuz the police have been called!"

Nona winced to have this woman screaming in her ear, but absolutely lost it to hear sirens in the distance.

"You actually called the police?" Nona cried out, the two of them facing each other off on the wet lawn of Sonja's abandoned house. As the Santa Ana winds started up, Nona closed Daniel's coat even tighter around her, which he'd given her to wear when they'd made their great escape. Now she and this woman were nose to nose, surrounded by curious neighbors parked on their steps, the sidewalks, the driveway. Daniel had his battles inside with Arthur, and she had to deal with the neighborhood loudmouth.

"You have no idea what's going on here," said Nona.

"Oh, I don't?" the woman spat back indignantly, as she waved her overly long fingernails in Nona's face, reminding Nona of the *Hey Babys* that she and Kai used to know in high school. If you lived in Santa Monica in the early eighties, fourteen blocks inland from the Pacific, off Pico, chances are you knew the girls who pasted their hair down the side of their faces with Dippity-Do to effect the "good hair" look, and sported a single gold tooth and ridiculous press-on nails, who hung out idly on their front porches in hot pants, midriffs, and furry slippers, smacking their gum loudly and slinging their babies on their hips at age thirteen, whom their own mamas supported. They had names like Pooky and Dimples, but Nona and Kai called them *Hey Babys* because *"hey, baby!"* is what these freaks of nature loved to yell to the guys who drove by in their low riders.

As Nona revisited that image, she realized that these were also the girls who could fight, when she never could, so that thought lodged nervously in the back of her head as this woman screamed in her face.

"Who the fuck you think you is, tellin' me I don't know what's goin' on?"

"Why are you involving yourself in this?" Nona yelled, on the verge of tears she fought to resist, lest she show her fear. But she was afraid, and that quiver in the voice was giving her away.

"I live here, bitch!"

"Don't you have anything better to do than to get in everyone else's business?"

"I see this shit every day!"

They screamed at each other until they had no voices left, and they roused the rest of the neighbors, who only got more excitable as the sirens got louder. The woman continued her rant, even as Nona tried to walk away, and aggressively followed behind as Nona pled for more information from others in the crowd.

"Whenever that motha-fucka comes over here, there's a fight," the woman screamed from behind Nona. "Time'a day don't matter. He would pick a fight with Sonja every fuckin' time. And I told her, over and over again, she oughta have that niggah arrested! Cuz I will kill the motha-fucka that ever comes up in my face the way that crackhead would act with her! Lorca don't need to be around all'at shit!"

Nona couldn't make any sense of why she was so annoyed by this woman's "crackhead" remarks just because Arthur's drug of choice was not crack. Who cared about a ridiculous technicality here? Yet she found herself wincing with every utterance of it, as if one over the other was better.

When the woman started to shove at Nona, Nona gave her fear full away, and started to plead in a flight of tears, "please stop it! Stop it!" just as the police car was driving up. Two officers immediately separated them and warned them to behave, as the crowd egged them on, yelling, "It's a fight! It's a fight!" while others shouted that the real problem was not the catfight out here but the Hulk inside who was bashing windows and phones.

Nona couldn't think straight in this deranging melee. She only knew that these two officers were now on their way up the front steps of Sonja's house. Arthur's very life had been snatched away this evening, and now he was about to be taken away in handcuffs because of nosy-body neighbors.

"That's right! Arrest that motha-fucka!" screamed the woman Nona loathed. "He broke into this house!"

"He did not!" Nona lied. "His son lives here," was all she could offer to qualify it.

"Not no more!" the woman said, laughing. "And praise Jesus for that! Who knows what sick thing he mighta did with that child whenever he took him away from here."

The rage suddenly mushroomed in Nona so phenomenally at the notion that this gossipy shrew would insinuate what she did about a man she'd only ever observed from her snoopy window, and make such an unfounded accusation, especially considering Arthur's own childhood, about which this woman knew nothing, that before Nona knew her next thought, or better judgment, she had whirled around and cuffed the lights out of the woman. Unlike the huffy soap-opera slaps of most women, Nona's whole raging body went into this one, as the entire left side of the woman's head was suddenly slammed against Nona's red palm.

The lumbering body crashed to the ground, only to bounce back with an equal furor. Frighteningly sooner than Nona was ready for, her own face felt the prickly white explosion of a fist in retaliation. The sting was so profound that it blinded her for a flash and jarred her inner ear, careening her to her knees, in a disorienting stupor. The world was sideways and rumbling. The crowd became bedlam.

She worried about her reconstructed jaw, which had never been fully strong again after the rape. Yet in an instant, that worry was gone and was replaced instead with the impenetrable hunger to make pulp out of this loud, classless, clueless, detestable BITCH!

Dumbed by rage, which obliterated her earlier fear, Nona sucked in a gulp of air, held it in her lungs, closed her eyes, and dove back in. The absurdity of the sight of these two was not lost on her: The Hey Baby in signature furry slippers, hair curlers, shorts, and overly long acrylic nails; and Nona in her splendidly wild Galliano gown, and her Louboutin shoes that she'd spent a solid week shopping for, on Rodeo Drive, just for the occasion. (Not this occasion.)

As the two wildcats tore each other to fleshy shreds, and Nona worried about her return receipt, the officers were intercepting Arthur from Daniel's clutches. There was such a flurry of chaos that Nona could barely know where to direct her temper. At the Hey Baby? At the uniformed men who were cuffing Arthur? At Sonja? Or at God?

"What is going on here!" Daniel demanded.

"Sir, I'll ask the questions," remarked one officer, in that quintessentially arrogant manner of policemen. "And I'm asking you to step back. But I'm only asking once."

Nona heard this all in the distance, but was otherwise engaged. Suddenly Daniel looked up to see her dilemma and went madly awry, running out to pry the women apart. The two officers followed on his heels with Arthur's arms held tightly by each.

Nona was all the more confused when two arms swiftly grabbed her that were neither Daniel's, nor the Hey Baby's, nor the two cops. A second squad car had arrived on the scene, she realized, with many more officers in tow, and she was now being brusquely clutched at her arms, as Arthur had been, by a second pair of uniforms, and promptly handcuffed for assaulting the Madwoman of South Central.

A smug impulse leapt out of Nona suddenly as she calmed herself with the assurance that people like this woman probably never read a book in their lives, so that her anonymity in this mortifying scandal could remain intact. And she wasn't even allowed to turn around to see if they'd cuffed the madwoman too. How many cops were even here?

"This is an outrage!" Daniel spat at the gathering of law enforcement, before Nona could beg him to shut up.

"Say one more word, asshole, and you'll be hauled in too."

And he was. Daniel could never shut up when shutting up was needed.

Nona could only muse to herself the ridiculous irony of this evening. Here they were, the three celebrated artists, who had, only hours ago, clinked glasses with the country's royalty, now somewhere off Manchester being arrested as common thugs for disturbing the peace.

As this horrifying scene grew larger and uglier, one of the officers placed a hand on her head and guided it into a squad car, as her wrists burned from being bound behind her. She watched them handcuff Daniel and shove Arthur to the ground. Her mind reeled, *this is not happening!* Beyond the greasy glass of the squad car window — her first — she watched Arthur lying on the ground, his own hands manacled behind him, quaking and sweating from the need for a fix that would not come this night. She saw him resign from life and become passive, his will resolutely leaving his sick body and abandoning him. As they all had. Arthur's mother and father. God. Now Sonja.

She and Daniel caught a glimpse of each other, he in one car, she in the second. Both their hearts were clearly broken, and not for their own trivial plights, but for the put-upon man who'd been fraught with so much despair already, and now lay like an animal against the asphalt, once more afflicted.

She had always thought of Arthur as one who slithered through life like so many lizards who got trampled by the boots of big men. He was too low to the ground to be considered worthy of not being trampled. No one caught lizards the way they caught butterflies — to admire their beauty. Arthur only blended into the foliage like the many lizards who prayed that one more day might be theirs without being stomped or stalked for their hides. She'd often thought that perhaps that was why Arthur desecrated his own hide with so many needles. To insure that no one would want his. To insure that he might be left alone in this life.

Tonight that image became realized with the most brilliant clarity, because she watched Arthur's colors change before her eyes to blend into the cement so that they would not find him. And though his body was theirs for the time being, his soul had dissolved from their sights. His eyes were empty. He looked Nona's and Daniel's way, and she clearly saw all volition gone, vaporized by the great heist of his only son.

How had the night — a night they'd all anticipated with jubilation — gone so wrong?

THIRTY NINE

The phone call to Harper felt like a joke. Safe to assume the woman never expected to hear from Nona via Parker Center.

"You're where?"

Nona had to convince her it was real.

At four in the morning she stood in the cramped cell, cocooned herself inside Daniel's greatcoat, and shivered from shock. Arrest. Her. She still couldn't make it real in her head. Her hair was a twiggy, matted mess. Her Galliano, which was barely containable beneath the coat, had dried blood and mud upon it. She rolled her eyes disgustedly that this was the only time in her life that she'd ever invested in couture, she of the boho aesthetic, and the ensemble didn't even survive the first wearing.

There was no way to sleep in the cell, as it was wall-to-wall detainees. They must've put the Hey Baby elsewhere, which relieved her. She couldn't have slept anyway, as the adrenaline and fear still pumped through her like a pressured hose and her face pounded. A swollen cut decorated her right eyelid, the same one that had been tumored and patched two years ago, and she couldn't believe she was revisiting that place of black eyes and bloody noses and busted jaws. These were not the realities of refinement, the snob in her assessed. She looked no better than the other smelly humans pushing and shoving for a tiny crawl of cell space to call their own, and that was her only shot at feeling safe in this frightening place.

She didn't dare look around or connect with anyone's eyes. Connecting would mean engagement, and she feared some Crazy catching her eye and deciding that she needed dealing with.

At just about dawn, a guard came for her and opened the cell doors, leading her down several dingy hallways to the reception desk where Harper stood waiting. She hadn't expected to break down upon sight of Harper, but as their eyes met Nona's whole composure collapsed and she cried hard in Harper's embrace.

They collected Nona's things from the desk clerk, signed her out, and Harper proceeded to explain that Daniel and Arthur, who had been taken to Men's Central, were also being released on bail and that Neville was picking them up, and meeting back at the house. Nona asked if she could be taken for a cup of coffee before heading home so that she could get her bearings first.

"I feel so wide awake," Nona muttered, shaken, over her 99¢ breakfast and mediocre coffee at the all-night Norms on La Cienega, but trying her damnedest to regain a little edge. "I feel like I've been syringed with a dose of Freon. I mean, my veins are just so spliced open and screaming. I just, I feel like I'm ready to bite."

"Take a deep breath. It's gonna be okay," Harper assured with that maternal hum that could usually soothe Nona. Not tonight. Harper reached for Nona's hands, which were trembling, but the frothing animal pulled them away.

"Just, just, let me get my thoughts out, Harper, please."

"Of course."

Another several deep breaths were required, however, before Nona was capable.

"I just...I can't believe all the miseries Arthur has had in his life. Just one after another, after another. Jesus, what doomed straw did he draw?"

A silence followed, as Harper assessed Nona's state then cautiously responded.

"What about Sonja's miseries?" Harper asked politely.

Nona stared at Harper for some seconds, and suddenly felt ridiculous that it had never occurred to her to concern herself with Sonja's position.

"I—I—" she stammered. "I—I don't—"

"I don't mean to put you on the spot. I'm only suggesting that you put yourself in Sonja's shoes for a moment. Lorca is her only child too. And Arthur is..." Harper hesitated. "Look, I mean no disrespect toward Arthur when I say this, okay? I've known him a long time. But he *is* a drug addict."

Harper snickered, which shoved Nona back some feet.

"I'm sorry. I am not laughing at Arthur...or even the situa—"

"You don't know him!" Nona bit, shaking her head in sad disappointment.

"Nona, I've known him longer than you have."

"Have you ever been there, in the flesh, to see him fix? Huh? Have you? Because, I have. He doesn't show that part of his life to just anybody. I'm sorry, Harper, I don't mean to one-up. I just don't think you really have a proper vantage point to comment."

"Oh my God, are you listening to yourself? Is that supposed to be some sort of street cred calling card? That if he has allowed you to watch him shoot up, then it means you get to be in the coveted inner circle? Come on, don't you see what you're doing? What you're rationalizing? I was laughing—and I apologize—at the lunacy of life that would make me have to be so delicate and diplomatic about the issue of a drug-addict parent. In any other scenario, and with any other person, wouldn't the answer be obvious? Yet we seem to be placing Arthur on some sort of pedestal, and challenging people's up-till-now fairly solid position that drug addicts should probably not be allowed to influence children. Honey, I know as well as you do how incredibly wonderful Arthur is with Lorca, but—"

"The greatest part of Lorca is everything that Arthur has given him."

"I know that, Nona."

"A lust for life, a questioning mind, a respect for people, a love for learning—"

"I know all of that. But just answer one question. If you were Sonja, wouldn't you be just the least bit concerned that your child's father cooks up an H cocktail every morning?"

Nona stared at Harper, pie-eyed and thin-lipped. *Yes! Hell yes! Of course!* But she couldn't say those words to Harper. Saying them would mean giving in that Arthur should probably lose. Again.

"But to take him and just escape—" was all she could utter instead, and still save face.

"Honey, I'm not saying Sonja should've handled it the way she did. But this is a woman in desperation. We aren't always blessed with finesse when we're desperate. And this is a mother using fierce maternal instincts. You know good and well that you and I both would do anything, just or unjust, in the belief that we were protecting our child."

This coming from the exchange of two childless women, Nona couldn't help but note.

She dropped her head into the palms of her hands, and sighed.

"Honey, in your fight to support Arthur," Harper offered, knowing Nona was weary, "which I support, just remember that Sonja is not necessarily the enemy here."

"Hey—" Nona suddenly thought, or she wanted to suddenly think, as this conversation grew thick, "—how did it look, you know, us leaving the gallery so abruptly? I mean, was everything—"

"Not to worry," Harper assured. "It was such a remarkable evening that no one noticed any alarm. Are you kidding? Exiting in the presence of everyone? Oh, very chic, very high fashion, very haute couture, very *très, très.*"

Harper actually made Nona laugh for an instant, amidst all the Hell of this night. Then, just as quickly, the laugh was gone.

"What she did, really, Harper, would be considered kidnapping."

Harper reached for Nona's hands again, and this time Nona didn't pull away. Harper knew Nona was beaten, unable to be calmed or humored this dark morning. It was a warm and windy dawn. The strange Santa Anas of L.A. winters. Lovely on the back of the neck if the mood were just right.

Nona and Harper arrived back in the Palisades some time after daylight to a roused and pacing Daniel. Neville was still with him, but Arthur had already gone home. Surely to do that thing he did, which Nona never wanted to hear about again, frankly, for as long as she lived.

After embracing his wife long and hard, and asking if she was okay, Daniel immediately commenced presenting his campaign to discredit Sonja. He scrutinized every angle and mapped out all the logical places Sonja might head.

"Of course, there's the mother in D.C. But there's also some family in St. Louis and Wichita, which is where I think we should start. I have every intention of investigating Sonja's background to see if there's anything comparable to Arthur's drug use that can be used against her. I mean, the mental competence factor, alone, has got to count for something."

"Daniel, maybe that's not the way we want to go," Nona cautiously slipped in, then posed the same question to him that Harper had posed to her, who had, by this time, and with Neville, left them to this conversation.

"Is it possible that we're—distorted—about Arthur? I mean, maybe we're the ones who are guilty of, I don't know, believing that his brilliance as an artist gives him the permission to rewrite the laws of moral code and absolves him from having to play by the same rules as the rest of us. Maybe we're just not thinking rationally."

Daniel looked at her as though she'd betrayed his very heart. More a surprise than a wounding, really. But the wounding followed quickly enough.

"Well, let me see," Daniel offered up, with a humiliated sarcasm. "I guess I'm trying to decide if I should be offended that you would infer such a lacking in insight from me."

"What? No, Daniel, this is not an attack on you. I'm accusing myself of the same thing."

"If you can even entertain the belief that Arthur gets away with anything because of his—what?—brilliance? Is that the theory? Then you don't know him at all. Have you not been paying attention to the molested child? The abandoned father? The man who can barely make ends meet most days? He has never had a break in his life!"

"I never said that Arthur gets everything he wants. I only suggested that perhaps you and I think that because he is the man he is, that he deserves to!"

"He does, goddamn it! You have no idea what that man has been through!"

"Yes, I do!" she yelled, furiously following behind Daniel as he began to rant the dimensions of their house. "I *have* been paying attention to the molested boy, the abandoned father—"

"You have no clue—"

"—AND I know about Viet Nam, and the beginnings of his heroin use, and how many times he's been homeless—"

"You have no clue—"

"—I know the things that haunt him, the lifetime nightmares—"

"You have no clue," was all he kept muttering in a kind of cryptic tone, as though his ego needed to convince itself that he was still a closer friend to Arthur than she. Or that there were certain bonds between the two of them she could never penetrate. So be it. Who cared! This was not a contest to see who could be the better friend to Arthur.

"I love Arthur," she assured, calmer. "It's him that I support in this battle. I'm merely asking you—us—to just breathe deeply for a minute and support him without getting on the warpath toward Sonja. It'll only fuel what is already some pretty monstrous hate in his heart. That's not what he needs from us."

She didn't dare continue the line of thinking that there just might be, somewhere deeply hidden, *maybe*, some tiny grace note of an empathic side to Sonja. Daniel hated Sonja. And only a few hours ago Nona had hated her too. But Harper had been right. They needed to see this thing deeper than the simpleminded archetypes of good and evil.

And her poor husband was only on his way to a stroke if he didn't quell his passions somewhat in order to accommodate that truth. There was no dragon to slay here, except fate maybe. But she quickly came to learn that as long as Daniel believed there was one, he had vowed to face it with sword and shield, for the brother he deeply loved.

FORTY

He began to see that he was in this thing alone. He couldn't count on the support of his wife, as he'd hoped, because she had begun to throw her feminist issues in his face. If she was accusing him of taking the position that Arthur should be allowed to get away with anything he wanted because he was an artist, then she was guilty of taking the position that Sonja should be allowed to get away with anything she wanted because Sonja was a mother. Suddenly the mythical, sacred, holy anointment of motherhood was being placed at the head of the line as the primary issue here.

He was a mere man, so how could he possibly comprehend the maternal pull that would do anything to save a child? Nona never actually asked him that question, but it reeked loudly from her argument. He tried calmly enough to suggest that maybe the maternal pull wasn't operating at its best that would compel a mother to kidnap her child from his own father.

"Where the Hell is this position suddenly coming from anyway, Nona? You and I both used to grumble that the height of literary culture for Sonja was of the supermarket romance brand. We used to cringe when she would take Lorca to those overwrought Christian tent revival extravaganzas and have the nerve to call it theatre. We used to tease that she wouldn't know the difference between Karl Marx and Groucho Marx. D'you remember any of that?"

"Yes, Daniel, unfortunately I do. We should really be proud of ourselves that laughing at other people is what props us up. When did we get to be such snobs?"

"That's not what I'm saying at all. Sonja has never encouraged Lorca to read books. We're not snobs to frown on that."

"I know, I know," she conceded, but it wasn't good enough.

"Sonja has taken for granted, in that passive, spineless, welfare-mentality way, that Lorca's school will take care of all of that and therefore he doesn't need any of that influence at home."

"I know, Daniel."

"Her only guidance for him is her insistence that he go to church every Sunday morning and praise some God."

"Daniel—"

"She's not teaching him to have pride in himself, or, or, or, or making any attempts to help him thwart the rage and self-hate that's rapidly growing around him. Lorca would be classically on his way to gang life if it wasn't for his father. And now you're Sonja's ally?"

"I am not Sonja's ally!"

They argued like this for three solid days, and he quickly began to resent that the *Murmuration* splash had come and passed without so much as a moment to decompress and relish its success. He didn't know where to direct his bitterness about it. At his wife, for dividing them on this thing, therefore wasting much valuable time in combat? At Sonja, for creating this crisis in the first place, and on the very night that was all-important to Arthur? Or at Arthur, for running out on *Murmuration*'s opening, and not timing his retaliation to happen at some later date?

And suddenly Daniel was dumbfounded by his own self-centeredness, and the horrible dawning that his anger was probably not nearly as altruistic an impulse as he'd surely strutted. It was at this dawning that he knew he couldn't, in all good conscience, go on with this charade of an argument any longer. And with that, he dropped his tirade, and the yelling finally ceased.

He'd been so caught up in his narcissistic volley for three huffing days that it wasn't until he and Nona finally went to neutral corners that either of them even realized they'd not heard a word from Arthur since their bail.

They drove to his apartment, but there was no answer. For the next two days after that, they either rang him up or went by, but found nothing. Then a solid week passed with still no word. Had Arthur actually chased Sonja across the United States, as he'd threatened, hopping a plane to Washington, D.C. to deal with her mother? Daniel shuddered to think of it.

Of course, there was also the matter of a pending arraignment from their arrests. It was sure to be just paperwork and a few hefty fines, but Arthur's sudden disappearance was not about to score him any points with the custody issue.

They spun all wheels, frantically overturning each stone, checking every hole in the wall, when ultimately, after a second week had passed, they decided to just stop this already, leave Arthur to his life and his choices, and be there for him when he resurfaced and asked for their help, but until such time turn their attentions inward and to each other.

Daniel tried, but worrying about Arthur could never completely leave his mind. And as much as he wanted to hold stubbornly to his case that Nona wasn't being a true friend in all of this, he knew it was tough for her too.

Over the next several weeks, Daniel fought the urge to butt his nose any further in Arthur's business, and instead held his wife, who fought to do the same. They took long walks in an attempt to find some peace and to help each other recover from that tumultuous night of street brawling, and jail cells, and the breaking heart of their dear friend, and the abyss that had begun again between the two of them. Each time Arthur came into their thoughts, they simply reminded themselves that he was a grown man who could handle his own life. Wherever Arthur was and whatever he was doing, he would survive it as he had survived all else.

They went to the Thursday night drum circles. They told themselves it was for healing and anchor and strength. But Daniel knew that each of them had, as their sole secret quest, the hope of finding Arthur there. As much as they tried to relax in their lives, it simply wasn't possible as long as Arthur was missing.

"Paint!" she demanded of him.

"Write!" he demanded back, each insisting that the other throw all energy into the task of calming their stresses through work.

One afternoon, several weeks into this, they drove into Beverly Hills and by the Benton Gallery to see if any interest at all was being generated for *Murmuration*. Since the opening, it had been practically ignored by the two of them.

There seemed to be some traffic inside, but they didn't go in.

They next drove to the Miracle Mile District and went into the LACMA gift shop to see how the book was being displayed. There it sat prominently between a catalogue for the new show by Industrial Abstractionist Sophie Schiller, and *Van Gogh's Van Goghs*. Fucking Van Gogh he was next to! He was beginning to feel a little significant. The *Murmuration* book had released three weeks after the opening into every major bookstore across the country. They'd simply been too busy indulging in domestic dramas to pay attention.

Daniel thumbed through a copy and read the monograph by June Steele for the hundredth time. She had described him as the elusive gentleman painter, tossing words around such as *fury* and *carnal* and *meat*. He reflected back to the beginning of all this, when they'd first started assembling the project. He had expressed to Ms. Steele over a glass of wine at the Ivy one evening what he had tried to create. In the midst of their conversation, June Steele had flirted with him in that *"I'm so turned on by your brilliance"* kind of way. She may've even said those exact words. What a laugh, he had thought that night. But he was eating it up now, wasn't he?

He remembered thinking at the time that in an earlier day, when there was no woman all-important to him, he would have bedded June Steele without a second thought. Even if he did believe she was full of shit, which generally tended to be his impression of Ms. Steele; he knew better than anyone how to offer just the precise bullshit compliment to someone whose cute ass he wanted. Who cared whether June Steele's flatteries about his work were genuine or simply uttered to woo? Certainly not he.

But he had gotten through that evening without defacing his marriage, and had been proud of himself. He had also, however, wondered how many more of those challenges would come his way that he might not be able to get through. Women had always been his weakness, and the strains at that time between him and Nona could certainly have threatened to trip him from his footing.

Funny how those were the concerns of yesterday. A lifetime ago. Those strains were nothing compared to their recent ones. Today there was so much more complexly woven into the fabric of their marriage that the idea of an adultery to take him away from it all suddenly seemed so juvenile and unassuaging. Did it mean he'd finally grown up? Or was he just too weary to get it up?

As he glanced over her monograph, he was just grateful that June Steele had been kind, and didn't care a whit if her words were genuine or not. If he was, however, feeling just a bit intoxicated having this influential critic gush over him, and having his name proudly stamped on the cover of this handsome book, and being next to Van-Fucking-Gogh, then he was completely flatlining over the next set of events.

Customers actually recognized him and Nona and began asking for their autographs. As if they were rock stars or some ridiculous thing. Nona was accustomed to this; she'd done book tours and the talk show circuit for *Champion* just a few years prior. But Daniel was flustered. This strange animal known as celebrity made him queasy.

Even more profoundly was the sensation that hit them both when people began asking about the third party of the *Murmuration* trio. At simply the mention of Arthur's name, the gloom in each returned. He saw it in Nona's face, and he felt it in his bones. For Daniel, it was not only that Arthur was gone, possibly forever, as far as anyone knew, but that for the first time ever the name of Arthur Hughes Dufresne was being known and admired, and Arthur Hughes Dufresne was nowhere to be found, to even know that it was so.

FORTY ONE

As the weeks continued to pass, growing into months, their worry over Arthur's disappearance grew as their handholding walks diminished. Daniel spent inordinate amounts of time at Santee under the guise of creating something but never quite producing anything, while Nona spent inordinate amounts of time at the Orchid Club alone. She wrote incessantly these days, but Daniel couldn't figure what. He was sure she didn't either. He doubted it was a new novel, because he would overhear terse phone conversations between her and her editor. *"I'm writing every day!"* followed by, *"I know, I know, I'm sorry."* And before they knew it, five astonishing months had passed. He couldn't remember five months ever passing without seeing or hearing from Arthur in the nearly twenty years they'd known each other.

On one unusually hot June day, somewhere in the compass of time known as the Waiting For Arthur era, Daniel paced his flat, in between stretches of constructing a frame for a canvas, and went through several fifths and an easy carton of cigarettes before he got much accomplished. After much nailing and hammering, he finally got to the business of stretching a canvas onto a 10 ft. x 10 ft. plywood frame, which was followed by more hammering. So huge and unmanageable was the thing that he literally had to crouch on top of it.

He mixed paint and linseed with such a flurry that he practically stumbled clops of swirly color onto the canvas before it had even been given the chance to be completely mixed. Streaks and hues of every conceivable shading and variation surfaced, and impulses toppled over one another to get to the canvas. He recalled the way Kandinsky first discovered the enigma of the abstract. So it goes that Kandinsky had unwittingly come across a painting he'd been suddenly moved by, only to discover that it had been one of his very own, lying unrecognizably on its side. The idea of form wholly upheaved, Kandinsky had uncovered an alternate way for the senses to receive images. Or even Jean Dubuffet,

Daniel's first inspiration to paint, who had largely garnered his own inspiration from the art of unschooled children and the insane. There had existed something concrete in the honest chaos of their paintings and scribblings, Dubuffet had observed; something untouched by ego and cognition, which had given their work a naked power Dubuffet, himself, had hoped to claim.

What was Daniel hoping to claim on this blistering June afternoon, air dirty and stagnant, sun just to that point on the horizon that it gave annoying glare? *What the Hell happened to June Gloom?* He paced further and suddenly felt the creeping urge to shag somebody. It had been creeping for some time, but he had denied it, shaken it off, told himself he could make love to his wife whenever he decided to take himself home. But to his irritating discovery, it was only someone he didn't care for whom he craved now; some nameless face who meant nothing to him, and to whom he meant equally, coldly, nothing.

For an instant Christianne popped into his thoughts. In a weird sense they'd been so irreverently perfect for one another, neither of them giving two shits about anything except to shag. On this angry, 103-degree day, too annoyingly early in the summer for this kind of heat, sun slapping his canvas and bubbling his paints, he was so ready to ring her up. Instead (*instead* was definitely best) he grabbed his cock with a firm grip and squeezed it. He swilled bourbon in a futile attempt to kill his erection and sweated the smell of Old Forester and body odor from his aroused pores.

Ultimately he couldn't avoid jerking off if he wanted to get back to work, so he stepped onto the canvas with his bare feet into the mad fury of wet paint globs, letting the semen sprinkle itself about the canvas, and smearing it with his toes into the persimmon that was dominant. Who knew what lethal chemical compound he might be producing?

And persimmon. The first time he'd ever heard that word was when Yvette corrected him for saying he thought her red fingernails were sexy.

"They're not red, little man; they're persimmon, the color of my favorite juicy fruit. Except for you, that is."

Yvette had called him little man because he was twelve years old, and she was somewhere in her ancient thirties. Yvette had taken his virginity, compliments of his father, on one of what was to become routine visits to whorehouses. Daniel had ejaculated within seconds of her touching him with her long red (*pardon, persimmon*) nails and had grown erect again in another second.

The official story was that his grandfather Leviticus had taken him to his very first museum, but in secret truth it was Yvette. Odd juxtaposition, one might suppose, but in later years, thinking back on her, which he seemed to do often, he concluded that it must've been her way of giving him back a bit of something she had assuredly taken away. A piece of innocence, perhaps. Or wonder. Awe. She knew he was on his way to becoming a hard, turned-out youth. It's what happened to all little boys who grew into manhood by way of a prostitute. She knew she was the maker of many hard, turned-out youths. So perhaps she felt that if she could offer up her hearty dose of grit with the balance of some beauty, she might actually succeed in giving up the guilt of her profession. Or maybe it was just a means of getting out of the cold, and he only remembered it his way because he was a romantic at his core, with a weakness for hookers-with-a-heart-of-gold clichés.

On that visit, the National Gallery of all first experiences, he remembered being instantly absorbed in the netherworld of this phenomenon called art, which countered his street kid existence of confiscated rye, and thievery, and drunken parents, and no hot water, and black eyes, and bloody noses, and Bromley Fucking Hall. He dove willingly into the azure sea of Manet's *Blue Venice* and drank up that electric blue. He sunned under a tree in the spring of Renoir's *Oarsmen at Chatou*. He lounged with Cèzanne's *Large Bathers* and caressed each of those round women. He strolled in the meadow of Pissarro's *Landscape at Chaponval*, unburdened for one blessed moment by his ugly life. He could walk right into any painting he might want and live there. And he did.

That was the singular experience that would change the course of his life. And after that first day at the National Gallery, which would turn out to be only the first in an obsessive lot, he dove into Yvette with an abandon only a youth can know. On one occasion he sucked her nipples so hard he bruised them.

"Slow down, little man."

Goddamn it! Images were bombarding the present-day Daniel. Smells. Colors. He paced the floor further, splattering paint when and where memories told him, and begged Nona not to come over when she'd called earlier. He'd been jerking off, chugging whisky, chain-smoking, creating carcinogens in the ozone-depleted air with his brush cleaners and turpentine, and making a general mess of the floor and walls while nursing old memories of large-breasted whores. He did not wish for his wife to get caught in the line of that indulgent fire.

Then his ulcers started in. Christ, were they taking him down today. He could barely catch his breath at one point, and he stumbled about ransacking the place for a bottle of Maalox that never surfaced. What did surface during the search was his autographed copy of *Champion*, the book that spat in his face every time it turned up; and the character that, though not flesh, would plague him more than any other in his lifetime. But he cherished it as a junkie cherishes his fix. And on this baking day, he grabbed it up, thumbed through it, and found the passage that would do him well in this instant.

At one point, during the abduction of Champion, while holding the gun to his head, Will Speck begins to dream, to envision blowing Champion's head right open and watching it blossom like an iris and part like great biblical waters. In Speck's imagining he jumps inside, submerging into the restless sea of blood, pulp, and brain matter. He bathes in it, breathes it in, drinks from it until the well is dry. He then jumps out and begins to glow, recognizing the transformation and that he no longer needs Champion. So he pushes the rest of the gutted artist aside to let the dried-up Champion whither away like some old speck. Like his old Speck. Suddenly, however, Speck jolts and realizes it has only been a dream. Either that, or it is an alter-reality that the book's authoress leaves deliciously unclear.

Daniel proceeded to tear the pages out of this particular passage and glue them onto the canvas. He literally had to kneel onto it in order to reach certain corners, so huge was the thing. He sprinkled the torn and pasted fragments of Nona's words with spindly smatterings of greens and deep blues. Marc Chagall blues. And black. Lots of black. And reds, even redder than his Yvette's luscious persimmon.

The last wave of an ulcer attack suddenly hit him like a fist to the gut, and he collapsed onto the wet canvas and couldn't move. His body was now a submissive part of this painting. All he could do was lie in the center of this animal, this explosion of his head, this blasted effort at saying…who knew? His ulcerated innards, and the flesh that housed them, mixed easily with the persimmon, and the greens, and so many blues, and much flaky semen, and the crises of Gabriel Champion and Will Speck, and the unmistakable essence of their creator Nona Childe, and thoughts of Arthur.

Suddenly, thoughts of Arthur.

His collapse onto this canvas reminded him of one of the pieces for *Murmuration*. It was a portrait of Arthur, naked and nailed to a garishly pointillistic canvas, as though nailed to a cross, his needle-tracked arms, darkened and scarred and wretched, stretched beyond the outer edges of the piece. The colors were ruddy oranges and brutal blacks and deranged reds. The shape of the image was angular with sharp edges, as if Arthur were a cutout, or shards of glass. His dreadlocked head bowed to one side as in all the portraits of the slain Christ, but Arthur's crown of thorns was made of hypodermics, and across his cruciform were the words from a Christian hymn, crudely penned in dripping ink: *The Comforter has come. The Comforter has come. Proclaim the joyful sound that the Comforter has come.*

Daniel lay on top of his canvas for near to an hour, staring up at the ceiling, arms spread out as in surrender, hypnotized by thoughts of his dearest friend, until every bit of paint dried and his body was stuck in his own psychedelic crucifixion. He wanted drums badly today. He wanted to hear that waterphone sigh its female sigh. He wanted to smell a pungent cunt. He could brilliantly whiff some quim in his fertile imaginings. He then winced until he lost his breath from the pain in his gut.

Life seemed fairly meaningless right now — but not without a good, stiff shot of gastric anguish to remind him that he was, at least, still here.

FORTY TWO

She and Daniel were ravenously hoarding their solitudes lately, neither spending much time together, nor sharing of themselves when they were. Both tried frantically to grab the hem of their runaway lives and get back to the business of creating something. Daniel spent most of his time lately in his studio, and Nona was all but barricaded in their home with this or that writing idea, although not one steady theme could seem to materialize.

She was frustrated beyond belief, with Seward Press all but ready to sue her for recompense of her rather hefty advance. It had been almost three years since she'd handed in an outline. Three years! *My God, what happened to me?* There had already been press releases sent out more than a year ago about her forthcoming follow-up to *Champion*, and here she was with crap for pages, or no pages at all. She no longer had *Murmuration* as her excuse for not getting anything done.

She wondered what happened to writers who breached contracts. Were they relegated to the B-minus assignments of ghostwriting for the lucky dimwits of lurid news headlines who had no writing skills whatsoever but who had a sellable story? Or worse, "novelizations" of movies? Or was it as simple as just being sued for her advance and then kicked to the curb? It stunned her to contemplate how easy it was to go from celebrated to vilified. It felt akin to having one's mug shot up on the wall of the neighborhood Chinese take-out place for writing a bad check.

Maybe her agent was onto something when she'd suggested Nona write romance novels. At least there was a formula. Plug in the numbers and you've got a book. She hated that this was what the writing industry had become. Or perhaps it was always this way, and she'd been merely naïve to have assigned her industry the Dorothy Parker fantasy.

The only thing that stood a chance of keeping a lawsuit at bay was the fact of Seward Press and *Murmuration*'s publishers collaborating to release a companion edition of *Murmuration* and *Champion*.

"An artist's book about writers with a writer's book about artists. AND they're husband and wife!" had been the proposal hook.

It was Harper's brainchild, and it virtually guaranteed a second life for *Champion*. Still, nothing seemed to be on her side in this quest for getting a word written, and she knew Daniel was feeling just as foiled in his work.

She and he had grown remote from each other, singly obsessed in their own individual journeys. It led her to the depressing conclusion that it was no accident most of the world's artists, the great to the passable, were unhinged narcissists. She'd always found it curious that every artist from Van Gogh to Frida had always had as many self-portraits in his or her body of work as any other theme. Today she got it. It was a pursuit that guaranteed self-absorption.

This afternoon — while laboring deeply over which adjective, of several choices, would most intimately express her thought, and stubbornly ignoring the reality that any good, upstanding Evelyn Wood Speed Reading alumnus would breeze right over it anyway — Daniel's phone rang.

The voices that came blaring loudly over his machine, usually when she'd be in the middle of some crucial writer's thought, were the distracting reality she had learned to tune out. This time, though, the hairs on the back of her neck danced as she suddenly heard Arthur's voice. She stared at the phone, paralyzed.

"Danny boy. Arturo. Just saw that film about the mathematician who goes insane. You gotta check it out, man. It's somethin' else. I'll tell you all about it when we talk (*Pause*). I'm fine (*Pause again*). No murders committed (*Arthur harrumph*). So rest easy, brotha. Love to Nona. I'll try you at the studio."

By the time she struggled loose from whatever weird fear had curled its tendrils around her, and she grabbed the receiver, he'd already hung up.

"Arthur, Arthur! Damn it!"

She slammed the phone down and star-69'd him, but there was no answer and no voice mail. Must've been a payphone.

She dialed Daniel, stabbing the buttons with a frantic finger. No answer on Santee.

"Goddamn it, where are you? A little afternoon repast at the Orchid?" she mumbled sarcastically, though she was the one spending the most time there of late.

Or maybe Arthur had already reached Daniel, and they were talking this very minute, and Daniel was just ignoring his call-waiting.

"Somebody tell me something!"

She dropped everything, got in her car, and headed to Arthur's. She would deal with Daniel later. As she found herself caught in the sludge of Los Angeles interstates, she decided that this had to be the smoggiest day L.A. had seen. People were more irritable in the smog. Their eyes burned, their noses dripped, their patience waned. Hers too. And she honked her grating car-horn right alongside the best of them on the crammed Santa Monica Freeway.

She exited at Vermont and headed south to find an event of some kind happening at either the Coliseum or the Sports Arena. It was hard to tell from where exactly the traffic was generating. Exposition Boulevard was a mess to get across, and King Boulevard was worse, not to mention the surrounding disaster area of Harbor Freeway Metro construction, which went on endlessly, and was the reason she avoided it. It seemed as though every time she attempted to get to Arthur's apartment, the world was trying to stop her.

She ended up parking four blocks away and paid five dollars to some sniggling opportunist who'd decided to claim a stretch of several parking spaces as his own, taking full capitalistic advantage of the crowded event nearby. Sometimes she hated this city.

She jogged the four blocks, approached Arthur's building out of breath, ascended the staircase two steps at a time, and banged on his door. No answer. *Shit!* She was sick of no answers today. She had to see him, had to look in his eyes to know that he was all right. That's how you knew with Arthur. His eyes betrayed all.

Ranting and panting, she took a moment to calm her thumping chest. She leaned against the opposite wall, facing the whitewashed wooden door she'd just been pounding. It was splintered and bowing in places. Warm to the touch from the day's heat. Swelling, as wood did. The hallway was damp and musty. Humid for L.A. And the smell of sizzling bacon grease coming from one of the other apartments made her think of her mother's kitchen on Sunday mornings. It also brought up the memory clearly of her first visit here, almost two years ago now, witnessing Arthur become that other animal.

When she couldn't take the vivid sense-memory any longer, she gave up and descended the staircase, pouring herself into the street like a jilted lover.

"Little Wing."

FORTY THREE

Her heart thumped vigorously and her palms sweated as she turned to see Arthur making his way up Figueroa and taking a seat on the stoop nearby, with a brown-bagged 40-oz. in his hand and a dullness in his eyes. To finally see that face after all these lost months was inexpressible. She wanted to grab him and hold him right on the spot, but thought it best not to rile the other Colt 45 swillers who were loitering the same stoop and talking audibly about the pussy they ate last night with her face, or some other part of her, in the corner of their eye.

"Ignore these ignant mu-fuckas. They got to buy it to get it, and can't afford a nickel's worth most times."

"Fuck you, junior," they all shouted, laughing. Arthur's friends. The collection of Arthur's varied alliances, which ranged from movers-&-shakers to hood rats, would always make him an enigma, or perhaps easily enough figured out if she ever bothered to take one minute off from being such a snob.

They walked back upstairs, and she said nothing until they stepped inside his door, then poured everything. Where had he been? Worried sick! Why hadn't he called? Who had been keeping the rent paid on his apartment for him?

And she fell to thankful tears, embracing him gustily.

"Did you ever reach Daniel?" she stammered.

He shook his head no.

"Cuz, I'm the one who got your message, and I tried to reach him, but I guess he's on one of his painting frenzies again. Me, I can't seem to get started with anything these days. Too busy worried about you. But he's creating like a mad scientist. Of course."

She rambled stupidly, and Arthur allowed it, smiling at her in that *"you are so precious"* way that she would've hated from anyone else. But from Arthur, any smile was the sun. She stopped practically mid-phrase, and they simply looked at each other for some minutes.

"So, you and Danny changin' the world?" he asked.

Her eyes glistened. *Changing the world.* That was a good one. If anything, she and Daniel were quickly becoming flotsam. What came out of her mouth was barely a crackle.

"Not without you."

He didn't want to hear that. He hated sentimentality. Always called it a demon sugar. Sumptuously sweet, but empty of anything beneficial. Instead, he took another swig from his bag and, with a slick flick of the wrist, tossed it in a trashcan on the other side of the room. She watched it hit the bull's-eye without touching the rim.

"Please tell me you found Lorca."

She asked it in a manner that begged release, because she got the feeling she already knew the answer. When he shook his head no, her chest caved.

"Then where have you been for six months?" she asked in a defeated whisper.

"Thinkin' about my life. Makin' decisions."

His tone was flippant, and there was that unmistakable mask men wear when they're being threatened with emotion. Tough. Too cool. A bad mother-fucker.

"Like what?" she asked.

"Like, I'm tired."

He looked at her pointedly. Awkward minutes passed as she waited for him to elaborate. Whenever she and Arthur were alone, like clockwork some foul tale about his life would come out, and she would shudder to witness it. Happened every time. What horrible reality was she about to bear witness to today?

She actually began racking her brain for a way to comfort a heartbreak she knew was there even if it did its best to hide, until she remembered that there was no comforting Arthur. He never allowed anyone close.

He suddenly moved about the room, unsuccessfully searching for the right words with which to finish his thought; either unsuccessfully searching, or willfully avoiding, because he never did. Instead, he sat in front of the television and turned it on, collapsing lazily onto his sofa and popping another can of malt liquor.

"Want one?"

"No."

She watched him watch television, and she grew irritated. After several minutes, she plopped herself on the coffee table directly in front of him, blocking his view. She took his hands in hers and exhaled exhaustedly. He was the one to speak this time, however, before she had the chance to start the diatribe he knew she'd start.

"Look, Nona, I can't scour the earth for 'em."

"You can't give up, Art!"

"Who said I was givin' up art?" he threw at her, laughing lazily. She didn't laugh.

"S'just the search I'm givin' up," he finished more seriously. "I actually gave it up months ago."

The swelling in her tear ducts kicked off again. Everything in her face burned.

"How can you, Arthur? Lorca is everything to you. You have never quit anything in your whole life. What happened to you? Did some spirit you called up in a drum circle tell you that? This is wrong. You can't give him up. He's your flesh."

"No, THIS is my flesh!" he suddenly exploded, moving forcefully away from her and knocking over the can of Olde English in the process.

A glacial spread soared outward from her limbs. She feared him.

He stretched out his arms and shoved them at her.

"This is my flesh, and this is what I've done to it! Now, it's MY flesh and I ain't complainin'. But that boy doesn't need this shit!"

His virility was thundering, voice rumbling and deep, instinct feral. He was a severely lean man, no doubt the drugs, but his ferocity made him imposing.

"What does that boy need with a junkie father?"

"Who's been feeding this to you?"

She had to forget everything Harper had said to her. He couldn't be doing this!

"Nobody feeds me anything, Nona. It's just what it is, okay? I've been through too much shit in this life to top it off by chasin' some woman half way around the world, cuz she fears I'm a danger to her kid, which, fuck, maybe I am!" He laughed in his anger. Then calm. "Shit, Nona, this just wasn't meant to be."

"What wasn't meant to be, Art?"

"All of it. The whole parent thing. I'm not supposed to raise a kid."

He laughed again, that disgusted laugh, as if the most obvious truth had been under his nose all along and he'd been a fool for not seeing it.

"See…Moses struck the rock with his rod, instead of speaking to it…in the wilderness…at the water—"

"What?"

"—and because o' that, though he had lived his life in the service of God, though he had done everything in his means to redeem his sins through works, though he had literally been God's messenger, he still could not enter the Promised Land. And it wasn't that he couldn't be forgiven. At that point, it was larger than him. It was a symbol. But if it was gonna have any meaning at all, it had to BE."

"What the Hell are you talking about?"

"See, this is the way it was always supposed to be. And it only just recently hit me why there's always been this huge blockade in my path with every goddamned step I've ever tried to take to build a life. This is what I can't have. Being a parent is what I can't have, because of what I did."

"What? Arthur! What?" she bit. "Becoming an addict? God knows I wish you weren't, but it's hardly akin to whatever sins of Moses you're talking about. And since when have you ever followed the conceits of biblical proverb? You're the one who said God failed you! Now you're gonna let God guilt you into giving up your son because you haven't led a pristine life. That's bullshit! You can't do this!"

He looked her squarely in the eye, grabbed her hands, and held them to his chest.

"Listen to me," he whispered. "You're absolutely right. I can't do this. I cannot do any of this anymore."

He chuckled at some dreadful irony into which she was not clued.

"You think what I write is poetry? Naw, baby girl, *this* is poetry. This is so fuckin' beautiful I can barely stand myself. See, the one thing I took away from somebody once is now being taken away from me. It was only a matter of time. And me tryin' to fight that, I finally realize, is laughable. Cuz it's bigger than me. And it's bigger than you, my beautiful little rescuer. So please stop tryin'."

"I don't know what you're talking about," she crackled feebly.

"It doesn't matter."

The tears rolled down her cheeks, but she didn't sob outwardly. If anything, she steeled her demeanor and looked away from Arthur, as if looking away might actually stop his awful words from entering her ears.

"I'm okay, Little Wing. Hey, hey. Look at me. I'm okay. And my boy's gonna to be okay too. Don't you worry about him. Sonja'll do right by him. I mean, that's all that matters, right? Not my rights or hers. But *his* life. Yeah?"

"You did find him, didn't you?" she cried. "And you just gave him up."

She looked into Arthur's eyes. Bloodshot and thick with fluids, his were a pair that had resigned. They threatened to weep, but he was such a man. He only allowed them to glaze, never to let go completely. She could see the muscle move up his cheek as his jaw clenched, doing its best not to let him fall. When she looked into those eyes, she saw the wall.

She thought about the people in this world who wasted their lives daily, heaping senseless violence on humanity, people who had no contributions to offer the history books, to beauty, people who simply fell off the edge of their meaningless lives. But Arthur was different. And Daniel was right. Life had been unusually malevolent toward this peaceful man who had only ever wanted to give life, not take it away, who only wanted to write words that would move and transcend and uplift souls. Life never loved Arthur. Not the way Arthur loved life. And this was unbelievably cruel.

Angry interrogations began to flood her head. Who did love Arthur? If life didn't. If God didn't. If his own parents didn't. Who caressed his face at the end of the day when the world had beaten him down? Who held him at night when the rest of the world held someone else?

While she and Daniel had certainly secured their place in the gooey circus of love songs and love stories, Arthur walked through this world alone. Never asking for a thing except to love the people he loved. The one person in this world he loved the most, maybe the only person truly, was his son. And now he was willing to give the boy up?

She looked again into Arthur's eyes. Little did he know that they betrayed a secret. Walls always did. For while his pride would never allow his heart to admit it, while he might've been a man who habitually shunned affection, presently he screamed to be loved, to be reckoned with, to be someone's complication. She heard it loud and clear.

And at the instant of those words in her ear, she suddenly brought herself closer to him. He looked at her puzzled, and steeled his stance. He wondered what she was up to, eyeing her suspiciously. He allowed her to look into his eyes, but cautiously. He let her caress his craggy face, but wondering.

She placed her mouth gingerly on his and kissed it softly. It wasn't a horny impulse. Not trivial or transient. It wasn't escape. It held the weight of something else.

From the corner of her eye, she saw a shiny trail trickle across his clenched jaw. He might've said no. She was certain he would have, had the lure of something soothing not been as intoxicating as his narcotic. Instead, in this battled instant, as he clearly wrestled with his love for his brother, she saw him, after a lifetime of relying upon only himself, surrender.

When her mouth touched his, his lips parted only slightly at first. Uncertain. Her body quivered with a tingle. Holding him, him holding her, she was astonished to feel just how unimposing he really was. This fragile man was not the virile brute who'd been raving only minutes before. That man had been ten feet tall and had shot fire from his nostrils. This man here was breakable.

He tasted like warm malt liquor and salt. But all she could think was that she was tasting tragedy. An old, tired tragedy that was just crying to be picked up, and held, and kneaded, and fixed, and delivered.

They clung to each other and ultimately settled onto his mattress, undressing nervously. *Fragile* was the word that kept returning. This was not the lustful, torrid sex that she and Daniel had lately been having. And as soon as she thought her husband's name, her sin screamed at her. She had to shove him from her thoughts so that this moment could be for Arthur.

As Arthur leaned into her, she caught the awful glimpse of his ravaged arms, pinched and punctured beyond recognition. Lean, brown arms glowing of sweat from the heat outside and in, decorated violently with dark needle marks that pulled and twisted the flesh and caused the raising of black keloids. She stared at these little craters, trying furiously to see inside them. When her mouth kissed them, the hairs on Arthur's arms raised and the man himself had the impulse to pull away, but her grip held more intention than his resistance. For one crazy moment, she wondered if kissing these veins into which Arthur daily poured his poisons might not just pour the poisons into her. And if so, she was willing. It would be a small price to pay for the man who had likened himself not to the Prophet Moses but the Sinner Moses.

She felt his body tremble with weeping, but she wouldn't look into his eyes because she knew he needed to weep alone. She also knew that his weeping was not for her. They both had, as their primary thought, after that of the comforting, their betrayal. They didn't speak it, but it crept upon them. They both loved Daniel completely. But that could never support this. *Go away!* she demanded of the thought.

As Arthur made the move to be inside of her, her first thought upon entry was how much she wanted to grow old with her husband. Her love for Daniel was not in danger. People get over indiscretions. What they never get over is a life unloved, and Arthur had been talking like someone at the end of his. Arthur's ramblings earlier had frightened her so outright that she'd almost begun looking around the apartment for a bottle of pills or a gun. This was a man completing his life. He deserved to be held and kissed and comforted and loved and shown that his life was not yet over. He deserved to have someone cling to him as if life depended on it.

This was the reel that ran in a loop as the man with whom she would betray her husband lay on top of her.

FORTY FOUR

He ran up the staircase and proceeded to open the door with his own key, which Arthur had always given him in the case of drug emergencies. When he'd returned home to find Arthur's voice on his machine, he'd been riled, to say the least. Riled into happiness, relief, anger for the worries Arthur had caused them.

He'd tried to wait for Nona to come home, but didn't know where she was or when she'd be back, and after a time had simply given up waiting. He needed to see Arthur immediately to find out what had happened in six months, and if Lorca was back. And since he and his wife didn't exactly agree on the Lorca situation, anyway, he figured it was probably best, for now, that he not find Arthur with her.

Find him with her.

If only, at the time Daniel had thought it, he could've foreseen the cruel portent. At first it didn't seem real. In that instant in which reality is swiftly warped, he thought surely he must've been having a nightmare.

There they lay, asleep, unclothed, wrapped in each other, in a kind of desperate grip: His hand on the mountain of her hip, hers tucked into his chest, her face snuggled in the crevice of his neck; a used condom on the coffee table beside them that burdened the eyes even more than the two sleeping figures, who were unaware of Daniel's presence at the door.

The sight was so astonishing that a white-hot bolt shot through Daniel from his groin to the tips of his fingers, and his face stung with that atomic slap that comes from nowhere. As the two people he loved most in this world were quickly killing him, they only lay in oblivious slumber.

He couldn't gather his thoughts rationally to determine what this was before him. A momentary insanity? Or an ongoing affair to which he'd been stupidly ignorant all along? As if one over the other could've made the difference. He was barely able to catch his breath before he realized that it was happening again. Just when he'd finally allowed himself to let his guard down with a woman, after all of those fucked up years trying to recuperate from Chelsea.

No. This couldn't even be compared to that. Chelsea had not been his wife, and the bloke she'd fucked had been a nobody. Nona was the world to him! Arthur was the world to him! What in Hell was this!

He couldn't look at them without getting ill. Everything in his gut sucked itself inward, pulling and tearing at vital organs, until it cut off the flow of air. He was driven to stare further at the sight, to somehow get inside of it, to find the reason for it. To give them, even in this moment of his implosion, a way out, if only he could be made to understand it. If he didn't leave this room right now, he feared it would be the end of him.

He backed quietly out and disappeared through the door, leaving it wide open for the world to see. He descended the stairs and fell onto Figueroa, where the streets were beginning to fill with a rowdy crowd from a game at the Coliseum that was just letting out. He was dizzied by rage, and as he approached his car, against the floating tide of game-goers, he hyperventilated with such ferocity that he vomited on the sidewalk. His eyes felt as if they were about to catapult from his head. A few drunken hoots and laughs came from passersby, who assumed he'd been partying with the throng and were showing their stupored solidarity. With each expulsion of his gut, his body convulsed savagely, trying its damnedest to purge the unbelievable reality.

Eventually he rose from his state of retching, confounded and sweating, nose clogged with acidic bile, throat burning, and he paced the dimensions around his car, paralyzed and unable to decipher what was happening.

Move. Move. Just keep moving.

He squeezed his eyes tightly shut and tried to shake it from his head. But it was like some crude effigy from a distorted fright house mirror. It was not about to go away.

What do I do, goddamn it! What do I do!

Nothing was clear.

He wondered if he should kill her with his dignity and leave quietly, only asking her later, politely, where she'd been. Or should he go back up there and explode before them, relishing the sight of them scrambling shamefully for their clothes? Goddamn it, there was no relish in this at all.

Where were they? Where were they!!! His wife and his friend? Because it was NOT them upstairs in that sex-stenched apartment. It was not Nona, and it was not Arthur. They would never do this to him. Those two filthy creatures up there were not the family that he loved.

He got in his car and started to pull out, to run from his life, where his wife was an adulteress and his dearest friend, for whom he had fought, for whom he had gone to jail, whom he called brother, was a betrayer of the most Judas kind. Suddenly he noticed his camera in the passenger seat. Without thinking it through to a rational end, he jerked the car into park again, grabbed the camera, and headed back into the building and up the vile stairs.

Should anyone ever ask, the corridors of Hell are not fiery and red, at all, but are whitewashed with flat house-paint and reek of putrefied bacon grease and sharp cum.

As he peered into the doorway once again, quietly closing it behind him, the two of them remained sleeping, even now unwary of activity. They slept like the dead, as if delivered from some long-suffered prison of the spirit. What was this deliverance? And whose was it? Arthur's or hers? But he couldn't advance that thought. To do so would be to give validity to their deed.

He aimed the camera and began clicking. He would catch them in all of their nakedness, and he would plaster their slutting likeness over the walls of the entire fucking world, and he would blow up the picture so huge that his wife's pussy would be as large as she, matching cunt for cunt.

Arthur stirred, no doubt from the sound of rapid clicking, but Daniel never stopped to acknowledge it, and suddenly Arthur was fully awake and stunned by Daniel's intrusion.

"Shit, Danny!"

Arthur jumped up startled and came at him. The camera was instantly knocked from his hand, but Daniel was done with that perversion anyway. He thrust Arthur's naked self up against the wall with both hands around Arthur's neck, whose own hands, in a reflex, fastened around Daniel's grip. He suddenly heard Nona screaming behind him to know that she had finally stirred too.

"My God, Daniel!" was all he could hear from her. It had to be a mixture of the horror of being caught and the horror of Arthur and him killing each other, which they surely both intended. She scrambled for her clothes, while a messy tangle of stumbled wrestling and aggressive blows were struck by both men. It was a savage brawl.

In movies, they embellish fist punches with grandiloquent sound effects, accented with furious musical underscoring, designed to amp up the drama, but there is nothing so ugly and horrid as the dully thumping, unadorned sound of flesh hitting flesh. With each blow that Daniel struck, trying his damnedest to shatter Arthur, another piece of his own heart chipped away under the weight of Arthur's treason. With each blow to some part of Arthur's naked body, astonishingly rail-thin, he recalled the countless occasions that he had come to Arthur's rescue or that Arthur had come to his; the endless episodes of seeing Arthur through his withdrawals, or bailing him out of a holding cell, or paying his rent for him. With each blow, their entire history was recalled, and it screamed in Daniel's bloodied face.

With each blow that Arthur struck to some part of him, Daniel was reminded of the animal of survival that Arthur was. Heroin addicts will kill their own for the fix that is life and death, and Arthur had lived his entire life as that animal. So, why should it have surprised Daniel that if his own wife was the fix Arthur needed, this time, that Arthur would simply take her, with no moral dilemma? Each blow that Arthur struck, which damaged Daniel's heart far more than it ever could his face or ribs, reminded Daniel that no amount of love and bond in the world could curb the animal instinct of the feral beast. They were quite the murdering team, his wife and his dearest friend. Hers was a betrayal slightly more baffling, but he couldn't decode that at this moment.

She managed to slip literally between them without getting hit in the crossfire, but barely, and all Daniel could do was storm to the other side of the room, to get away from them both, to catch his breath, to collect sanity.

"My God! Daniel—" she cried.

"This is rich!" he suddenly bellowed, half laughing at his stupid gullibility, half raving with dizziness. He whirred around and punched his fist against the mirrored wall behind him. It smashed into bits, spraying flecks and shards about the room, bloodying his hand, but not even beginning to work cathartic for him.

"Here, all along, it was me I worried about. ME! I was certain I would be the one. Begging my will every day of my life to do right by you. Trying my damnedest not to stain our marriage with infidelities. I was so afraid of Daniel the Rogue. It never, ever occurred to me that, that—this is a joke! This has to be a joke!"

"Please, Daniel—" she begged.

"Shut up! You shut your fucking mouth!"

"Calm down, Danny!" Arthur barked, quickly putting on his pants but keeping a keen eye in case Daniel tried to strike Nona. Daniel could read him like a book, *and how dare you!* He knew that Arthur believed all men were as capable of woman-violence as he'd once been. Then again, maybe Arthur was right, for at this moment Daniel could easily picture the demise of the woman he called wife, and by his own hands.

"You!" he threw Arthur's way. "Talk to me!"

He fumed back and forth in a space too small, really, for fuming. They stared at each other for several minutes.

"I have been your friend, your BROTHER, for twenty years!" Daniel poured. "Does that count for nothing? I have pulled you out of the fucking trenches every time you've ever been buried deep, which is more often than any human should be allowed in a lifetime. Shit, I was the goddamned president of your Get Lorca Back campaign, when this one here thought we should reeeaaallly give Sonja the benefit of the doubt. After all, you are just a junkie! Isn't that right, my darling wife? When no one else was there for you, I was there for you! When my wife wasn't even there for you—" He was seeing double. "—and you take her?"

"Daniel—"

There it was again. That female din he was loathing. And if he heard it one more time, he would fasten his hands around her lying neck.

"—Daniel, please, let's just go home and talk. This is for you and me to talk about. Please!"

"How long have you been fucking him!" he threw at her.

"That's not what it is, man," Arthur intercepted.

"Has this been going on the entire time he's been supposedly gone?"

"Daniel! Oh, God, this is not THAT."

"Well, I sure bought it."

"No, Daniel, this just happened," she cried.

"This just happened? Are you fucking kidding me? Christ, honey, you're a writer. Surely you can come up with a less predictable cliché than that."

"Danny, you're outta line, man."

"I'm outta line? You're a fucking interloper, and I'm the one who's outta line? That is rich! Where were you for six months?"

Arthur wouldn't answer. Of course his lover jumped in to cover for him.

"Daniel, please listen. He decided to give up on Lorca, and—"

"Do you honestly think I give two shits about any o' that right now?"

It was such a melee that neighbors began banging on the door, demanding for them to quiet down. It wasn't the first time the three of them had performed rousing street theatre for the locals.

"Do you love her?" Daniel asked Arthur pointedly.

"Daniel, don't do this!" she begged, still trying to fasten buttons, but unable, really, to function at all.

"Shut up!" Daniel yelled her way. "Do you love her!" he shoved at Arthur one more time.

Nona melted into a wall, hands up to her face, and the room was suddenly silent, as the men faced each other off. Daniel stared at the conflict in Arthur's face, though Arthur tried hard to be a stone. And when he glanced again at his wife, it seemed as though they were both awaiting the answer like a ticking bomb.

"No," Arthur whispered.

Daniel's breathing instantly stopped, as a frost blew through the room and everyone felt it. The stubborn tears finally gave up their fight and flowed, as he faced not merely a thief but a cold-blooded one. Or a liar.

Nona's face gave no reaction away, though if Daniel were a betting man he might've sworn that he glimpsed just the faintest jaw clinch of rejection.

"And she doesn't love me either, Danny. She loves you," Arthur offered, as if Daniel could accept any offering now.

"Did you tell her about the rape?" Daniel tossed out. But calm. It was the trump card he alone possessed. And he instantly saw it. Subtle. Just a shift in the eyes, really, but he could tell that he'd lanced Arthur clear through. He had now betrayed his brother as deeply as that brother had betrayed him. Wasn't that only fair?

He didn't bother to notice what his wife's reaction was to the sound of the very word that had haunted her ever since her own rape. He was too busy trying to rescue himself from the swamp of his own agony, even busier trying to yank Arthur down into it with him. He knew she'd fall. Women fell easily. So, for the moment, he ignored her.

"Did you tell her that no one could even recognize the ruin that had once been a woman, so badly had she been beaten? And by your own two hands? Those same hands that have touched my wife in ways only her husband should be touching her."

He saw life fold up within Arthur, as Daniel not only hurled the haunted memory vividly back at him, but was now sharing it with another. The only other in this world with whom it had ever been shared. And her.

If there was any life left in Arthur, Daniel was surely driving the rest out. But as they had driven it out of him, he no longer cared what careless thing he did or said.

Now he saw the face of his wife, barely recognizable.

"What are you doing, Daniel?" she whispered in a tremble, as she approached. She stood between them and faced Daniel, but he only looked past her to the man of the hour, and the men's eyes never varied.

"Why are you doing this?" she demanded, more forcefully.

"You don't believe me?" Daniel challenged, though he never took his eyes off of Arthur. "Go ahead. Ask him."

He waited to see if Nona would turn to Arthur, but she never did nor asked the question. He got the feeling she didn't truly understand what he was revealing. In the next instant he was certain of it.

"I did the deed! All right?" she suddenly exploded. "I am an adulterous wife! And I will spend the rest of my life begging your forgiveness because I love you. But don't do this vile thing. Being raped almost flattened me. You know that! And not being able to put a face to who did it…and you would use that black spot in my life as a weapon to wield at your dearest friend?"

Daniel saw the flinch in Arthur's eyes. Now Arthur knew about hers. Daniel hadn't even intended this perk. But she couldn't hear what Daniel had to say about Arthur's, because there was only hers in the world.

"You're the one who said that my beaten face wasn't really mine, and that I should refuse to own it. That's been your little self-empowerment rhetoric to me all along. Or maybe it was just your way of getting inside.

And now you would describe me as some sort of…how did you put it? *The ruin that had once been a woman*? How does such a vile thing come from you? How do you toss rape around here like it's a toy you play with? Who ARE you?"

But he didn't need to hear her pleadings, or feel her disgust, to know that what he'd done was vile. And even though it was impossible in this moment for her to really understand what he was revealing, it didn't matter. He'd done what he'd come back up to do. He'd injured them both, possibly beyond repair. After all, for twenty years he had kept the secret that had meant the difference in Arthur's sanity. Arthur had genuinely redeemed himself of those crimes of thirty years ago. Yet all it took was a woman for them both to breach their sacred trust in each other. And that woman now grabbed up the rest of her clothing, hating him surely, beaten, possibly irreparably, and walked out.

He thought to catch her by the arm, to call her a typical rape-victim narcissist, to tell her that hers wasn't the only rape in the world, but he would have his wife to face at home, if he ever decided to go back there. In all excruciating honesty, he couldn't truly look in her eyes yet to deal with her at all, so for the moment he let her go.

The door slammed, and he and Arthur were alone. For an unbearable minute they stared at each other. Twenty hard years between them. Of love. Hurt. History. Loathing.

"Don't ever forget what I did, Danny," Arthur finally said.

What?!

Daniel's brow folded. What did that mean? Why was Arthur not falling prostrate and humbly begging his forgiveness? The bastard fucking well owed him a good beg!

He looked at Arthur pointedly and was about to ask the question, when Arthur resumed.

"Don't ever forget. What I am is what I am, and you know that. The nature of a man does not change. That's what I went away to find out. That's why I know I can never be a father to Lorca. And apparently you knew that all along, or it wouldn't'a been in you to spill out so easily. I just wish you woulda clued me in a whole lot sooner instead of bein' so goddamn polite all these years."

What the Hell was Arthur doing? And what was this ominous riddle?

That's what I went away to find out. What the fuck was that! And why, for fuck's sake, did Arthur not want his forgiveness! Or even lash out at him for *his* betrayal! What the fuck was going on!

"But that li'l girl out there," Arthur continued, "man, I've seen you through the Chelseas and the Christiannes and all the other nameless women, and Nona is the best thing that's ever happened to you. She loves you more than the whole world, Danny. Believe that. I seduced her. Not the other way around. Do not throw her away. Cuz you won't find another woman like her. She's the real deal. Purest thing you or I will ever know. And I know that's hard for you to hear right now. But you'll see I'm right. In time. You'll see."

Daniel couldn't listen any longer. Arthur was screwing with his head. For a second he almost felt inclined to comfort the friend he'd always comforted. He almost had to remind himself that this man before him had just bedded his wife and still smelled of it.

He couldn't go any further with this, and apparently neither could Arthur, because they each turned away from the other at the same instant, Arthur toward the kitchenette, Daniel toward the door. And as Daniel moved to storm out, he heard Arthur mutter to himself:

"I'm done."

The magnitude of those tiny words jerked Daniel back around. Or maybe it was the suspicious sound of something being picked up from a kitchen drawer. Or maybe it was his greater voice saying, *pay attention!* But when he finally did, before Arthur had even finished the word *done*, the gun was to Arthur's head and the trigger was being pulled.

He swore to God, as if in a slow-motion dream, he saw Arthur's finger slip right inside that steel loop and squeeze that trigger, and advance that barrel, and his head take that bullet. But he couldn't have seen that kind of detail, could he?

His hands rushed up like a tidal wave to stop it.

"NNNNOOOOOOO!!!!"

There was no drama to the fall. No pomp. No pageantry. Arthur's body simply fell, quickly in a dull thud to the ground. Unmusical. Unpoetic.

The blood from Arthur's head squirted in every direction. Daniel frantically grabbed the limp body and held his own hands to the exploded temples. He screamed at the face that was so suddenly blank. Did death really happen this fast?

"ART! ART! ARTHUR!"

Daniel shook him violently, trying to hold Arthur's head together, and screamed over and over until his voice was sandpaper. He did his best to hold Arthur as they slipped and slid against the sticky blood, which now spread across the linoleum in a great flood. And fast. Arthur wouldn't help!

As Daniel held him, he could see, from the corner of a crazed eye, pieces of dark red brain and skull clinging to Arthur's filthy walls. He had the mad impulse to gather it all up and piece it back together, like some batty Dr. Frankenstein, because there were still brilliant words to write, still Arthur's son to love, still Arthur's magnificent life to live.

FORTY FIVE

"I did the deed! All right? I am an adulterous wife! And I will spend the rest of my life begging your forgiveness because I love you. But don't do this vile thing. Being raped almost killed me. You know that! And not being able to put a face to who did it—and you would use that black spot in my life as a weapon to wield at your dearest friend? Because, how on earth can I possibly tell you you're wrong? It could be him, right? Isn't that what you're insinuating? Well, guess what? For that matter IT COULD BE YOU!"

She shoved a crazed finger in Daniel's face and couldn't believe that this was her husband standing before her, or that she was even going where he had just gone. He'd called her a ruined woman. The man she'd fallen for in the produce aisle of a grocery store, who had painted her brilliantly time and time again, whose heart could swoon when listening to Callas.

"How do you throw rape around like it's a toy you play with? Who ARE you?"

She knew they'd hurt him badly, but to have sent him to this? A sweaty chill flushed her face and quickly soared southward, alerting the rest of her functions that catastrophe was at hand. And catastrophe was always dizzy. She couldn't tell which way was up.

As she faced her husband, all she could think was that she would never be able to make him know what was in her heart when she had chosen to do this. There was no sense to it, no excusable reason, at least not one that he would ever accept. How could she say to him that Arthur's state was so much more frightening than either of them had ever seen before? That she'd felt in her gut that Arthur was completing his affairs? Daniel would sneer at that word, wouldn't he? Find an inappropriate humor to shove into the dreadful moment, a weapon. How could she tell him that Arthur had so panicked her this afternoon that she couldn't let him go from their lives?

She tried to look in Daniel's eyes, but couldn't find him anywhere in that hateful face that had just used rape against them both. He was gone from her. And she couldn't look at Arthur at all. One glance his way would only be interpreted by Daniel as some lover's thing.

She yanked past them both, out of the apartment, slamming the door behind her, and down the stairs, passing nosy neighbors in the hallway but unable to look their way. The sickness in her stomach churned as she realized that she'd lost her husband today. But did she even want him this way? This creature that was unrecognizable to her? This werewolf that had just turned? Both thoughts made her lose breath.

As she fell outside, she noticed Daniel's car at the instant curb. Her own car was five or six blocks away. It irked her with a weird jealousy that Daniel had found a spot when she hadn't. It was all about timing, wasn't it? It irked her even further that this was the dialogue in her brain in this instant of the Great Cataclysm. Did cataclysms always bring with them thoughts of mundanities like grocery lists and toilet seats left up?

She walked agitatedly, trying to get her bearings. After two long blocks, the chaos in her head finally began to calm somewhat and she felt more steadied. *Only three more blocks to go*, she kept mumbling. These were not the right shoes for such a hike.

As she continued to walk, thoughts of the three of them, and what they had been to each other, bombarded her. Each had always made the other two stronger, and now she had managed single-handedly to blow all of that to mere shrapneled fragments of the trio they'd once been.

One hundred years from now, or a thousand, in some bookstore or library, someone might dust off the ancient art book entitled *Murmuration* (the fleeting phenomenon of a collection of starlings was the actual definition of the word, and was how each of them had reverently thought of the other) and string together the names of Daniel Cross, Nona Childe, and Arthur Hughes Dufresne. One hundred years from now, or a thousand, they might still be a trio. But as for now, on this day, they had been mortally blown apart.

Then she heard it. It came from blocks away. She jumped, jarred by the sound. Such a finite, mythical sound. *Arthur.* Her eyes shut at the instant that his assuredly must have.

And suddenly she was blasted into gear, in spite of the blister that was beginning on her foot. Her head reverberated with screams, as she turned and ran back in the direction from whence she'd come, huffing rhythmically, with the pounding of her heart in concert.

She would never have left that apartment had she truly believed he could do it. After all, wasn't she Nona the Rescuer? Always insisting on saving Arthur from himself? She should be there right now. But no, *goddamn it*, she'd allowed Daniel to distract her with his wounded fucking play.

I'm wrong. I've got to be wrong. It's not Arthur. It's not Arthur.

It served as mantra, as engine, which had her sprinting, sweating, and panting the four blocks back up Figueroa. Midway up, she kicked off her shoes and continued in her bare feet. Gunshots were routinely heard in this neighborhood. Crackhouse raids. Drive-bys. Gang retaliations. Drunken lovers. Her brain furiously worked on willing this horror on some other household, some other domestic drama that had simply unfolded itself nearby. A cramp in her side stabbed her and took her to the ground. She frantically breathed it out, pounding her side with a fist and struggling to get back to a standing position. The remainder of her sprint was labored, as she held her ribs and continued.

She could already see the commotion of a crowd forming in the distance and of sirens approaching. *Jesus, they never respond this fast!* Or was her hysteria simply warping time? She dodged her way in and out of the swiftly growing swarm of neighbors, spilling out of nearby buildings and from the Sports Arena parking lot across the wide stretch of boulevard, the stopping of cars, forming traffic jams, the irritating honking of horns, the milling of voices yelling, *"Somebody got shot,"* and *"What happened? What happened?"*

The nausea hit as she reached Arthur's building and realized that this was, indeed, the destination of the swelling riot. She was ready to explode when she had to break stride to allow for medics, police, gurneys. Excruciating minutes passed in this rite.

"Goddamn it! I have to get in there!" she screamed to a crowd that did not notice. She followed as directly forward as she could, pushing her way up the narrow staircase, squeezing and wrestling through the hubbub, fighting and shoving even, until she made it to the doorway of Arthur's apartment, nearly underneath the trampled boots of an agitated crowd.

There Arthur lay, confirming the very thing she had feared.

The blood-spattered tableau was breathtaking. She had never seen so much garish red in all her life. Dark, fuming red. Like Martin's *The Great Day of His Wrath*.

And Daniel. Holding him. Cradling his head, as though about to perform a baptism. The hysterical babbles that Daniel screamed at Arthur might as well have been the speaking-in-tongues that usually accompanied such a rite. She'd never heard Daniel cry like that. It was a thunderous sob, like the eerie remembrance of Mr. and Mrs. Wenda's donkey on the Bagamoyo farm, baying mournfully into the sad night when its mate had been slaughtered by a stalking lion. Even then, Nona knew it was a sound that would haunt her forever, follow her through life, reemerge in some other form, like a cleansing that, once in awhile, simply needed a good wringing out. Here it was.

Seeing Daniel destroyed by this act wiped away whatever glint of a suspicion she might've entertained that he could've been the one to pull the trigger in an ugly crime of passion. To know, at least, that her broken husband could not be a murderer was some pitiful drop of consolation in a day of few.

No, this was Arthur's doing. A doing she had fully predicted.

She had to wait in the sea of nosy-bodies, as no one was allowed past the doorway. From her undignified post she stared at the limp body that had once contained Arthur but was now emptied of the exquisite man who'd housed it for fifty-something years. It lay eerily still. His head was blasted right through the knotty dreadlocks, stuck together by the sticky, red glue. Not much of his face was left, as it had caved in, in a kind of weary collapse, but his eyes remained intact, and were still open. She looked deeply into them now. Try as she might to conjure, there was nothing there. Only two glassed orbs.

He had been her lover for one day. A love no one would ever understand. And to ask her husband to understand would be asking too much. It would only be a profound solipsism that would insist he consider her reasons. So she would never ask it, nor try to explain. It was right that he be angry at her weakness and her heartlessness, and to believe those things of her. She swore to spend the rest of her life begging his forgiveness, but could never utter this truth — that Arthur would live in her heart always. There was a spot for him tucked deeply away, which even her husband could not touch. It was only for the profound and afflicted man to whom she now had to say goodbye.

Her chest heaved at the notion of never hearing him utter *"Little Wing"* again, and she was furious with God for never having been, with regard to Arthur Hughes Dufresne, quite fair.

As she tried to say her goodbyes, she watched Daniel struggle to do the same. It was much harder for him. There was history. A brotherhood. Now betrayal.

Daniel wouldn't let Arthur go willingly, even when the police tried to pry him loose. Eventually he stood, making his way awkwardly in the viscous blood, though not toward her. And the smell of death slowly crept.

The paramedics covered Arthur's body with a sheet and tried to make the crowd disperse. Some cooperated, others didn't. Nona wasn't about to budge.

In the ensuing hours — culminating in zipping Arthur's body into the coroner's bag, and Daniel being intensely interrogated by the police, and the flashes of forensic and reporter cameras going off like a round of firecrackers — the crowd slowly began to drift away until there was only Daniel and her and the authorities. They both stayed to answer whatever questions the police had, but as for, or to, each other, they never spoke. They only stared from opposite sides of the room, with the death of their friend and a breach between them.

As the turgid hours passed and the red walls closed in, the last of Arthur was zipped and shipped, and the night was bold with stars. Nona stepped into it, leaving Daniel to talk further with the authorities, who were detaining him but not her. She'd wanted to stay, but he'd simply shaken his head, never looking her way.

She floated, hovering above the city, looking down on it as she passed over, and squatting to take a pee on its head. She descended onto her car, climbed inside, and was numb behind the wheel, bare toes gripping gas pedal and clutch, wafting the length of Los Angeles's freeways, not knowing or caring where she ventured, and feeling oddly inebriated.

Floating, drifting, spinning. She thought for a moment that she might actually achieve flying away. Instead, somewhere in the early morning hours, she pulled into their driveway clear on the other side of town, got out of her car, glared at the dark orange sun, and crawled into their house, up the stairs, into bed. This was the time of day when coffee brewed, showers ran, and newspapers were retrieved from wet lawns. But this was the end, not the beginning, of Nona's day, as she pulled covers over her head and shivered in a nightmare-plagued sleep.

FORTY SIX

When she awoke, she thought days and nights had passed her by, but it had been only a few hours. Daniel was not in bed beside her. Had the police taken him to the station for further questioning, and were detaining him indefinitely? After all, his face had been bloodied too, and scenarios surely suspected. Or was he wandering the streets somewhere, in a different kind of trouble? Her fingertips were numb. She couldn't move. She lay so still that she became hyper-aware of the rising and lowering of her chest, the rattling of her lungs, the sounds of the house creaking, the growing clamor of sanitation trucks and lawn mowers and car horns.

She stared at a picture on the wall, which hypnotized her. It was a framed album cover of the only solo recording her mother had ever made. *Ruby Chan: Live from Shelly's Manne-Hole, 1968.* If she stared at it long enough, she could conjure her mother's voice, and see it seep through the album jacket like a smoke stream, and wrap itself around her, and sing to her.

From out of the blanketed din, there suddenly came a fierce pounding on the front door downstairs, rudely slapping her out of her momentary reverie. She jumped, but was too desensitized to respond any further. She knew it was only a matter of time before word would spread and her door would be pounding, but she couldn't engage. It continued to pound until she heard a key in the lock. *Daniel!* Her heart thumped quickly to remind her she was still alive. She followed the sound of his footsteps on the staircase.

"Nona, honey," Kai panted, bursting into the room.

Nona suddenly blurted her first cries, which swelled to an unstoppable balling. Kai threw her arms around Nona tightly.

"Daniel called me. He was calling everybody, and I immediately went over to his studio—"

His studio. Of course.

"—And Harper was already there, but when I arrived he was only on the phone with somebody else. It was like he was trying to round up the cavalry. And I wondered where you were, but every time I tried to ask he would just ramble on about Arthur, and I could never get a straight answer from him. So I left him to Harper and came straight here."

"He's gone," Nona poured.

There was more than one to the meaning, but Kai didn't know that. Or did she? Had Kai been clued in that in one sorely misjudged gesture Nona had lost both Arthur and Daniel? They held each other and stayed that way for so long that Nona actually thought she might be comforted. Finally Kai sat back on the edge of the bed and held Nona's hands.

"You know, I just don't get it," Kai started, shaking her head. "I mean, we were just starting to click, you know—"

Click?...*Wait.*

"—we'd only gone out a couple of times, and he seemed pretty happy to me. I mean, you know, happy for Arthur. At least having a good time when we'd hang. And then, aagghhh, God, this impulse of mine! I feel selfish and despicable that the only thing I can think of right now is how this all affects me. I mean, the man is dead, and—"

"Wait a minute," Nona interrupted. "What about you and Arthur? Were you dating?"

"Oh, shit..." Kai responded. "I forgot I hadn't told you. I mean, for the longest time we just wanted to keep it under wraps—"

The longest time?

"—I just hadn't been ready to say anything yet, because you didn't think it was such a good idea when I first asked you about him. And I just didn't want to hear *'told you so,'* if he started dicking me around or something. I knew he had this reputation for being tormented and aloof. And then, of course, he goes and disappears forever after that crazy night you guys had. I fucking showed up to that opening with him, and he just ditched me. I mean, of course I realize he had other things on his mind that night. But I just—I was too embarrassed to ever say anything. The only thing I could think was, *'Well, there he goes, Mister Tormented and Aloof, just like Nona warned me.'* And then he was gone for so long, and I honestly never thought anybody would hear from him again, so then there was no point in saying anything. I mean, we only slept together maybe a handful of times."

Oh God.

"And I knew that for him there was never gonna be anything serious. Arthur just didn't do serious. I knew that. But I kind of thought that maybe we were starting to have a little something. I mean, he was laughing and smiling a lot in those days. And I thought, well, maybe…this is embarrassing, but I kinda thought…maybe I was the one who was bringing some sun into this guy's perpetual bleakness. Ecchh, it really sounds ridiculous when I hear myself say that out loud. Anyway, I'm the one who asked him not to say anything. And, and—"

"Oh God—"

"—I know. I just had no clue he was that on the edge."

"I'm sorry!" Nona cried, but cut it off quickly, lest she give away that there was more ulterior than condolence in her motive. After all, Kai was here, holding and consoling *her*, which meant that Daniel hadn't spilled the rest.

"Honey, we're all gonna be okay," Kai offered tenderly. But Nona didn't deserve tender. She had managed to betray both husband and best friend in one stellar gesture.

"I would like to know one thing, though," Kai pressed. "Why are you here grieving alone? And why is Daniel ranting like a madman in his studio, clear on the other side of this city? You two should be supporting each other right now. You were the only family Arthur really had, and you're here, and Daniel's there. Why is that?"

"Please, don't ask me that right now," Nona struggled to get out, as the world began to blacken in front of her. Kai held her to steady her, then got her some water from the nearby bathroom sink, which Nona couldn't drink.

"He's trying to make these funeral arrangements all by himself," Kai resumed, "and I'm watching him pace that studio like a crazy man—"

"—Please, not now—"

"—And Harper can't even calm him down. He's just in such a bad way, Nona. And so are you, honey. I mean, you guys need to come together on this thing—"

"All right," Nona finally bit. "I'll go over there!"

Kai was jolted by Nona's outburst, and they both stared at each other, as Nona's hands came up to a lathering mouth.

"Oh my friend, I'm so sorry," she broke, falling apart.

"It's okay, honey."

But none of it was okay. The last person on earth Daniel wanted to see today was his wife, and she couldn't even confess why. She did, however, know that Kai was right. As impossible as it was for her and Daniel to come together in their hearts right now, a man who had been family was dead. These next few days would prove crucial, and would require that she and Daniel do right by Arthur's memory and set aside their estrangement for the time being to do just that. She needed to hold her husband in this time of his crumbling, even if he wouldn't want it of her. She needed to let him know that she'd never been looking to escape their marriage.

He would consider that a joke, wouldn't he? And she didn't. Their marriage was everything to her. But how would Daniel ever be able to believe that again? And how would she ever be able to make him understand that it had been her purest instinct to hold and comfort Arthur without contempt for the untouchable love she had for their marriage vows? It could never be viewed that way. The institution precluded any and all other moments of the heart; those were the rules. According to that institution, she had allowed someone to come between her husband and her, let his troubles pound a crack in their foundation. And not just any someone, either, but the only man Daniel had ever called brother.

The one consolation, and thank God, was that Arthur hadn't confessed some tortured, secret love for her that he'd been harboring all this time. At least his answer to Daniel's question had been *no*. It was the smallest of blessings. No need to fuel Daniel's fury beyond its current blood red.

But she couldn't help an itch. It niggled at her, this notion of Arthur saying *no*, so directly corresponding with their intimacy, which she had been willing to risk her wedding vows to offer him. She wondered if Arthur's answer hadn't been a lie. Even in this indignant instant of proclaiming her undying love and commitment to her husband, even as she stared into the face of Arthur's own secret girlfriend, her dearest friend, the idea of a *yes* was proving too intoxicating to resist. She felt entitled to a *yes*. And ultimately, she rationalized his *no* as a lie, a device to protect the woman he loved.

The greedy child could've snuggled in that one for awhile longer had she not been struck suddenly with a horrible thought: What if sleeping with

Arthur not only failed to save his life, which had been the foolish notion, what if it tripped up his heart even more? A heart she was damned well insisting on claiming, in spite of his answer. What if Arthur knew, in that moment of her choice, what was just dawning on her now? That what they did could not possibly have happened again, because this had never intended to be an affair. If Arthur truly did love her, as he'd confessed (it would never dawn on her again that she was choosing to remember it differently), then did she send him to this?

After all, he'd once said to her: *"The last thing I need is to start feeling too good in somebody's arms, and then get to that point where I have to have that goodness every day or I'll die."*

She moved away from Kai with a jerk, shaking off the thought and wiping away sopping eyes. She tried to piece together what business needed to be taken care of first, because she feared her own head. Better to focus on the living, anyway. Arthur was no longer here, but Daniel was. She had dedicated her life and love to her husband, and she would go to that service now, even if unwelcomed.

"Okay, I'm gonna go," she stumbled, as she tried to get her bearings, and searched around the room, but didn't know for what.

"I'll go with you," Kai offered, as Nona squeezed herself into a pair of jeans.

"No, I'll be all right. I need to do this alone. But, hey—"

Nona abandoned her zipper to put her arms full around Kai.

"—thank you. For always being here for me. And don't worry. I'll be here for you too. I promise."

FORTY SEVEN

Stepping outside was bitter. All she wanted to do was disappear into a cave. Yet here she was again, back on the Santa Monica Freeway for the second time in twenty-four hours, steeped in the hot, dusty July of Los Angeles, no longer able to ignore dealing with life.

The stretch of freeway she was driving was currently undergoing earthquake reinforcing, even though it had now been five years since the big Northridge quake. Huge orange and rust-colored trucks and tractors slept on the side of the shoulder, looking like grotesque sculptures. The grayness of the city stood stagnant, waiting for someone to climb aboard it and ride it out of itself, into some kind of movement, some kind of life. She listened to Carlos Santana on an AM station, and his guitar hypnotized her.

Her eyes burned from the smog, and the air-conditioning in her car drew too much juice from the small foreign engine, thus driving her along sluggishly enough to notice three separate piles of fly-swarmed road kill littering the highway between the Westside and Downtown. Death seemed everywhere. As she passed the National-to-Robertson stretch, she glanced north across the city's vista toward the distant gallery that had once housed *Murmuration*. The exhibit had now been moved to a space on the LACMA grounds, bringing even more traffic to it. But that life, the life of growing celebrity, seemed so long ago now; so disconnected from her present reality.

She barely remembered exiting the freeway, parking, and stepping out of her car, but she must have, because she was now helping herself to the freight elevator of Daniel's building, and that sunken feeling in her gut hit her again. If she was in a fog driving over, she was now as clear and awake as if on a cocaine high. Between heat and grief she thought she might just pass out on the floor of this thing, but she was too agitated to faint. Her hands were so sweaty that she couldn't work the ropes and levers properly, and fitting her key in the access hole to get herself to Daniel's floor proved near impossible.

She tried to take a deep breath and second-guess what state he would be in. Daniel wasn't a violent man. A wall-basher and a glass-breaker, yes, but never toward people. There was a different kind of violence she feared today. The violence of will. His loathing of her, alone, might do her in more effectively than anything physical could; to stand before him, look in his eyes, and know that the gleam in those eyes was the gleam of shock and unfathomable hurt. That was what she knew she'd have to face.

The elevator door opened onto aggravated activity. There were only Harper and Daniel, her trying to take over phone responsibilities, and him refusing to let her help. But all movement stopped when Nona entered. She looked at Harper first. She was afraid to catch Daniel's eyes in her glance and see that gleam. Harper walked briskly her way, and they fell into an aggressive embrace. As much as Nona wanted to, she wouldn't let herself break down. She refused to cry in front of Daniel, lest he interpret it as a weeping for her lover. It wasn't a lover she grieved for. She had loved Arthur on a much different plane than sex, yet because she took it down that road, in a fit of desperation she still couldn't explain even to herself, there would be no way to convince Daniel of that distinction. So she remained as ungrievous in front of him as possible.

Daniel busied himself on the phone, and she and Harper took in each other's eyes. Refusing to cry was more painful than crying.

"It's good that you're here," Harper whispered.

"Is it?"

"He's trying to make funeral arrangements and is accepting no one's help. Neville was here earlier, and Kai—"

"I know." *Who cares about particulars!* "How much did he tell you?"

There was no rush to answer.

"Harper," Nona bit in a spitting whisper, half irked that she already knew the truth, and half disgusted with every inch of herself. Harper knew she was here for answers.

"He told me about you and Arthur," Harper reluctantly confessed.

Nona's eyes shut tightly, mortified.

"I love my husband!" was all she could muster.

"I know you do."

The whispered volley went on for minutes.

"Whatever he's told you, it isn't as conniving or malicious as he believes."

"Okay."

"He's your best friend, Harper. And I've hurt him. So I don't blame you if you hate me."

"Well, I don't. I love you."

Daniel stormed in the background, yelling at someone on the phone and doing his best to ignore them.

"I've ruined so many people's lives in the past twenty-four hours."

"Stop," Harper chastised. "That's the last thing anybody needs. A little life went on, is all."

"A little life? Bit of an understatement, don't you think?"

"Yes, it is. But someone has got to level this penchant the two of you have for wanting to play out some Shakespearean tragedy."

"Arthur is dead and my marriage is over! It *is* tragic!"

"I know."

"I miss Arthur terribly."

"Yes, honey. I know."

"And I can't tell Daniel that."

All Harper could do was nod her head in reluctant agreement. Over Harper's shoulder, Nona finally had the nerve to look Daniel's way, and though he was still on the phone she caught him suddenly staring at her. It startled her that he was already glaring her way, and a shiver crawled up her skin to have those gray eyes upon her. It was their first true eye contact since she'd stormed out of Arthur's apartment. She couldn't read him, and that was agonizing. It was a blank face. An empty heart. A pair of hollows for eyes. A stranger, which was the biggest heartbreak of all.

When Harper realized that Daniel was ready to deal with Nona, she held Nona's face in her hands.

"Call me tomorrow. Let's you and I talk alone. For now, be here with him. He may not know that he needs you, and he may not want to need you, but he does need you."

Nona shook her head obediently and turned to watch Harper descend in Daniel's elevator. She took a deep breath and turned back in Daniel's direction. Minutes later he hung up the phone. They stared at each other. She felt the swell in her bones of an impending explosion. He wasn't about to be the first to speak, so she eventually did, otherwise they could've stood forever like two wax museum figures.

"Do you need any help with the funeral arrangements?" she offered as gently as possible.

"No," was his quick answer.

More silence. He didn't go on about his business, though, like someone who really didn't wish to be bothered. He simply stood, staring at her, challenging her to say something that might actually do him good. She knew there was no such thing.

"Sure, all right," she stammered. "Do you mind if I just ask you what those arrangements are?"

"Why?" he asked practically on top of her inquiry.

"I—just because, there are, are, are things that I happen to know Arthur wouldn't want."

"Yeah? Such as?"

"Well, um, such as, I overheard you talking just now about caskets, on the phone, and I just think that he should be cremated."

"Yeah, well, you know, it's already been taken care of," he threw at her, annoyed.

"Well, I—but I just think—"

"I've handled everything, all right?"

"He doesn't want to be buried," she shoved through gritted teeth; pushed, aggravated.

"All right, know what? I don't need your help. But, gee, thanks a heap, anyway."

Her face grew hot and prickly.

"Daniel, yesterday you were ready to throw the both of us into the den of lions. And now you are clinging to him like he's your own precious property."

"Christ! Do I really have to suffer this?"

"I'm not trying to hurt you."

"Well, now, what would ever make me think you'd do anything to try and hurt me?"

"Okay, crucify me if you need to. I certainly deserve it. But do right by him. I'm only trying to offer that maybe a traditional funeral isn't what he would want."

"What would you know about what Arthur would want? Oh, wait," he sneered. "Was that possibly the most ridiculous question of the year?"

"Look Daniel," she forced. She had to keep forging ahead, or she'd crumble from his hate. "Arthur was haunted by the whole idea of funerals. He used to have nightmares about them, because his father, the undertaker, if you'll remember, used to take him to work and force him to watch them embalm corpses, and, and, and, and—"

She was close to hysterical now, just trying to get it all out before Daniel had the chance to stop her again with another poisoned dart.

"—and, and, and he used to gag from the smell of carnations because he only ever associated them with death. He doesn't want to be lying in state in some funeral parlor, for the world to come and gawk. He doesn't want his insides taken out and replaced with fluids and make-up and a wig. He doesn't want to be stuffing. I'm, I'm, I'm—"

Was it even worth it? She was ready to collapse.

"—I'm, I'm just saying don't do this to him. Don't put him in the one place he feared his whole life."

She knew Daniel was choking on the idea that there just might be something about Arthur that she knew and he didn't. Some intimacy between Arthur and her, alone, that would only ring up that other unspeakable intimacy in Daniel's vivid head. She knew she was doing her own case no good by saying these things, but they had to do right by Arthur. He would want no traces of himself left on this earth, which had done him no good.

"Please don't make these decisions out of hate."

Daniel stared at her and she saw the heartbreak in his eyes, the heartbreak that his dearest friend and brother was gone, whose last act on this earth was one of betrayal, and with his brother's own wife, whose infidelity was equally inexplicable. Now, to top it off, that she just might have something better to offer in this moment of needed organization than he.

"Fine. It's all yours. Handle it however you please."

He stormed toward the elevator.

"All it took for Arthur to be pardoned was for him to kill himself," she said, hastily. "Is that what I'll have to do to be forgiven?"

That stopped him cold. He turned around and headed back toward her in an ominous stampede. And she actually did fear for her life in this frightful instant, watching the horror in his face, the twitching in his jaws, the nostrils flaring. His hands came up to hold her face on either side, shaking her. His face was so close to hers that she could feel the sprinkles of his spittle across the bridge of her nose as he screamed at her.

"Goddamn you! What! You're gonna leave me now, too? Is this the sick game you plan to play? You wanna stick a gun to your head, as well?"

He held the nape of her neck with one hand, and with the other pressed an index finger, like a gun, deeply against her temple.

"Is it turning you on, to do this?" he cried. "Goddamn you, don't you ever threaten me like that!"

He bellowed loud and long, as he looked into her eyes, his own darting desperately back and forth. She saw those searing eyes searching frantically for her somewhere in there, but he couldn't find her and she saw the alarm in his face.

I'm right here, she wanted to whisper.

When he finally let go of his grasp, she fell off her balance and he stormed back across the room. It was a cruel thing she'd said, but it was the only way she could keep him from walking out on her. He leaned against his worktable, holding his side and catching his breath. She stood back up, but cautious, and kept her eye on him.

A long silence followed. She hoped that maybe this outburst was some sign that he was not done with her yet. He didn't want her to die. He'd made that clear. It didn't necessarily mean he was forgiving her, but she was praying it all meant the same. Ultimately he turned her way and the look of sadness overshadowed all rage. She saw him weaken. She saw him want to forgive her, to understand. He was still so far from it.

"Why?" was all he could muster.

It was the one question she had hoped he'd never ask. Because to answer him honestly would be to say that Arthur had been a man who had known no love, and that she had wanted to give him love. That, in that one afternoon, she had seen Arthur slip from the grasp of everyone who had known and cared for him. That, in her silly vanity, she had thought her love might save his life. Her love. Daniel would never stand to hear those words. But it was the truth. She had loved Arthur, and always would. It was not the same kind of love she felt for her husband, but Daniel would never bother with the difference. Who would?

Her only answer instead — and she couldn't really say she knew what it meant — was that she was lost. She whispered it in a tremble.

"I just felt lost."

They looked at each other, both knowing that the past several months had not been harmonious. Maybe even the past couple of years. It had been an era fraught with the looming angst of two befuddled artists, whose temperaments daily clashed. In between those clashes were the moments of thrilling connection and deepest sympatico, but those had been so rare lately.

How they'd come to be in such a predicament was a bafflement to Nona still. They'd had all the ingredients of perfection in an alliance: A fiery duo whose love and passion and reverence for each other was unequaled; two artists who lived to push the envelope and challenge each other daily to do the same; kindred hearts who breathed the same politics and laughed at the same humor; a pair of shoppers who met in a grocery market one day, three years ago now, and fell in love.

They'd had no business complaining about their lives. Art had been treating them wonderfully. The Los Angeles County Museum would certainly tell you so. Likewise, Seward Press, which had strategized *Champion* straight to the bestseller list. The people they loved were the most stimulating minds they knew, and every day had been an incredible odyssey.

It was Arthur. He walked into their lives and shook them all off of their cozy foundations. Made them trip just a little from their steady footing, and wake up from their deep sleep of comfort and perfect planning. Arthur never just lived life, he *was* life. And perhaps it seemed a sham to say that a man who has just committed suicide was life, but he was. Because he made every one of them fall just a tiny bit into the sand, get their feet a little dirty and their souls a little stimulated.

So, saying to Daniel that she felt lost wasn't completely untrue. It simply wasn't the whole of it. And honestly, it had been a good kind of lost. Until now.

She knew Daniel felt lost, too, because all of a sudden he simply sank onto his mattress to great sobbing, as if to concede that he couldn't really refute her on that one. His wide shoulders shook as he sat on the edge, facing away from her, and buried his head in his hands, his mopped black hair tangled within the folds of his fingers, and his gruff man's voice barked out its cries. To experience a man weep was always painful, so basso profundo was the timbre; it shook the very room in which one stood and was, therefore, a hundred times sadder.

With no return blow that he could find, it must've meant that the battle was finished. For now. So she advanced. She prayed to know if this was the right move to make, but decided to make it anyway, without awaiting the answer, and gingerly sat beside him. She leaned her head to his shoulder. No fight. She breathed. A moment later she placed her arms full around him. His sweating hands found hers. Their fingers braided. She lifted her chin to rest on his shoulder, and her face leaned into his, with his tangled hair falling between his swollen cheek and hers.

He didn't really want her here, but wouldn't let her go. And they grieved together: For the unknown whereabouts of Lorca, and that he was now a fatherless boy. For their petty, indulgent natures, and having taken for granted an invigorating life, which could easily have been theirs, but instead they'd insisted on walking through it as tormented *artistes*, moaning at everything. For their love, which had been shaken off of its foundation, though she felt certain they could steady it someday. And for the loss of Arthur, a loss that was a hole in both their hearts.

Suddenly, after sitting for interminable minutes, Daniel began to babble.

"Please forgive me. It's my fault. It's all my fault. I'm so sorry. I'm soooo soorrrryyyy!"

Long, sung syllables of *sorry* moaned about like a dirge.

"Pleeeeeeeeaaase forgive me. I never meant to utter that word. Never meant to bring up THAT THING. I'd made a vow, and look what I did."

"It's okay, Daniel. It's okay."

He shook his head, and she rocked him like a baby, caressing his brow and purposefully breathing slowly, so that she might encourage him to breathe slowly.

Hours must have passed with them crouched in their embrace, in silence and unaware of the world around them, because when Daniel's phone suddenly rang, they both jumped out of their daze and it was dark out. After several rings, and the realization that he had no intention of acknowledging it, she pried herself away, aching from the joints of her elbows and knees. As she walked toward the phone, he collapsed resigned into the hollow of his mattress.

"Hello?" she tried to whisper. "Yes...uh...I'm his wife...yes...yes. Sure, um, but do you think you could call back in a bit? I don't think he's quite made a decision yet—"

"Is that the mortuary?" Daniel suddenly muttered from beneath a buried face and flaccid state.

"They don't mind calling back—"

"No, it's all right," he interrupted. "Tell them we've decided to cremate. We'll have a memorial in our garden, or—somewhere—I don't know. But yeah—cremation."

He didn't look up; just mumbled it in a fog. She took a deep breath. It was rattled and torn. She hoped that in this gesture of agreeance lay the promise of a truce, so that they could do right by Arthur and perhaps even begin to heal each other.

FORTY EIGHT

She knew that the next five days would be difficult, so she gave herself and Daniel a little test. If they could manage through them and come out relatively unscathed, then she believed they could manage through the rest of their lives. And if the answer to that was yes, then she'd offer him her proposition.

They'd agreed to organize Arthur's memorial together, even though Daniel chose not to sleep in their home and they only spoke when it regarded some detail for the service. Still, miraculously, they did manage to be a kind of support for one another.

She put on the best act she knew how around Kai, to the point of treating her friend like the grieving widow, but Kai wasn't the type to bask in that kind of attention and kept insisting, besides, that her 'thing' with Arthur had never been more than a few dates.

"Stop looking at me with puppy-dog stares every time you glance my way. You and Daniel were much closer to him."

But Nona could see how disheartened Kai was at the very idea that her romantic presence in Arthur's life hadn't been enough to keep him here, that he'd simply disappeared without a word her way and it wasn't even her he'd contacted upon returning.

Had Kai been keen enough, she'd have recognized the guilt in Nona's clumsy gestures, but Kai was a pure heart who rarely mistrusted anyone's behavior as ulterior. And that was Nona's only hope that her friend would never be the wiser, since she was horrible at this game of deceit. Was it even possible to be here for Kai with any other motive than her selfish one? If so, she couldn't figure out how, and that sank her even lower.

There were overwhelming particulars to attend to for laying Arthur to rest. Harper scoured Arthur's apartment over several trips, when neither of the Crosses could take themselves to that blighted return, but found no will to indicate what Arthur would've wanted accomplished. Their instincts were all they had to trust in making decisions about Arthur's estate, the notion of which was fairly frightening considering that the very best of Nona's lately had proven calamitous. All that seemed to remain of Arthur's life, besides the remnants of police tape on his apartment floor, was his body of work.

But God, the works.

Harper had suggested that a volume be posthumously published. Something that, along with the royalties from *Murmuration*, could potentially set Lorca up nicely for college. The tomes and notebooks and journals that Harper dug up were voluminous. She would heap mountains of Arthur's unpublished scribblings onto Nona's desk, because Daniel couldn't take it on, and Nona would spend hours, stretching long into the night, after an even longer day of dealing with her heartsick husband, reading the astonishing works Arthur had composed.

As she faced the mountain, Nona realized just how urgent poetry had been to Arthur. Sheer volume alone told her that there probably wasn't a single day in his life that hadn't brought with it some unmercifully transformative take on the world. A world that, clearly for Arthur, was ripe, and bursting with color, and dizzying in scope, and dubious at best, and which really did require some kind of elegiac musing on it just to filter out its unbearable rays of light and render it receivable. She imagined a furious scribbler who gave hours of his life every day in some coffeehouse, or Laundromat, or park, probably routinely shooed away by the authorities for loitering, while burying his face in his notebooks. Just to stay alive.

It rang with hints of graphomania, frankly, a compulsive disorder she also believed Basquiat suffered, and she couldn't help but see a theme. Both lived on the fringes. Both self-medicated. Both shot the world through with ridiculous flights of fancy. Both died too young. Only the ones that society called crazy seemed to have exceptional capacity to be visionaries.

This poetry before her was dark and hallucinatory. An expedition. Scary at its least and transcendent at its most profound. She came to realize, as she read these works that she'd spread out on her bed, and she read every last one, that though Arthur had often claimed not to have much use for this world, it was not so. If anything, he had learned to extract from its center a door, for all to walk through who had the courage to read him.

While it may have been a door that he himself couldn't seem to squeeze through very easily, this threshold was, for the reader, a kind of baptism.

Cantankerous, which was dated 4/15/71, speaks of sleeping on discarded sofas in alleys, and black money riding on the 'horse.' Of brushing his smell against society and watching its neck hairs rise. She noticed that the date of the composition was tax day, except that the human being in this portrait is so far below that common middle-class preoccupation. And she wondered if Arthur had purposefully constructed this, or if it wasn't just some unconscious alignment of the forces that simply drove him.

Wake up Ophelia begs a woman to do just that. It is a crying ode of such desperation, screaming out from mere words. In it he speaks of arms erupting and being lost inside dead eyes. Nona got the feeling that this woman, whoever she was, drove much of Arthur's poetry. As in *Requiem for O?* Or *She*, a delicate piece of verse that tells of a woman who lives unblemished by the sun. Could all of these have been about the same woman? Some secret love from his past that he could never share? She thought of Shakespeare's lady of the sonnets, who reveals herself as both dark beauty and fair light, and wanted to know more about this dark/fair lady of Arthur's sonnets.

A Curtsy to My Shaky Love weeps of smelling her in the folds of curtains and the scent of trees. In this case, Nona wasn't sure if the *her* of Arthur's iambic lament referred to this O woman, spoken of in so many of his others…or his habit. Which he elaborates on, most pungently and in no uncertain metaphor, in *Arthur's Bitch*. It isn't a misogynist rant, but is about peeling the crust off of his disease.

She could barely keep her grip on the rein of Arthur's wild horse, for it cutting her hand, while also realizing that her own too consciously heavy-handed metaphors shamefully paled to the clear, unforced call of Arthur's expression.

As she lay amidst the mountain of his poetry, the breadth of his life, she tried to find his presence in these thousand words; in the feel of old, crumpled paper, in the peculiar squiggle of his penmanship, because if she could draw him up, then maybe she could talk to him and tell him that she wished he'd chosen life.

She knew that an estate needed to be established, something tangible and legal that could be passed on to Lorca, but it seemed somehow improper and obscene to secure information on Arthur's copyrights, and to deal with lawyers and probate courts and the State regarding his intellectual property, which she knew they'd eventually have to do. It felt like a violation of something holy.

Though it had originally been his idea, Daniel eventually rejected the notion of having the memorial in their garden. Nona knew it was hard for him to even be in their home. He never once came there in this five days; they either spoke over the phone or she'd go to Santee. She even brought him some clothes on his request, though it made her ill to think that the prospect of his being in their home made him ill.

They ultimately settled on the Talking Drum, the coffeehouse that had first given them the drum circles. A circle seemed the most appropriate happening to occur at a memorial for Arthur. They wanted no men of the cloth officiating, committing his ashes to the earth and his soul to God, because Arthur had felt that religion failed him. So Daniel asked Mbarata Maseeka, the Elder of the drum circle, if he would deliver a eulogy. It was hoped that Maseeka's words would inspire a drumming. They all agreed that whoever felt the inclination to say, read, sing, or play anything should feel the freedom to step into the circle and commence. It would be the very kind of event that Arthur himself had always loved attending.

Some of the storytellers from the Griot Society offered to tell tales about Arthur and take the congregation on Arthur journeys. He had carved for himself an illustrious place in the Society and had been their good friend, spinning yarns of his own, in his day, which were the greatest of his gifts.

Harper asked Daniel if he would be willing to speak, but Daniel's feelings were ambivalent at best; all bound up in the fabric of confusion, and deceit, and tragedy, and love, and hate. No matter how hard he tried, he couldn't reconcile what had compelled Arthur toward such a betrayal. He knew Arthur loved him, but perhaps Arthur defined love differently. Daniel's head was much too cluttered with these musings to be able to offer any words of worth, so after hedging the suggestion for some time he respectfully declined. Harper knew better than to ask Nona, who was quickly mastering the art of near-invisibility so that she wouldn't inflame Daniel's image of Arthur and her any further, and Harper knew it.

On the morning of the memorial, Nona drove to Leimert Park alone.

She wanted to walk in by herself and take a seat next to her husband, who would need support today. She actually arrived before Daniel, but felt greatly soothed when, upon his arrival, he sat next to her. There hadn't been much in the way of affection since that fateful day, so his sitting next to her, of all the places he could sit, was large.

Mbarata Maseeka and the drum circle turned out to be the greatest gift they could've given to Arthur's tribute. The old man spoke powerfully, as he had that first thrilling evening.

"The man I know as Arthur Hughes Dufresne is a great warrior. He has warred always against the forces of intolerance, imprisonment, willful complacency, and fear. He has fought always for beauty and love and light. And it is greatly apparent to me today that all has not been lost in his warring efforts. For, as I look before me, I see clearly that in his spiritual transition he has assembled the greatest beauties he knew together in this place..."

When Nona looked around, the place was wall to wall, with crowds spilling out onto the street: Drum circle folk, Griot Society folk, coffeehouse circuit folk, friends from Arthur's neighborhood, artists, poets, musicians, groupies clutching their *Murmuration* books. But no family. Not a mother or father in sight, if they were even still alive. No Lorca, though word had been sent to Sonja's mother in D.C. Nona and Daniel and Kai and Harper had been Arthur's only true family in the end.

"...Many have thought Arthur a violent man. They have likened him to a rumbling volcano or a restless, hungry leopard. And I could contradict that popular belief with the niceties that are the obligation of the eulogist. But the truth is, people, he was. And he heaped violence upon no one more brilliantly than himself. Though I ask you this: How does one become a triumphant warrior without it? You must tear down and destroy the crumbling temple, so that it can be built again, stronger, better..."

Drumming had already begun by the time they were into the heart of the old man's eulogy, but neither Nona nor Daniel moved to join in. All Nona could accomplish today was watching everyone else pay tribute. She soaked in Arthur's presence, which had been remarkably called up by Maseeka's efforts, and her heart embraced this presence. Arthur, in turn, must've embraced Daniel's heart, on her behalf, as angels do, because just as she thought it Daniel placed his hand on top of hers, which had been resting on the bench by her side. The gesture was laughably simple. Nothing, really. But it started a tremor within her. She had wanted so badly to sing, and weep, and celebrate Arthur, and scream at him for leaving them, and indulge every emotion she had, but she'd felt paralyzed for a solid week by the fear of continuing to wound her husband. When Daniel saw her struggle to be a stone, he whispered to her in a kind of weakened stumble.

"Don't wait for my permission to grieve for him. I already know that you do, and I would only think you callous if you didn't. Not, not that what I think should determine—I, I, I don't know what I'm saying. I'm just— don't consider me today, if that's what you're doing. Feel what you feel."

At his invitation, the rush of painful release fell from her. Partly she cried for Arthur, but partly, as well, it was to hear her sweet husband's voice again, tender for the first time since this tragedy, his breath in her ear, and his anger with her subsided.

"...Good people, you must choose what is in your hearts to believe," Maseeka continued. "As for me, I believe that in destroying his earthly body Arthur was merely setting the stage for a much greater masterpiece. Perhaps this creation has already been in the works and is simply for each of us to discover in the days and years to come. Look far and wide for it, my friends. When it is found, we will all celebrate."

The old man's words made Nona think of Arthur as still alive, of his work yet being done here on this earth. It made her realize exactly what was so powerful about art. It was divinity and immortality. Not only for the artist, but for the witness. It was magnificent energy, which never dies.

And there was more. Poets read Arthur's poetry and their own. Dorothy Favor sang, and others joined her. Storytellers from the Griot Society told tales about Arthur, which made the congregation laugh, and testify, and sometimes cry, but mostly smile.

Kai and Harper had been as quiet and as pensive as Nona and Daniel had been. The foursome simply sat and watched the world around them celebrate their brother, but Nona could tell that each was caught up in the tide of sweet reminiscences in her own individual way.

When Leonard Cohen's haunting *Hallelujah* was performed by a folk duo, with the congregation joining in on its iconic choruses, Nona's tears quite overtook her and she made certain to remember every bit of this because she was determined to recall this celebration some day for Lorca, who would want to know how many people's lives had been touched by his father.

As they came to the close of the memorial, and as people began to mill and embrace, Daniel abruptly let go of Nona's hand and, without a word, walked out of the Talking Drum. She was suddenly hit with the prickly-hot dawning that his intention, all along, had been to be kind only until this difficult day was done. And that now that it was over, so were they.

Nona did her best to maneuver through the crowd, lungs seizing and heart thumping, but it wasn't easy, as she and Daniel got separated by more and more people.

"Wasn't it an amazing tribute?"

"Yes. Yes, it was. Can you just give me a moment, please?"

She didn't see who was talking to her, for doing her best to make sure she didn't lose Daniel from her sights, as he moved swiftly through the front door.

"Daniel!" she barked, once outside. He was already down the street and sticking the key into his car door.

He turned around with that annoyed glance that says *I knew you'd follow*. This was her only chance. The proposition.

"I have two airline tickets," she spilled abruptly. "Already bought. Already ours, if we want them. To Paris."

She could barely get it out without that little tremor in the chin that abhors risk. Daniel knew how much Paris had been the only fantasy she'd ever shared with him. They used to say they'd do it just as soon as a book was launched or an exhibit did well. He knew it was a city that held sentimental ties for her. He'd always promised it to her. This plea may have been manipulative, but she had no moral qualms about playing this game viciously if it meant she could fix her marriage.

"Let's just go away. Escape all of this. Give ourselves a proper chance to heal."

His eyes tightened.

"Think of it, Daniel, the city where my parents met. The city of love."

"It's the city of light," he corrected like an irritated schoolmarm. And cold. "Well, this is about as maudlin as it gets, wouldn't you say? You might be losin' your touch, though, darlin'. You're soundin' a bit like a romance novel."

For a minute she'd actually forgotten just how hurt he really was, and how cruel he could be. This one yanked her right back into the unmerciful present.

"Please," she pled with little dignity. "If we can just escape this place and really focus in on each other, I think we could get a better perspective on things."

"Let's see if I get this straight. Life makes absolutely no sense to me right now. I have never been in more despair. And your answer would be to just fuck all and go on holiday. Have I got that right? Isn't that your M.O.? Life gets rough, skip the country? How effortless to do when you're well-heeled."

It was in this instant that she realized he'd already left her.

"I love you, Daniel. That's all I know. Please, let's just do this."

It was a garbled plea. As he watched her curiously, Nona couldn't tell if it was loathing or pity that made him stare the way he did. Maybe he was memorizing her. The way people do you when they're intending never to see you again.

"No," was all he said after. He hopped in his car and pulled out, almost clipping a passing vehicle, and drove away.

FORTY NINE

Goddamn you! CUNT! He loved his wife. He really did. So fucking much it hurt. *SLAG!* Why did she even bother marrying him? If she just couldn't do it? Bouquets of roses be damned, "Will you marry me?" was every woman's sucker punch. Except that he was the sucker this time. *BITCH!* He called her every vile name he could think of. Never out loud, but whenever she conjured in his thoughts. *SLUT!* And it was never enough. To call her a cunt only worked to a limply cathartic degree, and then he was just as sick as before.

Sick of betrayal. Sick of death. Sick of them both scratching each other's eyes out for the position of principle affliction.

The blasted image was in his head again. The trigger against Arthur's skull. The entire measure of a man gone in an instant.

Death of *that* nature seemed to be a theme in Daniel's family. When he was a boy, he'd heard tales of his grandfather, Leviticus Rankin, witnessing the suicide of someone he'd loved. It was apparently quite the scandal in Rankin's small town. Daniel was never sure if the story was truth or myth because his mother had always had a penchant for colorful tales. If it were true, then it made him wonder if this couldn't possibly be some twisted cosmic tradition that was simply getting handed down generations, like a fucking genetic disorder. And if so, then his mother would've been counted before him, wouldn't she?

His imagination flew. After all, he hadn't seen his parents in thirty years. What if his mother had witnessed the suicide of someone she loved? And what if that someone were, say, his father? Or even the other way around? The profile was perfect, really. His parents had always been on the verge of some self-destructive drama.

He would never really have any way of knowing, but today his imagination was as colorful as his mother's, and that thought only made him curse her. Suddenly he cursed every woman in existence, with their maudlin natures that painted themselves pretty and romantic on the outside, but which only shrouded some other conniving agenda. Their smiles were more delicate than a man's, therefore greater at the game of deceit. His wife was no different.

And he cursed Arthur. Every night the ghastly image reproduced itself clearly and perfectly in Daniel's dreams. Seeing Arthur's very head open up and leap right out of there and attach itself to a foreign wall. Seeing Arthur's cognition leave him more quickly than Daniel's eyes could keep up. Every night that Daniel slept alone, in his old bed, in his old digs, he awoke in a fevered sweat at Arthur's words, *"I'm done."* Those fucking words. Every night that he slept without her, he watched Arthur's index finger depress that trigger.

Arthur had never been the suicidal type. He was a survivor. He was the biggest proponent of, *"You do what you have to do to stay alive, BUT YOU STAY ALIVE."* If spending eight years in prison didn't do him in, if becoming the slave to his drug didn't do him in, if the crime-of-passion of the woman he loved could not do him in, how could Daniel's stupid utterance do it?

For the five unbearable days of preparing for Arthur's memorial, he had walked around in a fog, pretending to take interest in the arrangements. He could give two shits! What would Arthur care about special tributes paid, loving words, fond anecdotes? Sentimentalities weren't going to bring him back. And Daniel wanted Arthur back. He wanted Arthur back so that he could hold his friend and say, *"Don't worry, mate, we'll find your son."* He wanted Arthur back so that they could laugh the way they always had, and commiserate on the miserable plight yet wondrous resplendency of artists, and whine in their cocktails over it all. Most of all, he wanted Arthur back so that he could hate his friend, his brother, for betraying him.

That was really it, wasn't it? Arthur had snatched Daniel's moment to rail against him clear away. And with nowhere else for that rage to go, Daniel had to figure out if it would all now aim at her, the one still here. And if that was fair, or if he even cared about fair.

An airline ticket to Paris. Christ, it was so like the affluent to wave a first-class ticket in your face and say, *"Here's the solution to all our problems, darling."*

After walking away from her at the memorial, he'd decided he was no longer required to play nice. For a week following it, he drank till drunk, never left his flat, and thought of her only in sexual ways. Yet every time she came into his imaginings, Arthur was right there with her. The image would hit him like a brick and knock him off his feet repeatedly. Picturing their bodies lying together made him puke. It was either that or the whisky.

He knew she'd be coming by. One whole week couldn't possibly pass without her showing her face, especially after the way they'd parted, so he prepared for her arrival. As large as a vengeful God he rendered it in his sight, just waiting for her to show up. It took eight days.

"Oh, my God!" she recoiled in shock, as she stepped from the lift one week to the day after Arthur's memorial. She turned, and flinched, and covered her terrified mouth with her hand, and looked up again, and winced, and stood agape. The dance of humiliation was sort of beautiful, he thought.

She had walked in and found him sitting in his huge chair in the center of his dungeon, unbathed for days, smoking his thousandth cigarette before it had even struck noon, mouth dry and ashy, and staring at a photographic mural of Arthur and her. It covered one entire wall from ceiling to floor on the far side of Daniel's flat. This was not any one of the photos he'd taken during the creation of *Murmuration*, or the hundreds he'd ever snapped at parties. But *that* photo. He'd actually shot an entire roll on that awful day, but in his fury of the moment most of the roll had ended up a blur. One came out, though. One was all he needed.

It wasn't until the day after the memorial, wallowing in thoughts of Arthur, that he even remembered shooting his camera on that sight. As soon as he did, he searched it out, ripped the film from the casing, a man on fire, and commenced developing the roll.

There before them was sprawled his wife and brother in all their slumbering after-sex, mounted on a billboard-sized sheet of foam-board, against the only of his walls that had no windows. The blow-up was so huge that it had to be assembled in pieces, and the image was now just a grainy haze, but still identifiable, which rendered it somewhat impressionistic.

"Daniel!" she cried, hand immediately shooting up to her mouth aghast. She couldn't advance beyond that exclamation.

He saw the chaos in her head as she tried to decipher his madness.

Was he mad? Who else would do this? And all he had done for seven days was stare at it. Try to get inside of it. Beg to understand why this all happened. Attempt to flush the image from his gut by saturating himself with it. At least that had been the rationalization. When he would awaken every morning, it was to that image. When he'd fall asleep in his drunken stupor every night, it was to that image. And now, she would have to bear it as he had borne it. Or leave. These were the choices.

"Why?" she warbled in a defeated whisper, unbelieving of his state, whatever she perceived that to be. Whatever in Hell it was. He didn't answer her. All he did was continue to stare at the photo. And after several minutes of deadly silence — her staring at him, him staring at it — she walked over to stand between billboard and man, though the appalled look on her face indicated that she was in no condition for a fight. She towered above him as he slunk carelessly in his chair. He only shifted his glower from photograph to her.

"Is there really that much hate in you?" she asked, beaten. He continued to leer. Took a slow drag from his Viceroy. Flicked a tobacco flake from his tongue. Sank even lower into the chair. Lazily scratched his crotch. He saw the life drain from her and instantly recognized a perverse pattern coming to form. Couldn't something this repugnant possibly drive her to the same tragic edge of a gun, and a bullet, and a trigger, and an *'I'm done,"* as it had Arthur? He was becoming the master at murder.

"Well," she could barely get out, for the trembling in her cheek, "it's certainly a long way we've come from an iced tea at Erewhon, isn't it?"

Don't do that, he thought, as he looked away again.

"—a long way from another photograph you once shot. One that was used to comfort me. To show love."

Bring it on, then. I can take it.

"There's no hope for us, is there?"

Wait a fucking minute. Was she no longer begging? He'd been so stiffly stroked all this time by the notion that she was so proverbially on her knees that this sudden resignation scared him.

"I don't know," was all he could answer, as the rules of this game got muddier by the minute. The most selfish of all realities was that while he didn't know if he could forgive her, he knew he didn't want to live without her.

"Goddamn it, Daniel!" she finally exploded. "Yes or no!" The tears fell from her in a race to the dirted earth. She stomped feet like a child. "You either want to try, or you don't, because I will not live in this sick limbo of yours!" She shoved a pointed finger at his masterpiece on the far wall. "This is sickness."

The leopard in him finally pounced.

"You're in limbo? Really?! Well, I'm in Hell! And in Hell there is only sickness. So guess what? I'm allowed to be as sick as I goddamned well please! But I'd gladly trade places with you. Let's see, in order to do that, all I have to do is shag your dearest friend and rip out your heart and everything and everyone you've ever believed in! And then you can be the one to watch them kill themselves right before your very eyes, close enough to taste the blood that has spattered on your face. Glad to trade places with you, darlin'. Really!"

There followed a wretched silence. It would give no inch of mercy to the air that connected them. It was an odorous air. Still. He knew he'd knocked the wind out of her. He'd knocked it out of himself.

From out of her inertia, there rashly leapt her last patience with him. Without saying another word, she ran over to his worktable, swooping up buckets of paint, charcoal sticks, hammers, pliers, whatever she could find, stormed over to the mural, and violently shoved her booted foot against it. There was only the brick wall behind it, so it shoved her back and down onto the floor, causing everything in her arms' grip to spill around her. Her body was suddenly monstrous as she leapt back up, the fall only fueling her rage. She pried open paint gallons and doused the effigy with deranged color, hurling not only paint but also the cans they came in, which dripped like blood against the corporeal landscape. She wielded an ax hammer, slicing through the innocent foam board, with shards of drywall exploding about and snowing down upon her. Brick wall still there. So it rattled her very brain. Dropping the ax hammer, she placed her hands to her temples and screamed her warbles of how they were doing a masterful job of slaughtering each other, and that to look at them now no one could possibly believe that there had ever been love here. She was vehemence and impetuosity in one quaking body.

After watching her absurd vandalism for some minutes, Daniel grabbed up the same tools and the same buckets of paint, and helped her.

"Yes! Kill it!" he screamed. "Because I can't bear this any longer, either!"

He tore into it, matching her, riot for riot. And the two of them pillaged and plundered, with his paints serving destruction far more effortlessly than they had ever served creation.

Fifty

He couldn't say what happened to the game he'd been playing, but it had turned on him. And with that dawning, he collapsed. Gave it all up. Fell to his knees, suppliant.

He cried for minutes, days, even, maybe, for all his head could tell, before anything else was said by anyone. She stared at the broken man on the floor, her own face bloated and red, unsure of how to advance. As the volume got turned down on the surrounding air, suddenly nothing could be heard except the last of the foam board falling from its hinges, the dripping of paint, the heavy panting of two soldiers that had been to war, and the gruff tears of the afflicted man on the floor. Once more.

"Bugger all! This is the least of it," he cried. "And it's a pretty fucking sad state of things when an affair can be the least of your torments."

"I know," she tried to offer up. "A man is dead—"

"And I killed him."

"No, Daniel."

"And it would seem that I'm trying to do the same to you. Why else this insanity?"

"Daniel, you're not responsible."

"Then why've I been living with that?" he spat in the direction of the destroyed blow-up. "Am I trying to kill myself, as well? Or drive myself mad? Maybe I already am! What is wrong with meeeeeee!"

He wavered somewhere between misery and mania, letting his defenses down and knowing it, giving her the opportunity, and she was an opportunist, to slide right in and comfort him. Was she a snake, or his loving wife? He could scarcely tell.

"Why do you keep insisting that Arthur's death was your fault?"

Was she talking again? He didn't want to talk. He just wanted to be held, and he didn't care who did it. He wanted to cry like a baby in her arms, and feel her breast against his wet face, and maybe take her nipple in his mouth. *Goddamn it, Nona, don't speak to me now.* But she would.

"Why do you keep insisting—"

"Stop! Stop it! Stop asking! Please!"

"Daniel, just talk to me. I'm here for you. Just tell me—"

"Aaaaaggggggghhhhhhhhhh!" he screamed, as the roof of his life opened wide like a departed earth. "Because! I betrayed him far worse than he could ever have betrayed me. Christ, I can't have this conversation with you. Don't you understand? I need for you to know how badly the two of you hurt me. I can't have you believing that any betrayal could be worse. Except that one was. My betrayal of him was far worse. His betrayal didn't kill me. But mine killed him!"

"What betrayal?"

"I dug up his worst canker after he had, FINALLY, over years' time, managed to bury it deep, maybe even heal it. And all it took was a handful of words from me, out of petty vengeance, to unearth it—"

"I'm sorry, Daniel. You're talking in riddles. Please calm down and speak to me clearly."

"For twenty years. And all it took from me—"

"Stop it, Daniel. It wasn't you. Think about it. What was the one thing Arthur lived for? What was the one thing that kept him from ending his life years ago? A natural survival instinct? Bullshit! Being a parent did that. Having a son is what helped him to bear up all the tragedies in his life."

"You don't understand—"

"No, listen to me. He gave up on his life because he had given up on his son, Daniel. It wasn't because of any slanders you might've uttered. You were angry and hurt. You would've said anything—"

"No, no, no, no, fuck, you don't know! Slanders? I wish that's all they'd—"

"Lorca was his only reason for living. And you knew that. Otherwise you wouldn't have been so obsessed with finding that kid. It was, like, it was your own crusade."

"I loved him, and that's what family does!"

"But it was more than that. It was because you knew that not finding Lorca was the one thing that could kill him."

"No, no, there was another—"

"This campaign of yours wasn't about arranging some teary reunion or even getting back at Sonja. It was about saving Arthur's life. And even I couldn't see it at the time. But you knew. Daniel, it wasn't anything you could've possibly said that killed him. That's crazy to think. Believe me, it was something that had already occurred before you or I had walked into that apartment."

"Then why would he do it in front of me? Tell me that. Was he just that fucking twisted? When you're ready to check out of this fucking life, you do it alone in a room somewhere and you leave a note. You don't make it theatre. No. It happened right when it did for a reason. It was payback. For MY treachery. Arthur would never have been capable of standing anybody down who challenged him about Ophelia. It was the one weapon that could topple him with one tiny breath. I was the only one on this earth that he'd ever entrusted with that weapon, and I used it on him. And I don't buy for one second that he had given up on Lorca. He'd never do that. It was himself that he gave up on. Because of me!"

It wasn't until he finished his breakneck ranting that he even realized Nona had stopped arguing with him and now simply looked at him puzzled, brow pursed, head cocked. They stared at each other for some seconds. So many deadly seconds that he nearly screamed.

"Who is Ophelia?"

His heart skipped.

"What?" he asked perplexed. Caught.

"Ophelia," she repeated. "You just said—wait, Ophelia is the woman Arthur wrote tons of poetry about."

He stared at his wife with a stunning that was just that.

"So, who is she? And why wouldn't Arthur have been able to stand anyone challenging him about her?"

Daniel shook his head, started to deny it.

"No, no, no, no, no, don't do that, Daniel. That's what you just said. So, who is she?" Her breath grew short and rapid.

What on earth had he just done? How had he allowed that name to slip? He'd been on such a bullet train that he wasn't even aware of what he'd said. When he'd tried to spill on Arthur the first time, she hadn't gotten it. A second chance to maintain Arthur's good name, to redeem his own sins, and fuck all if he didn't blow it again! Was he just that determined to drive her mad? Shatter her even further with the answer to her question? Or was he getting back at the dead man after all?

He processed thoughts. Eyes darted agitatedly. His and hers. She was panicked.

"All right," he whispered in a beaten rasp, head hung in shame. "I'll tell you everything."

He scooped up a shaky breath.

"That day in his apartment...I...I...I..."

How on earth would he start? He never again in his life wanted to revisit that day.

"I...I...he...fucking Hell! Nona, it wasn't YOUR rape I was bringing up that day."

Her eyes shifted. It was subtle. But he saw her finally begin to comprehend that he was about to send her deeper into a Hell already architected.

"What do you mean by MY—"

"Just—please, let me just get this out."

More deep breaths. It didn't help.

"Arthur did rape a woman," he uttered finitely. "And, and, and—she died—I mean—he, he, he—killed her."

Then with a new energy.

"But it was all just a, a, a confused, em, em, it was a moment of drugged and desolate passion, a kind of horrible mistake. He, he never meant, I mean—"

He didn't wait for breath to catch up.

"—You have to understand where he was at that time in his life. He'd just come back from Viet Nam, he was wrecked in the head, practically homeless, he was strung out with a brand new addiction, and still facing the demons of his father's abuse. He was at his lowest ebb possible. And, and, and—it wasn't anything like your situation. She wasn't just some stranger walking on some dark street, and he wasn't a predator. They, they, they, they'd had a history, and, and, and—it was a lifetime ago. Like, thirty years or something. Maybe more, even. I don't, you know, I don't really remember any longer."

Liar. It lived in him every day of his life, in cartographic detail.

He was afraid to look at her, but when he eventually did he saw the dread well up, and her eyes glaze with disbelief.

And Arthur. What had he now done to his dear brother's name? A name which that brother had lived his entire life to redeem.

"Nona, even though you and I vowed never to keep any secrets, I'd vowed one to him first. I never intended on telling a soul, because he deserves a better memory. And especially you, because with your own history—I knew you'd never be able to see past that to know the truly remarkable man Arthur became. And I broke that vow. And out of what? A lover's scorn?"

Nothing from her. Did she think him a liar? Or was she digesting this poison?

"Redemption is real, Nona," he continued. All he could do was keep talking. *Keep talking or go mad.* "I've witnessed it firsthand. Arthur paid his penance a thousand times over, through the horrors of prison and the horrors of his addiction and his poverty. His entire life was atonement, for Christ's sake. And yet he managed to lift himself out of that fortune and become a remarkable artist, and raise a remarkable son."

Still nothing.

For a clear hour Nona stood, unmoving, and stared at some unseen thing, as Daniel did his rash best to preach the glory of Arthur, and to flog himself for his own crimes.

"Even now, as I hope and pray for your forgiveness, and his, I see how much bigger a man he was than me. Do you know that in the minutes before his death, he didn't even want my forgiveness? He wanted me to hate him, because he wanted to make what he was about to do easier for me."

Daniel tried to get her to sit, and she didn't fight him. She was limp. In shock, surely. He went for the phone to call Kai, Harper, anyone who could get through to her, when she uttered her first word in that hour.

"Don't. I'm fine."

She looked at him, but spoke nothing more. He couldn't read her, but it was the first moment since that fateful day that he could feel anything for her other than rage. He wanted to hold and protect her. Her own rape had remained a mystery, though she'd recently made great strides toward liberating herself from it. What if he had just sent her all the way back to the beginning?

They had two choices, really. They could persist in carelessly opening their mouths every time some new weapon needed deploying, and in doing so continue bit by bit to destroy each other. Or they could, as she had suggested a week ago, quit all this madness and be with each other, to heal each other.

His indignation had left him, so he offered to her that if the invitation was still open he would be willing for them to go away. He frankly didn't know what they'd hope to accomplish "away," but he was willing to try. Perhaps just to be on foreign shores where the distraction of their lives couldn't get in the way of their focus on one another was all the remedy they needed. After all, she'd done that very thing once before. Her sojourn to Africa had been meant to be a healing pilgrimage, and she'd returned taller. Even his own, to America, almost thirty years before, had proven to give him new life.

She seemed somewhat consoled by his change of heart, though he could see that it was hard for her to catch her wind. Who wouldn't be paralyzed from the neck down?

For the rest of the day, and into the night, they held each other. She wouldn't speak. Wouldn't give a single sign of what she thought of all this. And he didn't force it.

They had created quite a plexus. Two people in pieces. Struggling hard to gather up the shards of their indulgent lives and paste them back together.

FIFTY ONE

He stared out of his tiny window on this difficult day, as Los Angeles grew small and checkered below them. It would be the second time in his life that he had escaped an entire continent in order to save that life. All he knew for certain was that he had never known any pain as great as the one he felt sitting in his roomy, business-class seat, taking off from the Tom Bradley terminal, headed for what his wife had believed would be their redemption. That was before the bombs came crashing in, and now he wasn't sure what she felt at all. Or himself, for that matter.

They ordered their first of many rounds of something stiffly alcoholic and retreated away from each other to their own respective Hells. They gripped each other's hands tightly and often, with the anxiety of two alley cats, and prayed to make it to Paris without losing all hope. But while their hands may have been in the same vicinity, their heads were as far away from each other as humanly achievable.

He could barely decipher his own mental state. On the one hand he was still angry, still hurt, confused, betrayed by the two people he had loved most in the world. On the other hand he was the villain, sending Arthur to his death, and telling Nona about Ophelia, knowing it could well wreck her. On the third hand — and yes, there is always a third in the inbred anatomy of unfair life — he wanted badly for his wife and him, together, to throw their wrath at Arthur, and wallow in their romantic suffering, a team. It was a mad bewilderment.

This maudlin Paris vision had been his wife's fantasy for as long as he'd known her: Clichéd notions of beautiful architecture, and vibrant museums, and love ballads on accordions, and moonlit reflections on the Seine, nursing them back to health and love. He didn't believe in it the way she always had, but now he prayed for it just as foolhardily.

He noticed she'd brought with her paperbacks of *Giovanni's Room, Tropic of Cancer, Nightwood, A Moveable Feast.* She was trying so hard to get a taste of Paris before actually having to swallow it whole, and was perhaps depending a little too furiously on her favorite writers to carry it out. It seemed that she desperately wanted the romantic antidote of Paris, some Cartier-Bresson ideal of overcast skies and moody cobblestone streets. He just wanted to hide away with her forever in a little Latin Quarter flat and forget all about Los Angeles.

As they soared across the Continental U.S., he had no idea what to make of her state. After that night in his flat, him spinning the story of Arthur and Ophelia like some Fright Night host, it took them exactly seventy-two hours to round up passports, pack luggage, and get the Hell out of town. And in all that time, she'd barely spoken beyond a few limp monosyllables.

He wondered if their tale had completely destroyed whatever progress she'd made in her own healing, and if he was about to have a catatonic on his hands. And yes, he'd even begun calling it 'their' tale, because he surely felt Arthur's accomplice in this crime.

He tried his damnedest to conjure some fond memory of his wife and their marriage, and to recall how her presence in his life had made it that much richer, because it was now up to him to take care of her, and to undo all that he had done. But every time it seemed as though he might be on the verge of softening to her again, he would instead graphically relive the terrible killing of his dearest friend and most potent betrayer. A man he loathed and loved simultaneously.

And the betraying act itself. The image of it replayed for Daniel over and again in full burdening color and motion. Even the smell and sound of it was digitally clear. He wondered petty, contemptible things, like: Was Arthur a more virile lover than he? Was Arthur's touch more sensitive? Would she think of Arthur from now on whenever they made love? And really, the least ridiculous question Daniel asked himself, the question that truly did matter when all the others were merely an illustration in what can make a man go insane, was: Would they ever be able to make love again? He'd have to answer it at some point, since she was pretty much leaving this all up to him.

He still had no grasp of why. When he'd asked her that day after Arthur died, her answer to him had been that she was lost. For two weeks he'd tried to decode that puzzle. He knew that he and his wife had not been connecting in those weeks prior to Arthur coming back, but it wasn't out of any kind of anger. The Lorca dilemma had divided them, but could hardly count as an estrangement. It was really that they'd both just felt lost. Back to that word. He supposed he understood her feeling alone and needing to connect. He knew that he could be stubborn in his isolation. He couldn't blame her for feeling restless and unfulfilled. But why Arthur? Of all the blokes in the world who'd have begged for time spent with her?

He glanced over and watched her bury her head in tales of Paris, as they ordered one numbing cocktail after another. He wanted her to talk, just to know that she was okay, but she would not engage. Instead, as they each prepared to stare away from each other for the next eleven hours, Daniel rummaged through his own pile of airplane reading. Among the lot was *The Assassination of Gabriel Champion*, the very book that had brought them together.

He pulled it out and hoped she'd notice out of her periphery, and perhaps display some flattery that would tell him she was still with the living, but nothing came from her way.

She had always apologized for, as she'd put it, the *"garish heavy-handedness of the names Speck and Champion"* but he'd always defended it, assuring her that it was the proper way of all tales of expressionistic symbolism. Gone seemed to be the days when they spoke of such things, gaily deconstructing and analyzing the art around them, their own work the most.

He opened up this bloody assailant of literature that had spilled his life onto four hundred pages, by now easily his third or fourth paperback copy, and probably thrice as many times reading it, and proceeded again.

In the opening chapter, the reader is introduced to an old warehouse, where one man holds another hostage at gunpoint. The kidnapper doesn't bind his victim or tie him down. The hostage is allowed to walk freely about, pacing, jogging in place, so as not to atrophy about the legs. The kidnapper simply watches him, gun aimed, eyes following the hostage around that dungeon like radar. It isn't known yet why this kidnapping has occurred until the conversation begins to unfold. When it does, it is no ordinary Prime Time kidnapping dialogue of, *"Tell me where you've hid the money!"* and grumblings about unmarked bills and street blokes named Rooster. They argue on the governing nature of art. This is salon dialectic, the stuff of literary roundtables and copious shots of absinthe, yet it has dressed itself in 70's TV-cop-show clothing. Does art govern, or is it governed? Does it create the moral code of the day, or merely reflect what is already established? The reader is immediately thrust into a deranged and thrilling Theatre of the Absurd. Jean Genet meets Quinn Martin.

Then the question of art's healing or damaging effect riles the kidnapper, Will Speck. He wonders at the injustice of life that selectively gives the gift of brilliance to some and not to others. He plans to defy what he calls the elitism of natural selection by pressing the barrel of his gun deeper into the flesh of Champion's temple and whispering in a sinister threat: *"What if I blast all of that brilliance right out of that head and onto that far wall there? Whose is it, then?"*

Daniel jerked away from the book, the ice in his glass jangling as his hands trembled. Hadn't it been his own deranged impulse, in a moment's delirium, to gather up Arthur's brains that had clung bloodily to a far wall, and sift the brilliance from all of that veiny mess? As if such a thing could be done.

His heart thumped fiercely, as his breathing grew fitful, and he refused to have his life any further laid on the slab by this book. Nona never even noticed his agitation, which was best. He needed to be left alone with the disgust he felt at the undeniable parallels between Will Speck and Daniel Cross. He thought of Mozart's Salieri, who tries to drive the composer mad so that he can steal Mozart's gift; or Joe Orton's jealous lover, who hammers the playwright to death out of the unbearable frustration of not being as gifted. He did kill Arthur. And only another swig of bourbon might lessen that exclamation.

After five straight, he slept. The only place life didn't hurt right now was in his lushed unconsciousness. And he awoke again somewhere over the Atlantic. He'd missed a meal and apparently one of the in-flight movies. He picked the book up again, but with a new tremble in his hands, and continued to read this work that talked of art as a matter of life and death and had the nerve to realize that motif literally. That belief had been his religion.

He cautiously turned pages he'd already turned so many times, and came upon the chapter where the reader finally gets to be inside Champion's head. The turning point chapter. As brilliant as Speck may find him, as the world may find him, Champion knows what even Speck doesn't, that there's never been real exigency in his work, that the madman has given him an unexpected gift by sticking a gun to his temple and creating that consequence of life or death, of paint or die. And though Speck believes that he is looting Champion of that brilliance, thieving it under the gun like some tangible thing one can hold or feel or squeeze, what he is actually doing is aiding Champion by waking the artist up from his deep sleep of comfort and fame and adulation. He is making Champion know, for the first time ever, what it truly means to create as a matter of life and death.

So, while Champion may be imploring God on the one hand not to be killed, he is imploring on the other not to be rescued.

But what a bloody fucking existence, Daniel thought. He came away from the page exhausted. Who had the energy to live in that kind of suffering? If he, Daniel Cross, lived but one life and made no contributions to its persevering self, which would persevere with or without him, but instead lived it blissfully, wouldn't that be just as fine? And, goddamn it, without the ulcers! Why had changing the world always been so important to Daniel? And what made him think he was even built of such stuff? Will Speck needed so badly to change the world that he held a gun to a man's head. Was Daniel as desperate as this character is? Desperate enough for destruction? Or had he already shown himself to be? As in that day in Arthur's apartment? When he feared the answer just might be yes, he realized a beastly truth. He actually had to run it in his head a few times just to convince himself that he'd really deduced such.

"Art is evil," he mumbled in a fever.

It tasted blasphemous on the lips.

"Huh?" she muttered, looking up from her journals.

Art had been everything he'd ever lived for.

"Nothing. Sorry."

Yet when he really thought about it, all that art had ever offered him in return was despair. What other conclusion could he make?

He listened to his own tremulous breathing for several minutes, not even obscured by the high-pitched hum of the airplane cabin. Fear was a loud, loud siren.

Art is evil.

He wondered if this was how Nietzsche felt the first time the philosopher concluded that God was dead. A little terrified, perhaps? Waiting for the lightning bolts? Just in case he was wrong?

FIFTY TWO

Her head rang with the Yeats. The one her college professor had turned her onto just before he attempted his seduction. For the purpose, she supposed, of giving it all a poetic credence just in case she resisted. It turns out she didn't resist. She could always be counted on to fall for the brooding intellectuals, and so proceeded to carry on an affair with him throughout the entirety of her junior year. But she also remembered being vaguely disconcerted by his psycho-sexual instincts to manipulate her with words as breathtaking as — *The great wings beating still Above the staggering girl, her thighs caressed By the dark webs, her nape caught in his bill...How can those terrified vague fingers push The feathered glory from her loosening thighs?* — just to buttress any potential case.

How was it that this theme would repeat itself so insidiously throughout her life? Or maybe the epiphany was that all of life rang with themes of rape. That it was, in the larger, symbolic context, the very definition. A reprehensible negation of everything she'd ever believed in, it did nonetheless seem that the most basic modality of life was far more Darwinian than Chopraesque.

It was not one of those epiphanies that parted the gates of Heaven. It was the other kind.

Arthur.

His name had reeled in her mind for three days unrelenting. She shook her head, as if tossing off beads of sweat, and did her best to replace the numbing litany of that name with thoughts of Paris.

She sat next to Daniel in a plane seat, alternately consoled that he'd been willing to do this, and unsure if there was even a point any longer. That he would reveal this tale to her made her want to throw her wrath at him as much for being the destroyer of her illusions and the wretched deliverer, as she wanted to hate Arthur for the deed.

She squeezed her eyes shut as the mortified crept over her that she had once again been so laughably out of touch with reality. How on earth had she managed to misunderstand? To assemble in her twisted head that Daniel had been naming Arthur as her...*God!* She couldn't even finish the thought; it was so embarrassing.

As she thought back on it now, it was so clear this thing Daniel was trying to spill, and right in front of her during all the rest of it, too: Arthur's constant self-flagellation, his abhorrence to affection, all the little cryptic riddles that she'd waved away as the genius' mind at work, even through *Murmuration,* come to think of it, considering the brilliant exposer of souls that Daniel's work was. And Daniel literally had to smack her on the head and say, *"Wake up, idiot!"*

She'd felt so out-of-body listening to Daniel tell it. The tale simply wouldn't register in her brain. She'd watched his words float out of his mouth, but could only see them as disconnected letters, dancing in front of her, refusing to actually form words and make sense. An ill wind.

And Ophelia. The Muse that had haunted Arthur's poetry. The dark lady whom Nona had wanted so badly to know about. Ophelia hadn't been Muse, at all, but a lingering ghost, refusing to sleep until Arthur had successfully undone himself for his deeds.

Would Ophelia be able to rest now that Arthur had done it? And was this what Nona could look forward to being, toward her rapist? Some restless phantom that wouldn't suffice to advance to Heaven until revenge was won?

Breathe.

Paris.

As they touched the ground of Orly's runway onto an overcast July morning, so drastically different from the baking smog of recent Los Angeles, she wondered what made a man capable of such an act? She had asked herself that same question countless times after her own rape, and now she had to ask it of someone she thought she'd known inside and out. Except that he was no longer even here for her to really ask him. All the dreadful questions that now swirled in her head and made her dizzy had no place to go. And if Arthur were still here, could she have even asked him? Or would she have been filled with such a fear and hate and disillusionment that she could never have put herself in a room with him again?

She felt hostile that this new snag only made her grieving ambivalent, and guilty that ambivalent was the right word, because even as much as she shuddered in the Hell that this new revelation had encased her in, she could still see the man she had known only as poet and friend. Not rapist. Not murderer. Or it was all she could allow herself to see. It served her right for having been the one to create an even greater ambivalence in Daniel's grief.

Maybe Daniel had been right to say that her desire for Paris had bordered on the sentimental. Maybe she had been ridiculous to think they could rehabilitate. At this point she no longer even cared about Paris. She was numb. But she had to at least try to make them lustful about life and each other again, if for no other reason than to have the chance to drive out that other story.

They pried their hands loose from the cocktail glasses they'd been clutching since LAX, gathered up their crumbling wits, glassed eyes, and thick tongues, and exited the plane into Orly's drab warehouse of a terminal. They took care of baggage claim, customs, currency exchange, and a taxi ride into town with barely a word between them, but always gripping each other's hands like two alcoholics on their way out of one shaky binge and into the darling next.

As they traveled north along the highway from Orly, she looked wearily for the Paris that would heal them. This place where Hemingway and Sartre and de Beauvoir had once chatted over lunch while writing amazing words. Where Van Gogh and Gauguin had shared a flat in the very section of town she and Daniel would be staying. Where James Baldwin and Richard Wright and Josephine Baker had made their homes after their own home had shown no love for them as African-Americans. Where Daniel's beloved Impressionists had made their radical mark on the world. History aside, however, and perhaps the result of engaging too much film-noir romance, it was a place that for Nona had always evoked sounds of a muted trumpet. Some Miles Davis sentiment that slid and slipped in and out of the silence. She needed it badly right now.

Lastly, it was the place where her mother and father had met and fallen in love. Perhaps even the place where she was conceived. So, her disconnect with it, at this moment, felt like a slaying.

Maybe if she just saw a monument, something defining and historical and legendary, something worth a photo-op. An Eiffel Tower. A Notre

Dame. But the only wonders this part of town seemed to boast were drab, square blocks of building monstrosities, huge billboards, ugly airport motels on the side of the road. They were far outside the city still, which was a teasing and tawdry floozy, and of course behind every tawdry floozy there always followed that muted trumpet.

Her eyes lazily swooped left and right, trying to find some recognizable thing. When her heart thumped at the idea that her Romantic Paris might've been a hoax, she realized that there was the seed of hope in her yet, even as buried as it clearly was under everything else.

Then they saw it. As their driver pointed it out, she and Daniel both turned their heads in obedient formation and stared at the monstrous obelisk in the distance. Neither of them looked at each other nor responded. To their north, as they now headed west along the Périphérique, the Eiffel Tower barely pierced itself through a fog and was far more remarkable than Doisneau had ever captured it.

She defied that huge, girded structure to give her and Daniel the promise of their healing and reconciliation, and their willingness to temporarily abandon the world they had known so that they could get back to themselves and each other. She dared it and Paris to work their magic.

The taxi exited the highway and spilled out onto the irresistible streets of Paris Proper. The deeper into the city they were driven, the more looming the Eiffel Tower grew above them, casting its giant shadows across entire landscapes. When a cluster of trees caught her eye surrounding an especially stately palace of breathtaking architecture, their driver offered that they were approaching the Sorbonne and the Latin Quarter, and would be to their hotel soon. Her heart raced and she couldn't slow it. She wasn't sure if it was fear and dread, or anticipation and hope, that made it race so.

As they turned onto Rue de la Harpe, she knew for certain that she had arrived in Hemingway's Paris. This tiny cobblestone alley was almost too small for a car to drive through, and, clearly out of a movie, lined itself on all sides with endless sidewalk bistros and street musicians and lively, loud-talking men who whistled at earthy women.

The cabman stopped in front of a perfectly ordinary storefront hotel with shuttered windows and home-stitched curtains, and it instantly felt like home. Anything will when you're desperate to hibernate.

When Daniel had first told Harper that they were leaving immediately for Paris just to get away for a bit, Harper had wanted to arrange an elegant suite for them somewhere off the Champs-Élysée, but he'd told her that extravagance was not welcomed on this trip. Nona hadn't been good for much conversation during their hasty preparations to get out of town, but was grateful that her husband had at least been on the same page as she. She needed to forget all about money and luxury and the growing celebrity that was clearly becoming theirs in Los Angeles. Perhaps she'd felt that if they could get comfortable enough in their humble accommodations at the Hotel du Levant, then Paris might give her the same itch it had given Anaïs Nin, or inspire Daniel to look out of a window once in awhile onto Rue de la Harpe's richly Bohemian life and find his way back to painting, and in doing so perhaps make them whole again. As for Daniel's reasons, he had always tended to eschew affluence.

The elevator was too small to fit two adults and luggage, so they hiked three stories up, lugging two garment bags and three large totes. By the time they opened the door onto the flat that would be their home for a while, they were spent. Daniel was sweating the way men sweat; profusely, and it smelled of digested bourbon. She wanted a bath instantly, but all Daniel wanted to do was lean out of their window and watch the Parisians below stroll by. They had still barely spoken. She knew he was waiting for her, but silence seemed to be the food she gobbled up like the starved.

She drew a hot bath with salts, closed the door behind her, and sank deeply into it, trying to calm her wits. No one told her you couldn't soak away aches of the soul with hot water.

The bathroom window looked out onto the main thoroughfare, and from the street below she could just faintly hear an accordion player pumping out *The Anniversary Song*, a lovely little three-quarter-time ditty. She almost laughed at such a cliché. The annoying man kept dropping or adding beats indiscriminately, however, making it a lopsided waltz. Still, it was caressing to hear music, even faintly, even unremarkably, outside her window in this city.

She knew why Daniel had finally changed his mind about this trip. He'd felt sinister. Her muteness, once he'd unleashed that tale, had convinced him that he had thrust her into some kind of catatonia. Maybe he had. She just didn't know what to say to him. He had knocked the complete wind out of her. But here they were. He was trying. And so she needed to.

She must've lain in the tub for a clear hour, because the water was chilled by the time she noticed. She wasn't ready yet to deal with Daniel, so she reached forward to turn on more hot.

Arthur.

There was no way in this quiet moment to keep him from her thoughts. That was the problem with silence. And she had spent the past three days in this state, either shooing Arthur away whenever he would invade, or forcing his entire life and legacy to play itself over and over in her warring head. It was a yes-no, come-go derangement.

This time something was different. Maybe it was the soothing salt bath that made it so. Maybe the music outside. Maybe the Parisian air, as she'd always been a sucker for a sensual play. All she knew was that as Arthur attempted once more to invade, and for the first time since all of this, she gently invited him. But as one invites a lion that is supposedly trained not to kill — there is still fear, and there'd best be a backup plan.

Three days of a maddening roller coaster ride, of furiously trying to connect dots, assemble letters into words, arrange pieces into some kind of order, finally reminded her of something Mrs. Wenda had said months ago in a letter when they'd been talking about the rape. The old woman had suggested that perhaps Nona no longer needed to affect punishment on her assailant. That perhaps she no longer even needed to put face to deed, in order to put it to bed. And all Nona's brain could interpret from that letter, that day, was, *"tuck it away, Nona, forget, pretend it didn't happen,"* which she had told herself she couldn't listen to, that it was the one piece of ill-gotten advice Mrs. Wenda had ever deployed. It happens.

Today, as she lay immersed — watching the foamy water slowly turn opaque and the pewter faucet weep its periodic tear, staring into the face of this New Age that she would hereafter come to regard as After Knowing, much as historians measure history with Before Christ and Anno Domini, and realizing that she would never think, feel, hear, or see anything the same again — she suddenly heard Mrs. Wenda's message with new ears. This tale of Arthur's, this certain chimera, finally made her understand that Mrs. Wenda hadn't asked her to forget. The old woman had asked her to realize that while retribution might've been what her assailant deserved, maybe even fulfilled some sense of payback, it wasn't what Nona needed. What

Nona needed was for the darkness to be ripped out of her assailant that could've compelled him to such a deed.

Arthur's bitter life had been *his* long, merciless ripping of that darkness. His atonement had extended far beyond whatever prison stint he'd done. His atonement had been his entire life. In the end, with harsh nicks and scabs along the way from the rip, this remarkable person had bloomed.

The man she knew as Arthur Hughes Dufresne had been an authentic light, and to suddenly learn that this same ray had once been the pit of wretchedness made her know, unequivocally, that from out of the pit one *could* emerge. It was possible. She'd witnessed the very proof.

Her faceless attacker's life had to be in the midst of its own long, merciless ripping for its hateful deeds. It was the way she'd always believed karma worked. If the journey didn't kill him, then at least it had every chance to transform him.

She suddenly sat up in this Paris water-closet, pruned and dimpled as her bath water grew cold for the second time, turned her head toward the window again, and stared at this epiphany, until it changed shape and color and played tricks on her eyes. She turned it inside out, shook it of all lint, played it backwards like a record, and stretched it like taffy, to see if it would fall apart too easily. Or stay.

She listened to the sound of her breath, and watched for signs of treachery.

This was what Arthur's tale had done to her. *To* her? *For* her? At some point, she realized, she would have to decide if this epiphany was something graced or afflicted.

She hadn't heard a stir in the main room for more than an hour. She wondered what Daniel was doing in there. Still staring out of his window? Contemplating the poet, as she was? She knew that until they could resolve their ambivalence about Arthur, they would be forever wedged in a kind a miasma, and would never be able to rejoin the living.

As for her grieving husband, he had not slept in a bed with her since Arthur's death. Tonight they would have to, unless his plan was to sleep on the floor or put her there. She wondered how the awkward transition of lying down for the night would unfold.

She didn't need to wait for night to find out. At the height of noon, when she finally emerged from her icy bath, pulled the kink out of her legs, and dried off, she stepped into the main room to find Daniel passed out across the bed, clothes and shoes still on.

She stared at him. He looked grateful to be passed out. She crept over and touched his face. A two-day growth had lain hairs down in one direction on his cheek. She traced the direction with her fingers and realized she couldn't blame Daniel for any part of this. She wanted to. But she knew he was suffering, still spinning from her adultery, still blaming himself for Arthur's exit.

Was there even a little satisfaction at having gained the wounded lead, after a solid two weeks of her husband wearing the crown?

You'd think so.

There was nothing simple on either of their plates.

The appropriately sullen minor-key waltz still serenaded them in odd meter, as she crept gently upon the bed, towel draped about her pimpled skin, and nestled herself in Daniel's sleeping embrace.

Oh how we danced on the night we were wed.

At one point the sound of the amateur accordion halted, and she glanced out of the window from her horizontal state to see the scraggly musician trudging up the street with his squeeze box slung over his shoulder and a few francs in his hand. Now there was only the mesh of discordant street noise. She wanted to be lulled to a peaceful slumber by the hum, but life was too vibrant down below, too turbid in her head, so she lay awake for hours, hypnotized by Daniel's sleeping breath on her neck and the sound of Paris outside.

She glanced around at what would be their home for awhile. The entire room was some variation of white. Some grays, some off-whites, perhaps from dullness and age. White walls; white Formica nightstands with aluminum knobs, recently buffed and shined; sheer, white lace curtains, which presently danced against the breeze that came in from the opened window; white blankets and pillow slips; two white vinyl chairs, very fifties modern. It invoked the starkness and melancholy of a Raskolnikov existence. The only dash of color in the entire room was a faded Modigliani print in a rickety frame on the west wall. Earth tones. Brown women with elongated faces, like herself. She watched the gradual shift of the sun from left to right, as the day passed, casting shadows on their tiny white room.

Was this to be their existence here, then? Opening their eyes only briefly to acknowledge that, *yes, we are indeed in Paris,* only to roll back over and sleep the day through? They could both probably sleep through the rest of their given years and never rejuvenate from their recent lives. Maybe this was Daniel's plan, for he slept now as heavily as a corpse. He never once stirred, not even when plates began to be dashed in the streets below, in this heart of Greek Alley. Only his tranquilizing breath on her neck assured her he was still alive.

She tried to smell Paris, but all she got was the whiff of stale bourbon from her pores and Daniel's sweat. She thought about their growing renown back home. They'd completely abandoned it. They were irresponsible and spoiled. The *Murmuration* investors, the museum curators, and all those blue-blooded philanthropists, who were just clamoring to suck Daniel's artistic dick, would be shortly in an uproar to find that their golden boy had skipped town and left the wine-and-cheese schmoozing to his agent. After all, the exhibit had finally gotten a fifteen-page spread in last month's Vanity Fair, and *where the Hell is Daniel Cross?*

Likewise, Seward Press had all but given up on Nona, and now this unexplained disappearance. She hadn't even had the decency to call her editor, who had been an incredible support system through the launching of *Champion.* Seward had three more books contracted with her, one of which she'd already been given an advance for, and which had been publicized to hit the bookstands next year, but with no draft yet, and *where the Hell is Nona Childe?*

Eventually, on this first day in Paris, she did sleep. But the whole world had to spin on its heels in her active head before she was sufficiently dizzy enough to fall unconscious.

When she awoke, she was alone.

FIFTY THREE

He must've passed out shortly after their arrival at the hotel, because the next thing he remembered was waking up with a horrible stiffness about the legs and spine and his clothes pasted to his body from sweat. Strange designs reflected on the walls of their dark room from streetlights flooding through the lacy curtains. It was night, and he realized instantly that he'd slept clear through their first day in Paris.

She was asleep beside him, wrapped in a towel that had fallen tangled about her. The sexiest thing in the world was that tiny glimpse beneath the tousled terrycloth of the closely cropped coif between her thighs, little kinky black hairs that smelled sweetly of a woman, and the slit that peeked out in a smile. Only young women excreted pheromones so feverishly that you could see the cloak around them. He might've theoretically preferred someone his own age with whom to wax intellectually, but it was only his wife's age or younger that screamed at his groin and demanded that he procreate. He also knew that his thought was cruel, as Nona was one of the most intellectually stimulating women he'd ever known, but all he could see right now was the means to his sexually and emotionally frustrated end. He wanted to climb inside of her and disappear.

What stopped him was his warring head. He couldn't fathom intimacy with her after what had happened between her and Arthur, whose name, every time he thought it, would hit him in the gut. Instead, he got the Hell out of their cramped room, leaving her to sleep off her own burdens.

The very least he owed his wife, who seemed barely conscious these last three days, because of him, was everything. And he was prepared to give it all to her, anything she needed: Polite strolls along the Seine; quiet, early dusk dinners at sidewalk cafés; clinking wine glasses to toast new beginnings and a swift healing of their loss. He would be right there with her when she was ready to open up the symbolic family album and shed a tear at the Slow Club and the Opal Room for the memory of her mother and father. He would indulge beauty with her at the Louvre and the Orsay for long coveted glimpses of da Vincis and Vermeers. Against his inclination to crawl in a hole and die, he would give his wife what she had begged of him. It was the least he could do for the contagion with which he, and those in his life, had infected her. So this night was his last opportunity to get shitting drunk before he'd have to begin his sojourn into gallantry.

The time was somewhere around eleven-thirty. He stepped out onto Rue de la Harpe and into a Paris nightlife with which he was completely unfamiliar, but was eager to learn. As he breathed in the air, he tried to conjure the memory of his one and only boyhood visit to this city. It was 1960, and his grandfather, Leviticus Rankin, had taken Duncan and him to visit a friend who'd lived near a cemetery on the outskirts of town. A cello maker this fellow was. Rankin had been trying his damnedest to generate some interest in either boy to play a musical instrument, so every afternoon he made his grandsons watch the artisan at his craft. But all Duncan and Daniel had wanted to do was run through Père Lachaise and terrorize the young women who were earnestly paying their respects to departed loved ones.

It would seem that the only two trips he'd ever made to this city had both begged an important duty, when all he'd been inclined to do was escape it.

Le Chouchou looked promising. It hid itself down an alley adjacent to their street, which littered itself with Greek restaurants and dense crowds. The alley bustled madly, even as the hour approached midnight, and in every window there could be seen a glistening beast rotating above the flame and lamb slivers being shorn away from monstrous skewers. Every restaurateur stood proudly in front of his establishment and beckoned passersby to taste his fare. One place was only more colorful than the next, but the call of a simple bar was all Daniel could hear this night, and Le Chouchou looked promising enough.

He nursed one beer for near to an hour, until it fell warm and flat. He couldn't even get enthusiastic about getting drunk, and he worried about his malaise. The most extraordinary woman he knew slept naked in a bed half a block from here, and the only thing he could muster was the energy to sneak limply away. Getting drunk had been his excuse to get out of there, but finally none of it made any sense because all he could think about was her.

Every woman who walked past him or took a seat at the bar gave him an erection that shrieked at him. But each time he caught someone's eye, who might smile his way and invite him with those eyes, he would only see his wife's face instead, and turn away. By the end of several hours of this rude dance, his seventh or eighth ale, all of which had been allowed to grow as warm and flat as the first, plus as many shots of whisky and a good slump across the bar, he looked out and saw the daylight. So much for their first twenty-four hours in Paris.

The days that followed were all right enough. Nona was at least talking now, though it was still with an efficiency of language that held no adornments, no frills, no dynamism — this coming from the woman whose life had been words.

The language of this household was now the language of fragility.

A language of sparsity.

A haiku.

It was, at least, preferable to the silence that had accompanied the past several days, and which would've eaten them both alive in time.

By day, Daniel actually came close to feeling soothed by this city, or pretended so well that he started believing it. He had to admit that it felt wonderful clutching his wife's hand as they strolled through St-Germain-des-Prés. She was right about there being something of a balm here, which came damned close to inspiring romance.

The nights were harder, because that's when couples held each other, and he could only do so superficially, as thoughts of Arthur would always invade just at the point of some relief.

Their first week here, he simply couldn't do the museums, even though he'd sworn to be up to the task. When she would suggest it, he'd politely beg out with, "let's wait a bit," and her laconic self would simply nod head and go about something else. He just wasn't ready to let himself be slapped in the face by all the painting legends who'd housed their wonders in this city's great halls, telling him just how mediocre a human being he was. *Not yet, please.* He was still too overwhelmed by the notion of holding his wife and NOT envisioning her adultery in his mischievous imagination. Wasn't that task enough for now?

And she never fought him. Or begged him. Or anything. He got the feeling this was as much obligation for her as it felt to him. Something they were supposed to do. She seemed to have lost her whole reason for wanting to come here in the first place, and he knew it was his fault.

He could barely get through the days for waiting to soak his aches in a shot or two of something stiff by night. Nona never came with him on his jaunts to the bars. She preferred to stay in their flat, after a day of strolling through the Tuilleries or the Marais, and read or study her Paris guidebook or write in her journals. Was she writing about Arthur? They still hadn't spoken about him after what Daniel had unfolded. At first he'd worried that he'd sent her toward some kind of breakdown. At this point he was grateful for her economy of words, yet afraid of every corner they'd turn, because around each one might just lurk the moment when she would be ready to talk, and then the real work would have to begin. A project he just wasn't sure he was up for.

Was this it, then? Deed done? Confessed and revealed? And suddenly Arthur was wiped from their consciousness? As if their friend had never been here at all?

He wasn't sure how he felt about that. It was a heavy uncertainty. Burdensome about the eyes and gut. Just one more wrinkle to ponder in his new monastic life.

Once Nona was able to successfully set up her laptop in their flat and obtain an internet connection, she and Harper emailed each other regularly, which gave him some ease. Any activity to keep her busy enough to relieve him of his job for a moment or two was a good thing. He had told Harper about the adultery but not about Arthur's past. Maybe Nona would be the one to spill it to Harper. And at that bleak thought, he realized just how much momentum this damage potentially had, to grow like a cancer. Still, anything to keep his wife engaged and connected to someone was welcomed, since he was barely functioning as husband these days.

So, their first two weeks basically entailed emails from Harper making sure they were all right; long walks through the city; a glass of wine with every meal; smiles that took great effort; a bar scene he'd usually indulge alone; and on home to their flat on Rue de la Harpe, where they'd roll over in bed, she to the left, he to the right, until the next day of forced smiles and polite behavior.

He wasn't always polite. Once in awhile, because the tension was so palpable that it would bring him close to screaming, he would offer a cursory answer to some comment she'd make, then smile quickly to show that no sarcasm was intended. It wasn't sarcasm he felt, anyway. It was just the only way he usually knew how to deal with uncomfortable situations. With her, with this, he didn't know what to do, or how to be. Or who he was.

Their conversations began to conjure his days with Christianne, who'd had no conversation. And at that thought, he knew assuredly that he and Nona had dismantled each other's spirits, perhaps for good.

They filled up on baguettes and exotic cheeses and cognac day after day, listened to outdoor bands on the quad of the Georges Pompidou, and on one miraculous night made a connection. They'd found a delicious cassis sorbet at a little ice cream shop on the Ile St-Louis, which they consumed with champagne. As they left the ice cream parlour and crossed the Seine on the Pont St-Louis, they came upon the rear of Notre Dame, which really was the most breathtaking angle of the thing. Only a block and a half from their flat, it was a sight that had caused Nona's eyes to glisten the first time she saw it, and to tell him of her plan to begin each day by lighting a candle in the vestibule of the holy place, clearly a desperate ploy for groundedness. Though she'd always claimed to be "not terribly religious," there was a sentimental stripe to his wife that belied whatever claims of roguery she undoubtedly thought bold. With defenses and game-faces down, her reliance on a godly world had betrayed itself.

In lighting her candles, she always said that she prayed for beauty and for them. He wondered if she also prayed for Arthur. If she did, she never said. And though he'd always been a confirmed atheist, he secretly hoped that she was taking care of Arthur's soul for those who didn't know how. Daniel had never been a believer in God, but, like her, he was sure betting on God now. Or maybe he was only betting on his wife, the true savior in his life.

Up to this point, they had never seen Notre Dame by night, and coming upon it this evening, as it grew larger in their midst to tower over them, was an eerie affair. At first they backed up from it, to consider it as one considers a painting, not knowing quite what to make of it or how to digest its puissance.

It chilled him that this edifice, but mortar and stone, held in its walls an ominous might that gave it life. God or no God, a great power lived in this stony wonder, and the power was its beauty, which was of such sway that Daniel saw it breathe. Nona saw it too; he could tell by her eyes. It was an inexplicable something that anyone else would've waved away as some artist's nutty head. But when he read his wife's eyes, and knew she was feeling the same awe that he was feeling, and acted upon the exact instinct as his to approach and touch its ancient, sooty walls and beg its vibrancy to penetrate her palms and rush through her veins, he wanted to love her so madly that he almost broke. But he fucking hated tears, so he grabbed her hand, instead, took her around to the front of the church, which, ironically, was camouflaged in scaffolding from a massive renovation it had been undergoing for several years already, and went right into the small talk he'd learned to master.

He pointed up to the rows of carved saints and angels and kings that adorned the three grand portals. Among the sea of them, dark and sooted and ancient, every one, there could periodically be seen a clean, white angel or saint shimmering out from the rest. He explained to her that these had been rebuilt out of a mixture of plaster and fiberglass to replace the crumbled ones, which had no doubt met their slow demise from centuries of a tempestuous history and bad weather.

Some bloke on the street had explained it to him one day walking, and it seemed a tiny enough anecdote to qualify as small talk. But he quickly saw where Nona was going with this; she could make a maudlin stew out of any old, thin broth. She looked up at these angels that gleamed brightly amidst the ancient ones, with the light of the moon giving them a fluorescent-blue, nether-real hue, and he knew she was standing there naming them. Pretty fucking sappy. She never said a word, but he'd always known how to read her eyes. One for her. One for him. Maybe one for Arthur. Maybe not. Lorca. Her mother and father, surely. She saw in these angels everyone she had ever loved.

All it evoked for him was Picasso's *Vue de Notre-Dame de Paris*, a severely cubist portrait of Notre Dame at night, a masterpiece, a turquoise and deep blue tempest. He recognized instantly how the Muse worked for the Spaniard. He saw Paris this night through Picasso's eyes, and ached that he couldn't see it through his own.

Before he knew it, he had taken her face in his hands and kissed her.

He took her by surprise, though she responded willingly. His kiss begged to feel her, frantic to locate her again. She smelled like coconut and tasted like champagne and tart, warm sorbet.

Ultimately it was all too painful. Trying to find intimacy with his wife and recommit his heart to hers, experiencing this city that Picasso had painted, knowing he could never paint it, and feeling completely impotent on both counts, he broke away and stormed off from her as abruptly as he'd grabbed her.

"Daniel."

But he briskly walked, unable to respond or even turn around. *This* was their first true moment in Paris. Not all the other bullshit. Though he was fairly certain this wasn't what his wife had in mind. And he knew this moment was inevitable, because just how much longer could he take behaving remarkably and smiling quaintly? He couldn't stand to have both the mystifying Nona Childe and the mystifying Notre Dame looming over him on this turquoise, cubist night, reminding him how small a man he was.

FIFTY FOUR

He left her there, surely wondering if he'd gone insane. He crossed the bridge onto the Quai de Montebello and headed west along the Seine. He was afraid to look back and see her face and the pain it might've held. Or even worse, the apathy it might've held. Besides, he knew she'd be all right. She'd simply walk back to their flat, cry herself to sleep, or not, and he'd apologize in the morning.

As quickly as he could, he hailed a taxi to get away from his wife and his life, and told the cabman to take him to the other side of town. The bar he was delivered to, where he paid a man at the door an amount of francs he didn't even bother to count, had blood red walls and situated itself on a remote street somewhere behind the Arc de Triomphe. This place was haunted. And there was something sexy in its mustiness. It was the scent of horny men and ripe women. Too dark to see anyone's faces, really, but that was the point.

He ordered a double shot with an ale chaser, sat on a sofa that smelled of cunt, lit a Viceroy, and sank down in the cushioned couch, hoping to rub the smell on him and maybe smother himself in some woman notion until he couldn't breathe.

Thrashy, Euro-punk drum machines pounded out mechanical hip-hop beats to thumping basses and chanting voices that screamed from the ceiling. A mirrored ball dizzied him as it spun spots around the red walls. He watched couples dance, and he smirked at the stories he made up for them. There was the older, ruddy-faced man who had consumed one too many whiskies, and who entertained a much younger woman, obviously a pro. They danced politely, subdued. For her, this was the weariest part of her job. For him, there was simply too much alcohol in his system to muster even a simple erection, much less give her a good go on the dance floor. There were the greasy gents who ground their erections against girls too young to be in holes like this but had breasts so suckable that *who cared?*

And lastly, there were Pixie and Trixie, he called them, two lovely young things in short skirts, midriffs, and Doc Marten boots. One Black, one White. Both enticing, with strong, thin legs, navel piercings, and equal hardware on their faces. They danced with each other. Actually they danced side by side, staring into a mirror on the wall behind him. Not into each other, but into themselves. They moved identically, some choreographed routine they were obviously proud of, and relished the attention they got from every man in the room.

For one brief second he flashed on Nona and Kai, who had danced together on the night of the drum circle. That moment, however, had been one of elevated purpose, of cleansing and rebirthing. How had he gotten from there to here?

These lovely peaches before him wriggled their asses beneath schoolgirl skirts, periodically flinging those skirts to reveal a glimpse of panty, and arching their backs to simulate orgasms. He was hypnotized. He ordered more shots and more chasers, and by the time he had licked the salt off the crest of his hand, and sucked the lime wedge until it was pruned and depleted, he was potent with his own erection. But he didn't want Pixie and Trixie's attentions. Getting their attentions would only get him into trouble. So he slid even further down on the sofa, and dropped his head sloppily back against it.

He just wanted to watch them dance and see their pointy nipples puncturing the shape of their blouses, bare stomachs writhing, hands slipping down their legs, eyes closed, mouths open, hair swooshing and pasting itself to the sweat on their necks. Were he a lecher, he'd beat off on the spot.

The world spun around him. Or was it the disco ball? He was lightheaded and narcotized. An hour passed. The room grew thicker as he tried to picture shagging the one with the peridot eyes. If either of them caught his stare, he'd be a goner.

"Another shot," he mumbled to a passing waitress. He needed to get sufficiently pissed enough to get the Hell out. He began to spin from the alcohol, and a pair of breasts was all he could think about now.

After another hour he finally succeeded in disgusting himself enough to exit this place, and he stumbled to a taxi. Did he have a visible erection? Some big, stupid-looking knot in his trousers that gave it all away? He didn't know, and he didn't care. *Just get me to my wife, please!*

When his cab pulled up to the Hotel Du Levant, he gave the cabman a wrinkled wad of paper money he once again did not bother to count, and fell out of the car as it sped away. Rudely finding the front door locked, he stood drunken and confused, but his head was too dizzy to be able to focus clearly enough to figure out why it was locked or what to do about it.

He glared into the front window. This place was like some liniment-smelling granny's house, with its tiny living room lobby, ivory-colored brocade sofa and matching chairs, all covered in plastic, and quaint little doilies on the end tables. Beyond all that quaintness, enfolded in the distance, he could see the front desk and the snoozing Algerian who usually took the graveyard post. He pounded on the front window, antsy to be inside, and nearly gave the man a heart attack, when, in very rapid French, the Algerian stormed to the door, cursing him.

"*Il y a une sonnette, idiot!*" was all Daniel caught. Something about a bell, and something else again about an idiot, whom he got the feeling was supposed to be him. The man opened the door brusquely and banged on the doorbell, which Daniel hadn't seen, to illustrate that it was right there in front of him. Daniel mumbled sweaty apologies, stumbled inside, and dragged himself to the matchbox elevator, melting into the wall of the tiny lift, as he closed its accordioned door.

He entered the flat as quietly as his drunkenness would allow, and surely enough Nona slept soundly, with the blanket half about her. He crept like a prowler to hover over her, inspecting every inch of her and liking the way the reflections of the designs from the illumined lacy curtains danced on her skin.

The ceaseless hum in the streets below seemed suddenly absent, as if it were willing to give him some small measure of mercy for just an instant. There was such a silence in this room, in fact, that he could hear her breathing magnified. The rhythm aroused him. His erection returned.

The most beautiful woman in Paris slept before him, half nude, and all he could do was collapse into one of the chairs across from her and take his erection from his pants and into his hand.

Her skin tingled and moved as he slowly stroked himself. Or he thought it did, for his brain was surely fried by now and likely hallucinating. The heat of arousal rushed into his thighs, and Nona's breath resonated rhythmically to counter his own increasing breaths, which grew louder and more heightened.

The closer he came to climax, the farther away it seemed, and the torture began to exhaust him as he stroked harder and faster. If he didn't come soon, this was going to kill him. In a fit of noiseless hysteria, he reached over with one hand, the other never leaving its mission, and gently pulled the covers away from her to reveal even more skin. Now a breast stared his way, and that stunning pubis. She never stirred, just sort of shifted in her sleep, and her legs slid against each other to reveal even more of what he needed.

Though he stroked in a frenzy, it still wasn't enough. And sooner than he wanted, his irrepressible woes were upon him. Erection gone. Cock limped.

Sexual frustration screamed at him, but his pathetic life screamed even louder. The abuse of his wife, which was surely abuse now that he'd begun using her as a sex thing with which to get himself off in the creepy shadows, became too much. The only thing he could do was sob that all grace was gone, and that there was no lower he could possibly sink.

He held his flaccid penis in his hand and cursed his flaccid life for not being able to get itself together enough to forgive this woman before him and love her again. Only, he did love her. He loved her so deeply that it made his head spin. He stuffed himself back in his pants and reached over to place his hand on her face. All he wanted was to feel her skin against his fingers. He spilled a few stupid tears on her neck. Not wanting to wake her, his face contorted in that uncontrollable way that wants to bring about hearty wails but refuses.

He wanted to love her completely; to dive right in there and find his place in her heart again, and hers in his. It was only himself in the way. He couldn't reconcile the grief and guilt he carried over Arthur's suicide. And he couldn't reconcile adultery. Arthur had taken her and had pried open some part of her and had claimed it as his own, some part that could never be Daniel's now. And Daniel wanted every inch of her. He was greedy, and gluttonous, and spoiled, and unforgiving, and spitting a lather of rancor that would not cease. What on earth had Arthur rationalized and sold her on, to get her to do this thing he knew she was incapable of on her own?

As he was about to collapse his aching head onto her chest and cling to her as he hadn't in some long time, she stirred. Awakened, surely, by his feeble attempts to quell his squalling. She startled him, and he hopped away from her in a flash, turning to rummage in a nearby closet and camouflage his state.

"Daniel, are you okay?" she asked, thick-tongued and hazy.

"I'm fine. Go back to sleep."

"What are you doing? What time—it's too dark. I can't—"

"I'm just stumbling around for a lighter. It's—go, go back to sleep. I'm fine. Sorry I woke you."

He stayed facing the closet, pretending to rummage through coat pockets, as she propped herself up on one elbow. She stared his way, though it was really too dark to see much of anything. In this awkward moment of silence, she was suddenly more awake.

"Daniel, what happened tonight?" she asked, the sound of sleepy distress oozing from her voice.

"Please," he begged of her gently. *Goddamn it!* he screamed in his head. "Could we just, could we talk about it in the morning?"

Silence. Longer than he wanted.

"Okay," she finally whispered.

Though, really, what would he have to offer her then, that he couldn't now?

FIFTY FIVE

"Daniel," she uttered.

This kiss, in front of the most magnificent cathedral in the world, was their hope. The only that they'd had in some miserable weeks. But instead of seeing it through, Daniel aborted it and stormed away, across Notre Dame Square, over the bridge, and out of her sight. She thought to be devastated, but upon further examination realized that she was mainly numb. She knew the moment had to come when it would all erupt before them. They'd done well to last this long.

She walked torpidly back to the hotel and climbed into their bed, covering herself with the thin blankets that hotels were always known for. She brought them up to her chin, turned the lights out, and stared at the reflection of neon from the street below that colored their dark room with an orange wash. But it was a hot night, and covering herself, she suddenly realized, was only out of habit. Or perhaps the instinct to cocoon.

She couldn't possibly know what was going on with Daniel. She didn't know what going on with herself. She knew he felt just as foiled in figuring out what exactly they were trying to accomplish here. She'd spent the past couple of weeks trying to do the small talk with him, just to anchor herself, get a footing, stop wavering, but she still came out dizzy, and the small talk would invariably only sting more from the sheer tragedy of what they'd been reduced to.

When the kiss happened, their first since all of this, she'd thought for certain they were finally about to be given some relief from the hole they'd buried themselves in. Some actual oxygen that might breathe life and love back into their blue, suffocating faces.

She hadn't wanted to let go of his embrace, but she could see him beginning to choke. She understood. It would've been so nice had she *not* understood, had she been able to get angry enough to start a fight with him, yell and scream, kick-start some kind of life between them again. But she did understand: A woman's betrayal never leaves a man.

Was she giving up?

After a bit, realizing that she couldn't answer that question, and that sleep was beyond her, she got up and sat at her laptop.

She knew she had to face some of the crises back home that their hiatus had created. Harper's emails lately spoke of Seward Press threatening to sue Nona for breach of contract, and for the return of her advance if she didn't come home soon and hand them something resembling a novel. And *Murmuration* was being readied for its move to New York, and the investors were nervous. The only thing keeping all parties from litigation was perhaps the most twisted of all phenomena. Apparently suicide and mysterious disappearances made good tabloid copy. *Murmuration* was more talked about than ever before, and lines at LACMA, according to Harper's reports, were around the block.

Nona had never bothered sharing any of this with Daniel, because it was just too much bogging down and had made her queasy to contemplate. She could only imagine what it would've done to Daniel. She wished she'd never been made privy to all the crap, but since she had, and since she couldn't sleep, she decided to correspond with Harper, perhaps try to put some of those fires out so that she could concentrate on the one burning here.

> Harper,
>
> Please call Seward Press and ask for Gentry Hall. She's my editor. A wonderful woman who's been more patient with me than I deserve. Explain to her that it's a matter of family emergency my not being in the States right now. And tell her that I do plan to correspond while away. And that I am actually producing something. Scratch that. I keep making promises that I can't seem to honor these days.
>
> Daniel grows more remote every day, though I'm not really much better, and we've scarcely done anything together of value. I had hoped that the museums here might remind us of the life we had, maybe even wake up some fire in him to paint again, but he won't even go with me to them. He seems not to want to be awakened. Or afraid. I can't tell which.

You, my dear friend, have become my diary. I'm so grateful for your friendship. It seems empty anymore to pour these feelings into a journal, which can't offer recompense or wisdom. Funny, isn't it? I've always been the biggest advocate of journal writing I know. I thought for sure it could help Daniel, but I was never able to inspire him toward it. These days he disappears into the night like some vampire, after a day that tries hard to be of worth, but is rarely gratifying. This place is so incredibly rich, and all we're doing is wasting the experience.

I wasn't even sure I had it in me to save my marriage when we first arrived. But after weeks of being here, and cloistered away from everything we've ever known except each other, I have to fight for us. And even as I write this, I'm trying my damnedest to be my own pep rally and convince myself that I have to fight, because I truly don't know if I have it in me. So I guess I really can't complain about Daniel, can I?

Have I sounded schizophrenic enough yet?

My mother and father's spirits are here. I feel them. Or I want to feel them. I tried to visit the Slow Club and the Opal Room, the clubs of my parents' employ during the late fifties and early sixties. I was told by a cabman, much to my sadness, that the Opal Room had been torn down years ago to make room for a video outlet. That was where my father had worked. But he also told me that just down the street from it, only a block and a half from the Louvre, one could still find the Slow Club. So I went one evening. Without Daniel, of course. Harper, I walked into this cave of an establishment, and tried to feel my mother's spirit lurking in the walls. But it's not anything like she used to describe it. There was a band playing rock & roll, for God's sake. I don't know what I expected to find. I guess the lesson I'm meant to learn is that everything changes. Every one, too, apparently.

And as always in my letters to you, I come back to Daniel, don't I? You're his dearest friend, Harper. And you're all he has now that Arthur is gone and I've proven to be someone he can't trust. Please help me. What do we do to reconnect again? We never speak of Arthur. Frankly, I don't know what to do with all my feelings about him, which are dubious at best. And I know Daniel feels the same. But Arthur is the key, isn't he? To speak about him. Harper, how do we do that?

All my love,
Nona

P.S. Christ, I'm so self-absorbed! Forgive me. How is YOUR life?

She pressed 'send' and sank defeated in her disgusted narcissism, curling up in the white, vinyl chair and pondering what she'd just written. She'd barely gotten in two sentences about work, before she'd segued right into SOS mode. The crises back home, it turns out, would have to wait.

Daniel had said that she and he were the only two in the world to now know Arthur's story, so she realized the second she typed it that describing her feelings about Arthur as dubious might be giving away something she shouldn't. But she left the word in, because she decided it was no longer her job to try and protect Arthur. It was a job he'd never wanted her to have, anyway, and at this moment she couldn't even be sure it wasn't spite that made her so willing to be this careless.

Yes, Arthur, anger toward you is a part of my reality now.

And just as she thought it, the anger commenced to a slow boil. She rested her head in her hands and started to cry.

Bless her heart, Harper's return email beeped its presence within the hour, to save Nona from resorting to babbling to herself in the mirror. Or smashing it.

Hey there, Beauty!
Don't worry about things here. I'm handling everything. I had a conference call with Gentry Hall. Bottom line is, kismet or karma or something is on your side. Oh, wait, that would be talent, wouldn't it?

(wink!) Right now Seward and your agent are fielding offers for screenplay options on "Champion," and the foreign deals are in full swing, and that alone is what's keeping a lawsuit at bay regarding your second book. It's nothing I'm doing. They realize they're still making money on you. They would be insane to drop their bestseller phenomenon. But you can't stay away forever. They aren't letting this go altogether. You still owe them a second book. Your talent has simply bought them, and you, a little bit more time, is all.

What I'm saying is, for now, concentrate on you and Daniel. Concentrate on Paris. Get the most out of it that you can. It was my mistake sharing all of this stateside drama with you. You don't need any of that right now.

To be honest, I don't know what insights I could possibly give you about Daniel's state. He didn't want to talk about Arthur after the suicide. It was as if he couldn't exactly assemble all the pieces to figure out just what had happened.

Give him space. Give yourself some, for that matter. You love the museums as passionately as he does. If you can't get him there, leave him at home. You go. Don't let him cut you in half just because he insists on cutting himself in half.

He wants to be there, Nona. You couldn't have dragged him kicking and screaming if he hadn't wanted to be there. He may not believe in the power of healing, but he desperately hopes for it. Hopes against all hope that his cynicism is wrong and that Paris can, indeed, romance the two of you back to each other.

As for you, my dear, I'm sorry, but I don't believe for one second that you've given up hope. You are the eternal optimist. And thank God for ya'. Always the one with *"Love everyone"* messages on your phone machine, and *"Be happy"* on your license plate, and who's always claimed to be able to see a light around people with good hearts and a cloud around people with dark souls. The rest of us may be cynics, honey, but we count on you when our own worlds get bleak in front of us. I have faith in you, even if you don't.

I do agree that Arthur needs to be talked about between the two of you. But not yet. Let some time pass. Daniel's anger and loss is still fresh. And while you let some of it pass, be good to yourself. Go to those museums, eat wonderful food, take boat rides, hear great music. Do all those things that have always been your heart. Even if it presently feels burdensome. If Daniel won't do them with you, do them without him. He'll come around. Because whatever else has happened, he knows you're dedicated to him and your marriage. Let him be angry. When he's empty of it, the only thing his heart will have left is love. Have I sounded enough like a self-help bible yet? Or like my dear friend, the eternal optimist? :)

Nona, I understand what happened between you and Arthur. I also know that it's nothing you could ever share with Daniel, so I'm glad I could be someone you could share it with. But in spite of your intentions, honey, you have to know that Daniel has a right to his hurt. Be patient with him, and don't worry about things here.

Although, just to insert business for one more second only, Seward does have some waivers for you to sign, since the Whitney is doing their own re-issue of the Murmuration catalogue. But I'll send those to you International Express. I've already run them by your lawyers. It's just signatures, is all.

Which, of course, means that it's all a go. Murmuration officially opens the Whitney's biennial on the 14th. I suppose Daniel's not interested in hearing that, is he? It's so ironic. He has struggled his whole life to lay some kind of significant foundation in art. And now that he's done so, he isn't in a place where he can celebrate it.

He needs to find beauty again. That's what the problem is, Nona, he thinks he's lost it completely. So I take it back. Get him to those museums after all! Remind him what he does. And that when he does it, just like every artist on those walls of the Louvre, he changes people's lives. He makes them know that there is something on this earth richer and deeper than just the biological. Walk him through those corridors and remind him that he belongs in that company.

His forehead needs much soothing. But I know you're up to it. Stay strong, my friend. But I already know you will.

Love, Harper

Great. Why was it all up to her to nurse Daniel back to health? What about her health? What about the blow she'd been dealt? Who was going to soothe her forehead? Of course, she couldn't express any of that because Harper did not know about Arthur's past, and Nona's earlier "dubious" comment hadn't signaled any alarm.

"I know you have a right to your hurt," Nona said to a Daniel who wasn't even there, pacing her floor. "I don't need Harper to tell me that. But if only you could know that fooling around with other men is not AT ALL what I'm interested in. I love our marriage! But it's a goddamned tricky proposition, isn't it? It would not allow me to engage in an expression of love that touched nothing and no one else, certainly not my love for you, which is untouchable, but nonetheless opened up the fucking earth, with fires burning in the fucking hills, and Moses tossing his goddamned tablets into the goddamned crowd of sinners."

A bitterness was growing. One she hadn't allowed herself to notice in all these weeks, because she'd been so busy castigating herself in an entertaining show before the feet of her wounded husband. And now that it was finally waking up from its dormancy, she realized that not only did she feel bitter toward the miserable fates, toward the laws of morality, toward Arthur, toward this new snag in her grieving for him, toward even herself, she was now also growing bitter toward Daniel.

"How could I have known about Arthur when I made the choice I made? I know you have to be thinking the irony is just what I deserve for being unfaithful. *Talk about poetry. Now they've slept together. Ha, ha, the rapist and the raped.*' Well, fuck you! Fuck Arthur, and fuck you! My only sin in this whole goddamned world is that I am too willing to believe that people are basically good and healthy and normal. And when they turn out to be less than that, I am the one who gets stung! I'm not fit for this world. I am meant for a better one—"

She stomped her feet like the spoiled and the privileged. A knock on the wall told her she was disturbing the peace. She froze in her proverbial pounding of the walls, fists clenched in mid air, and felt unglued that her rages had actually become audible. All she needed was to be kicked out of here tonight for ranting like a mental case.

She sat on the edge of the bed, stared at the wall, and fell apart. Then fell asleep.

She could barely even lift herself from her whipped slumber when Daniel finally came home and she found him rummaging through the closet.

Was he rummaging? Or was she hallucinating?

FIFTY SIX

Another week passed with them going through their mechanized motions. Nona tried to heed Harper's advice and give Daniel her patience, but the days grew longer and the nights were excruciating. Her only comforts were her letters to Harper. She also wrote to Kai, but their exchanges were filled with such a sorrowful falsity, as she couldn't find an authentic way to pour her heart out to her best friend without including the crucial factor of her infidelity.

In twenty years of being practically sisters, there'd never been a subject they couldn't talk about until now, and that only fed Nona's cantankerousness. On top of grieving the loss of Arthur, the loss of who she thought Arthur was, and possibly the loss of her husband, she could now also include the loss of her childhood friend, who seemed to be replaced by a mere polite acquaintance. She shared this with Harper one day via instant messaging.

Harper:
But they'd only dated a few times, hadn't they?

Nona:
I saw it in her eyes the day he died. That pain was as much hers as anybody's. She and Arthur had connected. Maybe not in his heart. Honestly, it's hard to know. But it certainly was so in hers. And that's enough.

Harper:
I think you need to give Kai more credit than that, and trust your friendship.

Nona:
How can I take that chance? And of course, it's even worse because I was the one who begged her not to pursue that interest with Arthur in the first place. I would look like a hypocrite with an agenda. I really have no recourse except to keep her at a distance. And miss her deeply. Maybe that's meant to be my punishment.

Harper:
Ouch.

Nona:
Ouch? What?

Harper:
Are you sure you're not trying to emulate Arthur's famous penchant for public prostration and self-flagellation?

Nona:
Excuse me? What do you take me for?!

Harper:
Honey, I don't take you for anything less than the friend I love and respect. But you have had the tendency in the past to romanticize Arthur and his life. And all I'm saying is that we don't get to give ourselves our own sentence of atonement. That's God's job.

Nona:
God? You're throwing God-talk at me now?

Harper:
Okay, I see. Daniel's atheism has finally rubbed off on you. Fine. All I'm saying is, we don't get the luxury of custom-designing our life lessons.

Nona:
I need to go now.

Are you freaking kidding me?

Nona logged off curtly, and stared at the blank screen.

She avoided her computer and Miss Self-Righteous for days. She seemed to be checking confidantes off the list like a mad spree at the grocery market. Daniel was still coming home drunk practically every night, and in the mornings he'd be so irritable from his hangovers that she'd end up taking off without him.

One morning she got up long before Daniel did, showered, and escaped their hole, which it was slowly becoming, for the streets of the Latin Quarter. She decided that from now on, unless her husband could see his way to coming home sober, she would do just that, and eat all of her breakfasts alone. One morning turned into a solid week of this lone sojourn, and she was starting to get accustomed to a certain Lonely Lady in Café with Newspaper routine. In fact, the Lonely Lady routine began to feel a little good to her, as she steeled herself with a martyr's piety. Nothing coats a broken heart like a velvety layer of The Wound.

This particular late-August morning was already hot, and it wasn't even noon. She strolled casually up the Boulevard St-Germain until she came upon Les Deux Magots and sat for a meal. She'd found herself an L.A. and New York Times at a corner Tabac, and she opened her morning papers and ordered tartines with strawberry jam and an espresso. She wondered if her mother and father had ever eaten here. The truth was that every step she took in this city conjured a wondering of her mother and father. Had they strolled the same stretch of block she strolled every day? Had they lived in the same arrondissement as her? Had they fought and been parted? Had they wandered the streets lost in all the best and worst ways, as this city tended to inspire?

"*Comment ça va, Princesse?*" he asked flirtatiously. Thank God she was interrupted. It was an easy hole to fall into.

"*René, ça va?*" she'd learned to return to her waiter, who'd become her regular waiter here of late.

He was a very young French punk, with two pieced ears, a silver stud in his tongue, tattoos abounding his skinny, muscular frame, the perpetual bed-head look to his hair, and a soul patch neatly adorning the dent between his lower lip and chin. Over this ten days or so of solitude they'd become friends, and she now looked forward to René's greeting every morning. On days he didn't work, she would take her breakfasts at Café de Flore. But Les Deux Magots was always her first choice, because Anaïs Nin used to hang out here, and because Paul Newman mentions it in one of his classic movies, and because her only friend in Paris thus far was the bright smile presently gleaming her way.

"When are you going to leave that myth of an 'usband of yours and take me back to America with you?" he asked regularly with his dense Parisian accent and a flirty humor.

She liked René. He was twenty-two years old, and terribly flirtatious, but without any agenda other than to flatter the older woman he called Princess.

She shared with him none of the messier particulars of her life, such as her troubled marriage, or the suicide of her dear friend. Or the affair. Or the rape. Both hers and...*Christ!*

All she told René was that she was a writer, and that she did have a husband, whom she loved very much, although she got the feeling he didn't really believe her on that count, since he never saw her with Daniel.

René had never heard of *Champion,* even though it had now been translated into a handful of other languages, including French. It disheartened her for an instant, but then what did she expect from a twenty-two-year-old punk? In truth, what little he knew about her dreadful life was definitely preferable to him knowing more.

About René she'd learned everything. He was animated and charismatic, and when she'd asked him about himself he never stopped talking. He was a musician in a thrash band who yearned to go to America to make his fortune. Anyone else might've thought him vain, the way he talked about becoming the next big thing, but she found him to be simply a lover of life. He didn't walk through it with some permanent glower tattooed on his forehead the way Mr. and Mrs. Cross had lately been doing, and that refreshed her.

She was antsy to attach herself once again to a community of some sort, after having lived in moody seclusion for the past eight weeks. Was that how long they'd been here already? It was a number that heightened her anxiety, and all she knew was that she needed to be stimulated again, to be reminded that she was alive. She sorely missed the Orchid Club roundtables of her other life, the conversations with Arthur and Neville and

Otto Matic, the German bartender. She missed going to see the newest permutation of a Kai performance piece, or doing the Venice Art Walks with Harper, or attending exhibits of the newest art world sensations with Daniel, and loving the debates they'd have over the work. And here was a young man before her today in a waiter's apron, also an artist, a musician. She had no idea if René was any good, but he had lust for life. And he was eagerly offering her a community she'd been longing for, so when he invited her to hear his band play at a club near Place de la Bastille, she told him to name the time and place and she'd be there.

The time and place turned out to be later that night, at Le Bataclan, a hole in the wall that would turn out to remind her of the old Madame Wong's in L.A.'s Chinatown. She was told that it would be midnight before René's band went on, so she waited until Daniel slithered out of their flat like a shiny night crawler to go wherever he went. And she made her getaway by taxi to the 12th arrondissement.

This place was crowded, loud, and manic. She didn't see René until he was on stage with his electric bass and two other band members. René was a little spitfire of testosterone and ropey muscles, as he flew about the stage clad in beaten leather pants, motorcycle boots, an equally beaten up leather jacket, no shirt, which revealed a hairless chest, two pierced nipples, and a pocket watch chain hanging from his belt loops. He was not only the bass player of this grungy trio but the lead singer as well, and he screamed French lyrics into a decidedly British punk sound. What else could she possibly have expected from a band called Evangelust? It was loud. It was fast. It was not her kind of music. Ordinarily. Tonight it electrified her.

It was music of the one-chord, heavy-distortion variety, but his band was adventurous and shamelessly bold. The drummer pumped out a beat faster than a man's hands could hit a snare, and he had some sort of double bass drum thing going on that sounded like fired ammunition. The guitar player created a wall of fuzz that put a crawl up her spine. René's bass pounded the walls, and his voice was tempered with a rasp that made it virtually unlistenable in any other music form. She couldn't say there was much skill in René's playing or singing, but for sheer gall he was utterly beautiful to watch.

This bashy, assaultive music was certainly a different experience for her, daughter of jazz musicians and a music snob, and her ears began to ache.

Until at one point she realized that, earache aside, she was actually getting into it.

Senses were ripe tonight, heightened by the propulsion of chaotic sound that pinched that delicate spot right between the genitals and the anus. It riled her, and it made her excited by something again.

SO THIS IS WHAT PEOPLE GET FROM THIS KIND OF MUSIC. I ALWAYS WONDERED.

Even her thoughts were loud.

When the set was done, René exited the stage and bounded over to her, though how he found her in this crowded hole was a wonder.

"Nona, I want you to meet my friends!" he screamed over the din. "This is Mimi, and this is Fairuza!"

Suddenly she was facing a spirited pair of young women.

To them he yelled: "This is my *princesse* from America."

Nona wondered if that clarification was meant as compliment or condescension. Did he think her rich and unapproachable? Had he prior described her that way to his two girlfriends, and therefore with this introduction came the winning of a bet?

In thirty seconds flat, and miraculously over the wall of noise, she learned that both these girls were also in their early twenties; neither from France originally; both students, Mimi at the Sorbonne, Fairuza at the American College of Paris; and both waited tables for their living, while Fairuza augmented her income with a second job at the gift shop of the Musée des Arts Decoratif.

"Sounds like life is really working for the two of you here!" Nona yelled.

"What!" they clucked, like a pair of twin birds. The noise was insane.

Nona would come to learn that René, Mimi, and Fairuza were an inseparable trio. What was it about trios?

Once conversation was possible, she learned that Fairuza was from Connecticut, so between them there was the automatic kinship of both being Americans in Paris. Fairuza was also the only White woman Nona had ever met who dreadlocked her hair. These locks were derriere-lengthed, blondly knotty, like thick vines of gingerroot, and for just an instant skittishly reminiscent of Arthur. Fairuza was that earthy brand of woman who never shaved her armpits or legs, wore no makeup, and could get away with that, being so young and fresh-faced, sported Birkenstocks and coveralls, and always had a good stash of pot on her.

Mimi, by contrast, was a stunning Ethiopian beauty, a sloe-eyed enchantress in unfair possession of a rich coffee hue, massive coiled hair, perfect white teeth, and a high forehead that made her look like some kind of ancient royalty. She spoke English as fluently as she spoke French, but Nona would come to love it most when she rambled in Amharic.

They asked Nona everything about herself, but she could barely get answers out before they were stumbling over one another with more questions. They liked her. She liked them.

It was a circle she was eager to join, for they were full of life and she was just about empty and in emergency need of a refill.

She taxied home at five a.m. to an empty flat and was actually more grateful than annoyed that Daniel had chosen to stay out all night, as the alcohol was fairly denting her skull right now, and she needed to digest her evening alone. René. Mimi. Fairuza. She was easily fifteen years older than these kids, and wasn't sure yet how she felt about that. They would either make her feel very old, or jolt her back into a youthful zest she desperately needed. They were all to meet for lunch tomorrow. She felt newly exhilarated. For the first time in forever. Then she slept. Like a corpse.

FIFTY SEVEN

"*Monsieur! Entrez!*" the little man sang loudly. "The most beautiful women in the world are behind this curtain. *Seulement deux-cent cinquante francs, monsieur!*"

Two hundred and fifty francs. What was that, like, ten dollars or something? It wasn't until after Daniel had handed the man his money that he realized it was closer to fifty dollars, not ten. *Shit!* Fifty dollars to see a woman he couldn't even touch. *Ecchhh, fuck it.* It wasn't the end of the world.

He slumped inside this dark palace, descended the strobe-lighted staircase, and sat to a tiny table right up front of the stage. A single highland malt scotch would do him this time out.

When the show began, the lights dimmed. They came back up in obscured crimson from an annoying red light bulb; a dark, ugly setting for an empty stage that was dressed in blackly painted floorboards and filthy drapes. A lone woman sat on a chair center stage and proceeded to slide against it, dance with it, twirl around it. Her boredom pissed him off. She fondled herself apathetically, stripped herself completely naked, sporting the requisite landing strip coif that stretched from Cesarean scar to perineum, encircled the chair, lay across it, and dizzied herself in twirls and turns to cheesy, synthesized dance music.

He heard the low moans of men in their corners with their hands underneath their little tables and the look of agony on their faces. He smelled semen. And there were women alone in this place too. When the first stripper finished, the smattering audience of mostly men could barely muster applause, so occupied were their palms. The second stripper was as bored as the first. She didn't even bother to lift her sliding feet off the floor to strut across the stage, and at one point the heel of her stiletto broke off. In a pissy fashion, she snatched off the shoe and tossed it behind her into the sea of lechers, to some applause, and it fell in Daniel's lap. He slumped out of that hole with her broken shoe. He figured he might as well get something for his money.

Back on the street, his eyes found this part of town more blinding than Vegas. The legendary Pigalle of the 18^e. From behind every soiled curtain would appear a man beckoning loudly for one and all to come inside and see the most beautiful women in the world.

"Live sex shows where they fuck right on the stage!" were the enticements these bar owners employed. Ugly men luring pedestrians in to see ugly women.

The second bar he visited, even nastier than the first, offered a voyeuristic treat of orgies. *Just don't fucking lie to me.* Most of the women had wooden teeth and fresh canker sores. Most of the men looked either too emaciated or too red-faced to be of any enticement to their partners. The lot of them only fraudulently rubbed themselves against each other in a simulation that wasn't nearly inspired. *Or if you're going to lie to me, goddamn it, at least fool me. At least be gifted about it.* But there was no gift here. No art. No greater reason. Nothing mystical or transcendental. Nothing even hedonistic, since the players were bored shitless.

Coltrane played overhead. Coltrane? John Coltrane? They were playing John-Sodding-Coltrane for this foul ritual? He loved Coltrane, but he wanted to walk behind the curtain to where they likely kept their stereo, and rip out the tape of *A Love Supreme*, and throw it in their faces, and warn them not to tread filthily on John William Coltrane but to do him some fucking good!

Instead he ordered a beer.

The beautiful jewel, whose name was Jewel, caught his eye. She sat alone, as did the handful of other women who graced this lie of a place. Jewel was a delicate fawn, so tiny and breakable that her bracelet kept sliding right past her hand and off her arm. He had picked it up and handed it to her, still holding the broken stiletto in his other hand, when she invited him to sit with her.

"*Merci, monsieur. Voulez-vous, vous asseoir?*"

He didn't know much French and she knew no English, but she motioned forth with her meek hand and he sat beside her in a crescent booth. To feel her against him gave him a tingle. She ordered herself a glass of wine, and he ordered another whisky from a waitress who, at least, and thankfully, spoke some English. The interesting thing about sex was that no one need ever say a word. An actual conversation between the lovely Jewel and him would've been a struggle, but her sex or his could be easily coveted, and the desire communicated, without so much as a grunt. Now, *that* was art.

She made all the moves. She took his hand in hers and leaned her breasts into his arm, and he didn't resist her. He wanted to be pricked. Awakened. Frightened. He was walking through his life like a zombie, and numbed by grief and rage from being able to do anything creative or productive. Not painting, not reconnecting with his wife, not allowing this city to inspire him, only allowing it to piss him off, which he supposed was good, but a fragrant cunt would do him even better.

Jewel was ginger-haired and green-eyed, with a round face and a floral scent. Lilac maybe? Hell, what did he know of scents? The only important one was emanating from between her legs, ripely. He was sweating the scent of his own arousal, and this was all the language he or she needed.

"*Jewel—em—c'est un mot anglais,*" he offered, in likely incorrect French, when she wrote it on a napkin.

"*Oui, monsieur. Mon pére etait Americain, mais je n'ai jamais voyagé dehors de cette vie.*"

He caught that her father was American, hence the English spelling of what should probably have been Jule. But she never knew him? And that she'd...grown up here? He couldn't really catch that last part.

"*Jewel—est le—meme—chose que—joyau,*" he tried to pluck out, telling her what the word jewel meant in her language.

"*Je sais, monsieur.*"

She already knew that. The only reason Daniel knew it was because of a tender memory. *Joyau,* the French word for jewel, had been the title of the first portrait he'd ever painted of his wife. Nona had been his jewel. Now he sat next to a Jewel in a Pigalle strip joint, and together they watched the orgy of fake sex between uncomely people on a stage not ten feet away. He wanted to whisk her away from here, but instead he leaned in to kiss her just as the drinks arrived. Had he been about his better wits, he'd have caught the subtle way in which she moved back just slightly at his attempt. She wasn't about to be kissed, but he barely took notice as their waitress presented them with a chiller of Dom Perignon, opened and smoking.

"I think there's been a mistake," he fumbled, before remembering to try it in French. "*Em—erreur—*em—shit, bugger—*gaffe—un gaffe, UNE gaffe.*"

The waitress was confused by his objections, and rambled on rapidly in French, though her English earlier had been just fine. He didn't get one word she said, but quickly caught by her gestures that this could not possibly be a mistake. And suddenly he saw what was happening.

"I did not order—look, I ordered a scotch and a—shit—*je n'est pas—je ne—demandai pas—cette champagne, monsieur—*em, *pardon—mademoiselle—*I didn't order this."

"*Oui, monsieur!*"

He and the waitress were instantly thrust into an absurd debate, with his incorrect French and her sudden unwillingness to speak what English she knew. The fucking bottle cost six hundred dollars, and they were attempting to stick him with this, informing him that the lady he was with had ordered it, and now it was opened and would have to be paid for. Amazing how much of the other language you actually can understand when you're about to be fucked from the rear. Within minutes he realized that Jewel was a part of this scam. His sweet girlish Jewel, who spoke no English and had wanted him. Apparently not.

"You're trying to fuck me!" he yelled at the waitress. Like her, he no longer even tried to communicate in the other language, but with the strength of his own let her know his wrath. She stormed away and came back seconds later with a manager, a dapper gent in suit and tie. Daniel tried calmly to explain to the gentleman what had occurred, but the manager only shook his head to say that he wasn't intending to listen to any sob story.

"You fucking cocksucker!" Daniel yelled again. "You are not about to fuck me!"

The cacophony of French and English expletives coming from the cocksucker and him did nothing to interrupt the writhing bodies on stage, or the groaning audience of trench-coated men, but it did manage to stir a pair of bouncers from the front door. Daniel's mistake had been to give the waitress his credit card when he'd ordered. He swore to this fucker loudly that he was not leaving this dump until he'd gotten his card returned to him.

He had to laugh at how much like a movie this scene was trying so hard to be, because, just as their argument reached its swell, Elvin Jones's drum solo on the *Pursuance* track kicked in, big, bad and bold. It was as explosive as their yelling, and there really couldn't have been a better underscoring for Daniel's and the cocksucker's venom.

"You are tryin' to fuck me!" Daniel kept yelling, as his credit card was slapped on the table.

"The card you can have, monsieur. It's only the numbers that I need. And they've already been run through. Have a nice day, asshole!" Suddenly the cocksucker's English was better than Daniel's, and his arrogance audacious and smarmy.

"Well, for thirteen-hundred francs, do I at least get the whore thrown in?" Daniel spat, having no clue what the exchange rate was. Really, though, it would've been so much more stunning had he been able to utter it in fluent French. Still, the cocksucker got his meaning, because at that point Daniel was grabbed and carried up the flashing staircase by Prick One and Prick Two, who dug into his biceps with thick fingers.

They didn't just toss him out by his bootstraps either, rid of the trash and wiping their hands of it. They had to take their rambunctious pleasures with him, as well, by socking him hard in the stomach, then the face, right in broad neon light of the Boulevard de Clichy. He was on the ground. The salty taste in his mouth told him that his ulcers might've ruptured. The inability to breathe for several seconds was his other hint. Time seemed to dilate one minute and constrict the next. He was much too boozed and out of shape, besides, to fight back.

After the Pricks left him to his beaten self and swaggered back into the club like cowboys, he got to his standing feet, did his best to stumble on down the street, and was accosted by an African gentleman wanting to sell him some hash. And though he was just about flattened, humiliated, boozed, clutching his stomach, and bleeding from the mouth, Daniel stopped to do business.

FIFTY EIGHT

Minutes after his purchase, a hand slipped around Daniel's bicep as if to help him walk. He turned to see who this was, and snatched his arm away when he saw the cunt beside him.

"Monsieur, please let me explain," she begged. He could only laugh that he had been duped in so many more ways than he had originally assessed.

"You're an awfully quick study," was all he could muster between ulcer bites and a trip to one knee. "Amazing how many...words of...English you...have learned between...there and...here."

"I am so sorry, monsieur, for the way you were treated."

"Get away from...me," he stuttered, even as he was doubling over.

She grabbed his arm and got him back to a standing position. He had to confess to something tantalizing about this possibly dangerous woman, who only moments before had conned him, suddenly holding onto his arms and helping him down the crowded street, around a corner, down a smaller street, and into an apartment building of some sort. It was only then that he realized he'd stopped fighting.

This building reminded him of the council houses he'd known as a boy in London, but he didn't know what they were called here, simply that one walked into a huge set of wooden gates to enter a tall-walled courtyard, and that from that courtyard were accessed several clusters of tiny apartments.

He must've completely lost his mind. This woman was responsible for his being out six-hundred dollars. She could only be up to no further good, yet he was willing and bewitched.

As the whore helped him to her bed, where he collapsed in pain, he could see that her tiny flat was even smaller than his and Nona's on Rue de la Harpe.

"What do you...want from me?" he grumbled at her, even as she was tending to him. "The cash in my pockets? Rob a man while he's down?"

She sank into a chair, puzzling over the strange man curled up on her bed.

"Let me get for you a warm towel for your 'ead," she offered, as she got up again and disappeared behind a bathroom door.

"Why?" he yelled to her from the other room. "Why should I let you nurse me back to health? So you can fatten me up for slaughter?"

"Mister, please. Tell me your name."

"What·for, Jewel? Or is that really even your name?"

"Are you always this grumpy?" she asked, holding a wet cloth in her hand. "Or only when you are bleeding from the mouth?"

He couldn't believe she was being sarcastic with him. It was this whore who had put him in this condition in the first place. And she had the nerve to be sarcastic?

She tried to wipe his bleeding mouth with the cloth, but he was an uncooperative baby about this. Nevertheless, all throughout his resistance to any move she made, he was all the more enticed. He wanted to see what she had in store. The very real possibility that he might not come out of this night alive only whetted his appetite. He was teasing and cheap in his obstinacy. As much the slut as she.

Maybe Jewel would hold a gun to his head, as Will Speck does to Gabriel Champion. If he was lucky, she might just threaten his life, and by doing so awaken him from the deep sleep he'd been in these past two months, and scare the shit out of him so badly that he'd piss his pants, and run home with his tail between his quivering legs, and thank his lucky stars that he had a loving wife, and grab her, and hold her, and take up a canvas and some paints, and be useful again. *Goddamn it! Make me useful again.* His prayers, which the non-believer in him never considered prayers, always came out as barking demands. He figured the ether, surely the only force receiving said demands, required no courtesies.

He curled up on the whore's bed, clutching his gut. She caressed his head, wiped his face, and put on a pot of coffee. She took his wallet before he had the chance to snatch it from her, and riffled through it. She took no cash, only inspected his identification to get the name from it that he wouldn't offer up.

"Daniel Cross," she read.   "*D'accord*, Daniel Cross.   Now please understand me. I feel bad for what 'appened."

"Do ya' now?"

"I am trying to apologize to you. I do what I do, you know? But I liked you. Most men come over to my table and just start 'aving their way on me. There is no 'allo, or what is your name. Those men I don't care about to swindle them. They deserve it as much as I am concerned. But you were so, so charming. Respectful. I only wish you had not made them angry, because now look at you."

Was this whore for real?

"Who wouldn't be angry over what you people do?"

"Fair enough."

There was a matter-of-fact tedium about her. She whored, she played cons, she likely dealt with violent men on a daily basis, maybe even heaped a little of it, herself, and he could see the fatigue in her face that interestingly enough held no trace of the put-upon-ness that usually accompanied the weary. It was fatigue as fact, not trophy. He could also see for the first time that she was not nearly as pretty as he'd first assessed. Maybe once upon a time, but the ravages of her profession had done her in. She had dark circles under her big eyes and pocked skin. Her teeth were all right enough, though one near the front was chipped and slightly darkened, and many of them near the back were dressed in dental metals.

"On an average con," he asked, more calmly than he'd been all night, "how much of that money do you actually see?"

She gave him the stare that meant to give him nothing.

He shook his head in disgust.

"I was almost ready to respect what you did, thinking, hey, you do what you have to, to survive, right? But you're an idiot if that bloke is your pimp."

When she fought off the urge to cry, steeling her glare instead, he found it hard to tell if this was part of her game, or if he had actually gotten to her with his remark. The sucker in him reached out to her and gently pulled her head down to his chest, and they lay together unmoving.

"You can always call your credit card people and tell them that your card was stolen. You shoodant have to pay for that champagne."

"But your employer still gets to collect his money, doesn't he? That's how it works."

"Why do you care, as long as the credit card people gives it back to you?"

"Because I want the satisfaction of knowing that those fuckers didn't get away with their scam. And there's no way to get that satisfaction, is there?"

There was silence after his last comment, until she uttered: "I am one of those fuckers, Daniel Cross."

Should he be kind? Then, after another beat: "Yes, you are."

There was no place for kindness in an alliance such as this.

After a time, head still resting on his chest, she began to caress him. Her hands came up to unbutton his shirt and her face turned inward to kiss his chest, which sent a shiver up his legs. As she attempted to slide her hand down his torso, he suddenly grabbed her skinny wrist and startled her into a freeze.

"I am not paying for you. Do you understand me? I'm already out money because of you. I am not interested in getting my cock sucked for the rest of what's in my wallet."

She looked at him keenly. He could see in her face that he was hurting her wrist, but she did nothing to complain of the grip. She was accustomed to this treatment from men, and apparently he was no different; only the newest asshole she had to deal with.

"I know," she whispered. Her voice was luscious. "Tonight I am just tired. Coodant we just lay 'ere together?"

She looked doleful, and sounded like a cheap, sappy movie. Oh, if she was still playing him he was a sucker.

"I am not interested in taking you on a ride," she proclaimed.

"That's FOR a ride, darlin'," he spat, though actually considering her offer. "Look, I'm warning you. If you try to steal my wallet, you'll regret it."

What exactly she was going to regret, he couldn't have articulated.

"D'accord," was all she uttered after his bully's threat. With that contract signed, and all caution tossed to the winds, he took her face in his hands and kissed her mouth deeply, his tongue sliding right in there against her own.

His chin quivered and he was immediately hard. She kissed like a woman who did this as her art, and he was eager. His gut still burned, but at least his groin was quickly catching up.

Hungry and desperate, both, they kissed in that slovenly manner that says that sloppiness is sensual. Opening the mouth so wide as to devour; half kissing, half sucking the lower lip; darting the tongue combatively against the other's; biting indelicately; suckling voraciously at the cavern of the opened mouth, which has made itself soft and cushioned. They gnawed and consumed like two vultures on a carcass.

After a time, she slid herself down his torso, trailing her hooker's saliva from his mouth to his chest like a slug leaving its glistening path behind it, until she reached his pants and unfastened them with relish. She took him out, and began upon his erection her finer arts.

His entire being trembled in the wake of their difficult sex, which was especially difficult because, for one thing, he refused to take his clothes off. That was too much commitment. Who knew, after all? When they were done with each other, she might still hold a gun to his head or rob him blind. Then he'd be naked to boot? No thanks. If he had to go at all, he'd go with his clothes on. As if that alone were enough to hold onto dignity.

There was also the matter of his intoxication. He'd been solidly fermented by an evening of copious alcohol. And while that never did much to quell his arousal, it usually irked his temper. So, here was this woman before him now, whom he wanted to lash out against and fuck at the same time.

Is this how rape is born?

He immediately sickened at the thought. He was no rapist! Goddamn it! He would never harm this woman. He could abuse her verbally, though, without losing sleep, and had done so already this night. He was suddenly disgusted with himself that his impulse was really no different from a rapist's, and his mind surged with thoughts of Arthur's raping moment. Was he, Daniel, as potentially capable as Arthur had, at one time, been? Arthur had been at his lowest ebb in life. Wasn't Daniel presently at his?

His cluttered head danced this way and that. How did it get so full all of a sudden? Arthur. Rape. Loss. Hell. Jesus-Fucking-Christ! All he wanted was a fucking blow job. But this mess only thwarted any possible orgasm. He never actually lost the erection, but it would not explode for imploding.

His eyes squeezed shut, as Jewel increased her intensity on his unresponsive erection. He wanted to die. Maybe he was already dead. His hands and his soul were incapable of creating any longer; the woman he loved was somewhere in the bowels of this city, not being fairly dealt with by him; and his cock was being sucked by a dangerous stranger who'd already robbed him of his purse. He had to be dead and in Hell.

When it became painfully apparent that no orgasm would be achieved, no matter how hard they both tried, he hastily took Jewel up by her shoulders and away from his tortured cock and begged her to stop. This was no use.

"It's not you," he whispered.

All the apologies and excuses and clichés that a man gives. He sat on the edge of her bed, giving some mercy to his tired penis that was in no mood tonight.

Suddenly he broke into near-bawling tears. He'd never wept so much in his entire life as in this repugnant era of it. In fact, he had never been a man who cried. No longer. He wanted his own wife to be the woman crouching beside him. He wanted to be standing over a set of paints and looking out of a window onto some Paris scene that would reflower itself on a canvas. He wanted his friend and brother to be alive and debating with him the impact of critical theory on art, and to have *not* slept with his wife. But none of that was his reality. He couldn't even pay his wife back for her infidelity with a little infidelity of his own. It surely wasn't for lack of trying.

He fastened his pants and reached into his wallet, depositing a thick fold of francs onto the bed. He had no idea how much it was, only that he'd made sure to leave himself enough for a cab. Jewel didn't object.

"This is not payment for anything," he offered softly, needing to prove that he was a man of his tough-man's word. In truth, he was a sucker for a damsel in distress, even if the damsel act was just that.

"This is a gift," he rationalized, on his change of heart, "because you've given me one."

"What gift 'ave I given you?" she asked, looking as weary as he felt. Or perhaps she was simply done with him now that she had his money.

He just shook his head. To tell her that she'd shown him what a pampered prince he'd become, and had reminded him of what a crappy life really looked like, would be to insult this woman who had brought him into her home and had nursed his head.

"Look, you might as well be the one to use this money, cuz I don't do much, anyway, except piss the lot of it away most nights."

"Will I see you again?" she asked.

"No. I don't know."

He was a smarmy bastard. Even now, he couldn't truly commit to the promise that he would put all of this behind him and try to rebuild his life.

He left Jewel's apartment on the Rue de Douai, grateful, after all, that he was still alive. He reached into his breast pocket, retrieved his tiny pipe, and proceeded to stuff it with some of the hash he'd earlier purchased. As he lit it and smoked, he walked back up Place Blanche where he figured were his best shots for finding a cab. He walked slowly this approaching dawn, lazily sliding his feet and holding his gut with one hand, as does the headless drunk in his favorite Chagall, a rabid portrait in harsh reds, mustard yellows, and demon blacks. He wobbled up toward the Moulin Rouge, whose neon lights were already shut off for the impending daylight. Surrounding him was that early morning turquoise he loved. Or used to love. He didn't know if he loved anything anymore. All he really wanted was for all the whores of Pigalle to rally around him, and fire him up, and hold guns to his head, and give him screaming erections and broken hearts, and to have to be exorcised of the soul of Toulouse-Lautrec, who would inhabit his body and jostle his insides and make him squirm and fidget and paint.

Fuck! This hash was good.

As he shuffled past the famed hang-out of Monsieur Lautrec, he had to chuckle when he approached the broken shoe he'd confiscated off the stripper last night, lying forgotten in the stain of his own blood droplets, right outside the scam bar. A cat had sprayed it and was now slouching away, rather the way he was slouching away, until he attempted to pick the shoe up and was hissed at by the mangy ball of flesh.

Like this scurvied cat, he was distempered, ill, afraid, mistrusting of everyone, and ready. He'd been so ready to be beaten to death by those two bouncers. Ready to have the lovely Jewel rob him at gunpoint, or give him some disease from which he would not recover. Ready to *be* Gabriel Champion and to have the life frightened and the art propelled out of him.

But he wasn't Champion. He was Speck. Searching desperately in every alleyway for some kind of anchor. Looking everywhere except in his own hands and his own soul.

FIFTY NINE

As fall approached, Nona realized that she and her husband no longer lived together. No official estrangement marked the realization, no indignant proclamations or staged histrionics of packing up clothing and storming out onto the streets. An act like that might've actually stamped hope on their dismal plight. Some sign that both parties still had a pulse.

It was simply that she looked up one day and couldn't remember the last time she'd seen him. They had become two artful dodgers, skillfully living in the same flat without ever having a single encounter. They had come to memorize each other's comings and goings, and knew when to show up and when to stay away. They'd basically become timeshare holders.

Paris was supposed to have worked, but the wind had been so knocked out of each, in very different ways, that neither ever actually took a single step toward healing their divide. The best they could accomplish was merely staying afloat.

She had become a television zombie, lounging in bed for hours with the remote control in her hand during the nights on which she wasn't hanging out with René, Mimi, and Fairuza, or during most days when the threesome would be at work or school.

Watching cheesy French mysteries from the seventies was amusing enough. Watching Matt Dillon mumbling in over-dubbed French in *Drugstore Cowboy* was equally a hoot. Going to movies made by French filmmakers became Nona's newest obsession after Fairuza rescued her one night from her couch-potato Hell and took her to a local movie house that specialized in French Noir classics and the Nouvelle Vague. There was even a film house that played nothing but Cassavetes right around the corner from her flat. This was ritual for Fairuza, who was studying film as her major, and who had been kind enough to drag Nona along with her and out of a funk.

It served as no more than Band-Aid, but Nona was grateful.

It was, in fact, Fairuza who became her closest ally of the two women. And yet, even with Fairuza's rescues, Nona still tended to find herself with too much time alone. No matter how hard she tried to fill it with the company of friends, she could never completely avoid loneliness.

She used to crave solitude back in the days when she was actually useful in life. It was solitude alone in which she could write, and that was just it — she was no longer writing. Not prose, and certainly not the novel she'd been struggling to write. Not even the daily journal-jotting she had lived and breathed by.

Daniel had been right about diaries; they were the self-indulgent folly of one's poor-me pathos. He was always amazed that the public gobbled up the memoirs of so-called geniuses, their chicken-scratch scribblings that contained anything from contemplated suicides to grocery lists. He used to warn that if Nona kept holding so much virtue in her journals, she'd eventually start buying into that delusion herself and begin fantasizing about the world discovering them after her death. He said that it was a convenient way of not having to actually use skill with which to construct a beautiful sentence that might be worthy of publishing.

He said, he said, he said. None of that mattered, anyway, since nothing was presently being generated.

The only grace that saved her at all these days was her new company of comrades. She had grown to love René, Mimi, and Fairuza. And whenever she thought on them, their names always appeared in her mind in that precise order, like a comedy team or a law firm. She loved them so quickly, in fact, that she wondered if her hasty amour wasn't just confused gratitude for the three of them having saved her from despondency.

She seemed to have two lives now: The dead one — that of scorned woman, rejected wife, failed writer, and hermit, the perfect character for any sticky, dime-store, French novella. And her other — that of picnics at Butte-Chaumont with René, Mimi, and Fairuza; of night-clubbing in Montparnasse and being initiated into the French punk scene; of sunbathing along the Canal St-Martin, that is, until autumn hit.

It was the second life that was responsible for the day she dared to pick up a pen again, after months of a serious paralysis. She also realized that thinking in terms of months was kind. It had been six years since she'd written *Champion*. And, except for the *Murmuration* prose, not a single other word of note since.

Whatever it was that René, Mimi, and Fairuza's presence in her life did for her, she was thankful. She started taking herself to the canal during the days when they'd be at work. She'd sit on its banks and admire its footbridges. Or she'd rummage through the floor-to-ceiling shelves of books at the nearby Shakespeare and Company, stand in the eye of literary legend that the place held, and attempt to find some connection, reestablish her own presence in the world of books. As she did so, she was surprised to find herself staring down the one monster in the closet that truly did need facing, and realizing that this was the most current culprit behind her paralysis.

He hadn't left her alone in all these months. Oh, her husband certainly had, but not Arthur. Arthur haunted her. She'd known she couldn't avoid him forever, though it certainly hadn't stopped her from trying. She needed to face him head-on and demand that the rapist in him explain itself.

She scribbled insanely, tossed pages away, scribbled more, tossed more, until penmanship was unrecognizable and her notebook was a vomit of barely codable words. Not a one could come out of her that wasn't superficial and skittish at best.

The only epiphany she seemed to come away with was that all of her deeds to get inside of Arthur, which had finally cost her her marriage, and possibly his life, had been for naught. He was more of an enigma to her now than ever before.

Arthur, where are you? Gracing the Heavens? Redeemed and reborn? Or taking your penance in Hell, where you left off on earth? How does it work? Tell me something!

She spent weeks roaming the streets of the Left Bank in this effort, and often ended up crying until she hiccupped, then taxiing to the nearest bar. On any given day, she never knew which — the rapist or the poet — was going to come visiting.

In those instances she'd retreat to old journals, a practice that had often proven to render pearls back, some jotting that perhaps had no real meaning at the time jotted, but upon revisiting often spilled the very lesson needed at the moment. The practice required the daily toting of endless, dog-eared notebooks stuffed inside a backpack that she'd lug all over Paris with her like a college student. She opened one of those journals today, randomly, to a page that startled her from its sheer portentous proximity. This written in college:

The early 20th-century European philosopher Leviticus Rankin often speaks in his works of the futility of capturing everything in a single moment. That if we capture it, it ceases to be buoyant and self-governing and free.

But it does beg the question, "What, then, is the role of the artist, since he captures?"

An artist captures.

There have been moments in my life, though rare, when I have transcended the very map I've created for myself. And in transcending it, have experienced absolute purity.

When this has occurred, my tendency has been to conceptualize the experience as "capturing everything in a single moment." But maybe it was that I already had it in my clutches, and the REAL moment lay in the ability to release it. To open my greedy, hoarding palms, and let it go.

John Coltrane understood what it meant to let go.

She heeded the philosopher's words (*my grandfather-in-law!* she suddenly thought with a start), gave up writing for the day, and wasn't about to admit exhaustion, and not revelation, as the true catalyst.

She turned her fixations instead to René and Mimi, who were lovers as well as friends. They reminded her of the early Daniel and Nona, passionate balls of fire, which she badly needed to feel again in order to resurrect. Fairuza, the more cerebral of the trio, and decidedly uninterested in any sexual angle, could at times grow weary of René's and Mimi's company. And though Fairuza and Nona could expound for hours on the clinical deconstructionism of Buñuel's *Discreet Charm of the Bourgeoisie* or the dramatic significance of Jules Dassin's *A Dream of Passion* over a fumé blanc and salmon at Chez Jenny, the exact of which they'd recently done on an exhilarating lunch excursion, it was finally the mischievous fancy of René and Mimi that fed Nona the most, and succeeded in luring her into the next chapter of her second life.

It was a chapter that began on her first rainy night in Paris, and Leviticus Rankin's dictum to *let go* seemed clearly the engine. She wondered if Daniel, wherever he was, was being inspired by the rain, which had always charged him on to paint. It was only a momentary pining, as she was getting better at tucking pangs away.

This particular night gave the city one of those rains that hits suddenly, swiftly, then gone. Except that this one kept coming back. One hour, a pour. The next, calm. Then a pour again. It went on like this the entire evening.

She and the girls trekked to Le Bilboquet for some jazz and were planning later to catch Evangelust at a bar on the Isle St-Louis. Le Bilboquet was very Belle Epoque, with its red satin walls, velvet, gold-fringed drapes, layers and layers of Persian rugs, Hindu artifacts, and gilded statues of Ganesh gods and maharajahs. The girls immediately commenced to drinking and were tipsy within minutes. They rather enjoyed the state of their tipsiness, as they sat on Indonesian ottomans near the shallow stage and allowed the surrounding Frenchmen to flirt with them.

A beautiful English-speaking girl was the chanteuse at Le Bilboquet, who immediately rang up thoughts for Nona of her mother standing before a microphone in a place like this. With a peculiar dialect, not quite distinguishable as anything solidly this or that, Nona couldn't tell if this girl was American or French, but there was definitely the hint of some stateside sway. The elderly piano player had that same curve to his English. Nona wondered if they hadn't simply been here so long that they'd begun to submerge the rhythms and color of the French language into their American English.

And she wondered if it wouldn't eventually happen to her. How long was she planning to stay in Paris? And what kept her from going home? All of her reasons for coming here in the first place had been dashed to bits and the whereabouts of her husband unknown. Would she look up in twenty years and, like this old man striding his left hand on a baby grand, find herself still here and taking life at a Paris pace? Would she one day ask *"Kai who?"* or *"Harper who?"* afraid to remind herself of her former life? She wondered if that had happened to her sister, who had long ago abandoned the States.

This songstress was good, but not great. No Dorothy Favor. No Ruby Chan. Had the girl been great, she'd have been able to keep Nona's attention. But she was only good, so these crazy questions just kept dancing about Nona's brain.

They ordered a second round. Drinks were starting at two hundred francs, which was really insane, but Nona had come to learn that in Paris, if live music was involved, the prices were insanely padded. She always did the paying if the price was steep, because her friends were struggling students and she was the well-to-do author. Of course, being a bestselling writer didn't quite have the same cachet in their company. Her new friends weren't much on books, except for Fairuza, who was the only one to bother seeking out *Champion* from a local bookstore. And though it could now be found here in both French and English, Fairuza had been in Paris long enough to be considered somewhat bilingual, and was excited by the idea of buying a French-language copy and challenging herself to get through it. Nona loved that about her. That life's challenges were an excitement for Fairuza hinted vaguely of a spirit that used to be Nona's. She fell alternately between feeling valid again because someone wanted to read her, and grieving for a part of herself that had surely died.

Before Nona knew it, the band's set was over, and she'd missed most of it in favor of an intoxicated self-wallowing. She tried to make up for her introversion by treating the musicians to a round of drinks on their break, and blew an easy fortune assuaging her guilt.

Now effectively soused, the girls eventually said their goodbyes and hailed a taxi to René's gig. This gothic punk club on the Isle St-Louis was even wilder than Le Bataclan, where Nona had first seen René play. After two more shots, she was officially spinning. And dancing. And shouting catcalls with Mimi and Fairuza to every cute guy they'd see across the room. For about a second — but only a second — she flashed with a terrible pang on Kai. This would've been precisely the kind of life-is-fantastic hang in which the two of them would have engaged with zeal.

Evangelust was already into their set, and the girls were in belly-laugh hysterics when a hole in the mosh pit formed just as René was descending from air to floor. Not exactly the way mosh pits are supposed to work, but then Nona knew that René was feeling no pain; he had a ritual of indulging in Ecstasy before going on stage.

Thank God the bathroom found her, for she couldn't find it. She knew the world would stop twirling if she could just expurgate her body of its entire insides. She wanted to vomit, but couldn't even manage a little inconsequential bile. The fucking toilet didn't have a seat; just the naked porcelain bowl, unadorned except for someone else's redolent purging of stomach and soul. And she wondered where along the journey downward she'd dropped all of her standards for a clean commode.

The stench, a salty musk of flesh and seepage, was so thick that she could barely wade through it. Her limbs suddenly folded under her and she landed in a squalid cesspool. She lay on her back, staring at the cockeyed ceiling and surrounding walls, which were so close they invoked the curious wonder of what solitary confinement must feel like, and quickly sparked in her a mild case of claustrophobia. These walls were dark. The color of feces. As if the management had already foreseen the sludge that would end up spraying them and therefore camouflaged them with clever sludge hues.

She tried to grip the wall of this stinking offal, but the rough spackling only scratched her hands until she was so frustrated at her filthy predicament that she pounded it with her fists.

Time has no meaning, or redefines itself, in the state of extreme inebriation, so she couldn't tell if an hour, a week, or a year had passed, as she gurgled in her slobbery tears for someone's help. She still hadn't thrown up, but instead lay resigned in the floor's turbid mixture of piss, shit, barf, semen. If she didn't catch her death from cholera, it would be a miracle.

She suddenly heard René's voice from the other side of the stall, arguing rapidly in French with someone who was arguing equally as loudly. She couldn't tell what exactly was going on, only that a commotion was now occurring in the women's room of this dive and René was coming to her rescue. The stall door flung itself open and René stood over her, himself sweaty from a hard night's work of music-making and head-banging and mind-altering.

She was never happier to see anyone in her life. Even if it was the boy she was forming just the slightest crush on, rescuing her from the floor of a toilet, with her drunk on her ass and her dress surely up over her head. She knew that René didn't care a whit about any of that, however, when he uttered in mock horror: "Oh my God, *princesse*, don't just lie there, or you'll drown in your own vomit like Jimi Hendrix!"

Even in all of her suffering and tears and impending regurgitation, the princess laughed. And they laughed their way out of the place, as he grabbed her hand, yanked her to her feet, and flung her arm around his neck.

She was out of it for certain, but not so much so that she couldn't recognize her own stirrings. For the first time in forever she felt aroused to be touched by a man. His arm went around her waist in an attempt to hold her up, and the hand at the end of that arm touched so near the curve of her breast that it made her skin tingle. His leather jacket rubbed against her latex party dress, with his hips knocking against hers in a stumbling effort to get them both to his car. The pouring rain heightened her senses enough to notice every tiny detail, which only added to her sense of Paris amour, and she was just grateful to be allowed to remember what it was like to feel newly sexual toward someone again.

Was he driving her home? He didn't know where she lived. And where were Mimi and Fairuza? Maybe he would take her to his place. Before Nona could have any of her questions answered, she passed out in René's passenger seat.

SIXTY

Daniel took a studio near Place du Terte, something more conducive to painting than their hole-in-the-wall flat on Rue de la Harpe that only held reminders. If he didn't paint soon, he was surely on his way to Arthur's demise. And as difficult as life was these days, he still didn't want to be found dead in the bowels of Paris and buried next to Jim Morrison or some ridiculousness. If he was going to stay in this city any longer, Montmartre was where he needed to be.

Nona loved the Latin Quarter. It was the home of the intelligentsia, oozing the atmosphere of the Sorbonne, and ostensibly offering a romantic society of youth and learning and men of letters with carpe diem spirits. She'd always wanted to find that community and become a part of it. He used to tell her it no longer existed; that it was all just tourist-trap storefronts and McDonald's chains anymore.

Montmartre, on the other hand, was beginning to thrill him. Sex bars and dubious characters aside, this place had an itch and not just from the canker sores. Men of passion and cock and bravado created works of art and fucked their women with equal appetite. He was convinced Montmartre would be the antidote for his malaise.

It was also just far enough north of their flat on the Left Bank that he knew it would be safe to roam these neighborhoods without accidentally running into his wife and facing his failure.

Painting was on his mind for certain these days, but not in the way Nona had hoped for it. Frankly, he could give two shits about the museums. *Dusty old Masters who may have had something to say four hundred years ago, but today is today. Provoke me today!* Actually, it's not how he felt at all. He was frightened to death of visiting those palaces, but had to tell himself something so that he could keep feeling cocky and smug and in control.

Instead, he met a young man who took him to Lapin Agile, so that he could talk with the ghost of Picasso. And to Bateaux-Lavoir, so that he could talk with Braque.   And to Place Jean-Baptiste Clement, so that he could talk with Modigliani.   And to Vieux Montmartre, so that he could talk with Renoir and Utrillo.   These were the various studios and bars and hangouts and apartments of the legendary painters.

It wasn't the lofty lodgings of the Louvre or the Orsay that would speak to him right now.   Seeing Renoir or Matisse on a wall was only going to sock him where none but his ulcers should tread.   He needed to visit the places where these artists worked, where they drank and became drunk, where they took lovers, and lived lives, and were compelled in those lives to put paintbrush to canvas.   He needed to be scolded by their ghosts, which he knew still lived and breathed and haunted the halls where the men themselves had created their most astonishing work.   He needed to be reminded of what it meant to be compelled, pricked, urged on, angered.

He must've been a fairly boozy mumbler one evening, spouting into his whisky all this craziness, because Benoît approached him at a Rue des Saules bar one night prior to finding his studio and promised just the potion for an old, ailing, has-been artist.   Daniel's first encounter with Benoît was just about that obnoxious.   He thought for a moment to punch the insolent stranger, until he remembered that he was a coward and a weakling.   Benoît was also considerably younger than Daniel, maybe Nona's age, and could likely beat him to a pulp.

Benoît Belargent was a painter also, which was perhaps why Daniel's drunken mumblings caught the young man's attentions in a thickly peopled bar one evening.   As he'd been raised in the vineyard regions of Central France, Benoît was most interested in showing Daniel the one and only vineyard Paris could boast, which wasn't far, he offered.   Daniel suggested to this high-strung young Frenchman that perhaps they should seek out this vineyard in the daylight some time.   Though, in truth, Daniel expected never to see Benoît again.

Never seeing him again, it turns out, was not to be, as Benoît was a regular drinker at this establishment.   After a handful of encounters they became friends.   Benoît had a beautiful wife named Clothilde.   Daniel found out soon enough that besides painting, Benoît and the lovely Clothilde made their living from grifts and cons.   Some were described to him that were not all that dissimilar from the mousetrap he'd been victim to, involving the mysterious Jewel.   Most of theirs, however, were often far more complex deceptions and involved much greater sums of money.

Why this curious couple was so swiftly amiable with everyone they met, and had been so willing to share with Daniel what wisely should've been kept secret about one's endeavors, made him wonder if he wasn't about to become grifted himself. Therefore, whenever he was around Benoît, he held on to his wallet tightly and learned never to agree to any verbal contracts, even ones as harmless as agreeing to meet at a certain time, at a certain bar, for drinks. He caught on quickly to always suggest another bar, or another time, whenever he was ready to socialize. To never let Benoît be the decider of any definitive thing was the practice Daniel felt was best to employ.

It wasn't long, however, before he began to realize that it wasn't because of any cunning efforts on his part that he'd been kept safe from Mr. and Mrs. Belargent and their crafty arts, but that it had never been Benoît's intention to dupe him. It also quickly became clear that the Belargents were willing to bring him in on their chicanery, were he willing to go. A crafty threesome was what they had in mind, but all Daniel wanted from Benoît was the part of him that was the painter. He needed that society again, and this was exclusively why he hung on. He'd have skipped town on this couple from the start, when he'd first heard what they did for a living, had it not been for the painting.

It was during this spell that Daniel had been looking for a studio to rent. Benoît informed him that the community of artists was alive and well and living right here in Montmartre. Daniel was promised that he had chosen the right part of town to look, but that he'd best beware the schlock portrait-scribblers who loitered the square near Sacré-Coeur, as they were quickly beginning to warp Montmartre's reputation with their concession junk.

Benoît was the one to eventually find a space for him, in the part of Montmartre known for its famed steps and hilly terrain, and it was that gesture, plus the motive behind it, that had blown Daniel's mind.

When he'd first informed Benoît that he was looking, Benoît suggested he approach the Cité Internationale des Arts.

"Are you kidding me?" Benoît had shouted. "The Cité would not only jump at the chance to house you, they would probably offer to subsidize the famous Daniel Cross."

The famous Daniel Cross? Had Benoît realized how transparent he was being? If he was as clunky in his swindling, he couldn't be very good at it.

Then Daniel had the most startling revelation. He hadn't been sought out in the bar that first night because he was some random drunk who looked as if he needed a friend, though all of the above was true, nor because he was fresh meat for a nice grift. He had been sought out by a fan. Benoît Belargent, the apprentice painter, had known exactly who Daniel Cross was. Six thousand miles from home and Daniel's name was known in this dirty little town. But how? He hadn't been away from the States that long, and he was a nobody when he'd left.

"I am not famous."

"*Au contraire*, my Brit-expatriate, slash, American-expatriate, slash, newly French import friend. You have obviously closed your eyes to the world that adores you, and refuse to be aware that your exhibit is being visited by movie stars and heads of state. Made all the more sensational, of course, by your and your wife's sudden disappearance just as you were coming into prominence. That move alone catapulted you from art underground to pop mainstream. Not to mention the suicide of the poet. It's a culture that feeds on headlines and scandal. You are the rich fodder for all your American gossip television shows. Tell me you know all this already! Your humble pie is adorable, but, uh, I am not buying any of it—"

Daniel's body went white. To have a complete stranger mention his wife. Mention Arthur. Spell out his life.

"—and all in the art community here are anxiously awaiting *Murmuration*'s arrival in Paris, which could still be a year in the coming, according to La Revue. Of course, when that time does come, you'll only have to escape again, won't you, Monsieur Howard Hughes? You're the new Warhol. Everyone wants you at their parties. Everyone wants to own a Cross. Well, listen up, *mes amies*, he lives here now, in Paris, thousands of miles away from where the national search is on for the new art rave of the States. And I've got him! The tabloids would probably pay handsomely for information on the celebrated recluse. What do you think I should do about that?"

Daniel's stunning must have been apparent and glowering, because Benoît laughed outright.

"My humor is crude. Forgive me. I have no intentions of disturbing your hibernation. But if this act of yours is for real, then you should be made aware of your growing renown. The New York show has completely exploded, and *Murmuration* is slated for London early next year."

"New York show? What New York show?"

"Come now. Have you so truly abandoned your life that you don't know any of this? All one needs is to pick up a Revue d'Art once in awhile. The radicals love you, the bourgeoisie hate you. Oh, you're all the rave."

Peculiar that Benoît would mention Daniel's wife at that point, when he'd never inquired about her before. Peculiar that there hadn't been the natural curiosity to ask about the suicidal poet, with whom Ben was obviously familiar. Simply a cavalier mention in passing, which had made Daniel begin to dislike Benoît. It was Clothilde who, in confidence one day, shared with Daniel her husband's deepest heart.

"Benoît talks like a swindler because he is one. It is the art of this trade that you speak always as though you have something on someone. You dangle smiling threats like the blackmailer or counterfeiter simply to keep it always known that you are the one in charge. You never ask questions, so that it appears you already know the answers. He is arrogant. So am I. We have to be for what we do. But Benoît adores you. He has grown cynical and feisty about the world, and so says *'fuck you'* to it with his impostures. But the love affair he has with the world he wishes existed is all poured out in his painting. And you represent that world to him. He spits on the junk painters who scatter Place du Terte. I don't mean literally, of course, although he did once get in a fight with one of them, who sketched him and then showed him the ugly caricature, demanding money. You are the real thing, Daniel. And he doesn't believe there are too many of the real things left in this world. When he recognized you in the bar that first night from the photograph that every article about you uses, he sent himself through a million somersaults trying to decide if it was you or no, before he had the courage to approach you. You are better than a movie star to Benoît. And after having read all the stories about your disappearance, to think that he would be the one to spot you, here in some bar in Montmartre where he practically lives, I cannot tell you what a jubilant tailspin he put himself in. He prides himself on being one of the few people who might actually recognize you, because frankly you are still a largely underground sensation here. But I have never seen him feel so alive as since you have become his friend. Let him help you find a studio. He has some influence with the Cité, has done some research work for them in the past. He is not out to hurt you. He is in awe of you, Daniel, and only wants to learn from his hero."

Daniel remembered thinking, after that chat with Clothilde, that this couple was either the glorious salvation he needed from his doldrums or they were simply ingenious in their wooing game and about to lower the trickster's boom, because he'd been effectively seduced. He allowed Benoît to arrange the studio for him, while doing his best to shake off the dust of his hinted-at fame. From that moment on, the three of them were inseparable. Then there were more.

He was introduced to Marcello Rozat, a young transgender painter, whose looks were striking by their very paradox. A tall, thin, short-haired androgyny who eschewed enhanced femaleness, Marcello desired neither breasts nor hips, but was shy and restrained, a listener more than a talker, content with her boy's frame and requiring only the subtlest ornaments of femininity, as in the slim-cut Capri slacks, the simple silk scarf thrown haphazardly but artfully around her turtled neck, the smart pair of boots with just a hint of heel, and something just this side of a page boy about her meek head. *She* and *her* were the preferred classifications, even though, for now, a penis was still maintained.

Marcello loved cigars, therefore Daniel made sure always to present her with a fine one whenever the group met up. She did some artist's modeling herself, and Daniel soon discovered that they all sat for each other. He imagined Marcello the object of many an artists' enthrallment, considering the mystique she was driven to wear.

Next was Corky Campobasso, an American from Queens, who could've been Anthony Quinn's brother, with the bluster of a bull, just to give balance to the circle. Corky was seventy-five years old, with a thick mass of a body, ravaged skin, and fingers that looked like sausages. He had left his family behind when his wife died, and had never contacted them again. Now he was a Paris transplant and had been so for the past five years. Corky had been a carpet layer and construction builder, until he retired and started assembling nuts and bolts and lead pipes and carpet stripping into the craziest concoctions. Something just came over Corky one day. He'd been an upright guy his whole life, voting Republican, reporting every damned detail of his earnings to the IRS, and raising his sons not to be draft-dodging pussies. Then his wife died, not even sick, just stricken unexpectedly with an aneurysm. His grief had been so overwhelming that he'd begun to loathe his children for not having treated their mother better when she was alive. Whether that had been true or just his grief projecting was something Corky had never bothered to decipher.

Suddenly, one day, he just couldn't seem to get all of his miseries out of his system, and he thought he might go mad. He took every scrap of junk he'd ever saved from his days of laying carpet and tiles and installing piping, because he'd always been such a fastidious pack rat, and just started gluing and pasting and soldering and nailing. He couldn't make any sense of what was happening to him, because he'd always been a man who'd hated art. Especially the kind he was now making.

"An apple betta' look like an apple, for my taste. The rest is bullshit," he'd been the type to argue. "It don't take talent to scribble mess and throw some paint around. Most artists today should just go get a fuckin' job!"

That used to be Corky. And the next thing he knew, something had compelled this man to gather up his junk, collected for thirty-plus years, and from it create something. Was it art? Corky would say he could give a fuck what anybody called it, but it saved him from going crazy.

His kids were convinced that crazy had already claimed their father, and they tried to have him locked away, until one day, like Daniel, Corky simply disappeared. Paris just seemed to be the haven for societal refugees.

Daniel could only grin when Corky unfolded the tale of his life and the birth of an artist at the ripe old age of seventy-five. Something had told Corky that the Muse did indeed exist, and he'd better listen to her. Corky's crazy garage sculptures were exciting people, and currently being shown in a little gallery not far from the Espace Dali. Corky from Queens. Who'd been an Eisenhower man. Now he was a bona fide Beatnik who smoked opium, laughed and drank with his rag-tag family of con-artists, cross-dressers, and creative agitators at Le Bar Bachon, wore nothing but sandals on his severely arthritic feet, kept a mistress named Catherine, and loved the company of young people. Because it made him young.

After meeting Corky from Queens, Daniel was determined to let this seventy-five-year-old's interminable youth rub off on him.

It was a vibrant playpen, this circle of artists to whom Benoît had introduced him. They all lived in hippie warrens, sometimes three or four artists in a single space, taking money from their families or finding their earnings any way they could. And they were alive, without a care in the world, the least of which was where they might find their next meal. Art was all that was important to them.

SIXTY ONE

Nona remembered nothing of the trip across town to Rueil-Malmaison, or entering René's apartment. She only next recalled the sudden silence of an empty room. Sudden, as in, one minute there was the hoopla of a nightclub, and a drizzly night, and a drunken woman, and a staggering hike to an old, beaten up Renault; and the next was her horizontal state on a makeshift divan in an unfamiliar room, alone.

She peered up from her hungover state and perused what she instantly knew was René's flat because his bass was propped against its amplifier in the corner, though even the darting of her eyes around this quiet room was like a megaphone to the eardrum. Had he simply dumped her here and taken off? As she looked down and found herself wrapped in a man's robe, she wondered if she ever did vomit, and if someone else had to clean up the mess. It was a thought that made her skin crawl. Here were these young twenty-somethings, whose bodies were strong, and beautiful, and wiry, and able to withstand much more partying abuse than hers, and here she was foolishly trying to convince herself, and them, that she was as up to the task as they, and making a fool of herself in the effort.

As her eyes slowly made their way around this room, she realized it was almost daybreak. A soft blue shaft shot its way through a nearby window, and the early morning sounds of sanitation trucks and delivery carts sang for her.

This room was made up of a living room area and kitchenette combined. There was the requisite dinginess that spelled a man's apartment; unwashed dishes in the tiny sink, and every imaginable kind of paper and mail covering his table in a messy pile. She spotted two doors. One main door, through which they obviously entered from the storm outside, and one smaller other. As she managed to stand and make her way to the smaller door, which she hoped was a bathroom, she opened it slowly.

Thank God, yes, a bathroom. She closed the door behind her and switched on the light to a room so tiny she could barely sit and do her business without the cold porcelain of the sink against her shivering leg. When she was done, she flushed the toilet and simply stayed sitting. The toilet seat had quickly warmed up to her bare thighs, and the sound of the rain, which had begun again, only heightened her anxiety of the freezing chill. So, for now, the warmth of the toilet seat would do her just fine.

She leaned her head against the side of the sink, bearing the weight of her headache and her shame. Until she heard it. And when she did, her breath stopped. She wasn't alone. In a silent panic, she looked around in the direction of the sound and discovered the other door she hadn't noticed before. Through this bathroom one could access another room. And from behind that door she could hear the unmistakable sounds of erotic breathing.

As it became clear to her what she was overhearing, the soprano sighs and baritone moans of sexual fulfillment, she realized that a hot little dalliance between her and René had never been his agenda in bringing her here last night. How embarrassing to have thought it might. Before she knew it, she had involuntarily crept from her spot to lean her ear heedfully into the door. The word *involuntary* rang in her head because there was no way she was going to admit to having all the makings of a pitiful voyeur.

The sounds made her shiver, reminding her of how lonely she really was, and clearly conjuring a flirtation that never existed. She wanted to conjure Daniel. Wanted to smell his hair, feel the roughness of his painter's hands, taste his mouth. She was fairly certain that would never happen again, as their tiny room on Rue de la Harpe was hers alone now. All of Daniel's clothing and luggage had long been gone. His scent too. That one had taken awhile to leave, but she recalled now that when it finally did, when she looked up one day and couldn't smell him any longer, she'd been afraid to say it aloud, but knew.

Why couldn't Daniel be with her doing this loving thing, instead of out there somewhere drowning in booze, and sorrow, and women, for all she knew, and leaving her to the same sad end? Or had he jumped ship completely, and gone back to the States? This was the first time that scenario even dawned on her. He had, after all, never wanted this trip.

She sank down to the cold linoleum, skin breaking out in a flurry of goose bumps, and breathed in the sexual sounds as if they were cocaine.

Her knees drew up in front of her as she leaned against a wall space that wedged her between door and toilet bowl. She tried to remain as quiet as possible, with her ear glued to the door.

Slowly her hand crept up to the light switch and quietly flipped it off, then made its way just as cautiously over to the doorknob. She carefully turned the handle. The movement was so slow and studied that it must've taken a clear sixty seconds of turning before she finally heard the microscopic click. And the only other thing she could hear in this instant was her own nervous breathing. She was a cat burglar discovering the combination to the safe.

No stirrings except the sexual came from beyond the door; her violation hadn't been detected. Her head cocked to face the doorknob on which her grip was now cemented. She prayed that the door wouldn't creak as she inched it open to a tiny crack and thanked God that the rain outside hadn't yet begun to swell the wood.

Her eyes fell on them, shaded in dusk. There was only a mattress on the floor, and the blankets barely covered them as their nude bodies melded with one another. She couldn't determine who was the more beautiful, René or Mimi. And they didn't make the kind of love she imagined they would. She would've bet on raw, wild, id fucking.

It was nothing like that. René and Mimi loved each other tenderly. Nona saw the ache of ecstasy in René's face, the belligerent creed that life simply was not worth living without the love of the woman beneath him. In Mimi's face was the most exquisite beauty. Who couldn't love such beauty? Their lips folded into each other's. Their fingers intertwined. A wild river of tightly coiled black hair flowed from Mimi's head, and dark berried lips opened to sigh their delight. His muscular arms creased her gingerly, and she hung from him like a neatly folded pair of pants. In one pink hand was gently held a coffee-hued breast. Between one pair of lips there nestled an angry nipple, snuggled and sucked. His newly bleached buzz cut with the black roots was crowned by her long, delicate fingers, which braided themselves around his temples like the thorns of Christ.

Nona could feel him inside Mimi as though he were inside of her. Nona's own hips moved when his moved. Her own fingers punctured the wetness forming between her thighs, just as René's cock surely punctured the wetness between Mimi's. Nona was suddenly in awe of young love.

People approaching middle age loved differently. They fell in love with each other's spirits, what each other's thinking heads had to offer, maybe even each other's politics and belief systems. With kids in their supple, rebellious twenties, it was something else altogether, much more primal. What they fell in love with, she came to realize, was each other's scent.

The notion of that kind of animal appetite was suddenly so erotic. No heads need apply. No deeper erudition as the lure. Just wetness. And heat. And hunger.

His bare buttocks were so small and firm, nesting right atop and between her opened legs, which were strong and lean and spread open like breathtaking butterfly wings. As his buttocks thrust into her and out again, Nona's own hands were pinned tightly between her legs, trying furiously to unburden a stupid itch.

In Mimi's face she saw herself. In René's she saw Daniel. Her sense memory was so keen right now that she could feel Daniel's hair pasting itself against the sweat of her neck. She smelled his peculiar male scent. A combination of arousal, that marvelous tobacco-sandalwood-leather essence she'd first whiffed from him the day they met, and the sexy musk of having painted all day. She heard Daniel's teeth click the way they always did whenever he was at the height of climax. She used to tease him about his clicking teeth, and he got much joy from her teasing. She could hear his laugh, and she tried to elongate it and make it last. His arms would hold her so tightly that she would almost lose breath, but gladly, knowing that his grip was unbearably made so by his intent to keep her there. Because, for Daniel Cross, life had simply not been worth living without the love of the woman beneath him. At one time. The memory was crystal. Then gone.

As she sat alone on an icy bathroom floor, masturbating like some lonely guy in a porn booth to other people's sex, abandoned by the most passionate man she'd ever known, because of her own wrongs, she simply gave up and refused to take her pathetic self to an orgasm. Quietly she closed the door, holding its cold knob in her grip, cocked to the left. She turned the knob right. Millimicron by millimicron. Until some sixty seconds later she heard the faint click. She lay down on René's bathroom floor and was so empty of tears by now that she couldn't even cry.

Eventually she made her way back to the sofa without her presence ever known, but couldn't sleep. Except that she must have, because the next thing she knew was a bright sun shooting through the window and eggs being made on a hotplate only feet from her. René stood over the concoction as Mimi sat with a coffee.

"Ah, look who is back with the living," Mimi said, smiling, bringing a cup to her, and crouching down to offer it, leaning in close.

"Good morning."

Nona sat up and regarded them both, grateful that she hadn't been caught in her spying, and realizing that a new dynamic had officially entered their friendship — jealousy. That René and Mimi had each other, and that she was the third wheel being tended to on this hungover day. Why couldn't Fairuza have been the one to take her in last night? From here on out, if it wasn't going to be the foursome then she would no longer agree to hang out.

SIXTY TWO

Corky was Daniel's first attempt to paint again. The timing couldn't have been more perfect since the rains had begun, which had always given Daniel a creative jolt. He told Corky he wanted to capture that crusty old soul on a canvas, and Corky agreed to sit for him.

When the old man first walked into Daniel's studio, Daniel was playing the legendary *John Coltrane and Johnny Hartman* CD. It just about made Corky flip.

"Aw, Danny, you fuckin' guy! How do you know about this album?"

Daniel just smiled.

He situated Corky where he wanted him, told him to get comfortable, and then became the audience for Corky's nonstop talking.

"You know, everybody talks about Frank bein' The Voice, but nobody remembers Johnny Hartman's golden tones. And it's a fuckin' shame. Hey, and have I gotta Johnny Hartman story for you. I caught him, listen to this, gettin' out of a car at the NBC Entertainment Center in Manhattan, I think he was doin' a talk show or sump'n. I egged Maggie on to go over and ask for an autograph. She'd hate when I'd do shit like that, but I wanted him to know *'hey, somebody knows who you are,'* and I promised Maggie a steak dinner at the Hyatt if she'd do it. Wait, hold up, hold up, hold up!"

Corky put his hands up to quiet the room, though he'd been the only one talking. *Lush Life* had stopped him in his tracks, and a good minute had to have passed in his freeze.

"Nobody turns a phrase like this fucking guy," Corky finally offered wistfully. Daniel smiled and stared at the air as though he could actually see the luscious phrase.

"Anyway," Corky resumed, breaking the spell, "so, Maggie gets his autograph, and then takes two snapshots o' me and Johnny with the Polaroid. I give one to Johnny, you know. I say, *Hey Johnny, when I become famous like you, you're gonna remember this picture, you're gonna remember this day.*

You'll be able to get money for it.' I made him laugh. I also told him any time he needed carpet laid I'd be happy to do it for him on the house. I think he appreciated that. And to think he ended up workin' hotel bars and dyin' young. Anyways, Maggie, bless her heart, was a gem about the whole thing."

Whenever Corky spoke of Maggie, it was with a longing that told Daniel that if he ever mentioned the tales of woe with his own wife, Corky would kick the crap out of him and tell him to straighten up and fly right and appreciate her like a gem. So Daniel never mentioned Nona. The shameful truth was that he'd grown afraid of engaging with his wife, and he would never be able to make anyone understand that. He only ever thought of her every waking moment, but he knew he had to get the shakes and kinks out of his life before he could deign to approach her again. If he didn't, he'd only keep inflicting his baggage on her, the greatest of which was the sin of Arthur's killing, which was slowly eating him alive; it might as well have been his own finger that had pulled that trigger against Arthur's skull.

Christ, even with all this new energy in his life, he still went there.

For a moment, he got so lost in his morbid musings that he forgot Corky was still talking. When he looked at his canvas, and looked at the time, not much had been accomplished, so he suggested they fold for the night, grab their umbrellas, and go get a whisky.

They sat at Le Bar Bachon, waiting for Benoît and Clothilde. Marcello would join them, too, and her new lover, Uli. Corky was still on the music roll, and always loved passing his anecdotes around as if they were war medals to boast.

"Get this one," he spouted forth with a sandpaper irritant to his Queens English. "I was in Vegas at a carpet layers convention the day Sammy died. I think it was...1990, was it? Heard it on the news, broke my heart. Now, there was a man who successfully crossed the color barrier at a time when it was not bein' crossed by anybody. I can't say I appreciated that at the time, but even assholes can change. He paid his dues dearly too. Remember that whole Mae Britt hoopla?

"Anyway, I got to witness a historical event. At nine p.m. on the day he died, all'a Vegas was s'posed to dim their lights for a whole minute. You know how much juice that city pumps out? That one minute alone'a darkness pro'ly saved the whole country their energy shortage that year. Anyway, there's only two other times in the history'a Vegas, prior to that night, that they dimmed the lights. You know what they were?"

The question was not rhetorical. He looked around at each of them, Daniel, Benoît, Clothilde, Marcello, and Marcello's new boy, for they'd all arrived one by one and had ceremoniously sat and become his audience. Corky offered his question like a quiz; whoever gets this right gets a drink. But nobody here knew much of anything about Las Vegas history.

"Anybody? Nope? Okay. Here goes. The deaths of John Fitzgerald Kennedy and the Reverend Doctor Martin Luther King Junior, is all. Can you believe that? Jeeses, the company Sammy was keepin', even after the bastard croaked. And I was there to witness it. Only, and get this, the goddamned Flamingo, that's a casino, for you fuckin' frogs that've never bothered to leap over to the other side'a the world—"

Corky was the Don Rickles of their circle. The more he offended the group with his crude humor, the more they loved him, because Corky only made comments like that to shock. The truth was, and everybody knew it, there was no greater love affair than the one Corky had with the Parisians.

"—the goddamned Flamingo didn't bother to dim their lights, while everybody else around 'em did. Talk about some goddamned disrespect. I wrote a letter to the city. And don't think I was the only one. A lot'a people were very, very upset about that. 'Course, I'm sure they did the same thing when Frank died, but I wudn't there to see that one. I'd sure like to know, though, if the goddamned Flamingo fin'lly decided to get their act together for the Chairman o' the Board."

Whenever Corky was in a room, he was the center of attention. He spun endless yarns on a world about which they knew nothing. They all thought he'd been involved in the mob. He was *so* Italian-American and *so* East Coast, and to them that spelled Mafia. But Corky would never give them the satisfaction of affirming or denying. He liked that game. He also loved their curiosity, and they loved him. Whatever he was in those days, today he was a renegade for art, with his misshapen fedora and his big purse slung over his shoulder that he'd once purchased in Tijuana.

"And talk about a great musician, that Sammy. You think they're gonna dim the lights for the likes'a these gang-bangin', gold-chain-wearin', posin', pants halfway down their ass, struttin' rapper types. They don't know from music. They can't touch Dinah Washington or B.B. On My Word Of Honor Blues Boy KING, man!" he shouted with a laugh that was burdened with emphysema. "Not with a twenty-foot pole. And speakin'a twenty-foot poles, I gotta chubby the size'a the Eiffel Tower! Where's my girl?"

The minute he beckoned for her, his Catherine walked in the door. Daniel personally believed Corky to be a wizard. He was Shakespeare's Prospero, ancient conjurer, magician, and mischief-maker.

Marcello's boy, Uli, piped in. "Obviously, monsieur, you are not a fan of rap music. But would it not be fairer to say that it redefines music rather than to say it is not music at all?"

Daniel smiled, as he recalled a similar debate with Christianne Tensmith's father years ago about art.

"For, even you, monsieur, are considered by traditionalists to be a fraud."

"Who the Hell is sayin'at about me?" Corky barked jokingly, knowing full well his reputation. "Look, what I do pro'ly IS junk. Who gives a fuck? It keeps my head on straight. That's what I do it for. Is it art? Hey, what can I say? If somebody out there is affected by it...you know, the world works in strange ways, it could happen...then I fuckin' made some art, arright? The rest'a the world can say it's bullshit, and maybe they're right. But it got some shit outta my head, and maybe it's gettin' some shit outta somebody else's head too. I don't give a fuck about popularity. I'm fixin' my screwed-up life, which is feelin' pretty goddamn good right about now, so I must be doin' sump'n right. This rap music you're tryin' to defend, my friend, more power to them, and more power to you. I just personally happen to think it's shit. But that's arright. Like, it's arright for you to think my shit is shit. Ppfff! Whatever works. I ain't gonna get my feelin's hurt, cuz I ain't doin' it to win no votes."

What a revelation this seventy-five-year-old newborn was, spouting his creed like he owned the place. Corky had been truly baptized and was evangelizing his newfound religion. He was letting them all know in his crude way that beauty was what they did this for, and that it would always be within reach.

As Daniel strolled up the hill toward his flat later in the evening, his head was immersed in thoughts that lingered with a grateful bombardment.

Was beauty really always within reach? As someone who had fallen deep into a pit, far away from his wife and his life, Daniel was surely betting on it.

Corky had blown his mind tonight, and he considered his reluctant new role as mentor to Benoît. Ben was in awe of him? Hell, he was in awe of Corky Campobasso from Queens.

Later in his room alone, Daniel came awfully close to believing that he could dream about her again with relative peace. Maybe it meant that Nona might see her way to forgiving him. Soon. Not now. Not yet. For now, he was just beginning to regain a proper footing.

SIXTY THREE

Now that winter was officially in bloom, the little accordion player with his lopsided *Anniversary Waltz* was retired for the season, and the temperatures had suddenly turned a bit too south for an L.A. girl. For a good few weeks after her drunken night and demeaning voyeurism, Nona avoided René and Mimi. She just knew she wore the guilt on her forehead and was certain that in her presence they would know what she'd done. She didn't call them, or answer her phone when she was in the flat, or pick up her messages from the front desk after she'd been out.

She called Fairuza, though. Whenever she'd get too caught up in the intoxication of René and Mimi, Fairuza could be counted on to sober her. She and Fairuza spent many long hours together, especially during her avoidance week. They'd meet for lunch and haunt the corridors of the Louvre, a place Nona had dreamt of walking with Daniel, but it wasn't to be. They would stroll through the halls of the Grand Gallery, or sit on benches in the huge salon of sculptured gods and goddesses and chat about this or that.

The day did come, however, when she had to face René and Mimi. Someone was bound to get suspicious if she simply continued staying away. When the day arrived, she must've been a fairly twitchy ball of nervousness, because they started teasing her over lunch.

"I think our Nona may have found herself a French boy," Mimi remarked, playfully. "I've never seen her so frazzled."

She laughed with them, but couldn't be sure she wasn't a terrible actress. She began spending fewer nights out with them and more under the covers, watching television. She'd click the remote control frantically, trying to locate the periodic porn channel, or she'd open her laptop and try to write, but she'd just end up writing about masturbation. Boring. She was hardly as gifted as Anaïs.

Ultimately she couldn't avoid what had been awakened that Peeping

Tom night. More often than she wanted, the image of René and Mimi making love would visit her, and she'd promptly shove her hands between her legs. She needed badly to know passion again, but was ashamed of her impulses.

One fidgety middle-of-the-night, she went through an indulgent bottle of '66 Château Margaux, Orson Welles's *Touch of Evil* on the television, and countless wasted pages on her computer before she just about hit the walls. Too much undone desire was burdening her achy head.

In an impulse, she got dressed, stepped out onto the streets at four a.m., and hailed a taxi to René's flat in Rueil-Malmaison. She'd come to know the patterned comings and goings of her comrades and knew that this was a night that Mimi worked. It was alarmingly easy for her to dismiss Mimi's feelings, to be willing for deceit, in the pursuit of her own itch.

She knocked on René's door, and had, of course, awakened him. His disheveled state was even sexier than the leather-jacketed René. The ridged lines of his blanket had indented the pattern on one side of his puffy face, making him look like some ceremonial chief, and his eyes had that absence of focus about them. He had put on pants to answer the door, but the rest of him was bare and unbearable. She wanted to fall into his arms that second, though it really might be best if she allowed him to invite her in first.

"*Princesse*, are you okay?" he asked in hazy alarm.

"Yes, I'm fine—I'm sorry for this—at this hour—"

"*Non, c'est bien. Entrez.*"

René would speak in French about every other sentence, and she could barely think straight. What had she come here for? And what should she tell him she'd come here for? Then she pulled her most manipulative trick yet, and started to cry. It was all she could think to do, to get his arms around her. She loathed that she would even consider pulling the helpless girl stunt, but she didn't loathe it enough to stop.

Promptly, as she knew they would, and thank God, René's arms went around her blubbering self, and his chin rested on her head. He shut the door behind her, and held her at the threshold.

"Shhh, shhh, shhh. Did you suddenly have a bout of loneliness in the middle of the night, *chérie*?" he pampered, like a father talking to his child. It was the first time he hadn't called her princess. An invitation?

"I don't know," she muttered. "The nights are always harder. I'm turning into a pathetic loafer. I sleep with my television on and a bottle of wine by my side and I don't get a word written."

She gave him, as her reason for tears, the lesser of her pains. She wouldn't dare use her deeper sadnesses to woo René, such as the end of her marriage and touch of her sweet husband, or the death and disenchantment of her dear friend, one-time lover, and greatest symbolic nightmare. These realities were what truly made her weep every day.

"This has been the most difficult time of my life, and I just thank my lucky stars I have you guys, or I'd be slitting my wrists about now."

"Well, you know you can always come here, *Princesse.* Doesn't matter the time." He kissed her forehead. She hated that. More father/daughter stuff. She wanted him to kiss *her.* And there was the princess again, as imbued with the pedestal as ever. Maybe there was no invitation.

"You know, someone should really kick your husband's insolent ass for abandoning you like this. If you were my wife—"

He was bringing up her husband? This was not boding well for her agenda.

"Please don't—I, I don't—I can't talk about that."

Yes, there was much to loathe about Daniel's behavior, but the whole story would surely have made René loathe her too.

I am no saint!

Daniel had a right to his hurt. It wasn't born from nothing.

He's an incredible man.

Goddamn it, she didn't want to defend Daniel right now. At this point she was just as hurt by Daniel as he was by her. But there was so much René didn't know for him to be making such smug statements. This little nothing punk rocker wasn't half the man Daniel was.

Her head was instantly discombobulated. This was going all wrong. She cared deeply for René. He was not a nothing.

But goddamn it! Neither is Daniel!

She wished she could've been straightforward enough to simply say, "*I don't want to be reminded of the man I love while I'm looking to get fucked,*" but she had to play games instead. It's what adults do.

She shook her weeping head, and prayed he wouldn't continue. But he would. It gave René pleasure to malign Daniel's name.

"He is a failure as a husband, and a very stupid man. He can't be much of an artist."

The slap to his face sprang him forward in a way no other of her efforts had. He drew her to him with a kind of male jerk, and his mouth crashed into hers.

His hand flew up to crown the back of her head, and that quiver in her groin shot her like a poisoned dart, swiftly and with no mercy, as she felt his erection against her.

The sex was manic. Right there against the front door. On top of the kitchen table. On the sofa. On his mattress in the other room. They tripped, and fell, and ripped at clothing, and fucked as though they might die not to. It was the most achesome love she'd ever made, racked in her joints and in that spot just below the gut that says all is not well. It was pleasure of such a wicked and panicky kind that she could taste the soot of betrayal beneath her tongue. She felt like a drunkard. And like the drunkard, she was dangerous and capable of violence, willing to kill her young to be so quenched, consuming until she was bloated and gross.

In such a dizzy moment of doped nihilism it is easy to tell a man you love him. Easy to believe it.

SIXTY FOUR

Daniel went to the International Express office on the Champs-Élysées to pick up money. He had wired Harper to send him scheduled checks. It was the first time in all the months here that he had bothered to make any kind of contact, which only vaguely included an apology for his neglect. He had taken up a postbox, where she could send other correspondence if she chose.

Of course she chose, since Daniel wasn't the computer type. He read Harper's letters, but never answered them, and in this age where email conveniently eliminated the annoyances of envelopes, stamps, and trips to the corner postbox, he was amazed and thankful she even bothered. Because while he was absolutely incapable of speaking to anyone from his former life, her posts were a tonic, and he was just grateful that she could see past the shithead in him to be willing to continue.

The post that baffled him the most confirmed his apparently very real, very burgeoning renown to which Benoît had alluded, and included newspaper clippings and magazine articles that made his head spin. He hadn't even known that *Murmuration* had opened at the Whitney. Benoît had said something about New York, but considering what Ben did for a living he was an easy man not to believe. Daniel wondered if Nona knew. According to Harper the exhibit was huge, with every name in the business in attendance on opening night, and apparently their conspicuous absences from it had generated as big a buzz as the work itself. They were the Bobby Fischers of the art world.

The Whitechapel Gallery in London was its next stop. His hometown. He was a bit anxious at the prospect, to say the least. What if his father saw his name in a newspaper there? Or came seeking him, desiring some maudlin, drunken reunion after thirty years? He was afraid to know, honestly, if Franklin and Camilla were even still alive.

Harper never mentioned Nona in her letters, but he knew they regularly corresponded. Or maybe his wife had already gone back to the States. He'd never even considered that.

After leaving the In-Ex office, he met Benoît for lunch on the Boulevard Haussmann. Ben promptly showed Daniel a copy of *Murmuration*. Big. Garish. A proud cockstrutter of a book.

"Why didn't you tell me you were gonna order this? I could've gotten one for you."

"I didn't order it. I just walked into the Louvre bookstore and bought it."

"Careful, Ben, you're talking out of the side of your con-artist's mouth again."

"What are you talking about?"

"The exhibit hasn't even come here."

Benoît just shrugged his shoulders.

If this was true, and his book really was in Paris now, then this growing celebrity was going to prove a bit unnerving. He couldn't very well be left alone with his new life and self-destructive tendencies if he was going to be watched by all, could he?

"You don't believe me? Look for yourself."

Benoît opened the book and showed Daniel the text, all in French. Daniel had known from Harper that the book was scheduled to be released internationally, but had no idea it was already happening. Now, holding the proof in his hands, his head reeled with just the tiniest bit of frightened intoxication.

Benoît wanted him to autograph it, but he promptly lectured that the book Ben should be looking for was *The Assassination of Gabriel Champion* by Nona Childe.

"Nona Childe, your ex-wife, no? She's good," Ben offered, gesturing to the book. "So is the suicidal poet. You say she has a book of her own?"

Benoît often inspired the desire for strangulation. Besides which, regarding Ben's *ex-wife* qualifier, Daniel was utterly unprepared for anyone's assumption that he was no longer married. Except that, of course, why would Benoît think anything else?

"Bloody Hell, Ben. Are you so like every other ordinary person in this world that you don't bother to expose yourself to anything beyond your own immediate interests? You should know who Nona Childe is from more than just my little coffee table contrivance. There was a time not that long ago when her book was tucked under everyone's arm walking. She's been a writer of weight long before there ever was a *Murmuration*. And for that matter, I'm gonna sit you down and plop a pile of Arthur Hughes Dufresne's works in front of you too. Which, by the way, is his name. Not Suicidal Poet. He's not a headline. There's a world of beauties out there, Ben, and if you plan to paint then you'd better goddamned well open your bloody eyes."

He could get so angry with Benoît, and it wouldn't get Ben the least bit irritated. Daniel could spit phlegm, and to Ben he'd be spitting gold. He did not want this pedestal.

He autographed Benoît's book with annoyed flourish and walked him directly across the street to a small bookshop, where they purchased a paperback of *Champion*. He didn't dare tell Benoît that Nona Childe was right here in this city, as well, or the flood of questions would come pouring upon his head of why he and his wife would have bothered to travel across the ocean to this place, together, only to live estranged. In fact, the more he thought it outright to himself, the more ridiculous their predicament seemed.

What he was even more unprepared for were Benoît's questions about the other *Murmuration* writer. The poet. The man who had a name. The nightmare.

But Clothilde said you never ask questions. Please, go back to being THAT Ben.

"All the articles I've read say that he shot himself," Ben pressed. "Is it true? Were you close? Why was he so troubled? How did it happen? Who is he anyway? Where did he come from? How did you know him? Whatwhatwhatwhatwhatwhat whywhywhy!!!!!"

"If you want to know about him, read him. I've stacks," was all Daniel could offer, dizzied from the questions. He was weary suddenly. Too much of this damned day kept trying to convince him at every turn that he was on his way to a life of fame he no longer had a stomach for, and shoving the memory of his failed marriage and lost brother into his thoughts.

It was definitely time for a drink.

SIXTY FIVE

It became eight in the morning, and Nona and René were still at it. Her right leg had a kink in it, her insides were raw and stinging, her buttocks had red slap marks across them, and she was whipped into exhaustion. And he was whipped. And they were determined to whip each other into a pudding.

She felt stoned, but no mind-altering chemical had put her in this state. She swore she saw the ceiling move in a trippy wave, as she listened for her greater self to speak out and tell her to quit all this.

When a key was heard in the front door lock, and suddenly Mimi was standing in the harshness of morning light, casting a shadow over them, their world froze. The sudden silence pulsated with sharp breaths. Such a concert. And Nona knew she was at the very nadir of life when all she could think in this panicked instant, far beyond that of having betrayed her friend, was that she loved being caught.

To be discovered in the drench of their thick-smelling sex, with her legs wrapped around his torso and her cunt fairly biting his shaft, which was hard for her (*not you, Mimi!*), was too irresistibly coaxing. To not be the outsider, this time, looking in. In this moment of Nona's panic and her regret and her self-disgust — after all, this wasn't the first of such scenarios for her — and her viler instincts to stick her tongue out at Mimi like a vengeful child, she was the center of the world.

She couldn't read Mimi, which alarmed her. Mimi seemed unmoved. René's reaction was even odder. Calm.

He was, of course, still bolted to Nona. And as the minute passed that brought Nona frightfully close to a stroke, René assessed their predicament just as nonchalantly as he had answered the door hours before. With no trace of regret, he leaned in to caress her face and give her a gentle kiss, sucking at her bottom lip as he came away from it, and slid his cock casually out of her. Nona's legs instantly retracted inward, like a dying spider, and she pulled the covers over her naked self.

This confounding moment radically countered the squall that had blasted through Arthur's apartment on that unspeakable day. Daniel had been a mushroom cloud. One has no time to think out a plan of reaction in that circumstance, for limbs and torsos and bulging eyes and bloody, decapitated heads are flying this way and that. One simply acts to survive. Here, now, was baffling at best.

As René pulled his naked body off the bed, and shook a kink out of his own leg, Nona stared at Mimi, heart nearly tripped, trying furiously to get inside Mimi's head. René stumbled off to the bathroom without a word Mimi's way, but giving her a kiss, too, as he passed, which made Nona's eyes blink.

With only the two women now facing each other, she wondered if Mimi was waiting for her to speak, to offer her excuses, her lies, her blubbering apologies. She'd do it if Mimi wanted. She would beg on hands and knees for Mimi's forgiveness, as she'd done with Daniel, because even as much as she'd had an awful moment of loving the moment, her heart was breaking to have broken Mimi's.

She buried her face in one hand, which propped itself on a drawn-up knee, and cried. She didn't want to cry. She wanted to be a bad-ass bitch and stroll out of here with an attitude, and a chip, and a snapped finger, and a *whatever*. But she couldn't. She'd never been that woman. That woman was far more equipped for treason than this conflicted one.

"Why are you crying?" Mimi asked.

Nona looked up flummoxed. Why was Mimi talking to her without even the hint of rancor?

Mimi knelt to sit on the edge of the bed, which smelled so thickly of sex that Nona almost gagged to know that Mimi had to smell it too. Mimi brought her hand up to Nona's wet face and caressed it. Instinctively, her own hand closed on Mimi's, and she cried even harder.

"*Non, joliesse*. Oh, my *woudit*," Mimi sighed, with offerings of tiny kisses on Nona's face. There was such a sweet bend in the sound, and the seductive mixture of Mimi's many languages, and the absolute absence of hurt. Between it all, Nona was just about unglued.

Mimi's hands brought Nona's down from her face, which forced both pairs of eyes to meet, to regard each other, to determine what each could buttress. And in one considered move, Mimi leaned in and kissed Nona's mouth. A kiss that lingered, even grew.

Nona was shaking and panicked and confused. To touch a woman in this way was confounding. There was not the thickness of a massive chest cavity, and a firm trunk, and a blunt piercing, and all that went with touching a man. But Mimi, who clearly knew this territory well, guided her. Nona closed her eyes, and before she knew it Mimi had undressed to join her. She felt the dip in Mimi's waist, the swell of buttocks, the smoothness of skin, which did not erupt in tiny hairs all about it, as a man's did, but had the gentle constancy of silk. The women wrapped themselves in each other, one pair of curved hips against another, and without the familiar sforzando of male ramming.

What was this bizarre chain of events? Why was she having her achy pleasures with René one minute, and allowing her heterosexual self to be sweetly ravished by this woman the next? And why were one and the other being tolerated, fostered even, by either of her friends?

She began to suspect that she was the toy, passed from one child to the next, set up for some delirious orgy that had been planned all along, a plot that she had simply walked neatly into. If it were so, then it was a bewitching set-up and she seemed to be willing. When she looked up and saw the still naked René watching in the doorway, cigarette in hand, she gleaned delight from his face.

Hers and Mimi's wasn't the wild romp that she and René had just indulged in for the past several hours, but was a concentrated meditation. They lay on René's mattress, four legs intertwined, as René left them to their privacy. She imagined, in this indulgent moment, that in an earlier century she and Mimi would have been sketched and watercolored by Rodin, who loved drawing brown women. Or by Millet, who dealt in earthy subjects. An odd thought struck her, one that didn't belong: Were Daniel here, he'd have painted a masterpiece.

As she later taxied home, she felt pricked and ionized, shifting forward in her seat and clutching the driver's seatback with her jittery hands, trying to decipher her evening, morning, day. It had been twenty-four hours since she'd last slept, and the thrilling turbulence of those twenty-four hours raced through her like a bolt of lightning and replayed itself over and again in a loop. She was weirdly high. And itchy to write like never before.

SIXTY SIX

The conversation that Daniel and Benoît entered upon at Le Bar Bachon, after a day of roaming bookstores, involved some various riffs on critical popularity.

"—And he was told he only had one year to live," said Marcello.

They joined the party and ordered shots. Daniel had to down two and request a third before he could effectively tune in to the roundtable.

After his head felt properly slapped, he turned his attentions toward Corky.

"Every artist should be told he only has a year to live," Corky decreed. "That'll light a fire under somebody's stagnant ass, for sure. Mortality is the demon artists fear most. No wonder he wrote ten fuckin' novels in one year."

"Except that it made him a cynical bastard," chimed Uli.

"He pro'ly arready was."

"Ah, but monsieur, you are contradicting yourself by saying that on the one hand he was always cynical, when on the other that he was searching desperately for his immortality by writing all of those novels in one year. Cynics are not the ones searching for spiritual meaning."

"Are you fuckin' nuts? They're the ones searchin' for it the most! Don't let the hide fool you. Cuz, all the fuck cynicism is…is armor against some kinda wound. And anybody with a wound is gonna be searchin'."

"Uli, *mon cher*," Marcello chimed in, "being told he was dying is not what made him cynical. Being told it was all a mistake, that the doctors were wrong, that he would live, after all, this is what made him cynical."

"And to you, my darling, I would ask this," Uli returned affectionately. "If the doctors told YOU they were wrong, would you become a cynic?"

With a lover newly in the picture, every conversation now insisted on incorporating the condemnation of the HIV that was Marcello's reality, much to her non-attention-loving chagrin. And it became everyone else's job, a favor secretly begged by Marcello, to gently nudge the conversation away from it.

Daniel and Benoît jumped into the fray, and to the nudging task, without skipping a beat.

"Why are any of you assuming he was a cynic, at all?" asked Daniel, toward this debate they'd begun two nights before on one of Daniel's favorite writers.

"Come now," barked Uli, "who but a cynic would smash the beauty and meaning of critical theory to dust by critiquing his own books?"

"A simple opportunist," Daniel answered.

"It was such a brilliant set-up, really," offered Benoît. "I wish I'd thought of it. His publisher puts out all ten books at the same time, under ten different pseudonyms. Then the writer, himself, gets a job reviewing books for a major newspaper, under his own name, and among the books that come to him are HIS OWN, only the newspaper doesn't know this—"

"Are you saying that the publisher and writer planned this ruse purposefully?" asked Marcello of Benoît, and clenching the hand of her beautiful Uli.

"Well, that's not really known, is it?" Benoît answered. "But planned or accidental, the set-up was more perfect than perfection. And in his shoes, who here wouldn't have taken full advantage, as he did, and given yourself glowing reviews, insuring increased sales, and the popularity and success that a great review can give you? It put food on his table and probably more than a few diamonds on his wife's neck, you can be sure. Daniel is right. If he was a real cynic, he would've denounced his own books—"

This made them all laugh, which only fueled Ben's fun.

"—He would've ranted on and on about the triteness and the shallowness of their contents. *They read as if they've been cranked out ten at a time!*"

Benoît gesticulated grandly, with the circle in hysterics.

"He would have been showing how easy it is to create bullshit. Easier still for us ridiculous humans to buy it. THAT'S the true cynic. He was, as Daniel said, at best an opportunist."

"Is this the artist in you speaking?" asked Marcello, slyly. "Or the con-artist?"

"Exactly!" Uli added. "Because, there is no purity in your scenario."

"They are both me, dearest 'Cello, because they are one and the same. And to you, Uli, I say that there is no such thing as purity of critical theory. I'll say it again. I believe in bullshit. In fact, I'm going to start a church of bullshit—"

This busted the table up a second time. Benoît was in his element.

"—with bullshit followers, and men of the bullshit cloth, giving spiritual instruction in the practice OF…"

Upon Ben's conducting gesticulations, the whole table shouted, "BULLSHIT!"

Then from Benoît, more seriously: "This man can review his own work and call it brilliant. And simply because he deems it so, it suddenly becomes an invaluable piece of work. Don't think he wasn't *laughing all the way to the bank*', as the Americans say, at the gullibility of human beings and the unfounded power of critics. This very scenario proves that critical theory is fruitless, even dangerous, when it can be this easily manipulated."

"Hallelujah!" Daniel interjected. "We rely so helplessly on criticism and analysis, and give it so much omnipotence that it can shape a whole century's worth of art with one all-powerful word from Diderot, or Baudelaire, or, or, or…Siskel and Ebert, for chrissake!"

"Who?"

"Who?"

"Who?" the owls all cooed.

Corky laughed like jolly old St. Nick.

"Exactly! Goddamn, Danny, you fuckin' goofball. Exactly. So fuck 'em all!"

The entire table boisterously clinked their glasses and guzzled their spirits, except for Uli, who was not buying any of it. But then Uli was the single non-artist at the table.

"I think you are all full of shit," he threw their way. "It is only the sour grapes in each of you that make you thumb your nose at critical theory, because what you do are the targets. And each one of you has, at some time, been torn to shreds by a critic. Therefore it becomes easy to say that it is meaningless."

"So, are you saying that we should do cartwheels to tailor our work to meet the personal tastes and fetishes of a few uncredentialed reviewers," argued Benoît, "who, today, say it should be green, when tomorrow say '*now*

RED is what's in'?"

"I am saying," answered Uli, "that were it not for the Diderots and the Baudelaires, we in the modern world would have no structured understanding from which even to form our own. It is easy to dismiss something because it does not suit your ego's end. Yet, truly, critical analysis of art is quite crucial in keeping thought alive."

The argument would never end, and they all knew it to be so, and that wasn't really the point. They were awake, thinking, questioning, having the time of their lives, being the very critics they had just derided, which only illustrated Uli's point — even if they would be loath to admit it — that because of their opinions, thought was indeed alive.

A moment's satisfaction filled up the hollow of Daniel's caved chest, as he caught a glimmer, rare any longer, of what it was like to feel rich and vital again. It was the very sort of conversation in which his old Los Angeles cadre would've engaged. And at that thought, the moment was gone. Replaced with the pang of a wistful nostalgia.

SIXTY SEVEN

"What made it flawed for me," Fairuza began over lunch, "was its lack of resolution."

"What do you mean?" Nona asked.

"Don't get me wrong, I think you're a wonderful writer. It's just, it's not for me, this brand of art that just lays a problem out on the table, with no hope for a solution accompanying it. That's the reason I didn't especially care for *1984*. Here was this provocative and scary probability, and at the end Orwell simply says, *'Well there it is, people, deal with it.'* You walk away from that book with a new contempt for life. How does that serve anyone? Always, in the end, there has to exist that seed that promises and reminds that life is ultimately beautiful. Because, if not, then what's the reason to go on? Is that the impact you want from yours?"

Orwell's wasn't the only book Fairuza hadn't particularly cared for, in spite of her condescending qualifier.

Nona had encouraged her to be honest about *Champion*. What's the old adage? Be careful what you ask for? She was in no mood today for a critical slaying. She was already feeling dubious about her wild new sex life, which she could not shake from her thoughts, and which she knew would be fervently criticized by Fairuza, if Fairuza ever found out. And now her book was to take a lashing too?

"Fairuza, art that lays a scenario on the table and leaves it to thinking minds to decipher is the best kind of provocation. It incites thought and question and a dialectic. That's what makes Orwell so powerful. He creates this dystopia as a cautionary tale, which, by the way, is a perfectly legitimate literary device, as it serves up revelation. Are we supposed to only fill our libraries and museums and movie houses and concert halls with expressions that try to make us believe that it's all just a wonderful life? When, of course, that isn't so? What, then, gets provoked in us? We walk around with a false sense of ignorant bliss."

"You're missing my point," Fairuza tossed back.

At that, it was time to order another bottle of wine to drown it all out. Today was Fairuza's birthday, and they were gaily knocking heads (though Fairuza was significantly gayer about it than she) at the Jules Verne, Nona's treat, with their window seat and the shadow of the southeast grid of the Eiffel Tower looming over them.

"I'm not saying I only believe in happy endings and an idealist's portrait of the world according to Frank Capra," Fairuza continued. "Give me grim. Give me foreboding. But for the love of God, don't make me do all the work in finding the pearl. And the pearl must be found, you do realize that, right?"

Nona's eyes grew wide. *You're going to tell me about the rules of writing?*

"Fairuza, this may come as a shock to you, but art is not obligated to uplift. It is only obligated to awaken. And once awakened, it's up to YOU, now armed, to determine how it's fed you, and to cultivate your own state of grace."

"I beg to differ. I think an artist IS obligated to offer some glimmer of hope, some tool of beautiful irony or metaphor that renders the grim and foreboding only part of a grander scheme, which allows us to finally let go of this breath we've been holding. In *Champion*, what point are you making to finally have Speck turn the gun on himself? What's been achieved? Does he, the misguided one, the one who in drama has the lesson to learn, ever come to understand what makes the artist? His suicide makes every prior effort of his completely meaningless. And from a metaphorical standpoint, it is the ultimate minus. The negation of all things beautiful, all things art."

Nona's head bogged down with thoughts of Arthur.

"Your point, Nona, would seem to be that all, in the final chapter, is hopeless, and without a lesson learned. Ironic, isn't it?" Fairuza asked, smiling, and holding her hands out, as if introducing Nona to an audience. "The artist riffing on an artless world."

The girl was feeling clever.

"Well, I don't believe in an artless world," Fairuza continued. "So give me this explosive, suffering soul who only wants to create, BUT give him a dawning that is the result of his insane kidnapping and tormenting. Let the crime exist for a more elevated reason than just titillation."

"Titillation is not how I operate," Nona bit, defensively. "Give me a little credit. The most obvious and predictable character to have evolve is Speck. But fuck the predictable! We get enough of that on television. Speck is meant to be the catalyst for someone else's enlightenment. An unrecognized divinity, the way Christ was, or Joan of Arc. In Christ's day, his divinity was disguised in the robes of an ordinary teacher. In Joan's time, hers was the cloak of an ordinary soldier. What do we identify with today, in this age of the loner sociopath who wants to explode on society? Will Speck is divinity disguised in the garb of your ordinary outcast. There's your irony for you, Fairuza. And the one whose change occurs, because of Speck's actions, is Champion."

"But that position makes Speck's life meaningless."

"Not a bit. It makes him a martyr in the classic sense. He's never made aware of his own aftermath, his power to awaken."

"Martyrs don't choose death, Nona. They fight till death chooses them."

"Speck does fight till death chooses him. If suicides could speak, they would tell you that they had exhausted all attempts to live in the world until there was no choice!"

A huge wrinkle creased Fairuza's forehead.

"I just can't find satisfaction in that."

"Then what would be your satisfaction?"

"That Speck find HIS art because of this act."

"Oh, give me a break! And all he has to do is click his heals three times?" Nona blurted sarcastically. "Then I'd be sending the message that all any lost soul really needs to do, to find his way, is to commit a crime. Just kidnap somebody and put a gun to their head. That'll bring you enlightenment. That's not the statement I want to make."

"No, think about it, Nona. Speck opens Champion's eyes to his own complacency."

"Yes! Exactly! That IS the point I make—"

"No, no, no, no, no, no, let me finish. Take it one step further. In turn, that epiphany propels the teacher out of Champion that Speck needed him to be in the first place. The dialogue that would ensue, as we watch them both finding their way, teacher and student, would be awesome. The way it's written now, you have a man winning who didn't need a lesson learned in the first place. I mean, you portray Champion as brilliant and self-realized already, right? So then why does the change need to happen in him? You never give Speck that dawning that every protagonist must have. And Speck is your protagonist, Nona. Not Champion. You do realize that, right? I mean, it's easy to call Speck your antagonist, because he's the one with the gun. But it's his story. He's the one we've got to get inside of. Champion is merely this symbol of worship. He's the device. You negate your own protagonist's life from the very first breath to the very last. Even in titling the book *The Assassination of Gabriel Champion*. I mean, I get the clever thing you were going for. The death of artistic urgency, blah, blah, blah. But Speck is the one whose life is sacrificed in this search for truth. He's the one who is assassinated, in a sense, and his name doesn't even merit space in the title. You make Speck nothing, Nona. Even Jesus and Joan—YOUR examples —weren't *nothings*."

SIXTY EIGHT

As far as Daniel was concerned, *The Assassination of Gabriel Champion* should be taught in every art school and be as integral a part of its curriculum as Klee's *On Modern Art* or Shahn's *The Shape of Content.* So if Benoît was expecting Daniel to mentor him, then Benoît would have to read *Champion* first.

"*Mon Dieu!*" was Ben's exclamation after closing the book on the final page. "I can certainly see why this book has meant life and death to you. Every artist needs to be as wide awake as if they had a gun perpetually cocked to their temples."

"Yes! Will Speck is gold, right? Our fear, of course, is that we're the ones holding the gun, instead of the ones being provoked. Speck represents what's basest in our human instincts. To take by force what we are lacking and assume it to be ours for the taking—"

"Exactly! And he SHOULD die in the end, because the death of Will Speck symbolizes the greater death of that instinct to destroy and to usurp, rather than to create and to contribute —"

"Though, by his destroying, something is created. Talk about your final beauty, that it is determined to be found under every wormy rock."

They volleyed like this for hours, and Daniel finally found comfort in having a comrade-in-arms over the book that had upended his life. He turned the whole gang on to Nona's book, in fact, and they promptly tossed aside their current, ongoing literary debate and made *Champion* their new parlor game of choice. They analyzed it. They debated it. They tossed it back and forth like an overused tennis ball. Daniel loved that they all cherished it as much as he did, and that it could be appreciated from as many perspectives as there were pages in the book. Sometimes they'd go at it for days, on a piece they all agreed was an important work.

But there was something else, besides, that was also the reason he relished. He'd been mourning the willful loss of his wife, and had been unsuccessful thus far in rescuing himself from that self-inflicted quandary. So, in a certain sense, this animal that lived and breathed and called itself literary discourse succeeded in giving him his wife back. She was in the room with him whenever *Champion* was discussed, because *Champion* was her child, a child he had tried to adopt but had proven a miserable step-parent. He'd never been able to help nurture it, because he'd been too burdened by it.

Now he'd brought the book to others, though it had been his own salvation he'd sought in the gesture. Because of that, between wincing moments of some parable pang, which *Champion* had always given him, he was able to snuggle in the bosom of his wife's spirit as lustfully as he would his wife's bosom, if only he'd had the spine to go and find her.

"It's about redemption!"

"It's about love and death!"

"It's the ultimate peek into the torments of the creative process!"

"It's the search for God!"

Delirious was this dialogue, made even more so when the rounds of absinthe would commence. Some of the theories were insane, some laughable, some truly tantalizing, but the coterie feasted on the delights of exercising their heads, and no one was more falsely fulfilled than Daniel. Falsely, at least with regard to himself, because the nights in his flat that followed evenings with the gang at Le Bar Bachon were always hollow and painful, especially if the earlier evening had included a dense *Champion*-fest. In his loneliness, which would be even bleaker when he'd drag some woman home with him, Daniel would recall how it felt to hold his wife, while not actually going to find her so that he could really hold her. He'd sit against his far north wall, and draw on that image like a drag from a spliff, and stare forward, entertaining some fantasy of her and him.

He had learned to conjure her easily, without so much as a cockeyed glance, and had become somewhat skilled at tuning out the blow jobs, which were all he ever really wanted from the women he'd pick up. Too much effort to shag when his spirit was this broken. But every time he was close to arousing himself at the notion of going to find Nona, a pang would attack, usually involving thoughts of Arthur's death. A night still didn't go by without it invading his dreams, the image warping more garish each time, until a night didn't go by, as well, without padding his slumber with several stiff shots to help kill his consciousness. That would, of course, always follow an evening at Le Bachon, which was already consumed with much drink. His hands shook all the time now, and he could never approach Nona in this state.

His most recent efforts at painting were producing a body of work he doubted his wife would applaud. The jittery constancy he was getting on canvas was unrecognizable to him. It was someone else's hands doing this, he'd say to himself, then pose the question: Was severe self-ruining and madness what gave Van Gogh his squiggles? Or Seurat his dots?

His efforts looked like that of a psychotic's, muddied and self-pitying and screaming to be saved. No one could possibly look at these canvases and glean anything from them except pitiable concern for the mental state of the artist.

The more he tried to paint, the more nightmares he had. The more he sank into melancholy. The more he drank. The more his ulcers bled. The more his hands shook. And the further away he got from any notion of looking for his wife.

One night in Corky's flat, with only the two of them there, he begged a hit off the old man's opium pipe. Corky had tried to turn him on once before, but Daniel hadn't been able to fathom it. Tonight he was beyond fathoming. He just needed a break from his heartsickness. He was desperate to know ecstasy again, and the absence of distress and ulcer fits and alcoholic shakes and heartbreak and grief. He asked Corky to give him a crash course in the inhaling techniques of the hookah, and before he knew it every microscopic thing in this breathtaking world was suddenly a joy to him. He marveled at the walls, the ceiling, the floor, the air between.

They took a stroll up the hill toward the vineyard, a black and ominous bed at night. His sensations began, one by one, shutting down. Each valve shut like a dungeon door slamming closed. He was keenly aware of the physical sensation of his nerves being clamped off. He could feel the weight of the outside air and the heaviness of gravity. The sky was moonless this night, with a smattering of rolling clouds about it, which followed them. The stars were incredibly bright and growing brighter by the minute. Time elongated, as if a single minute were stretched into a taffy before advancing to the next. The sounds of crickets, the street traffic, the wind, the voices and grunts and coughs of people all around them were suddenly a detailed symphony in his ear.

He had hoped to discover what it would be like to paint in this state, but suddenly realized that he could give two shits about life at this glorious moment. An artist must feel urgency in order to create. No urgency here. And with that dawning came one crucial truth about opium. This thing he was experiencing was no passionate encounter, only the absence of it. There was no curiosity, no fervor or zeal to the queer sensations, only a tepid apathy, a gentle felicity, where every stupid word uttered was easy poetry. This was a feeling so free from concern that he frightened himself that he no longer cared about anything. When every taste, from the hearing and seeing to the doing, was already an experience in great art, when the ordinarily discriminating sensualist in him could now be so effortlessly awed by every flutter, every twitter, what further need was there to seek passion out?

He was suddenly scared to death and begging to be released from this painless paradise in which he could no longer feel even the ends of his fingertips without the accompanying tingle. Thought after thought only tripped over the next, or collided into the last, a lazy labyrinth of rowed dominoes, careening haphazardly, one into the other, laying the whole piece down flat.

In all the hours of this bizarre journey, he never did pick up a paint brush. Never got to know what it might be like to create without a care in the world. God help him, he never wanted to know. Never wanted to lose his sense of Champion.

SIXTY NINE

Mimi got up to light a pipe of hash, and Nona smoked with her, sucking huge drags from René's pipe and handing it back. They hung lazily about this drizzly morning in René's apartment, watching the rains outside his window, while he worked his shift at Les Deux Magot, and were to meet him there for breakfast after some time alone.

It was odd this arrangement the three of them had seemed to settle into without so much as a list of rules to say, *"This is allowed,"* or *"That is not allowed."* Each of them would make way for the privacy of the other two, in every combination, and this morning was for her and Mimi. They were wild and wanton and nestling into their romantic threesome as if they'd been doing it all their lives. And for all Nona knew, those two probably had been.

In the weeks that followed their first encounter, they had all but abandoned Fairuza, who'd been trying damned hard to be Nona's saving grace and the one person left in her life to offer up intellectual stimulation. Nona must've suddenly been afraid of that, because all she had allowed herself to do over time was get lost in beautiful bodies and horny impulses. She and Fairuza may have shared a pursuance of art; but she, René, and Mimi shared a great fuck. How do you compete with that?

She'd felt especially wounded by Fairuza for criticizing *Champion*, as though it weren't Fairuza's right to have an opinion. Something was changing in Nona. She no longer relished growth and challenge, as she once had. Her only interest, any longer, seemed to be for the immediate enticement, the automatic accolade, the quickie. Yet always the stroll home at the end of a day with the knot in her gut that warned her she was no longer listening to her greater self. That voice had been replaced by a high-pitched, drunken, warbling coloratura, wailing on about loss and entitlement.

Fairuza's comments had been naïve, Nona rationalized, then proceeded to compensate for that defensiveness by frantically scribbling down anything on the pretense that she was writing again. Except that because she resented it for interrupting her partying life, the challenge was met with anger instead of exuberance.

Every day since their lunch Nona opened up her novel and faced it. It was her first time reading it in years. Then the notebooks got opened up, and the scribbling commenced. In one were all of her attempts at saving *Champion*, her half-hearted endeavors at supplying the beauty that Fairuza had charged was missing. In another was her answer to that, her *"screw you"* to Fairuza. She brazenly broke every rule thought crucial for writing effective prose. No compositional balance, no narrative arc, no irony, no development and resolve, no clarity of voice. It may have been slaphappy and lunatic, but she was pissed off and willing.

She even made words up, à la Lewis Carroll or Anthony Burgess, created her own spelling system à la Ntozake Shange, and strung the whole lot of it together in nonsensical ways. She decided to be a barbaric enemy of grammar and the dictionary, as they weren't nearly massive enough in their provisions to accommodate all she had to say. Words — convention and *in*vention — were spattered to the winds willy-nilly. Jackson Pollock had nothing on Nona Childe.

She was ready to pounce these days. She was angry at her husband, at Fairuza, at *Champion*, maybe even at René and Mimi, and taking it out on them by fucking them, one and the other, without the slightest offering of love, and even angrier still that that's exactly the way those two wanted it. They had no interest in engaging. And periodically she also had to stop her ranting and correct herself, as she did right now. René, Mimi, and Fairuza were her dear friends. They had willingly invited her into their lives when she'd been at her lowest, and had offered her their fellowship. None of them were to blame for anything. It was her. Only her. She was simply on the verge.

She sucked up the contents of René's hash pipe as though she would die to be denied it, grabbed Mimi by the nape of the neck, kissed the girl, and felt ready to eat a slaughterhouse of beef, as she bade Mimi get dressed so they could go consume a massive breakfast.

When they arrived at Les Deux Magots, they took a table on the wet sidewalk, as the rain had just let up, and she shared with Mimi the newest bits of prose she'd been experimenting with, as René buzzed his way around the crowded café.

"Tell me what you think, Mimi. I'm feeling lit these days, like I just want to scream, you know? I feel hit by God, or something, like…I feel like a Holy Roller—"

Mimi looked quizzical.

"—It's a, a, a Southern thing. An American thing. Anyway, listen to this. What do you think?"

She read from a dog-eared notepad, semi-loudly over the din of French grunts and exclamations. What she'd written was only a beginning, hardly refined yet, but she gripped her notebook as if it were a bottle that would either soothe or kill her, and recited to Mimi all the mess she'd been scribbling. She even gave the recitation a little funereal, hip-hop flavor, clearly entertaining visions of Jim Carroll. Or Tupac. She played with words and twisted institutions into pretzels, bouncing from one theme to the next, without so much as a traffic warning. It wasn't remotely the focused meditation that had always been her method, where she carefully drafted outlines and made sure all of the elements of composition were in place. She was wired and unhinged, and sort of proud of herself for stepping out of her comfort zone.

When she finally looked up from her high-strung rap-a-thon, Mimi's head was turned, trying to get René's attention. Mimi suddenly turned back when she heard Nona's voice cease, and gave a sheepish smile, clearly asserting, *don't worry, I really am listening.*

"So, what do you think?" Nona asked, on the verge of fretting that Mimi had barely bothered to pay attention.

Mimi looked befuddled.

"I don't—I'm not sure I really understand it," Mimi confessed. "What is it?"

Goddamn it, don't make me have to work this hard!

Oh, if that sweet voice and that accent weren't so arousing Nona would've jumped up and stormed out, leaving Mimi to her air-headedness. Why wasn't this chick getting it?

"It's—it's—it's—it's—um—um—"

Maybe she wasn't getting it either.

She searched for words in the thick air, hoping to find them in the swirls of cigarette smoke.

"—it's, it's, it's, it's—in my—in my—life right now, just—chaos, this—this—"

"What's making you feel chaos, *woudif?*" Mimi interrupted, mercifully rescuing Nona from her idiotic stuttering.

I don't want a therapist, damn it! I want a fellow soldier in this war for art! But Mimi was no Fairuza. Mimi didn't have a clue what art was for.

"Aren't you having a good time with us?" Mimi continued.

Ever the vapid hedonist. Huh, sweetie?

"—I mean, I know there is the matter of your husband—"

Was that as deeply as Mimi knew her? Marital estrangement was but the beginning of it. Nona had lost her art and her soul, and was fighting like a street brawler to get it all back again, and losing the battle, and being shown that by Fairuza, and now *THIS CHICK DOESN'T GET IT EITHER?*

"Don't you get any gut sense from it at all?" Nona asked, calmly, leaving the rages to her own private thoughts.

Mimi seemed weary, probably wondering why Nona was throwing this head trip her way, after they'd just come from making pleasant love, and sitting before a pleasant breakfast, and about to engage in a pleasant day with their pleasant shared boyfriend.

"Oh, Nona, I don't know. It's too over my head, I guess," Mimi offered, even in this instant taking up the blame herself. Maybe it wasn't over Mimi's head. Maybe it was just mindless drivel, and dear Mimi was simply too kind to ever say it. But all Nona wanted to do was take her home, and fuck her, and tell her to shut up and stop trying to think, and disrespect her, and treat her the way bastards treat their women.

Instead, she told Mimi not to worry. She did decide, however, that she needed to be alone, and so she bade them both goodbye until tonight, when the three would meet up at a new bar in Place Pigalle, grabbed her umbrella, and took her wet walk up St-Germain toward the river.

Though she'd been few places in her life, she felt certain that there was no city lovelier for strolling in the rain than Paris. Even in her bleakest moments, it served as balm. She could never resist the kiosks that lined the Quai and sold prints and postcards of all the artist greats, and seemed always open no matter the weather. She stopped to browse, envisioning her lifelong fantasia of sitting for the likes of Braque or Picasso, and realized that she hadn't run that reel in a long time. Not since being painted by Cross. She smiled at the faraway moment, so far away that she wondered if she'd only dreamt that life, and the smile faded.

Suddenly she thought of the twins, her beloved Basquiats, whom she'd never before left alone for this long. Six months had past since the life she'd known in Los Angeles, and there had never been a symbol more emblematic of that life than her *deux ange*s. They had symbolized her lust for life and ridiculous flights of fancy. And of those traits she was presently empty, or quickly emptying. Who, today, got to gaze upon the twins' magnificence and emerge transformed? They hung on a lonely wall of a closed up house in Movie Star Town and entertained rude darkness instead.

When she approached the Seine, she glanced over the Pont de la Concorde and wondered if anyone would ever find her journals should she decide to jump. It was only a rhetorical thought, a wink of self-pity. Yet, just as Daniel had prophesied, she seemed to be depending on those journals to hail her, because at this moment she couldn't find any other way to reclaim the meaning in her life.

SEVENTY

He couldn't remember how long the high lasted. Only that at some point he fell asleep, and when he opened his eyes onto the sunlight his beautiful opium adventure was but a memory. He felt no repercussions, as in alcoholic hangovers or post-coke crashes. He was simply void and back to his old self, which was growing older every day.

After a shower in the curtainless basin that always soaked his entire bathroom, he went to Benoît's flat to sit for a series Ben was working on. The newest gimmick for Ben was that he wanted to paint painters. Ben loved a certain school and had spent the better part of his adult life honing a look to his work that could only be described as an attempt at Twombly or de Kooning. The body of work Daniel had seen so far had been a chaotic scream, a hue-fest Rorschach meant to awaken the darkest pathologies. Potent enough, sure. But Ben's problem, and Daniel had tried on more than one occasion to express this as delicately as possible, was that the younger had yet to find his own voice. He was merely copping. It was de Kooning's chaotic scream, down to the stroke, not Belargent's.

Ben was taking a class in nude studies and seemed to be constantly in battle with his instructor, who simply wanted Ben to release all of his old notions and comfortable habits. But Ben fought him at every turn.

"I don't do representational work. Leave that to advertisers and comic strippers. It's a bore. If I want my nude to look exactly like the nude standing there, I can just snap a photograph of her. *Fait accompli!*"

Ben's instructor tried to explain to him that Realism didn't have to be his chosen approach.

"Go the way you will, but go that way out of choice. Picasso went the way of his abstractions because the literal eventually stopped speaking to him and a more psychologically symbolic vision screamed his name. Go that way because it screams your name, not because you have no skill or craft with which to go any other. It's easy to scribble nonsense and throw some paint around and say that it symbolizes something, because who is to negate you? Or to draw some stick figures and claim that its crude simplicity is making a statement, when, really, its crudeness is because it is the only thing your pen and hand can accomplish. There is no purity in that kind of deceit."

Of course this teacher had no idea to whom he was speaking. Benoît Belargent, master forger and crowned pirate, was a devout believer in deceit, and this preaching only piqued his stance. It annoyed Daniel. There was gold in what Ben's instructor had to offer him, but Ben couldn't hear it. Today, as Daniel perused this current series that he was sitting for, he realized that the newest artist Benoît was trying to cop was Daniel Cross.

So, after six months of being in Paris, and now the Christmas season was upon them and the crowds ever more oppressive, Daniel finally took himself to the Musée d'Orsay and dragged Ben's obstinate ass with him. Ben needed to see what Daniel already knew. He literally snatched Ben's paintbrush from his hand and led him there bodily.

Upon approaching their first Cèzanne of the day, Daniel stopped stunned in his tracks and did what he knew he'd do and had avoided all these months. He choked up instantly, recalling every serenity he'd ever felt in a long life of few. Including the night before, with Corky's pipe. Including the first time Yvette the Whore took him as a boy to see these very Impressionists, and then took him to her bosom. Including that first evening with Nona, almost four years ago now. Opium, be damned. Art was his drug of choice. He finally let go of the breath he'd been holding for far too long.

"The Impressionists? Really?" asked Ben, assaulting Daniel's moment. "You brought me here to school me with the Impressionists? You have got to be kidding. They only replicate landscapes. Pretty, I'll give you that, but certainly offering no new takes on life."

"On the contrary, Ben. They were the rebels of their era. To you a simple landscape is nothing bold, hardly a *Piss Christ*. But in their day, the job of the artist was to hail the saints and nobles. The ordinary life of a field worker who might be on the verge of revolt, or a pair of nude lovers taking a picnic…these were not fit subject-matter for a painting. And these artists challenged that. They offered in their freely brushed strokes and shadings an emotional impression of nature in an era where emotions were considered dirty laundry, certainly not to be aired in public, rather than the realist canonization of subjects, which was the dictated school of the times. You don't have to be personally struck by them, Ben, but for God's sake realize what they are. In their day, they were as rebellious as you. D'you think you were the first artist to ever rile a critic? Shake up a society?"

"Hardly me. I'm nothing. But the artists I admire—"

"The artists you admire should include the Impressionists. They changed the face and shape of art. The very thing every artist should pray he is able to do in his lifetime. If not love them, which you are not obligated to do, at least *get* them."

Though how anyone could not love them was beyond Daniel. As for his own obstinate self, there was no turning back now. He had ignored this place and all the others, because he'd feared that seeing these works up close and personal would only dishearten him. Not so. He was — as art has always intended — transformed.

He'd started out this day by trying to teach Ben a lesson, and his own was now slapping him in the face. He sat on a bench in this magnanimous converted train station and wept. Not only from the sway of this rich palace, but from the enormity of his deeds all these months. He had chosen to ignore art. Then love. But the splendor of this vaulted Heaven would no longer allow him to ignore.

The Louvre was next. The Grand Palais. The Pompidou. The Musée Picasso, which housed *The Muse*, the very masterpiece he'd described to Nona the day he'd met her, as the painting he would probably never get to see in his lifetime.

He spent days, which turned into weeks, loitering the seemingly endless halls that housed what was religion to him. He went with Ben or he went alone because, truth told, this trek was no longer about Ben. He deliriously poured these artists over him, like a baptismal water, and drank up their very presence, which dripped from every pore of every masterpiece. Even the cathedrals that sprinkled Paris, the great ones to the dilapidated, had ancient frescoes hidden in their naves and chancels, where the unsuspecting art lover might never think to look. He haunted every one of those cathedrals, like some fevered Quasimodo, drinking it up and being replenished.

For these secret treasures his heart broke. Largely neglected and forgotten, especially in the smaller churches, many of the paintings were faded and faint now, the plaster on the frescoes peeling away in huge chunks, toward one day the promise of being completely disintegrated. What would happen if the day were to come when all the art of the world simply peeled itself away from age and neglect?

Thank God there were still artists who would create even as life came crashing down around them, who were not indulgent brooders like him, who were unrelenting and indomitable, who were the blessed assurance that this world would always be artful. He wanted to be counted among them.

In the weeks to follow, he took deep breaths and tried to remember what was important. He moved slowly, cautiously, afraid of disturbing the waters in his head, which had been, at least for the present, and mercifully, calmed by his visits to the museums and by the waters outside, which had always inspired.

He was reborn, and itchy to paint. Like a lousy groin he itched. It made him feel like some men, whose chests swelled at the confirmation that they'd just impregnated their women, because it promised them they were still potent, still men. He tried as hard as he could not to judge his shaky efforts too harshly. It was so out of his character to approach life this timidly that he felt like a diapered infant. Was this living? It must've been what rebirth felt like. Taking one's first new steps, wobbling, falling, stumbling back up.

Funny how just when his life was beginning to feel meaningful again, and just as he was ready to go find his wife, beg her forgiveness, show her that he was attempting to change, to bounce back, and to try and offer her better than he had before — she found him.

SEVENTY ONE

The meeting itself was chance, but not like one finds in a movie — *a bar, a lonely barstool, a lonely barfly, and in she walks.* Nothing like that. Actually when each of them looked up at some point in the evening and caught the other's eye, amidst the hubbub of bar life, they were both already deep into their drink and their respective company at Le Bar Bachon, which was Daniel's regular hangout. And he never, for one second, believed she would ever walk into the dive he now called home.

In the instant of their mutual notice, the glacial spread swelled throughout him and his breathing grew labored and short. To suddenly have it confirmed that his wife was still in this city hit him two ways. He wondered if she was still looking for him, still trying to make their marriage work. Or if she had, as he had, simply fallen through the cracks of Paris's earth and was too numbed from uneasy life to make any kind of meaningful movement.

He had not intended for their reunion to happen this accidentally. He had envisioned a brave and deliberate march her way, to reclaim his bride upon his return from war, to sweep her up into his battle-scarred arms and announce victory. He'd just needed a few drinks to take the edge off first. A few days to muster the bollocks to go home.

Now it was too late to be deliberate, and he hated that any move, at this point, would seem to her a mere afterthought. She had never been an afterthought, but she would have no reason to believe otherwise.

The heat in his face rushed quickly, though whenever he wept lately he never much had the appearance of it, as his eyes were already perpetually reddened and glassed from a fifth-a-day tradition. Only the heaviness in his breathing alarmed Marcello, who sat closest to him in the red leather booth along with the rest of the gang. Marcello placed her hand on his shoulder in the midst of some boisterous argument between Benoît and Corky, but all Daniel could do was adjust his shoulder politely to brush her hand away and indicate that he didn't wish to be noticed. As he glanced at his wife from afar, he knew he was unworthy of approaching.

It was ironic that at this very table sat fans of Nona Childe; he'd seen to that. Yet they would never know her to pass her on a street, and now here she sat, across a room merely, and they would remain unaware.

He wanted to throw himself on her mercy and not let her leave this bar until she forgave him, but she might just spit in his face for being a bastard and storm out. He loathed public scenes like the ones he'd had all of his life, first as a child with his drunken mother any given day of the week, then with Chelsea, and finally with Arthur. One more like those he simply couldn't stomach.

She sat at the bar with a young man and woman. She'd made friends. Of course, why wouldn't she? But it frightened him to think that she might've, as it would mean that she had managed to go on in her life without him. Although a shunned wife who only lay in her bed, day in and day out, never venturing outside, or combing her hair, or bathing, only lying in her grief and loneliness, pining away for him, was not a woman he would love anyway. It was certainly not Nona. He used to think she was delicate, but she turned out to be the most fearless creature he'd ever met. And now he had probably lost her because of it.

It was hard to tell what she thought of seeing him. That the prick is still alive? He couldn't blame her. And he knew he looked bad. He was drinking far too much these days, and was now Corky's reluctant opium pal, who had smuggled some into the American Hospital for him after he'd collapsed one evening from his ulcers. His belly had distended and he'd coughed up blood. He'd been sent home within a few uneventful hours, but had been promised pain. So, Corky took pity on his moaning self by offering him an escape out of his pain. And though he'd sworn off of it beyond that first night, the conversations that could be had with Corky around the pipe had been too fantastic to resist.

In spite of how he knew he must look, he decided to take his chance. When the young couple who sat with her moved to the dance floor to bump and grind as young punks did, he got up quietly and was barely missed, now that the debate between Ben and Corky had turned into a free-for-all. He made his way to the bar and cautiously took a seat next to her. For all of his morose indulgences over these months, which had selfishly involved her, he would fall suppliant and crawl to her forgiveness.

She stared into her drink and breathed as agitatedly as he'd been breathing. Her hands, which clinched her glass, shook. They weren't like the alcoholic shakes his hands displayed; they were the tremor of fear. *My own wife fears me.*

He flashed on Franklin and Camilla. His mother and father had feared each other so intensely that each had kept his and her own gun hidden away. He and his brother had both known about the guns, because each parent had privately confided in the boys, making them swear their allegiance if things got bad.

He wanted to apologize to his wife for having sent them the way of his parents, a way he had sworn they'd never go. *Please don't fear me,* he silently begged. Aloud, all he could offer her was what he'd already offered countless other women in this bar.

SEVENTY TWO

"May I get you another drink?"

The sound of his voice sent a shiver through Nona, pricking her ears. She closed her eyes tightly and clenched her jaw to keep from weeping out loud, but the tears only rolled faster.

When she'd first looked up and seen him across the room, she'd done a double-take because his hair was no longer the shoulder-lengthed swath of unruly waves, a look that had always given him a kind of gothic regality. It was now buzzed close to his head, exposing more gray than black, and with a day's growth about his beautiful face, like some rugged sailor. The man still gave her heart a frantic start.

Every day of their estrangement she'd fantasized about the moment when they'd see each other again. And she never knew whether it would be here in Paris, or back in the States. There'd been so many unknown variables. But the one variable she could never entertain — was never. Instead, she'd clung to weightless fantasy. And had apparently been clinging for all these months without even realizing it. Of course, in every one, they were both tear-drenched happy. Here, now, the moment finally realized, happy just wasn't the right word. It was more like drudging up the spirit of a dead loved one at a séance; fear plays a great part in the excited anticipation. Numbed was perhaps the better word. She had to tell herself repeatedly that this was no apparition trying to scare the wits out of her for all her recent hedonistic indulgences. This was her husband, whom she feared she'd lost forever. And he had willingly, in this unexpected moment, walked over to her.

"No thanks, this is plenty," was all she could give back to his offer. What she wanted to do was strangle him, scream at him, slap him, hold him, love him, enter his life again, and be his wife. She wanted their life back. She wanted to know where he'd been. She wanted to know if he was painting. If he'd made his peace with her. With Arthur. With himself. Or if he was coming over here to say, *"well, as long as you caught me, you might as well sign these divorce papers, sweetie."*

He had walked into this bar with a group of people he seemed genuinely to care about. This was where he'd chosen to be. Not with her, but with them. For all she knew, any one of the women at his table might've been his new reason to be. If one were, that woman would have a lot to learn about him. She'd have to be willing to dust off his demons once in awhile, because he was incapable of dusting off his own. Although, once dusted, one always found the most incredible man beneath. She'd have to make plenty of room for his genius and his passion, to boot, for both were large. But the idea of teacher to a new Mrs. Cross bent Nona sideways and stuck her in the ribs.

After excruciating minutes of gripping her glass and staring into the eye of it, of trying to slow her heart and catch a breath, she finally looked up at him. His health seemed poor. Those beautiful gray eyes, though still powerful and expressive, were now sunken and clouded, and his hands shook so tremulously that she wondered how he could ever paint again. He sat so near to her that she could feel his warm breath, a sensation she never expected to experience again. And his jittery hand moved to place itself on hers. She closed her fingers around his and shuddered at how much his hands trembled. And at how much she still loved them.

She prayed that René and Mimi wouldn't notice him here next to her, that they'd just continue dancing as they did every night. She needed this moment, because who knew what the next would bring?

She and Daniel looked at each other in handholding silence. There was so much to say, but neither knew how to advance. Instead they reverted to silly, first-date rhetoric.

"Would you like to dance?" asked the man who hated dancing.

It was surely that they both just needed to be held, and this was his way of asking without *really* asking. A slow enough song played that they could get away with holding each other in the slightest sway. They moved heedfully from their spot at the bar, perhaps fearing that if one of them made too sudden a move the other might just scamper away.

She recalled the first time they'd taken to a dance floor, nearly four years ago now, at The Factory, after one of Kai's shows. And she found it just the tiniest bit cruel of life's phenomenon that it always made one yearn for a past that was somehow fonder than the present.

Within an instant, she was in his arms. *Home.* After Arthur, she'd stopped believing that she could ever feel at home anywhere again. Perhaps there was life in each of them still.

As 4 Non Blondes pumped through the speaker system, asking *"what's going on?"* in a screaming appeal, and feeling too queerly apropos to this moment, Daniel's head leaned down to bury itself in Nona's neck, and his arms drew her into him. She reached up to put her hand behind his neck, her other wrapping within his, as she leaned her head into his chest, and was overloaded with a wild thankfulness. Suddenly she felt the rhythmic tremble of a man weeping but not wanting to be seen at the deed. It started it up in her. They were a gushy opera, for certain.

She could see from a sideways glance the curious stares of his friends. It was a mixture of knowing and wondering. Had they been aware he was married? Did he still wear his ring? She hadn't bothered to look. Or might she, in their minds, be just some other woman, of the many, that they'd witnessed him pick up in bars?

She closed her eyes to shut out every stinging image, because she couldn't bear to entertain thoughts of his new friends and possible romantic entanglements. She was afraid to know who these people were, who laughed and drank with him and were his new life. And she was just as sure that he wouldn't want to know about hers. She couldn't even see René and Mimi any longer. They'd probably sneaked off to a bathroom somewhere to fornicate against a wall.

Daniel turned his mouth to her ear and whispered something she didn't catch at first, but there was no need to ask him to repeat it, for in another second it was all purged.

"Forgive me," he whispered, every syllable pumped out like a percussive smoke stack. "Please, please, please for…give…me."

He tripped over himself like a child in snotty hysterics — or like a man who had been broken — mumbling it repeatedly. He was surely about to break her, and not just from the squeeze of his embrace.

"Forgive ME," she gave back in a teary whisper.

Before they could even begin to stumble over each other with plea and sympathy, from out of the gaudy blue the violent hand suddenly yanked Daniel by the nape of his collar and away from her, and the fist exploded on his face.   Nona's throat seized to see Daniel hit the ground like a felled boxer, and the glowing flush swelled in her cheeks when she looked up and saw René pounding her husband to a fruity pulp.   Daniel was helpless against this hopped-up twenty-two-year-old.

She and Mimi frantically tried to shove their bodies between them.   It was hard to tell if anyone from Daniel's table had joined the fray, but soon enough the whole place was bedlam.

"What the Hell are you doing!" she screamed at René, once they'd gotten him unglued from Daniel.   Several people were tending to Daniel, who was disoriented on the floor and a bloody mess, while Mimi faced René, trying to shove him back, but René was a roaring ball of masculine fuming who would not be tempered this night.   A true punk.   He got as much joy from this as from anything.

Out of breath and in his full mettle, he yelled back, "He was all over you!"

"What do you mean, he was all ov—oh my God, this is not what you think, René!"

Dear, precious René.   He was actually being chivalrous in a kind of thug way, defending her honor, which was sweet, but he was also beating the crap out of her husband, so she could only be so touched.

They screamed at each other in overlapped babble, while she tried to see if Daniel was all right.   Daniel clung to her even as he was being helped to his feet by a couple of young men, and so much was yelled every which way that she couldn't make out any one coherent thing.   One of the men who'd come to Daniel's aid wanted to start a fight with René, but the surrounding women foiled that idea.   René ignored him, anyway, as he and Nona continued yelling at each other.

"He was harassing you.   Putting his hand all over your ass."

"No, René.   Please.   He was not harassing me.   You don't understand."

One of the young men, perhaps the one trying to fight René, she couldn't tell, had Daniel to his full feet as Nona tried to swing Daniel's arm around her shoulders to support him.   This man wasn't so sure about her. He tried to pull Daniel away from her and take Daniel back to the table, engaging the two of them in a ridiculous tug-of-war.

Daniel finally clutched the man by the lapel with one hand, who was clearly his friend, even as he embraced Nona's shoulders with the other, and whispered something to the friend that she couldn't make out, but which made the man suddenly release Daniel to her and hand Daniel his overcoat.

As she grabbed her own coat from the bar stool, and she and Daniel made their way uneasily to the establishment door, she heard over her shoulder Mimi's chiding whispers to René:

"Let her go, idiot!" Even in reprimand, Mimi's voice was alluring. And then: "It's her husband."

Mimi knew. Her lovely friend, with whom she had charged air-headedness just this morning during her childish tantrum in the café, knew why she couldn't let René beat the life out of this man. Mimi knew why Nona had to walk out of here right now with him, no questions asked. No one had to explain it to Mimi, the way it had to be explained to René.

And from René in return: "Then I wish I had killed him."

The selfish reality that Nona had made enemies of total strangers sank her.

"Stop it, René!" Mimi bit. "Don't be such a child. And take a good long glance now, *chouchou*, because we will never see her again."

Nona swore she heard those words. She wanted to turn back immediately and assure Mimi it wasn't true, clutch her friend by the arms and fiercely swear that she would never let that happen. But the husband she thought was no longer hers was bleeding beside her. Her friends would have to wait.

As the bar's door swung closed behind them, she and Daniel entered the winter, even as they exited another kind, leaving behind them the din of loud music, raucous mischief, angry sport, and his friends and hers, all pondering, surely stupefied, on the perplexing exploits of Mr. and Mrs. Cross.

The winds were fierce, but at least the rain had stopped. Once curbside, she looked left then right, trying to figure where she should be taking him. She wasn't as familiar with Montmartre as with the Latin Quarter, but she knew enough to realize that they were too far away from their flat to get Daniel the immediate attention he needed. He was too disoriented to offer any help and was close to collapsing on the spot when the young man of earlier came bounding out after them. This was the same man who had wanted to fight René, the one who hadn't wanted to trust her with Daniel. Without a word their way he hailed a taxi for them, speaking rapidly to the cabman, yelling to be heard over the increasing wind.

"*Venez!*" the man beckoned to Nona. She didn't know what to make of him, but he was obviously Daniel's friend, and she decided to trust that he would do them no harm. As they approached the cab, he stuck his hand in the breast pocket of Daniel's coat, who was barely responsive. René had really cold-cocked him badly with only three swift blows.

"I've given the driver his address," the man offered, handing her a door key and struggling to keep his windblown hair out of his face. "It's just up the road. He lives in number fourteen."

"Thank you," she gave back, though to hear the words *"he lives in..."* gave her a pang. Daniel used to live with her.

"Are you Nona?" asked the man.

"Yes."

He looked at her keenly after that, as though he wanted to say more, but instead only proposed, "Get him home. Take care of him. I am Benoît, his friend. I'll be 'round tomorrow to see how he is doing."

"*Merci,*" she said, curious about this man, who was curious about her.

"It's an honor to meet you, Nona Childe," the man offered, clutching her hand. "But your friend in there...had best watch his fucking back."

And he was gone. She trembled a bit to wonder who these people were, whom Daniel had chosen to befriend, and who carried the hint of the mobster on them. A second later they stepped into the cab, and the Christmas carol *God Rest Ye Merry, Gentlemen* played on the cab's radio. All she could think, with a little bit of humor, but mostly trepidation, was... *good advice.*

The cab ride was only minutes long, and her bleeding husband shivered beside her. In spite of his injured state, she smiled at the notion of them holding each other again. Whatever Daniel's sojourn had been all these months, not to mention her own very odd one, something had brought them back into each other's lives and had healed their anger, and she was thankful. He clung to her in these few minutes, until it was time to exit the cab at the address he now called home.

Several ancient gateways, a ramshackle courtyard, and a rickety flight of steps led to number fourteen, and she couldn't help being struck by how strangely theatrical this burrow looked. She felt as though she were entering upon some *Streetcar Named Desire* movie set, where every bricked building and weedy sidewalk seemed larger than life and oddly artificial, but so mesmerizing. She wanted to see lingerie hanging from a line, or some drunken Stanley stumbling up the staircase in dramatic romance. Her own drunken Stanley was far too beaten, physically and spiritually, to excite any kind of romantic ballet.

Ironically, that had always been Daniel's anguish. He'd lived his life in the belief that the world expected him to perform on command, and he'd never felt up to the task. Now, as they made their way arduously up the stairs on this biting Christmas Eve, and as she fantasized their mise-en-scène, it would seem that he was once again being expected to play the tragic-comic leading man.

SEVENTY THREE

When he'd whispered in Ben's ear to *"leave me with her,"* he'd been ready to die in her arms right there in Le Bar Bachon. But she wouldn't let him die. She fought like Hell to keep him with her. And the next thing he knew, his front door was throwing itself open, as much from the determination of his wife as from the gusts of the windstorm, with his rude frame clumsily leaning against her, and he had no idea how they'd gotten here. He stumbled as quickly as he could to the bed, and gratefully collapsed.

The moon gleamed a shaft of soft light into his north window, which tempted for a moment to soothe him, until artificial light was suddenly turned on. It was too angry an invasion and his eyes shut instantly, as he huddled on top of the bed and tried his best to be unconscious.

The pain in his face, where the punk had done the most damage, almost rivaled the one in his gut, but couldn't even touch the one in his heart. His eyes opened again to look in her face. It was a face of great sadness. The lines in her forehead were deeper, the eyes dulled. She was so much older than the Nona who had stepped from a plane six months ago, and he was the one who had sent her the way of her weariness.

His head dripped with sweat. Was he dying? He felt like it. He wanted to grab her and hold her and make the grand gesture that would tell everything about his heart, but he didn't even have the strength to lift his head from the pillow. Instead he tried his damnedest to tell her with his eyes that he loved her.

She moved closer to help him with his coat, but left the rest of his clothing in tact, as she covered him with the blankets on his bed. It made him shiver more, and he couldn't stand to be inside his own hide. She left his boots on, probably fearing that she might have to whisk him away into hospital at any moment. He could only imagine that he must've looked like death.

She tried to help him gain some measure of comfort in his small bed by propping the pillows for him, and for a moment she began to fade from his sight. He struggled to hold her in his view, panicked that he might actually be dying at this second, and could barely piece together what had transpired to put him in this bloodied state in the first place. Had the punk completely knocked his lights out and left him with only stars? He tried to utter her name, but nothing more than a bubble of spit managed to peek out from his pursed lips. All he could do, to tell her how happy he was to see her, was to muster the tiniest smile.

It must've worked, because she returned it. In the whole of this entire Paris pilgrimage, including months of an abysmal estrangement and this very evening's event that brought her back into his life, this was the first truly peaceful moment between them. The first intimacy. He held her hands tightly. His were so cold that he knew he frightened her. She looked at him tearfully and wanted to caress his face, but he wouldn't release her from his grasp to allow it. This was the woman he was meant to love. The woman who had loved him in spite of himself.

Minutes passed with her in his clutches, though it might as well have been hours. At one point, she tried to move away from him to find a wet cloth for his face.

"Not yet," he managed to say.

He clasped her hands tighter in his own grip, and was afraid to look away because his face was swollen on one side, his left eyelid felt as if it was bearing the weight of something tumorous and bulging, and he knew that soon the offended eye would be swollen shut and he might not be able to see her at all.

He must've been fevered, because his very skin hurt, and he could taste the blood in his mouth. She caressed his forehead and ran her hand over the buzzed burrs of his newly shorn hair.

He reached over to clutch a bottle of bourbon that was sitting on a stack of books close by. He didn't even realize he was doing it until she tried to pry his fingers from it.

"Please don't," she whispered. "This is not what you need."

He knew it broke her heart to consider him a drunk, to suddenly learn that his instinct would be to medicate with this rotgut. She may as well know the truth. She gently took the bottle from him. Had he been stronger he might've resisted. Instead, he gave the bottle up to her and rolled over in shame. Closing his eyes, facing away from her now, and with no words but a beckoning of his shaky hand, he begged her to lie with him. If he died tonight, a very great possibility, it seemed, then at least it would be in her arms.

SEVENTY FOUR

As she lay down beside him, she held him until he fell asleep. She prayed he wouldn't die sleeping. Was he dying? It was a question she didn't want answered, but something told her she'd better consider the possibility. He seemed so close to it, even beyond the beating he'd taken.

What she did want answered was what he'd been up to all these months to put him in this state, but she'd been afraid to ask it. It was the same question put to Arthur after his disappearance, and to which they never got an answer. Those mysterious months remained unknown to them to this day, but what had been brought back with Arthur was his willingness to end his life. That's all they knew. Now, as she kissed and cradled her broken husband, she couldn't help fearing that his own reemergence might bring with it a similar end.

He had stared at her earlier as if he'd seen a ghost and had seemed confused by his surroundings. Now he slept, and she was grateful that he was finally being given some tiny measure of peace tonight.

She breathed deeply in this moment alone, and tried to assess this godforsaken dump that her husband now called home. As her eyes scanned the room that scared her, she suddenly noticed them for the first time. A tickle shot up her spine, as her eyes unfolded onto an army of canvases before her. All new, all different from anything she'd ever seen from Daniel's brush, her heart raced with the discovery that her husband was painting again.

She had to stand, as she cautiously crept away from his sleeping embrace. When she did, she stood in reverence. There must've been twenty canvases easily, each one a delirious Montmartre landscape or a startling portrait. The images were savagely harsh and brutal, grotesquely expressionistic, but with an eerie yet undeniably serene center, imbued with wild, phantasmal color. Powerful. Powerful. Too many adjectives, she knew, but there was no way to encompass it all with fewer words. Or she was no longer gifted.

The Paris of her childhood fancy, the one she'd urgently beseeched to heal their broken love, the one she'd given up on, was here after all. It had inspired this. As it would always do for its artists. Her eyes glassed.

This moment was a perfect étude, delicate and alarming, breaking and soothing her heart interchangeably. What struck her most profoundly was that this was the work of a man running from his mortality, fearing it is near. This was a frenzy not unlike the one she had created in Gabriel Champion, who fears that the end of his life is near because it has been threatened and menaced.

Daniel used to say how tormented he was by Champion and by this idea that to achieve brilliance one must be at the end of one's literal rope. It was her own book's premise, for God's sake, yet she'd always thought that Daniel's claim was just his edgy way of wooing her, artistic torment being so baroque and romantic. She'd never even thought to look for signs of a man's slow stumble from grace, his faint cry for salvation.

She crouched on the floor, the wind knocked out of her, and couldn't catch a breath. She reached over and snatched up the bottle of bourbon that she'd taken from Daniel, and finished it off herself. She figured that if she could numb her way through all of Christmas Day — if she could forget that this season was supposed to be about peace and goodwill, and that on this particular Christmas Day, René, Mimi, Fairuza, and she were supposed to prepare chicken liver and roast duck and *bûche de Noel* to celebrate her first Paris Yule; if she could just expel her friends from her consciousness for the time being, and with them this dread, which she prayed was just paranoia, that her husband was on his way out — *then* she'd be better prepared to help him get back up. To get back up, herself.

She knew she still needed to scope out a wet cloth and tend to Daniel's injuries, but he was passed out for the time being, and she just needed a moment to breathe. She got up, placed the empty bottle on his kitchenette counter, and crept over to his window to watch the sun rise on this Christmas morning. Here they were; the noted author and the celebrated painter, imprisoned away in a remote Paris hole, disappeared from the world they knew, and which knew them and had tried its best to hallow them.

SEVENTY FIVE

She fell asleep on the floor against the windowpane some time shortly after sunrise, sweated and pungent from a tumultuous night of surprise reconciliations, barroom brawls, great quantities of drink, more drink, huge life.

She dreamt of Arthur, a common condition, whose stark brown face was not demon this time, but Muse. And he stepped forth in his music form and begged the Crosses not to abuse themselves. He told them that he'd learned a thing or two from his tragic life and that it wasn't a requirement for brilliance. In this dream he was her own secret phantom, haunting every place she called home, never letting her sleep peacefully. And she wanted to be so haunted. He, likewise, haunted Daniel and reached inside Daniel's body with his lean, punctured arms, took Daniel's heart up in his palm, and soothed it like a master baker kneading a ball of dough. And the three of them were still a vibrant trio, still the saluted triumvirate of *Murmuration*, taking to the air, blessed angels, wild beasts, purged and purified by a rain that watered the earth steadfastly. A baptism. And the water poured. And it poured.

Suddenly she was jerked awake to find Daniel's face tilted over the edge of the bed, retching in his unconsciousness. Pouring. And pouring. She hastened over and shook him, as vomit flowed down the side and onto the floor. How could anyone sleep so soundly that their own convulsive hurling didn't stir them? She feared he was dead and that his body was simply expurgating the last of him. The floor beneath him became buried like volcanic acreage in the flow of his sick innards.

She shook him until he awoke, but he remained no good to himself or her. In a stupor he sat up, wavering, while she tried to gather every towel in the place. She needed to open a window but the temperature outside was cutting, so she endured the rotting smell, though it brought her close to her own heaving. She was even afraid to turn down his furnace for fear he might catch his death, as he was already a bundle of shivers. So the smell was not only the smell, but hot and sharp.

After cleaning him up, she dealt with the floor and the bed, which made her eyes water and her face prickle. She held her breath and worked hastily, helping him move to a chair, yanking up the ruined bed linens, and wondering how they'd ever gotten to such an awful place.

She redressed his bed with a couple of heavy blankets she'd found, but never located another set of sheets, so the bare mattress would have to do. She went to draw him a hot bath only to discover that he had no bathtub, only a strange floor basin with no curtain and an overhead spigot. This was all so dreadful. She wanted to whisk him away from this Hellhole, and throw him in a cab, and escape back to the Hotel du Levant, which was at least clean and had a tub, but he was in no condition to travel.

The man from the cab last night, Daniel's friend, whose name she'd already forgotten, had said he would drop by today, but it was Christmas. Surely the man hadn't realized that when he'd offered, but she prayed he would come anyway. Stuck here alone, she didn't know what to do for Daniel.

Once he was steadier, clearer, she managed to get him to the shower with some stumbling effort. Without even attempting to get his clothes off, or hers, she stepped onto the shower basin with him, holding him up with one arm, but ungracefully, and fumbling at the water knobs with the other hand. As the water shot forth, it shocked them both to yelling from being so cold. She was just about to jump out of her skin, but held onto him firmly. Why hadn't she thought to get the shower running first? Several seconds of frigid torture poured before warm water began to flow. Eventually the water became a steamy elixir they both craved. She prayed he would live through this day.

After a bit, and once he felt steadier, she prompted him to brace the surrounding walls while she pulled off his soaked shirt, belt, boots, trousers. As he stepped from his heavy clothing and she commenced lathering him, he started to caress her face. She looked into eyes that had seemed so cloudy before. They finally began to focus, to actually recognize her. There might be life in the old salty Englishman yet.

She held a cloth to his swollen eye, and washed the caked blood from his mouth and cheek. A wearied smile crept on both their faces as they each realized, and knew it of the other, that they'd lived through copious insanity and self-indulgence, and were still kicking and wanting to love each other. Smiles turned into laughter, but they were strained cackles and she knew he was still in pain. They had to laugh, though, in order to seal some measure of triumph to this deal. They laughed at how masterfully they had defied all of the rocks thrown their way. At how victoriously they stood here today, able to face each other and touch each other again after such a beastly estrangement, excruciating period of mourning, and much self-abuse. And finally, they laughed at how frightened they really were of each other still, because neither had ever before lived through a tempest as extreme as this alliance.

He touched her face then kissed her, and his erection grew against her, which she held gently in her hand and stroked. As he slid down to sit on the shower floor, she struggled with her own soaked clothes and gingerly climbed on top of him, steaming water still pouring forth. He trembled to slide himself inside of her. The first time since Arthur.

One would think that she could easily recall what making love with her husband was like, as many times as she'd called up the memory of it in her loneliness, but it had been six long months and this was unfamiliar. And she realized that it was because they were different people today. Perhaps wiser, certainly wizened, from hard life. Who cared about being young and wild? She rather liked the lines that were beginning around her eyes, and the gray that dusted Daniel's black hair, and the arduous life lessons of which they'd both been recent students. Only old pros could touch each other so artfully.

SEVENTY SIX

Sex was difficult because his body felt like it was dying, though simply to touch her again was all he needed to want to stay alive. Her. Nona. His wife. Not the faceless mouths that had each had their turns sucking his cock in these desolate months, but his one and only.

He felt like a thief, taking what he didn't deserve, which was her forgiving love. She gave it willingly. His hands wanted to caress her, but they shook so violently now that he was afraid he might hurt her. He made sure to see the agony of climax in her face, and actually did manage to reach it, himself, though it almost knocked the wind out of him. When they were done, she reached up and shut the shower water off, helped him to the bed, and nursed his head and his bruised face and itching body with a dry towel, while her very presence nursed his heart. Then they slept.

While they slept, his hand fastened around hers as if she were his prisoner. He knew she'd chosen to be here. She could simply have left him there pummeled on the bar floor and taken off with her friends, but instead she'd abandoned them in favor of bringing him home and loving him. Still, he feared in himself the impulse, had she not chosen it, to keep her here against her will.

At the height of noon he awoke, sweating and fevered beside her, silently screaming to be out of his intolerable skin. She slept like the dead. He knew he might explode on the walls if he couldn't meet with Corky for a little opiate repast, though the idea of the outside world was even more intolerable. It was quite enough to entertain the notion of his wife after all this time, without also entertaining the burdens of the rest of his life.

He stood to pace, cramped in the gut and legs, and staggered until the blood reached his brain. He made his way about the room, wandering, pacing, floating, goose-bumping about the arms, scratching his rashy skin until tiny dots of blood sprouted, trying his damnedest to make the walls stand still. He stared at her from every angle and couldn't believe she was really here. Her legs tangled themselves in blankets, under which she was buried from the cold. Her hair, which also peered out from the mountain of covers, was bent strangely in spots from having fallen asleep wet. Her disheveled state was irresistible and alluring, and he moved to another side of the room to stare more. She had always been worth painting. He wanted to pull the covers away, but it was far too cold and damp in here, even with the furnace blasting.

Besides, he couldn't stand still for long; certainly not for reminiscences. He grabbed a bottle of whisky from his cupboard and approached the mired spewings that dared to call themselves canvases. One in particular caught his eye. A demented mutation of Speck and Champion. Two amorphous images trying to be a Sears family portrait. Mother and father in smiling sincerity, and the cold steel carbine child in the middle. Surrealistic in nature, which was sort of new for him, his strokes were jittery now, savage and out of control, with lines that were never complete and smooth, but broken up, disjointing limbs from torsos. The colors were dark and severe, muddying any sense of definition with a deranged piling on of crazy paint, until the layers were so thick that the canvas had become an anthill.

Christ! A good splashing on of flat house-paint and a scraper would clear away that psychosis in one merciful move, and good-fucking-riddance. He picked up the bucket of gesso that he always kept close at hand, pried open the rubber top, and flung its contents at the mad canvas until the impasto was doused and draped in one clean sheet, and droplets dripped to the floor like white blood.

Sometimes his head truly frightened him.

SEVENTY SEVEN

She opened her eyes and was disoriented by her surroundings. Was it evening? Afternoon? Where were they? Until she looked up and saw the sight. Daniel painting. The first she had witnessed in all these months.

It had been her greatest Paris dream, and suddenly she remembered everything. She'd always felt honored to be allowed the privilege of watching him work, but as she stared now she realized that for the first time ever it was with fear, and she resented it. She tried to shove that earlier thought from her mischievous head. Tried instead to remember what greater thing they'd been put here to do.

He looked a sight. He was much thinner than she'd ever known him, and his skin was rashed and scabbed. He stood before her completely naked except for his work boots, which made him look slightly goofy. There was even a comical look to his willy, clumped there like a glob of clay waiting to be shaped into something. When she moved to turn the furnace up higher, fearing he might catch some dreaded pneumonia, because he seemed to be unaware that it was freezing outside and sweated like it was summer, he didn't even notice her.

A second later she was back to being mesmerized, back to staring at him unfold a rich flower of sensuous hues. The hairs on her neck rose as she watched him dab, dart, turn, dig fingers into, shift, whir, pace. It was a beautiful dance. But she couldn't put it behind her. Last night's thought. She got the creeping feeling that what was keeping him in this constant motion wasn't art, but some internal piranha trying to eat him alive. She frantically started looking for omens of her earlier suspicion. It was going on four years now of knowing this man and witnessing his process. He'd always been a ball of fire when he painted, could easily spit shrapnel your way if you weren't careful to dodge him. She'd always known how. But today it seemed as though her task was to extract from that mighty siege any signs of ruin.

She had to confess that even in all of the surrounding illness and abuse and inertia and stench that threatened to choke her, even with the threat of a man possibly setting his own landmines for sabotage, she couldn't help being romanced. Should she be ashamed for the impulse? She had long ago given up the belief that watching her husband paint would ever be possible again, and she would be damned if she'd allow some crazy notion to interfere with that.

Then she remembered something she'd once said to Arthur. Once believed. That art saves lives. She used to keep it scribbled on a post-it on her fridge, and had lived her entire life in the notion. As she watched Daniel sweep furious strokes onto a canvas, she suddenly realized that this was exactly what he was trying to do, and by the only means he knew how.

She got up at one juncture without bothering to dress, for now the place was warm enough from the screaming furnace. She crept over to Daniel's north window, which looked out over a tiny vineyard, and sat and stared. The rains were aggressive now and the window cold to the touch of her hand. The rains had always spurred Daniel on to paint, and so she clearly saw Paris's agenda this night. It loved feeding greatness. She and Paris, mightily arm-locked in this mission to re-embolden the artist. The city seemed almost as panicked as she, however, as the gusts of this rain whipped violently about and shook the shoulders of their room.

Daniel surprised her from behind when, though spattered with paint and in the throes of something crucial, he suddenly dropped his brushes and approached her. He ran his gnarled fingers over her back and breasts, smothering her neck with his hot breath and low moans, and slid his erection in her. They never said a word, but reveled in each other.

Night was day again when she next slept and then awoke. This time her head lay at the foot of the bed, and she glanced over to where Daniel now sat in a corner, staring out of the same north window. The rains were even more furious now. He sketched equally as furiously on a pad with a charcoal stick that blackened his hands. A race was clearly on.

She got up and attacked a project near the front door, where the rain had begun to seep inside and a puddle was forming on the floor. She gathered up and shoved towel after towel against the bottom of the door, and Daniel never even looked up.

She noticed that during his sleep earlier he'd fussed with the bandage she'd made for his eye, which had been cut during the bar brawl. As she approached him to fix it, he took her again. Just lifted her on top of him, though he barely had the strength. Smudgy charcoal fingerprints smeared across her stomach, waist, buttocks.

This time the sex was more labored. Too much booze, likely. Because, though she had polished off the one bottle, he apparently had a secret stash she hadn't known about, and had done his best to stay as tanked as possible. At first she'd tried to keep it away from him, but eventually grew weary from the effort. She simply couldn't fight him any longer. Besides, alcohol numbing had begun to show its appeal. At least he was producing.

He couldn't keep an erection. Of course, she didn't care about any of that. To hold him and caress him would've been plenty for her, but it angered him. She kissed him tenderly, but he didn't want tender and was irritated that he couldn't keep it up. Instead he tossed her on the bed with the strength of his ire, spread her knees with his blackened hands, and thrust his several-days growth between her legs. Her sighs must've ached at his groin, because his erection eventually returned, against everything his drunkenness had tried to dictate, and they were merely off to it again.

Seventy-two hypnotic hours passed in this existence. She ransacked his cupboards for food, finding very little but making sure they both ate the bread and cheese that he had. He needed to get stronger. In that time he never once answered his phone, though it had rung on several occasions. He probably hadn't heard it, from it being drowned out by the music he was playing on a boombox, but she also knew that he didn't want to speak to anyone from his recent life. She thought to ask him why, or to pick up the phone herself, but finally she never did. She realized that now was not the time to tread but to allow. She also refrained from asking him about the canvases that littered this room, because she knew he would only denigrate them, and she didn't want to tempt opening that door. To each other they barely spoke. It was almost liturgical, this speakless effort of theirs to lock the world out and reconnect.

Then the spell they were under was suddenly broken, after days with not a word. From out of the winter blue, Daniel threw down his paintbrushes, thrust his palms up to his temples, and bawled. She stared stunned at the man who had always despised tears yet had become insidiously plagued by them in this past year of his life. He couldn't stop.

His brushes simply lay on the fetid floor, with his canvases made to wait like some lonely woman in a bar, and he gave it all to his weeping. She began to panic, and honestly couldn't decide which storm was the more formidable.

SEVENTY EIGHT

His hands were gone.

And he couldn't help fearing that having them taken away was the penance he'd been given for his sins.

The thought flattened him. His winded self had been going back and forth for days now between giving in and taking his punishment, to stubbornly denying this sentence and doing his damnedest to defy his useless hands. He'd spent the past seventy-two hours doing everything in his power to be worthy of her. He'd violently thrown paint on canvases like a spoiled child, playing music loudly all through it, anything from screeching metal trash to burning bop lunacies, just to keep him moving forward. The more manic he'd become, the louder he'd cranked the music, the more he'd refused to let this be his punishment for seeking revenge. But it was, wasn't it? It was everything he deserved. Not only for what he'd done to Arthur, but to his marriage, as well.

A second goddamned shot at loving his wife, after months in a kind of mad purgatory. A second goddamned shot he had never thought possible. And now his hands were gone.

Shattering lives, he was starting to learn, will give you enlightenment. Though he was fairly certain the Buddha didn't have this particular blitzkrieg method in mind.

And his wife. Bless her heart, she never once said, *"turn that crap down!"* or begged him to paint when all he could do was pace, or told him to calm down when all he could do was paint. She knew why he couldn't simply relax and celebrate their reconciliation, because only she knew what he was made of, and that a true reconciliation required that he step up to the plate, be the artist and the man she deserved.

"I'm fucking trying!" he finally poured, as if he'd actually been having this conversation with her. "Goddamn it! Goddaammmmnniiitttt!"

He bellowed his degraded utterings between degraded hiccups, as he slammed his boombox against a wall, halting the music, and the blizzard outside rattled his windows in psychotic concert.

"They're gone. My hands. They're so fucking palsied that I don't, I don't, I don't even own them any more!" he blubbered, as much to the Devil on his shoulder as to her. And, though she knew what made him tick better than anyone, she looked frightened.

"Who even cares about art anymore, anyway?" he continued to wail to the whole world. "Nobody, goddamn it, that's who. In this ridiculous fucking age of Reality-fucking-TV-sensory-over-load-fucking-desensitized bullshit, what could possibly be exciting about some stupid little painting on a wall? *It's boring, mate. It doesn't move. It doesn't talk. It's not interactive. Dude, what does it DO?*' THIS is the generation that will dictate the cultural shift when you and I are old and fucking gray and in diapers! D'you realize that? So, what's the fucking point?"

His cries were suddenly that of a child's. Rheum dripped from his nostrils and stretched a sheet across the cavern of his opened mouth. His eyes bulged and glazed, his chest coughed up its sewage laboriously. It took every ounce of energy he had, which was already nil, to heave such tears. And he collapsed on the floor where she held him.

"Daniel, it's gonna be all right."

"No. It's not. This is my punishment for what I've done."

"Sshhhhh."

She rocked him like a baby. She wouldn't even entertain it. And bless her for it, but he knew the truth.

"And I miss him. I miss Arthur."

There it was. It was the first time since their own D-Day that he had let it be known to Nona that he loved Arthur still. Even when he'd done his best to soften the blow of the tale he'd spun for her by spouting all of his slick redemption rhetoric, he'd still made certain that she knew he'd been destroyed by their adultery. He'd done so well at making certain, in fact, that he had completely abandoned her to take up the bowels of this city. He'd done wounded to the hilt. And suddenly whatever strategies he'd entertained to keep his wife feeling guilty all these months were now instantaneously tossed out into the acrid winter. And with them, any tricks he might've had to keep her cowering beneath him.

"I miss him too," the wind blew his way in a gentle soprano.

It pricked his ears. He stared at the words that had leaked from her mouth in a crackled whisper. The first words she'd ever spoken of it.

SEVENTY NINE

They stayed cocooned in each other's arms for a solid day, night, and day again, only shakily peeling away to relieve themselves, then bustling back to the fold. They barely spoke, but took comfort in the silence. She'd managed to calm his fit, but he was fragile yet. It was when she finally suggested that they go back to the Hotel du Levant and clean out her belongings (*"no point keeping two rooms"*) that his anxiety returned. At even the hint that she might wish to walk out of this door he froze and wanted to take his contrition back, wanted to scream at her that she fucking well owed him.

He just knew that if they left this room, and she had two seconds away from the place to breathe fresh air, she would realize that she was crazy to stay with him and refuse to return.

"I'll send Ben to get your things. It's not a bother, he won't mind."

"Daniel, you've refused to answer your phone for a week. I'm sure Ben's been calling here all this time, trying to check up on you, and now you're suddenly gonna beg a favor from him? We don't need Ben. Let's just you and I go. You're climbing the walls. It'll be good for us to get out."

"I'll get you anything you want!" he spat back. He knew he sounded desperate.

"I don't need you to get me anything. I just think we could both use a breather. The rains have finally stopped. Please—all right—look, we won't go all the way across town. How about, let's just get out of here for awhile? Take a stroll. It'll do us good."

Even as she spoke it, she was slipping on her clothes and shoes and bidding him do the same, which meant that her decision was made. But he feared the outside now. Give him ten seconds of the rapacious smell of city grit and he was convinced he'd plunder a home or rob some innocent bystander for an opium bargain. He barely held onto his resolve, as it was, without also having to be teased by the Boulevard, where drugs floated everywhere for the easy buying. He was already purging his gut nearly every day, already scratching the life out of his rashy skin and hardening veins and atrophying muscles from what he figured must be withdrawal. What more did she want from him?

She had no clues about his newest little drug hobby, or was just too afraid to know. She was frightened to death. Not as frightened as he was. When she'd gently suggested three days before that she take him to hospital, he'd refused. This was what he'd wanted. To be alone in a room with his wife, to focus in, figure it all out. It would never happen if they left this hole for even a minute. She was threatening to upset a perfectly designed balance that was the only thing keeping him breathing.

But he also knew that the stench of this flat had become unbearable for her, and the last thing he wanted was to risk the chance of her running away, no longer able to withstand the Hell of this place or him. Reluctantly he agreed to go.

They peeled mildewed towels away from the doorway of their musty cave and stepped out into the cold night, bundled up in overcoats and clenching each other, to immerse themselves in the dizzying Sodom & Gomorrah of Clichy. The storm had now moved east, but not before downing trees all around them, crumbling chimneys and roof tiles, bending traffic lights, knocking over newspaper kiosks, and blacking out portions of the city. In spite of the storm's devastation, Pigalle was alive and electric, as if to boast that it could never be bested by any paltry tempest. They walked the wet, cluttered streets, awed by the catastrophe surrounding them and the hasty swarms of clean-up crews, and emergency vehicles, and red lights, and businesses still open and welcoming customers.

Nights up and down the Boulevard de Clichy had been his existence for some time now, in the company of stimulating minds, sensory overloads, women who would give themselves to him, absinthe rituals, and soothing little baggies of gummy, ropy knots of magic that he would go home and smoke, and spiraling whirlies. He gripped her hand with his own paralytic one and craved that existence now, which was exactly what he'd feared. But it could never be his again, because she would never venture, and he would not go without her.

Of course, now that they were out of seclusion the rules would be different. She would want to talk. Ask him where he'd been. Why he'd run away. What he'd been doing. And uncover the mysteries of Daniel Cross over the past months.

He couldn't talk. He didn't want to reveal his various recent debaucheries or to be told what he'd left behind when he ran away. It would only kill him to hear how he'd hurt and abandoned her. He already knew. And he didn't want to know, besides, who her friends at Le Bachon were that night. Or the identity of the prick who'd attacked him, as if he didn't already have some clue. He would never be able to endure having it confirmed that this handsome young punk had been her lover, defending her honor from the old, broken-down bloke with the palsied hands.

He just wanted a goddamned drink and to look into the eyes of his wife. *Please! Let's just get a drink and run back home, quick! And stop talking!*

She hadn't opened her mouth.

He avoided Le Bachon for obvious reasons, but definitely had a bar of some kind in mind. She might've ordinarily rebutted the idea, considering his deteriorated state, if it weren't for the fact that she needed a drink as badly.

They walked into their first, sat to the bar, and he took a deep breath. He was about to jump out of his skin, and she was fully aware of this, for she held onto him gingerly. They both gobbled up a handful of whisky shots. To take the edge off. Lots of edge. Steep, dangerous edge. She could keep up with him now, which had taken him aback when he'd first witnessed it in the flat. They had, indeed, become Franklin and Camilla.

"I'm so sorry."

"What?" she asked, grabbing another shot from the bar and downing it. She wasn't listening to him. He wasn't really saying anything.

After a few more shots between them, they stared at each other but spoke very little. She would, here and there, caress his forehead or run her hand over his close-cropped hair and simply ponder him. He could tell she looked at him pitiably, and every second of her pity hurt. But a couple more shots and he wouldn't give two shits.

He leaned over to kiss her, and wallowed in the feel of her tongue against his, which gave itself to him easily. She may have felt he was a sorry sot, but she still loved kissing him. His mother used to stamp obnoxiously slobbery whisky kisses on his and Duncan's faces, and now he planted one deeply onto his wife, biting her lip as he went along, and swallowing her whole. The tingle in his groin spread, which had been no easy feat these days.

At that, he slapped some money on the bar and whisked her out without a word. His cock was now so afflicted that it would need a cuntry shelter soon, or else rape some unsuspecting lamppost.

They got outside and darted down a tiny street, stepping over bested tree limbs that littered it, where he thrust her into the alcove of a stonewalled apartment complex that was camouflaged by a huge dump truck straddling the narrow sidewalk and the street. This alcove was unlit, and there against the wet wall he hiked up the dress beneath her heavy coat, as she ripped at his clothing and bit into his exposed chest. He wailed, but would not have her stop. The pain was irresistible, and she wanted it as reckless this night as he did.

They were drunk from trying feverishly to medicate their sores, and indignant with the world and each other. In their drunken belligerence, they dared each other to scare each other. They fucked in weather that could easily have given them hypothermia, not ten meters away from where drug dealers, grifters, and whores did their scores on credulous victims, and which was so violently carnal that both could've been up on charges.

When they were done they were still drunk, and catching their deaths in threatening pneumonia, and welcoming the thugs that swarmed not far, and daring any potential brawls, though he'd already proven he couldn't fight worth two shits, and not caring a fig, and stumbling on to the next bar. And the one after that. And the one after that.

He was just trying to keep from seizing between here and back home, which was his ultimate destination, but he knew she was afraid to go back to that flat — or Purgatory, Gehenna, Hades, the Infernal Pit, as it surely must've seemed to her. The real Les Martyres de Paris was not a horror gallery in Les Halles; it was right here in Montmartre, at No. 14 on Rue St-Vincent. And he knew she would come to fear it now that she'd had the chance to taste the outside world again. Even one as vile as this burg.

So, on they floated from bar to bar, until they could barely stand. For him, this was routine. But for her? He didn't know. Maybe she felt that if she sufficiently numbed herself, then the return to his flat might not seem so ghastly.

He saddened at the reality that he'd brought her to this dismal place. When he thought on her life before knowing him, her growing renown in the book world, her many awards, her peaceful singlehood and invigorating circle of friends and beautiful Zen cottage, he knew she deserved better than he had given her.

He almost harrumphed aloud when he thought back on the last post he'd received from Harper, which had been a sure sign that he had ruined their lives. The Whitney exhibit had been a smash, and *Murmuration* was now on its way to London, partly funded by the National Gallery, then Marseille, Berlin, and finally Paris. The book was already here. And optioning wars on the screenplay rights for *Champion* were being fought left and right, even without Nona's presence to commandeer it all. Yet they were here. Because of him. Not at home. Not taking care of business. Not eating up their successes. Not relishing their lives as celebrated artists.

That was the most insane phenomenon of all. No one knew where they were, which only fueled the art world's fascination with them. The tenor being attached to their names in the world of the living was laughably absurd, because they were no longer among the living. Their sole concern in the world at present was how to clean up his vomit, or whether he could get it up in order to give his wife a go. In the brief past days of their bittersweet reunion, they'd become two desert crabs, moving in some sideways fashion along the dust road, living their reptilian lives in an inebriated haze, fulfilling one sensual impulse after another, without regard for their higher moral will, which was really no will at all but an annoying parasite, of which they only tried to rid themselves by the numbing of their alcohol.

He suddenly stopped himself when he realized that he was projecting all of his own pathos onto her. He was the one who had ruined his own life because he could never figure out why his art had to change the world in order for his existence to matter. Why had he always been so covetous of everyone else's gift? Arthur's. Nona's. Why had he never believed in his own? For that matter, why had he never been satisfied to be a Regular Joe who loved his life, his passions, and the simple pleasures, instead of plagued with grand delusions? His wife was too beautiful for this, too much a light that he was succeeding, in his stupendous narcissism, in dimming.

Fucking Hell! That was an awful flood of verbose shit for one fried brain.

He shook it off just in time for them to enter the bar at Le Méridien Etoile Hotel, behind the Arc de Triomphe. He hadn't realized just how far they'd walked. Stumbled. They were miles now from the stinking red light district.

This place was packed with dancing, drinking, cackling party-goers. Leave it to the Parisians to be undaunted by a deadly gale. He had not intended to walk into this chaos, and was not inviting it, though he did need another drink right now, or he was in deep trouble.

They squeezed their way through the difficult crowd toward the bar area and demanded shots. It was so crowded that service was excruciatingly slow, and he tapped a steady beat on the bar top with his fingernails, even while being shoved and nudged by elbows and asses, until his own tapping was just about to undo him. Eventually they each downed a shot and took a second round with them to a tiny table not far from the bandstand that a couple had just abandoned. A violinist backed by a jazz quartet bellowed his swinging solo on *Autumn Leaves* above their heads, as Daniel quickly downed his second shot and watched Nona do the same.

Those earlier thoughts began to flood his brain again. Her beautiful life — His dark deeds and self-immolation — She deserved better — Blah, blah, blah. They flooded his brain even over the sonorous bed of this quintessentially Parisian jazz sound. He begged the electrifying music to drown out the thoughts and catch him up in it, instead, but it would not. It was doing well just to keep up with the clamor in the room; never mind the one in his head.

He and his wife were both so dizzy and wasted that they told each other witless jokes, and inane anecdotes, and laughed loudly at nothing, though he cried horribly inside, and he knew she did the same, and they were deranged by the maddening sound. And as he yelled some incoherent thing over the din of the partying crowd, incoherent even to himself, suddenly the pistol was out of his coat pocket and lying on the cocktail table. He slapped it there as one would a wad of money, revealing it swiftly as the punch line to whatever nonsense he'd been spewing.

He knew he'd paralyzed her. She'd been laughing with him, at his babbling and his sermonizing, and suddenly he was laughing alone. She stopped instantly and froze.

"See this?" he slurred, in sodden-eyed drama. "This is wha's gonna give you back your life, which I have robbed you of without remorse. Tha's what Arthur was tryin' to do. Tha's all he was tryin' to do. And I keep tryin' to tell him that I fin'ly get it, but he won't talk to me."

He danced the notion of the pistol in front of her like the bastard he could be, because he was too drunk to play this gracefully, to just disappear into a room alone, leave a nice note, and do it.

The place was so packed and chaotic that no one even noticed them. Or IT. Not that he cared if anyone did. He knew he could be arrested for a move like this, as France was extremely restrictive with its firearm laws, but it fed him to be this reckless.

Her eyes revealed her horror and panic, but he saw her try and con him. She didn't scream out, or try to snatch the pistol away, slap his face, wring his neck, any of the impulses that would ordinarily be hers. He knew his wife. Instead, she trod cautiously, attempting to still laugh when he laughed, while always with her nervous eye on the thing.

But I've been around Benoît and Clothilde Belargent, darlin'. I can spot a con at ten kilometers!

She wasn't very good at it. The glassiness of her reddened eyes gave her away, even as she tried to humor him.

"Daniel," she suddenly laughed, then cried.

EIGHTY

She was surely bleeding from the ears, as would any war victim who has narrowly survived a grenade explosion and now floats the streets in a daze. Deaf. Blind. One-armed. Shrapneled. But still here.

As she stared at a handgun on the glass tabletop within the shaky grip of his hands — those same hands that could raise the hairs on your neck with the strokes they created, and the hues they migrated toward, and the swirl of texture, and the breadth of passion — she knew in this instant that she'd been viciously duped by the man who called himself her husband and had pretended to try and rebuild his life. Their life!

Why hadn't she listened to her gut and gotten him to a hospital when she'd had the chance? Before he'd gotten to this brink? Why had she let him talk her out of it? Flashes of Arthur suddenly hit, and sneered at her that she had missed the warning signs again.

Daniel laughed in his drunkenness and rambled forth, practically screaming over the horrific buzz of partygoers, but the only thing that came out was incoherent babbling, a rapturous man speaking in tongues.

"You were my omen, Nona. My sign. You coming back. Reappearing in my life. Did you know that?"

She stared at the gun, refusing to believe in this moment, until in one heavily gestured instant, while he spouted off some foolish, drunken thing, he took his hand off of it. She tried to slip her own shaky hand in there and take it, but he was quicker. His large palm suddenly came down on hers, which had just clutched the thing, and now he had her hand and the gun pinned in his grasp.

The sensation of cold steel against her sweaty palm made her shiver. To touch it, to feel the sculpture of its barrel, the bend in its trigger, the smoothness of its hide, the evil in its purpose, made her recoil.

"Between everything tha's beautiful and everything tha's ugly is where I seem to live," he continued to slur, like some treacly, has-been poet. "But you, my love, are purity."

"Daniel!" she offered as prudently as possible, but had to shout it over the din. She could barely catch her breath to form a sentence, and couldn't hear her own trembling voice. "Someone is gonna see this."

"Careful, darlin'," he suddenly leaned in and warned in a whisper. "I'm half cocked!"

Before he even finished his exclamation, he snatched the gun away, nicking her hand, shoved the thing in his coat pocket, stood, and stumbled his way back into the crowd. She hastily followed him through the maze of bodies, up the steps, around the bend, through the lobby, and out of Le Méridien Etoile. He didn't even bother with whether she was coming or no. He knew she would. There was something smug in his certainty that she would.

He paced outside in the shivering cold, a drizzle starting up again, and tried to flag down a taxi, as she came bounding after him, fairly affrighted into a startling sobriety. It was even colder now than when they'd walked in, yet the party inside had now spilled out onto the streets. They couldn't escape this mad carnival.

"Daniel, let's not go home just yet," she threw out in a panic, amid the hubbub. She knew that if they went back to that hole, he would be swiftly to a foul deed. What deed specifically she refused entry. "How 'bout another drink somewhere? Maybe someplace quieter?"

Suddenly a hand was on her rear, and she shouted a general *"hey, asshole!"* to the throng and pulled away from some clamoring drunk, as Daniel paced in front of her, yelling his own epithets at not being able to get a cab.

"You don't want 'em to send us to the guillotine, do you?" she tried to joke, but was terrified and terrorized.

His irritation mounted that no cab could be gotten.

She couldn't ask him why he had this thing. She was afraid of the answer.

"Daniel—"

Or she knew the answer and couldn't bear to have it confirmed.

"Daniel—"

Maybe she was wrong. There were a hundred reasons he could have a gun.

"Daniel—"

Each utterance of his name grew fainter.

He started up the street and away from the crowd, finally giving up on a cab. On her. On life. He never even looked back to see if she would follow.

"Please, Daniel, let's not go home just yet," she called after him, following. Now her utterances grew the other way. "Daniel! Daniel! Let's not—did you hear me? Daniel, let's go get another drink. Daniel. Let's not go home yet!"

They must've walked for a clear hour, more maybe, up tiny wet streets, dark and shiny and shadowy. It was difficult for her to keep up with him, and her hands and feet grew numb from the cold and rain. She kept up an out-of-breath trot, just the same, and continued talking, babbling about nothing, anything, just trying to distract him. She begged him to slow down and talk to her, but he wouldn't.

"Daniel, please tell me what's happening?" she could only faintly hear her voice yelling, as if having floated out of herself. No answer. Eventually they turned up Boulevard des Batignolles, and up it they went, toward the apartment, though the hills were enervating.

Suddenly the question she'd feared asking, billowed with winter fog, spewed from her like a determined vomit.

"Why do you have this gun?"

He stopped dead and turned her way.

"Well, now," he offered with a cruel smirk, and that quirky way that he would sniff and purse his lips and clinch his teeth when troubled. "I wondered when the question would come. But it's still too polite to be quite honest, isn't it? What is it you really want to know?"

"What?" she bellowed to the stranger before her.

He made no sense. Her lips were numb even as she tried to ask it again, and he must've sensed her cold because suddenly his angry face softened. He approached her, taking her face tenderly in his icy hands and kissing her lips to warm them. She cried as he kissed her. She kissed him back, but couldn't let the question go.

"Why do you have this gun?" she asked again, pulling away.

"Because it's over," he finally spilled, but tenderly, resigned. "Because I have failed everyone I have ever loved. And my punishment seems to be that my body has now failed me. Have you seen my hands lately? They're a bloody palsy case. I can't even get paint to canvas any longer without spilling it everywhere else first. I can barely hold a brush, barely paint. The only thing I have ever lived to do. And I cannot live that way. I won't."

He was suddenly so calm in his confessions, so resolute, that her explosion was a violent sforzando against his gentle cadence.

"NNNOOOOOO!!!" she spilled in a roar of tears, when every fear she'd entertained became revealed.

And at the very instant that her scream thundered into the Parisian night, a blinding display of fireworks in the distance thundered into it as well. It fired off a deafening roar, which drowned hers out, and startled them both. They uniformly jerked their heads southwest to see a dazzle-hued sky surrounding the Eiffel Tower in the far distance. Only then did it hit her that this dismal evening was the millennial New Year's Eve, and that midnight had struck. They had been holed up in Daniel's apartment for so many numbing days that neither had paid much attention to where in time they were.

The midnight hour was now rung in, and while the entire globe celebrated this momentous passage into a 21st century — while everywhere people counted down to *"Happy New Year!"* with champagne glass in hand and a loved one to kiss; while the whole world nervously awaited the threatening impact of Y2K; while the hum of the city seemed suddenly to raise in volume around them, and the haze and smell of fire from the city's breathtaking pyrotechnic display filled the wet night air — she was having to face her husband's dreadful pronouncement that he was done with his life.

He turned back to her and stared, as startled by her scream as by the New Year rockets.

"Now, THAT would be the first honest moment you've had all evening." Tenderness instantly vanished.

He resumed walking, ignoring the crowds that had begun to form, people filing out of their apartments to look into the sky and savor a moment of history, and leaving her staggered.

"It's a new year, darlin', a new millennium—" he suddenly ranted like an amateur thespian, gesturing to the lit sky. He really could be so baroque when life was sucking for him.

"—A time of renewal. Of resolutions and all'at blah, blah bullshit? Well, then it's perfect, isn't it? I resolve to give my wife her life back, which I have selfishly robbed from her," he spouted to his audience of one.

She hustled after him, grabbing at his arms. He snatched them away and walked faster.

"Daniel, please don't do this," she pled behind him in a panic. Her eyes burned from the firework haze, and the streets were sprinkled liberally with people now, but no one looked their way. As they approached Rue Caulaincourt, she knew they were only minutes from Daniel's flat and he would be to this deed. "Please, please don't consider this."

"And please, please, don't YOU beg me!" he yelled.

Suddenly she stopped. He was right. It was time she was honest. With nothing else to lose, she spat it.

"Arthur didn't share it with anybody! Did he?" That stopped him. "He didn't cruelly tease the woman he loved by dangling threats of self-destruction in front of her. Because, though I am furious at Arthur for it, I have to give it to him. He meant his business. You, yourself, said it. When you mean it, you do it in a room alone. You don't make it theatre. And YOU are only doing this little drama right now because you are BEGGING ME TO SAVE YOU!"

He turned around and looked at her cockeyed. Those electrifying gray eyes. It was a strange stare. A stranger staring.

EIGHTY ONE

He stared at her for some seconds, then turned from her again and continued walking, this time faster. He could hear his own breath loudly, huffing and billowing like a great rhythmic wave, screaming for him to take it out of its misery. He studied the breath, kept with it, a meditation. The dancing skylight, and the sounds of a city in explosive celebration, and the inclement weather, and the panicked woman following on his heels threatened to hypnotize him, but he needed to stay on course.

Everything hurt. Every muscle felt as if it was drawing up. Every ligament stiffened. Every internal organ seemed on fire. His chest was tight and heavy, and he could barely catch his breath, as he weathered the hilly terrain of Montmartre. But intention will buck you up, will make you lift a car off its tires.

The rain was beginning to calm down, but not the woman behind him. Soon he was on Rue St-Vincent and passing the cemetery. As he did so, he glanced at the shadowed headstones and wondered if they would put him in a place like this, with weeds growing up all around the crypts and no one to tend them. Was she still behind him? Still pleading with him? Still shooting him with poisoned Arthur pellets? Did she actually have the nerve to say that Arthur hadn't made his suicide theatre?

He turned into his courtyard, blasted through the many gates, and climbed the steps to number fourteen, which winded him. He pulled his key out of one pocket and the pistol out of the other. He had barely made it inside the door of the flat before she was barreling over him and lunging his way, clumsily trying to grab the thing. He gripped her small wrists and flung her to the bed as he tore off his coat, tossing it on the floor, pistol still in hand, and slammed the door behind him. The thick heft of mildew and putrefaction hit his face. The fetor of the place nearly took him down.

He leered at the canvases that surrounded him, and cringed to see the brush strokes of a man who'd lost everything.

She was in the corner of his eye, crouching on the bed and keeping her own eyes on him, as he paced the room.

"You didn't have to come back here with me, Nona. You should go find your friends and celebrate with them. I know this place disgusts you. I don't want to keep you here. I just want to die in my own bed so they won't have to scoop me up from the street with the rest of the rubbish."

"Don't do this, Daniel."

"Don't do what!" he suddenly yelled, pacing and licking the sweat off his lips. "Better ask it of my hands! Look at them!"

He thrust them in her face, the palm of the one still gripping the pistol. Her head jerked back.

"What's the point of anything any longer if I can't do the only two things in this world that have ever mattered to me? To paint, and to love you. I can't even love you the way you deserve."

"It's not true," she cried.

"My body is in appalling pain every day of my life. I just want to be released from it, that's all."

"Please, Daniel—"

"I'm already dying. Why not quicken it? I've already given all I can fucking give in this life, and now I'm empty. And what has art given me in return, anyway? Happiness? Fulfillment? Bullshit! I'm the most tormented man I know. I've always been. It's never soothed me to paint."

"It has soothed others. It's changed lives. It's vital. Don't ever think it's not."

"But *I* want to be soothed. Me. Daniel. Why can't I be soothed?"

"We can soothe each other."

"Don't even pretend to be daft. Fucking is not what I mean."

He continued pacing the room, waving the pistol fatuously and sweating the whisky from his pores. The furnace was still blazing, but after having walked the entire night in the stinging cold, his body had grown accustomed to the bitter state, so it went haywire now. He sweated and shivered at once.

In spite of an earlier drunkenness, they were both now wider awake than either had ever been before.

"Arthur knew," he panted, talking more to himself than to her. And pacing. He had to keep moving. "Arthur knew. He said, *'fuck it, I'm tired.'*

Right? Yeah? Well, so the fuck am I! I don't want to be at odds with the world any longer."

"Daniel, what is it you think you're taking from Arthur? The wisdom in his decision to blow his brains out? Yeah, that was fucking wise."

"See, I don't blame you for your sarcasm and your bitterness toward him," he offered calmly. "Especially after what I told you about him. But it's right that I do this."

"Oh my God," she muttered, shaking her head.

He tried to reason with her. Tried to make her understand him. And Arthur. And Will Speck, for that matter. He had to plead the case for them all.

"Look at you, Nona. You've stopped living because of me. I need to do this—so that—so that I can give you back—you see, I mean, look at Speck. He knew he couldn't rob a man of his gift. Ultimately he knew it could never work—"

"God," she whispered, shutting her eyes. "Please don't talk to me about a book—"

"—Speck knew that the only way to give Champion his life back, the one he'd done his best to pilfer, was to end his own."

"Please! Don't be crazy on me," she pled, finally making the decision to screw diplomacy. "It's just a book. A piece of fiction."

"Some piece of fiction, eh?"

"God, Daniel, you've let that book become the demon in your head. And it isn't even—it isn't even—even—"

"What? What?"

"Worthy! Okay? It's hardly of enough power to make a man insane. Is anything? Please release this already. It's just a piece of fiction. It was never meant to torment anyone's life."

"You think I'm insane?"

"No."

She was no longer sure.

"It's a fucking mirror, is what it is," he continued. "Showing me exactly what I am. Showing plenty of us what we are. And if you didn't know that to be true, you could never have given birth to Will Speck."

"It's just a goddamned piece of pulp, Daniel!"

"No, darlin'. You're dead wrong. It has so much more portent than that. Art is God. It is vengeful and omnipotent. As much a destroyer as a creator. And Speck knew that. He knew art wouldn't heal him. He knew, because the gun allowed him to get inside Champion's head. It gave him an immediate intimacy. And d'you know what he found there?"

He offered the question to her like a quiz, but wouldn't even allow her the chance to pass or fail.

"Anguish," he revealed, as he started to laugh, the clarity of it so startling. "Not transcendence. Not elevation. Not healing. All that lofty rhetoric that art promises. But anguish. See, so, Speck just finally let it go. Released it. Like a—like a butterfly from a palm. He said, *'if this is what the GIFT does, then let's just be done with it all.'* And he was. Just as I am."

"This is so absurd, Daniel. Please, let this go—"

"—so he finally gave himself some ease. And that's all I want to do. That's all. So, why can't you just leave me THE FUCK ALONE!"

"No, no, no, no, Daniel, please! You can't put such stake in a book!"

"Look at you, the writer, saying such a sentence. You think that just because it's fiction, that it's not truth? You know better than that."

"Yes, you're right. But in my book's case, it isn't truth. The way I wrote it, is, is, is, is that Champion, losing that sense of urgency, once the gun is pointed away from him and onto Speck's pitiful self, grows paralyzed. Frozen. Again. No longer able to create. As he had been in the beginning, and so, is, is, is, is—"

She was wildly panicky.

"—is, is, is, is, is achieved the, the, the assassination Speck had intended. But you see, that's wrong. It should be the assassination of his stagnation and fear, not his gift. A friend of mine tried to point that out to me, but I couldn't hear her. I was so intoxicated by this idea of being the new Bleak Chic that I invested my whole ego toward defying everyone who tried to tell me not to end the book that way. But you see? That's what it is. That's all it is. A result of, of, of, of, of publishing boardroom meetings and votes and, and, and focus groups, and polls, and vetoes. And my ego. It has no resemblance to anything real."

"No. No. No. Your instincts as the writer were truer than the YOU now, who is only trying to CON ME—"

"Oh God—"

"—Don't you dare try to tell me that the goddamned publishing whores knew your characters better than their own creator did. Because I know all too well what you went through to give Speck and Champion their rightful story. And it IS right. You see, because now that Speck is gone, along with Champion's ability to create, the genius that had been so coveted now only glides through life like a, like a free-floating piece of airborne lint. And that's as it should be. Genius should be unclaimed—you see? It should be beyond these hands, which can't even hold a brush any longer. So, like Speck, I ask myself the question…In this world that woos genius… which I no longer am, if I ever was…what, then, is my reason to remain here?"

"For me!" she cried. "Goddamn it, how about for me? All right, don't paint anymore. Why should you have to? You've been brilliant already in this life. The world will be forever blessed with having had Daniel Cross as a part of its culture. Your body of work is already an amazing legacy. The world doesn't need any more of you. But I do! The people who love you do! Let's just relax from now on. Like you said, free it. Release it into the air. Forget *Champion!*"

"How can you ask that of me? I know you think me mad, but I'm not. What I'm speaking is, is, is—"

He paced agitatedly, the pistol still trembling in his palm; the steel handle warmed now and sort of soothing.

"—Artists weren't put on this earth just to be folly, Nona. Do you remember saying that to me the day we met? William Blake even believed artists to be divine, so how can you disavow the very book that's given me light? Your own creation? How can you think me silly by making this seem trivial? You're the one who gave birth to it, put it out there for people to be affected by. Well, darlin', somebody was. Deal with that."

"Daniel, art is not your enemy. You have been blessed with a gift. Speck didn't have that. He was only capable of destroying—"

"You are such—look at you. Such a liar. And not even good at it. One minute trying to disclaim the book, and the next referencing it to teach me some lesson? Which is it, wife?"

"Please, listen to me—Daniel—focus, and listen to me—"

"No, no, no—"

He shook his head to rid it of her talking.

"That's why Speck resorted to his terrorism," she insisted.

"No...no..."

"But that's not you."

"No...no...no..."

"THIS is not you."

"Shut up! Shut up! SHUT UP!" he roared, and shoved the pistol to her forehead.

She instantly dropped to her knees, arms thrown open wide in a crucified reflex. Here she froze prostrate, unbelieving that he would draw this weapon on her.

Suddenly the whole world stopped dead. Or his head was so deranged that he could only see the still tableau of horrors before him. All was quiet. Not even the millennial reveling outside could be heard. Only his breath. And hers. Frantic. Turned up. Agitated. Intimate. A duet.

He stared at her, as the barrel of the pistol glued itself to the center of her forehead, denting her flesh and taunting her skull, and he looked on that face that he loved. It was a sweet face, with expressive brown eyes that he could no longer even see because they were frightened shut; and the cheeks he used to caress, which presently quivered in a slow haze. That quiver hypnotized him. He would never hurt her, but she had no reason to know that.

Her body glistened of sweat, and when he glanced down at her legs, which knelt on the ground as if in prayer, he saw the golden urine run down the inside of her thigh beneath her dress.

The light that shined through his north window, just beyond her, lured him into a false high. It was warped, fluorescent, night color. The color of death, assuredly. The city hues of harsh reds, and sharp blues, and screaming greens, and muddy blacks and purples. Clusters of millions of little yellow squares of light dotted apartment windows in filthy, sooty buildings with exaggerated funhouse shapes. It was such a painting. He glanced again at the pee running down her leg. She never said a word but continued to tremble, eyes shut, clothes soiled, arms spread out like a slain Christ.

"What does it feel like?" he warbled, voice cracking.

Minutes passed. Not seconds, but an excruciating passage of time watched and waited for.

"Please," he cried. "Don't fear me. Don't think me mad. Just please tell me what it feels like—to be—frightened—alive—by this tease of death. To be so awakened by it that everything will look radiant to the eye from now on."

His chin quivered as he imagined such a thing, and those circus colors flashed at him and mutated every image in their wake. These colors tried to derange him.

"Tell me what it's like to piss yourself because you are so in love with life that you are terrified of losing it. I want to love life that badly."

He started to bawl, hard and gulping. Then he whispered. But it was an impotent whisper. Void of any real life. And like a jealous child.

"Tell me what it feels like to be Champion."

The question rang loudly and clanged in his head. In that second, she opened her eyes and stared at him. He could barely take looking in those eyes, which looked up at him and saw a murderer.

Dreadful more minutes passed. She wouldn't give it. The more she stared, the more the waiting was killing him. And he suddenly flashed on the night of the drum circle, a haunting that would never abate. A lifetime ago, it seemed. Another life, for sure. And the Elder's words:

A drum is a woman. Don't beat her. Caress her. Entice her to sing.

No wonder she couldn't give it.

He looked keenly into those eyes and remembered the first time he'd ever laid his own on her in a grocery market. She had flirted with him, a pixie so light of life and resplendent. Then she disappeared for months like some haunted vanishing. Like Arthur's haunted vanishing, just before he killed himself. And when she resurfaced, she'd been broken and damaged.

He wondered once again, as he had countless times before, about her rape. It remained a mystery to this day; a mystery that would probably never be solved, but she had long ago been delivered from the need for such a resolution.

It taught him something about this remarkable woman. Something no one else would ever know in quite the way he did. That whoever it was who had tried to rob her of her greatest self, that man, like the one who stood before her now, could never rape her of her extraordinary love for life. No matter how hard they'd both tried.

For witness the urine between her legs.

EIGHTY TWO

"All things are ready, if our minds be so."
— William Shakespeare, *Henry V*

Cruel. Compelling. Always. It had been that way since the beginning, she realized. Her tortured Heathcliff.

She watched him give her the horrible look of goodbye. Watched him pull the gun away from her forehead, its barrel almost pulling her flesh with it. Watched him draw it up and sweep it along the side of his own face. Watched his eyes close. Those bewitching gray eyes. Watched him place the gun to his temple, and cock it. Such a tableau.

In this tremendous moment, a brief blip in time opened up to encompass an entire life, it seemed as though he screamed at her to save him. Except that it wasn't his voice screaming. It came from someplace mightier than his conscious will. Perhaps it was his desire for beauty, which she believed was even greater than his desire to die.

All she knew for certain was that without thinking of the consequences, or even aware of what her own hands were doing, before she knew it she had leapt, and her hands had violently risen and rushed up to meet his. She swatted at the gun with clumsy fingers, half slapping his face, cutting his cheek with a fingernail, spraining a thumb, and watching the evil thing fumble out of both their trembling palms and slide across the floor, as their two bodies twisted and careened onto the bed.

She fell on top of him and screamed into his face, in disbelief that he was capable of such a deed, but couldn't even hear her own screaming. There was a mad silence in the room, a hypnotic mischief in her head that made colors and shapes loud and horrific. It drowned out all sound.

She held onto Daniel as he sobbed against her. His face completely buried itself in the fold of her chest, arms clinging and seizing. The sweat poured from her now. The urine already had.

And suddenly Bagamoyo. The poor, afflicted beast wailing mournfully into the sad night over its stricken mate. A visitation that would plague for a lifetime.

She held onto her husband until he eventually lost his shattered voice and his will and passed into a deep sleep. She couldn't tell if minutes or hours had advanced, but upon his unconsciousness she finally let herself collapse.

She stared at the ceiling, though she had no notion of it. What entered her head, a head already overfilled, bristling, and leaking from the lid, was: Would Daniel ever be able to see the poetry in this? In his failure to do the deed? That the shaking in his hands (*the fucking palsy case*, he'd called them) had been so uncooperative to his mission that he had never even been given the chance to depress the trigger? That those hands may well have failed the artist, as he had tragically claimed, though she would never give him that, but it would appear that they saved the man. Would he recognize that? Or had poetry left him forever?

For that matter, had it left her? Or worse, had it never existed? Her head sank further into the pillow, as she looked around this room that had held their eight-day exile, that still held his astonishing canvases, and realized that the only thing this world, a world her husband had tried to love by giving it his art, had given him in return was an unforgiving stumble from sanity. This world that boasted to be poetic. She had always claimed that the world was not artful on its own, that it was the existence of artists that infused the world with its beauty and poetry, but she had never truly believed it. She'd simply made it her claim because it was just so irresistibly radical. As long as such a claim remained an unproven abstract, however, a subject for roundtable debates and drunken bottles of wine, she could still live comfortably in the remotest of satisfactions that it wasn't really so, that the world would indeed prove itself artful all on its own.

She was no longer certain. After all, there once was a poet named Arthur Hughes Dufresne. And she just finished witnessing her husband, with her own eyes, put on that same madness like a cloak, a self-fulfilling fall, a baton passed from one walking wounded to the next, and become the madness that he wore.

For such a numbing blow, she felt ready to pull the gun back into the picture and threaten the same self-end — but for one thought suddenly striking her, one that perhaps had a chance of restoring her faith.

In that terrible second that the trigger of the gun attempted to be pulled, when Daniel actually, for one instant, believed he was about to die, he finally got to step inside Gabriel Champion's shoes. And now that he had done it, claimed that moment that seemed to be the ablution he'd been seeking all along, he would surely have to know that they weren't such epiphanous shoes after all. That it was, indeed, just a book. A character of fiction. A Holden Caulfield. A Sam Spade. Truth? Sure, maybe. Perhaps having no solid conviction about it, one way or the other, was why Nona Childe had no other book in her. Her punishment for being a lapsed believer. Still. A mere ream of paper and some ink.

Sticks and stones...

Perhaps now Daniel could finally purge the haunting from his gut, expel Gabriel Champion once and for all, and opt for peace.

As the first leaden hours of the new millennium crept by, and she held onto Daniel, her head spun crazy with notions of death. And art. And Art. And her husband's emotional break. And her love for him. And *what is it all for?* ruminations. Until eventually the sun rose. She watched it from the corner of their window, stubbornly insisting on a sentimental metaphor.

Their alliance had always been a love song, she mused, but one sung with a whisky-curdled voice on an old tack piano. Drenched in Sturm and Drang. Beautiful and awful.

Her eyes started to fade, as she began losing the battle to stay awake. She was afraid to sleep, for there was still the matter of a loaded gun, which now lay in a corner. Why on earth hadn't she yet grabbed it and thrown it down the trash chute?

And she realized that it was because there were two scenarios that vexed her:

The first found them lying peacefully in each other's indulgent clutches, having failed to deal with the world they'd been dealt, discovered by the French authorities and all of their aghast friends and fans. Two suicides. The celebrated painter. And the eminent author who, upon waking to find a dead husband, inconsolable, could not possibly think of living in the world without him. A gun by their side. And their work suddenly skyrocketing because, after all, the romance of spectacular tragedy is always so show-biz fabulous.

The second one had them awakening later in the day, a bit ripe and shaken from a night of copious boozing and self-wallowing drama and emotional breakdowns, but at least alive and grateful for the drudgery and rehabilitation of another day. Not nearly as fabulous. Except that from that moment forth they would both have been so awakened by that close call that, just as Daniel had earlier decreed, everything in the world would be radiant to their eyes from then on, and life cherished anew.

So the crucial question remained: Was Daniel actually capable of awakening at some point in the dawn while she slept and, still feeling shattered and hopeless and finished, taking his life after all? Or would he be able to recognize the hand of beauty reaching out to him? Assuring him that he had tenacious love for life in him still?

She needed the answer. For the sake of everything she'd ever believed in. And the only way to find out would be to leave the gun alone. To wait. To see. To let go.

Coltrane understood what it meant to let go.

And so the sun rose. And the very last image that her tired eyes caught — before she finally let her lids fall shut for the final time on an old millennium, an old life — was of that gun glaring at her like a fuming wildcat, ready to pounce.

She swore to God the angry thing had eyes, and was daring her to put all her faith in beauty.

OTHER WORKS BY ANGELA CAROLE BROWN

BOOKS

Trading Fours

The Kidney Journals: Memoirs of a Desperate Lifesaver

ALBUMS

The Slow Club

Resting on the Rock

Expressionism

Music for the Weeping Woman

Winter

Global Yoga

www.ingramcontent.com/pod-product-compliance
Lightning Source LLC
Chambersburg PA
CBHW020825030726
47496CB00001B/93